The
TRUTH
TELLER

The TRUTH TELLER

KATHERINE GOVIER

Vintage Canada
A Division of Random House of Canada Limited

13189527

VINTAGE CANADA EDITION, 2001

Copyright © 2000 by Katherine Govier

Vintage Canada and colophon are trademarks of Random House of Canada Limited.

Canadian Cataloguing in Publication Data

Govier, Katherine
The truth teller

ISBN 0-679-31099-1

I. Title.

PS8563.O875T78 2001   C813'.54   C00-932467-4
PR9199.3.G68T78 2001

Text design: Gordon Robertson
Cover design: CS Richardson

Printed and bound in the United States of America

2 4 6 8 9 7 5 3 1

TO MY PARENTS,
in the sixty-first year of their marriage.
With love and admiration,
thanks a lot.
Katherine

EGYPT'S MIGHT IS TUMBLED DOWN

Egypt's might is tumbled down
    Down a-down the deeps of thought;
Greece is fallen and Troy town,
Glorious Rome hath lost her crown,
    Venice's pride is nought.

But the dreams their children dreamed
    Fleeting, unsubstantial, vain.
Shadowy as the shadows seemed
Airy nothing, as they deemed,
    These remain.

Mary Coleridge

CONTENTS

BOOK ONE

I

HEROES
IN OUR PAST

"LADIES AND GENTLEMEN. We have inherited a vision."

Dr. Laird's voice resounded like the clapper of a bell, like the first chords of a hymn. Hearts rose to its beat. Backs straightened, chins lifted. Everyone knew what was to come. He always began that way. And his audience always sat on folding chairs, no less rapt for the discomfort or the repetition, which was anticipated, and annual. It was a glorious fall day. When was it not a glorious day for the Manor's commencement exercises?

October was perhaps a strange time for a commencement. School had been over for months; results were in; these students seated on stage were already history, off at universities across the country. But Commencement had always been on the third of October. To "commence" was not only to graduate, but to begin, and all beginnings at the Manor led back to the day Dr. Dugald Laird met Miss Francesca Morrow, his wife, Vice-Principal and Headmistress. Fifty years ago today fate caused their paths to cross right here on Taddle Creek Drive; they fell both in love and into eudaimonía, the state of being happy following their demons, in running the Manor School for Classical Studies in an unsuspecting Toronto.

As if to catch the glory, the giant Norway maple dominating the terraced lawn had leaves of gold worthy of Byzantium. So thought Amelia, general factotum of the school, seated in the second row. Weeks ago, its big, waxy, five-point paws had begun to dazzle and twist in the light winds of early autumn; now one by one the thin red stems snapped from the branches, each leaf taking a zigzag, fitful journey to the ground. The palm-sized gilt was piled up around the tree's enormous base. Gold above, gold below: it was as if, somewhere between sky and ground, there was the still, mirroring surface of an invisible lake.

Yes, as Amelia knew, a glimmer of prehistoric water did lie at the foot of the lawn, for the Manor sat atop the Escarpment, that ragged, ten-metre cliff marking the shore of the once-great Lake Iroquois. Many millennia ago the lake shrank southward leaving the sloping flatlands, which had been its bottom, traversed with lush, deep ravines and shallow creeks. The natives grew rice on the shore, and dried their fish. When the British sailed up they decided to build a fort at the mouth of a creek, the one with a bend in its path. This creek came by the name of Taddle, some say, from the Tattle family, which homesteaded nearby. Others claim the name referred to the tadpoles inhabiting the water, still others that the name was an imitation of the sound of water running over rocks. Or it could have been a variant of "tattle," a reference to the gossip exchanged on its banks.

No matter: at its mouth were the beginnings of a great city.

The sloping expanse between water and high ground began to fill with farms and wagons, with people and taverns. Amelia liked to picture it: the fields first ploughed and then paved; two hundred years passing until the people numbered two million, two and a half, plying trades from stock-trading to carpet-cleaning; the space clogged with factories, homes, a gothic pink-stone parliament, a glassed-in shopping mall and a streaming network of roads to carry those people back and forth. There were bank towers forty storeys high and ugly parking lots, but still there could be found gardens chock with roses and, in the deep ravines, vestiges of wilderness, foxes and even coyote. The city spread uphill unchecked, and along the banks of Taddle Creek were hospitals and museums and a university. The Taddle was buried as the clutter of untidy streets climbed to the escarpment, that old lake's lip. But there, *here*, thought Amelia, above the cliff, at the headwaters of the creek, the city stopped. Was forced by both landscape and human foresight to turn aside. That seemingly unstoppable growth made a detour, leaving untouched this quiet enclave with its circle of homes, its huge old trees and its atmosphere of genteel withdrawal. Within that circle the Manor was the prettiest house, its stuccoed walls overgrown with creepers, its dormers snug with casement windows and the sloping roof rising in two levels to flow elegantly into the contours of the hill.

Proud that the onrush of time might be slowed for even a breath, Amelia straightened her spine. Under the metallic slant of the October sun, students and parents listened with hands folded. Copies of Renaissance paintings flapped in the light breeze on the divider where they were displayed. Skirted martial artists with medieval bows bobbed on their toes on the side stairs, warming their tendons. Miranda and Prospero yawned and rolled their necks to prepare for their scene. And the old man waxed on. It hardly mattered what he said. He had said it last year and the year before and he would say it again next year. Though rapt, his audience was not listening to his words. It was listening instead to his heart; it was basking in his fervour, magnified as usual by the reverence of his wife, who gazed steadily at her husband, a small smile playing on her lips.

"To the vision of our founder, Marmaduke Matthews, to those who inspired him and who in turn—" said Dr. Laird, with a smile at Miss Morrow, "—were inspired by him, we owe our beautiful home in Wychwood Park. Be thankful that you have been schooled in a romantic suburb within the vastness of Toronto, in the polis, as the

Greeks would call it. What is a polis? An organization of mutually dependent men existing somewhere between the bestial and the divine...

"More than a century ago he dammed our creek to make a pond where the wild columbines cluster, and the swans glide unperturbed. He planned this suburb where artist and scholar could live independent of society. He fostered the art of teaching and passed on to his children a knowledge of the great works of Western civilization. To Marmaduke Matthews and his followers we owe our understanding of myth, our love of art, our faith in community. Today, our Wychwood is surrounded by city. And our Taddle Creek has been driven underground, detectable only as a faint gurgle under the sewer grate. But the Park is still the Park, and we, the Founders' Descendants, still believe. . . ."

It was hard to tell if the graduates believed; they were composed, at least, mortarboards level, faces blank, as if regarding some inner screen where futures flickered, still unreadable.

"Our forefathers shared a belief in the perfectibility of man. Oh, yes, Vida," Dr. Laird added, giving a nod to the school's radical feminist, "I could say woman here if I wished but I am old-fashioned: you must not mind me. Marmaduke Matthews' idea was good but it was not new. It came straight from the genetic coding of Homo erectus: Each member of your tribe is precious, whatever his frailty. He—or she, as the case may be—must be protected. If enemies set on him, fight for his life: it is your own."

There was a pause here for emphasis. In the still of the afternoon two more golden leaves detached themselves from the canopy overhead and, twirling, floated past Amelia's knees.

"Homo erectus understood these essentials. As should we students of the Manor. We are a tribe. We must care for one another. This is the simple truth that you must take from our teachings."

At this point Dugald pulled a handkerchief (white linen, freshly laundered) from his breast pocket and mopped his brow. Dr. Laird was living proof that to speak of weighty matters, to speak from the heart, was hard labour. The students and their parents remained attentive: would he rise to his heights? Would he get to the climax, the part about the underground water, the sacred spring?

"And as a tribe we cling to our roots. Our history is present in the here and now."

Please, yes, thought Amelia. The shorter version for once, a direct route to the inevitable conclusion.

"A sacred spring connects us to the great ages of mankind. To Mesopotamia where Gilgamesh sought eternal life, to the Greeks and the Romans, to the artists of the Renaissance. We—Miss Morrow and I—trace these waters in our very bloodlines. For you must know, my Uncle Marmaduke was the Utopian of Wychwood Park. And my bride is equally a part of our history, through the great painter, G. F. Watts, the English Michelangelo, who was her grandfather."

He mopped his brow again, and looked down at Francesca.

"No mere image . . . " she mouthed.

"As you see, the sacred spring is no mere image. It runs here beneath the grass we stand on. It drew my wife and I together to its banks, and it has kept us here. It is deep of spirit, and rich in inspiration. We have brought you to its source, and we urge you to stay within its murmurings your whole life."

Applause erupted. Eyes welled with tears. The graduates had been happy here. They had learned so much. They had loved their teachers. It was an odd school and they were not average, any of them. If they hadn't been proud of that fact when they came they were proud of it now. Some of them bent their heads, almost overcome. Dr. Laird held up his hand for silence. There was more. There was always more.

Pretty the way the tears came, thought Amelia. Annually, no less. No one understood better than Dr. Laird the power of rhetoric. *Inherited a vision. Homo erectus.* She only wished she had seen these ideals in action, seen the little savages stick together, co-operate in order to thrive. In fact it was hers to observe these same young people puking drunkenly by the streetcar barns, offering each other blow jobs, and bloody noses, buying drugs and selling out friends.

She sat with the unfinished ones, those for whom the murmurings of the sacred spring of the ages were still all but inaudible. Suffering in order of declining grade level, they were dry-eyed as they watched their schoolmates get away. They'd have Dr. Laird to listen to again on Monday. They'd hear the Commencement Day lecture again next year.

It was a first, allowing the "little rats," as Miss Morrow called them (a name borrowed from some musty European ballet school), to don cap and gown. The rats had begged to be allowed. The honour, they said, would inspire them. "Very well, but we shall have utter composure from the little rats if we are to have them gowned in the first row!" announced Miss Morrow. One could only hope: this was a particularly recalcitrant bunch. They sat, resplendent in mortarboards with gold tassels—Vida, Ashley, Maureen, Roxanne, Sara and the new girl. And in the row behind, beside Amelia, the boys—Dimitri, Chino, Darrin and Jacob the brain. The first three boys fidgeted. Jacob the brain had his hands in his lap, fingers laced, index fingers pointing up with the tips together. Like an undertaker, Amelia thought. Militant little Vida was erect as a sapling, the black square on her head perfectly balanced. Ashley, Maureen and Roxanne slouched in varying degrees of lassitude. They looked like headache victims, the mortarboards as taut as bandages across their foreheads.

Then there was the new girl. The gold tassel from her hat did not hang alongside her cheek as the others' did. Hers had worked itself along the edge of the flat square to bisect her forehead and drop between her eyes, falling alongside her nose and ending just above her lip. She turned her head to the left, away from the podium.

Amelia watched as the new girl's nose twitched and the left corner of her mouth twisted as if to bite off the fuzzy end of the tassel. Her left eye blinked every few seconds while she strove to remain poised, as Miss Morrow had instructed. She obviously did not dare raise her hand. But the thing tormented her. The eye began to tear. She jerked her head, an effort, no doubt, to dislodge the cord, but to no avail. The tassel remained.

Maureen turned and saw the new girl's eyes crossed and tongue stuck out toward the gold cord beside her left nostril. She snorted and elbowed Roxanne, who rolled her eyes and elbowed Ashley. Their shoulders began to shake with barely contained mirth.

Dr. Laird had moved on.

"I speak of visions. Well do I remember that fall day exactly fifty years ago when *my* vision cropped up on Taddle Creek Drive. She was the loveliest of creatures, a cloud of raven hair about her head, and damask cheeks. She stepped into the driveway and looked up at the Manor. She had measurements of thirty-seven, nineteen, thirty-five..."

There were usually titters when Dugald gave Francesca's measurements, and today was no exception. The new girl took advantage of the moment and flipped the tassel off her face, which made the other girls convulse, silently.

Ah, the mantra, thought Amelia. *Thirty-seven, nineteen, thirty-five.* It was like code, a locker combination. Science tells us that man is drawn to woman by the differential between her waist and hip measurements; that those females with a twelve-inch difference between waist and hip are more likely to arouse a man's interest than those with only a six-inch difference. This is an evolutionary thing; male instinct dimly grasps that wider hips will better house the developing offspring during the risky gestation period.

But, why, wondered Amelia, must the waist be indented? Why

did wide all the way down from breast to knee not do the trick? One had only to look at the pear-shaped goddess figures to see that prehistoric man did not need an hourglass, a body whittled to nothing between breast and pelvis. When were waists invented, she wondered, and by what agency were they added to the genetic coding of Homo erectus?

Did later man need women's breasts and hips set far apart, indeed nearly severed, as in the Barbie doll, so as not to confuse the functions of mother and lover? Amelia made a note to ask Dugald. He would undoubtedly have a theory. Miss Morrow for her part seemed to have grasped this from the word go, as she had preserved her wasp waist through workouts of murderous intensity.

But I digress, Amelia told herself, using a much-favoured phrase of the Manor. As much as the rats could not squirm, so the staff of the Manor could not drift. Never mind that the staff—composed entirely of one Amelia Holt, if you did not count James the janitor or Ferdinand of the canteen truck—was tired from her many jobs. These included teaching geography, substitute teaching everything else, being administrative assistant to Miss Morrow, and acting as guidance counsellor and general dog's body. It was Amelia who had organized the invitations, the caterers, the awning (in case of rain) and the displays of student work for today. The proceedings had to be perfect, as perfect as the myth of the school. She forced her mind back to the speech.

"Fifty years ago this young beauty and I discovered a mutual passion to teach the greatest works of Western civilization to the youth of Toronto."

Miss Morrow continued to gaze with love at her husband. Dr. Laird was Principal and she only his "vice," inspiring many a double entendre: Francesca had been his vice for so long that she was almost a virtue, and so on *ad nauseam*. But everyone knew that Francesca ruled the Manor. Her gazing affirmed the position he advanced: We worship works of art, ancient myths and the hourglass figure. Not necessarily in that order.

Amen, thought Amelia, gazing at him herself. Whatever your eccentricities, I am with you. With you, against the tide. Because in this metropolis yours are not the gods of choice; outside this garden, the glories of Western civilization have taken a back seat. The true gods in the here and now, as Dugald would call it, are Moreness, Money and Me. In any order you like.

Amelia was the realist. Someone had to be.

As Dugald Laird spoke, his audience grew. People entered at the back through the wrought-iron gate; others climbed the terraced lawn from the pond. Amelia was quite certain she had not invited all these guests. True, she had wanted to expand Commencement this year, to celebrate the fiftieth anniversary of the school. After all (she had said to Dugald, first, and then to Francesca) the Manor School was an extraordinary Toronto institution, a *world class* school for the gifted, the talented, the unruly and the truly off the wall, and it had survived for half a century. Attention must be paid, she said, and perhaps that was her mistake, the echo of *Death of a Salesman*. They loathed American literature.

"Amelia, my dear, we couldn't possibly," Dugald had begun. This had happened in the stairwell between the first and second floors. Dugald balanced on his toes, feet apart, and began to wave one arm (the other clutched an untidy pile of exam papers close to his chest). Right away she recognized the start of a rant.

"You, my dear, are an honest product of your time and place. Toronto loves nothing better than an anniversary. Don't you see? This attempt to create a feeling for history out of numbers, where no true feeling exists, is fuelled by a general bankruptcy of the imagination. Although quite possibly reticence and emotional stinginess also play a role. Have you not noticed that newspapers, magazines and the social calendar reflect this preoccupation? I myself believe that there is a minion at city hall whose job it is to comb the almanacs and arm himself with a full calendar of anniversaries, invasions and inventions of note, then to stir up celebration. Are outbursts of feeling permitted only on significant dates?" He smiled devilishly, bobbed his head, swept his gown off the banister, and passed by. Amelia suspected that by the time he'd finished speaking he had forgotten the question that got him started. She had no more luck with Francesca, to whom any mention of the passage of time must call attention to the fact that she was aging. Which she wasn't.

Consequently, alumni were not invited. Yet Amelia spotted some she knew, and others she'd simply heard of. She saw Connaught Bork, the industrialist, who had attended the Manor after being kicked out of Upper Canada College for setting fires. And Jim Byrd, renegade scion of a Fine Old Ontario Family (FOOF), who had become a Buddhist and made perfect little cabinets that sold for twenty thousand dollars each.

Yes, the Manor had its famous graduates. How could it not? The school drew from the bluebloods of Toronto, albeit from their more difficult offspring. Looking past the Headmaster and his wife, Amelia could see more uninvited guests. Mercy Rappaport, once the quintessential hippy, now reincarnated as head of an alternative school. Emma Knight, famed at the Manor for her drawings of male nudes, now a Supreme Court Justice. And was that not Forrest Bard, self-appointed Wychwood Park photographer, skulking in the rhododendrons? There was more here than inherited privilege, however. Rescues had been effected—outcasts brought into the fold, exotics coaxed to flower proudly—and all the while Latin and Greek ingested.

Of their successes, Dugald and Francesca never boasted. The were forbiddingly independent and intensely private, expending their energies daily in rooms full of high-maintenance teenagers, and withdrawing in the evenings to luxurious pursuits that were the constant subject of student speculation. They kept a distance even from devoted Amelia, who had been one of those students herself.

The gathering was so obviously larger than normal that Amelia began to worry. She was going to be blamed. But it was not her fault! To be sure the underground telegraph had been tapping away. She looked behind without fully turning her head and saw more arrivals, saw them nod and shake hands, saw their eyes seek out Dr. Laird and Miss Morrow at their accustomed podium. For so many the school had been a haven. For others, time here had been a penance, and the founders a misery. Thus did greatness inspire controversy: it was one of the lessons of history.

At its best the Manor was a hallowed enclave where great works were taught and young people grew wings; at any time of day you might poke your head into a classroom and see happy little scholars writing a description of a Greek statue or looking at pond scum under a microscope. At its worst it was—but who needs to know? It had been said that the student body was a collection of weirdos, that the school was the private fiefdom of two fanatics, the art classes simply daycare for high-school miscreants. You could hear Miss Morrow called a female Mussolini and her husband a madman. But envy is everywhere.

On the platform, Dugald seemed unaware of the growing crowd. "How blessed we are in what we have to work with," he was saying. "Great masters and great art, along with the sacred spring, establishing a direct link to the past. You all know that our lovely trees and the rock garden leading down to the pond were planted by Marmaduke Matthews himself, and that he and others had taken their inspiration for suburban utopia from William Morris. Of course you know that one of our inspirations, G. F. Watts, the Master, as we call him, was Lily's stepfather. He loved his ward dearly. I need hardly remind you that the Manor was built especially for Lily, Miss Morrow's mother, whose portrait hangs in our front hall."

Lily. Sulky, sultry Lily, the patron saint of the school, whose portrait Miss Morrow could not pass without her mysterious secret wave.

Francesca as his Lily's daughter had come into possession of certain paintings and reproductions that she would bring out on occasion from their apartment at the top of the house to dazzle an art class. Contrasting 'Lily,' and poised as if to eat her up, was his predatory 'Minotaur,' the very picture of seductive, self-pitying decadence. Watts' works were part of the landscape and his notions permeated the place. Elsewhere along the walls were pottery urns and bowls from the Master's workshops at Limnerslease in Surrey.

And the inspirations went further back. The halls were draped with tapestries Francesca had collected over the years, replicas of the Unicorn series—from the Cluny Museum in Paris. As a student, Amelia had spent many an hour gazing at the final panel with its mysterious emblem "A mon seul desire." It was usually pulled tight across the window in the front parlour, now transformed into a math room. Whenever she was alone in the place, she pulled the panel aside. The parlour would glow with golden light. A magical place the Manor was then, indeed an oasis at the sacred spring, an Eden. But Eden had not permitted knowledge.

Myth, Amelia reminded herself, exists to give order to life, which is chaotic. There are too many events for us to make sense of. Myth selects and arranges so that we may find pleasure in the shape lives take, even a dreadful fate arrived at by predictable means acquiring a certain elegance. Selection, direction, reverence, that is the function of myth. We could argue that love serves the same purpose: love says, here is the one you will attend to, cleave to, believe in. Now go ahead. *Forsake all others.*

That's fine for the chosen one, she thought. But what happens to the bits that don't fit the shapes, to the people outside the circle?

"The wrong of unshapely things is a wrong too great to be told," Francesca always said, quoting William Butler Yeats of course. He was now known as "Buster" around the school, since the new girl with her flair for malapropisms had renamed him. He was quoted all too frequently, as far as Amelia was concerned; she thought it had to do with Francesca's growing obsession with death, which mirrored Yeats' own. It is not easy to be a senior citizen and have a horror of "all things uncomely and broken, all things worn out and old."

Easier of course if you have love. And if in your love you beautify that other one, who is a mirror of yourself. Perhaps that is all love is, simply a way for people to find a replica of themselves. Conveniently created in the opposite sex. Or the same, as the case may be. In this case the opposite. Never was seen a more flagrant example of heterosexual romance than here in the Principals of the Manor.

But what did Amelia know of romance? Amelia was the Cheese.

On the subject of mirrors, she was well informed. She spent hours a day gazing in the mirror, and made no apologies for it. She was interesting to herself.

She was, arguably, a beauty. Red hair, which she rinsed with henna, turning it the shiny maroon that was as striking as the more common blonde among certain Swedes. Indeed, her father was Swedish, a man named Hult, changed to Holt because in Canada everyone spelt it wrong anyway. This hair, parted in the middle and falling evenly to each side in large waves, was intended to flatter her large, round face. Like a line drawn by a cartoonist, her mouth was expressive, turning comic, fearsome, morose by turns. Her forehead was wide, clear, flat, curtained at the temples by the gleaming panels of hair.

Her eyes, too, were round, not the long almond eyes one might expect to go with the mouth, but saucer eyes, of a chocolate brown that seemed surprised into focus. Above them, thin eyebrows formed two perfect curves. These curves were replicated under her eyes in deep hollows. The turn of her glance in her white face was like the rolling of large, weighted objects. There were no bones to speak of, only the roundness and width of cheeks. Her most delicate feature was her chin, which was long and pointed; when she thrust it forward, which she was more and more inclined to do, she showed a most beautiful arch atop the fabled neck. Her neck was her best feature, and she knew it, thanks to Miss Morrow.

When Amelia first arrived at the Manor, Miss Morrow sat her on a stool and walked back and forth in front of her, tapping her cane on the floor. Not for Leonardo or those who chose to replicate classical perfection. No, said Miss Morrow firmly, Amelia was not High Renaissance, she was Mannerist. Reminiscent of the Greeks but touched by something slightly mad, irrational, out of shape. Nothing here is to be measured by ordinary experience, the artist tells us. She is, declared Miss Morrow, who loved to address people in the third person, a Mannerist Madonna. She has come to us straight from the seventeenth century, where she sat as the model for Parmigianino's "Madonna with the Long Neck."

Miss Morrow made a habit of renaming the young people who came into her charge. This is done in cults, with something of the same effect. Leaders achieve power over their subordinates: it is as if they create them anew from the clay. At the time Amelia was dumpy, greasy-haired, sullen. She scoffed. But a subsequent visit to the tiny girls' washroom in the basement of the school showed her that she did have a long neck. It was set atop tiny shoulders, a small but rounded bust, and a narrow waist sloping to wide hips, wider thighs and long, almost tubular legs. She was a large girl with rare points of delicacy, grounded but wavering, flower-like at the top. She was not pretty in any way that her contemporaries could acknowledge.

For being unpretty and for other crimes, she was not sought after by her peers at any school she attended, and there were many. At first the Manor had not been much different; Miss Morrow named her a Parmigianino, which translated quickly to Parmesan, and led, of course, to "the Cheese." Amelia did not exactly mind being called the Cheese, even though over time the art history reference was forgotten. Today some believe that the name refers to her wide smile, to the self-consciousness that goes with being a teacher and the focus of many eyes, as in "say Cheese." Teaching can do that: years of basking in her students' adoration had led Amelia to see herself as the star of some ongoing, daily show.

And it was true that now, these fifteen years later, she was winsome and wildly attractive to men. Perhaps it was in the way she moved, the languid softness of her flesh, and the way it contrasted with her white, white skin and purpled lips. She had a look of mischief in her eye, and a siren appeal that she exerted on every man and boy in the school. To have power over men had come to her late, after that plain and lonely youth, and like so many women who discover their power late, she was not about to abandon it.

Yet she remained the Cheese.

The true significance of the name was other; it was accidental, and it was private to Amelia. When her peers made Parmigianino into a foodstuff, Amelia thought only of cheese as in the childhood game "The Farmer in the Dell." "The Farmer takes a wife, the Farmer takes a Wife, hi-ho, the derry-o, the Farmer takes a wife. The wife takes a child, the wife takes a child, hi-ho, the derry-o, the wife takes a child." And every one took someone or something until at last they came to the Cheese. And then they sang: "The Cheese stands alone, the Cheese stands alone, hi-ho, the derry-o, the Cheese stands alone."

Miss Holt. Single woman, over thirty. It was, in part, an illusion; the fact was, at any given time she didn't stand entirely alone. She was unpartnered, that was it. Not celibate. There was a difference. The truth was, she had unusual sexual tastes. So unusual that she must pass for a spinster? Certainly around the Manor. She was not interested in women and she would never prey on the girls at school. Or the boys. Well, probably not the boys. She slept with unsuitable men. That's all. It was very innocent, really. To pass Miss Morrow's test of acceptability, a lover must possess two of the following three: good family, good manners, good clothes. No lover of Amelia's made the grade. In fact, any two of these attributes would be guaranteed to turn her off. Her list, if she had one, might include two of the following: down at heel, dirt under fingernails, sensitive. And for this she stood apart. She allowed herself to become, and remain, the Cheese. Such is the power of naming.

"We are midstream," Dugald was saying. He was fond of water imagery. "We are midstream in the Taddle, its buried waters all around us. Tittle Tattle, piddle paddle..." He loved to pun. Half the time he thought he was Marshall McLuhan, his famous neighbour. McLuhan had said, "The park is a bell... and it resonates, it is a kind of theatre, a public way to create privacy." McLuhan loved those apparent contradictions, and so did Dugald. "Amidst-Dream," he went on, "in our theatre, we share a dream. My bride and I are always amidst a dream in our work. And what is that dream? To grow our youngsters as citizens of the world. To bring them to the sacred spring."

He paused and smiled down the long serious line of be-hatted, be-tasseled faces. "Some young people are leaving us, and we must bid them adieu. But others have just come to us. And we cannot abandon them, can we?" Here he smiled fondly at Vida, Roxanne and the new girl. "And so, while each year we do consider—"

Here it came. Would this be the year he would mention the dreaded r-word? *Retirement.* Amelia drew a breath and gazed around surreptitiously; she thought the onlookers had a signal air about them. The scene put her in mind of a French movie, *L'armée des ombres.* Simone Signoret played a French Resistance worker who after great service to the cause became a liability. Therefore the Resistance had to kill her. And it did, her colleagues suddenly appearing before her on a sidewalk. She had a second to register the affection and respect of this honour guard before being felled in a rattle of bullets. Yes, that was the sense of today's commencement, this honour guard summoned to recognize the Principal and Head-mistress before they fell.

But no. Missed again. Miss Morrow smiled demurely, eyes downcast.

"Who," demanded Dugald, his voice rising bravely, "would retire when there is a burning need for his services? Who would retire amidst a great work? Our great work is our students. Upcoming are some of the brightest minds, some of the great creative and scholarly talents, of their generation. This is the way it has always been at the Manor."

As his last words faded under tumultuous applause, the brown belts launched themselves to the shaky stage to kick and parry their way through mock battle. There's nothing like a good sparring: everyone loves the final bows when the combatants sweep off the face guard. After the karate the Shakespeare. Then the little rats doing their dance in masks they'd created themselves. Except they weren't little rats at all, truthfully. They were big galumphing girls with hips and breasts made slick in shiny unitards. Then the prizes, one after another, doled out to blushing granduands, the science prize, the arts prize, the all-round scholarship prize, named for a girl who'd had top honours thirty-five years ago and had then drowned on a canoe trip in Algonquin Park.

Then, over.

Damp of thigh from the heat and the plastic surface of the fold-ing chairs, the audience rose. Amelia loved to watch the rush for the party sandwiches. Those waspy, moist, white-bread triangles from Chapman's, with the crusts cut off and the slices of bread rolled flat with a rolling pin, with their traditional mild fillings of egg salad, cu-cumber, salmon and chicken paste, bring out the animal in Toronto-nians. People stuffed their faces and elbowed their neighbours. No one was immune. Connaught Bork, for instance, more accustomed to dining on ostrich loin in Vancouver while buying up old-growth forests to make matchsticks, shouldered aside aged grandparents in order to get within reach of the party sandwiches.

Jim Byrd, his bald pate covered with a little South American knitted skullcap, reclined against the wrought-iron fenceposts. Legendary in all that he had renounced, Byrd had refused an inherited fortune, or at least put it in a never-never trust, given up a seat on the Board of Directors, and eschewed the affections of numerous fine women about town. He had contracted some disease that made every single hair on his body fall out—he had no eyelashes, no facial hair, nothing to protect the fine white skin drawn taut over his hawk-like facial features. It was the perfect fit of an ailment; he could have chosen it himself. He was excessively thin, an ascetic, rumoured to eat nothing but celluloid noodles and vegetable juice. But aha! There went a cucumber sandwich into his hand, carried his way by a curious Vida with a paper plate.

Amelia watched them, Connaught all avarice and appetite, Jim all virtue and refusals, and wondered at the extremes. Yet the Manor had produced them, had harboured them both at difficult times in their lives. There were less successful alumni, to be sure, some taking their leisure in drug-rehabilitation programs, collecting employment insurance or leaping at car windshields wielding a squeegee. But all, no doubt, could recite "La Belle Dame sans Merci." What had they made of Francesca and Dugald's teachings? Where did the buried Taddle join the watershed of the great North American northeast?

Mercy Rappaport made her way amongst the young people, her fiery eyes fixed on Miss Morrow, her arms ready to embrace her. She simply didn't understand the inhibitions that kept others on the straight and narrow.

"My darling Francesca!"

Unsuspecting, Miss Morrow turned about, only to find herself seized by those octopus arms, muscular from pottery wheeling or skip-rope turning. Who knew what Mercy did in that school?

"Why, Mercy! How lovely to see you."

Francesca leaned back in an attempt to disentangle herself. But there were bangles involved in this, and long beads that hung from Mercy's neck. Inexorably, the four breasts met, Francesca's conical and exceedingly upright pair, which in no way admitted to being senior citizens, and Mercy's pendulous, beanbag variety. Amelia could feel the Headmistress recoil. Time for a diversion.

Francesca had always told the students they couldn't help themselves to the sandwiches until she gave the signal. The grown-ups had eaten enough, Amelia thought, moving to Francesca's side. She plucked her arm.

Francesca winched her neck toward Amelia, and then snapped it in a way that caused her whole torso to bend forward like an elastic. That loosened Mercy's hold and Francesca was out of her arms and six feet back in a trice. It was probably a karate move.

"Could we give the signal to let the students have a go at the food now?" Amelia asked. "They've worked very hard."

Francesca smiled gratefully. "Yes, Amelia, what a good idea." She raised her left hand high over her head and brought it down with a swish, as if she were a drag-race monitor. The students descended on the food table. Francesca's would-be embracer was lost in the crush.

The woman had no equal, thought Amelia. She never would have. Mercy was simply a welter of compassion and wooly ideals while Francesca had a heart as hard as a diamond and the mind of a chess master. Was it reason over passion, or passion over reason? Francesca had both in equal measure, and needed nothing less to run the school. She had inspired the worship of numerous young women, and had imitators who could put Mercy to shame. Amelia herself, for instance, appeared to be the chosen successor, she who would take over the school when its Principals stepped down. Not that one hoped for that time. Not that one could even imagine it.

Mouths full of sandwiches, the students milled about with cans of Coke, tripping on their gowns, stooping, great grown things that they were, to talk to their grandparents. Dugald smiled over the

heads of the crowd, happy and oblivious. The alumni made mysterious eye signals.

Amelia moved a little closer to Francesca. "There's something in
the wind. I fear there may be a speech. I mean by someone other
than the Headmaster."

"I sincerely hope you are wrong, Amelia."

Oh but I am not wrong, thought Amelia. She felt the tremor of
expectation in the air. One might imagine that an expression of love
from former students would be a good thing. But history teaches another lesson. No one wants to be bid goodbye; no king wants to give
up his throne, no queen her pedestal. It does not matter how kindly,
how well-intentioned the throngs who gather, whatever they say is
a sentence to exile. It is never too far a cry from "Happy Anniversary!" to "Time's up!," especially in Toronto. If you have done well
for a long time, we want no part of you. It was this way in Ancient
Athens, as well. A successful military campaign followed by a triumphant return to the polis was a virtual guarantee that your fellow
citizens would weary of you, that the little shards of pottery with
your name on them, *ostrakons*, would appear in the agora, and before long you'd find yourself outside the walls. *Ostracized.*

Francesca excused herself and went to Dugald's side. She stood
slender as an antenna, sensing danger. Waiting for whatever was in
store for them. Yes, today was a triumph. But the lessons of Greece
were all too clear. The gods are envious and disruptive. How does
Solon warn Croesus about assessing a man's life before his death? "If
man prospers till the end of his life he is truly fortunate and deserves
to be called happy. But till he does, do not call him happy but lucky.
In all things look to the end and final result. For gods often give men
a glimpse of happiness only to ruin them branch and root."

Even as his wife wrapped his arm in hers, Dugald's eye turned
away to the back of the crowd. Amelia followed his glance. It had
fallen on an old woman, a stranger as far as Amelia knew, supported
on either side by two middle-aged people. Her face was arresting;

in its lines were benevolence and calm. She had been a beauty, once, but she was heavy, and grey, *old*. She gazed around, her eyes clouded with white. Perhaps she had cataracts. Perhaps she was even blind. Her children—for the man and the woman who each held one of her arms must have been her children—were gentle with her. Dugald was riveted.

Bork was the one who took the microphone.

"We could not let this occasion pass without coming forward to give a public heartfelt congratulations to Miss Morrow and Dr. Laird for their tremendous success in maintaining the Manor School for half a century..."

Francesca stiffened and uttered a muffled protest. But Dugald wasn't listening. The old woman was not blind. Her eyes had settled on him, at first lightly, as if, to her, his face were simply one more in the crowd. But now those large, whitened, beautiful old eyes stopped their information-gathering and simply fixed on him.

Who was this?

Dugald turned his whole body toward her, as if compelled toward the hollowness of the woman's gaze. He went pale. There was no name for the look, although longing, devastation or, simply, pain made a start in describing it. Their eyes met. Between the two, each to each, passed a naked recognition, a simple yes, we meet again.

"...grateful for all they have done, and will continue to do, for young people, for the depth of their knowledge of the classical world, for their passion for the arts. I know personally I never see a pond without recalling Dr. Laird's lectures on the Circularity of Life..."

Some laughter here; the old Pond Lecture was always good for that.

Francesca, with her controlling forearm, held Dugald more tightly, turning her face to shield it from the applause that was surging, rising up from this little patio under the pergola.

"I cannot tell you how often, when at a loss for words at a formal dinner, I have resorted to my repertoire of lines of poetry memorized. '*Let me not to the marriage of true minds admit impediments.*' ..."

More laughter. Francesca vibrated like a tuning fork held up to sound middle C. To her, as to any perfectionist, the approbation of peers came preciously close to mockery, bringing to mind the ways in which she, Dugald and the Manor had failed. Living in the shadow of the Greeks, of Milton and Donne and Shakespeare and the Master, G. F. Watts, could not be easy. It made it difficult to appreciate one's own achievements.

"You must not thank us..." Francesca began, only to be drowned out in a roar of appreciation. In this way simpler hearts meaning well extended their clumsy warmth into deep waters and caused enormous offence. The noise rose up through the beams of the pergola and into the thinning leaf cover of the Norway maple. Francesca and Dugald, for his focus had come back to her now, bore the insult without flinching.

"Fifty years," Connaught continued, "is a very long time."

Not so very long, when it is your life. Here, Connaught showed his ignorance, his shallow focus on the ephemeral. Half a century may seem long to those whose ambitions are of this world alone, but in the great scheme of things it was only the winking of an eye. Dugald and Francesca suffered. Someone ought to rescue them. Amelia could not do it. Connaught blathered on.

The afternoon was growing chill: despite the earlier heat, summer was over, and the sun was dropping rapidly to the fringe of maple to the west. As it fell, a thin, grey mist sprang up from the pond. No doubt there was a scientific explanation—the unseasonable warmth, the coming change of season. These little fogs came and went, here in the park: upsurges of the buried Taddle, perhaps. Dugald would know. But Dugald was withdrawn and white, not within reach. Amelia saw his eyes return once more to the old woman's face, that remarkable face. Forrest Bard obviously thought so too; he trained his lens on her and snapped a photograph.

Connaught surely was winding to a conclusion. The little fog pressed up the terraces and caught the crowd around the ankles. It surged, while the champagne that Connaught had brought fizzed into rental flutes, and took hold, so that trouser legs and the blue hems of academic gowns, waistlines even, began to be swallowed in mist. Amelia turned her head to look for the old woman, but did not find her. When she looked back, all the right elbows were bent and raised for the toast, save Francesca's and Dugald's.

"Congratulations! On fifty years of patience! Fifty years of passion!"

Curiously, the little curls of fog avoided Amelia, stranding her on an island of grass, the Cheese, apart. Across the mist, she could see Dugald and Francesca, head and shoulders, holding fast to one another. That's when love swept Amelia's jaded heart once more and she wished she was the sort to protect these wonderful people from whatever was to come.

2

THE NAMING
CEREMONY

"THE TROJAN WAR has ended."

Miss Morrow stood, erect, beside the teacher's desk. Her gold-handled cane leaned against the chair, but she did not use it.

"Troy has been destroyed by the Greeks. There is no greater tragedy than the destruction of a great city. There has been mayhem and hideous violence; screams of terror and cries of grief have rent the air; the stones of the shrines run with blood.

"However, the victors are in trouble. The gods Athena and Poseidon are angry with them. One of their heroes, Ajax, has raped the seer Cassandra, a priestess at Athena's shrine. The gods have decided to teach the Greeks a lesson by making them suffer terrible journeys home. One of these will be the journey of Odysseus, which we know as the Odyssey. However, the gods' wrath provides no solace to the Trojans, whose city lies in ruins and whose women are about to be sent off to live in captivity."

It was an ordinary Monday. Amelia had stopped by the classroom door, on the excuse that she needed Miss Morrow's view on some administrative detail, but really just to listen to Francesca teach Euripides' *The Trojan Women*. In her classes, the students became accustomed to thinking in grand terms: emotions are enormous, so are flaws, mistakes have dire consequences, passions run riot, we are all playthings of the gods. It was a world view that fit well with the teenage mind.

"It is a play of lamentation," she pronounced. "Hecuba is at the centre: she was Queen of Troy but now her husband is dead, and her mad daughter Cassandra is to be married off to the victorious general. What do we know about Cassandra?"

Nobody knew about Cassandra, but the new girl blushed furiously.

"Recall," said Miss Morrow, "that the young priestess has been given the gift of prophecy by the god Apollo but because she spurned his advances, he made certain no one would ever believe what she said. What must it be like to see the future, to try to warn people, but to be ignored? A very special agony, hers . . ."

She felt Amelia's presence, and dipped her head without turning from her task.

"Picture it—the topless towers of Ilium are behind us." She gestured out the window and southward over the Park toward the smog-bound high-rises of the city. "The sea and the Greek ships lie ahead." The students looked northward out the windows; there lay the abandoned streetcar barns and beyond them, the jerk meat shop on St. Clair Avenue, now the waves of the Hellespont.

"Earlier, Cassandra tried to warn the people of Troy that the war would end in disaster. But King Priam, her father, shut her in a beehive tomb for her troubles. After she was released, she was raped, as we know, on the altar in Apollo's temple. Now, at the end of the war, she is to be taken by Agamemnon of the dreadful House of Atreus. She who has forsworn men! Imagine her terror! Imagine her mother's grief!"

Francesca opened her book, holding it in the palm of one hand. With the other slender hand she drew a quick circle around her face. It was mime for "a beautiful woman." She became Hecuba. She hardly needed to read: she knew the words by heart.

"Up, unhappy creature; lift your head and neck from the ground. This is Troy no more.... Set your course by the wind, sail as fate directs. Do not steer your ship of life head-on against the waves."

Amelia watched the new girl. She was twisting in her seat, sensing what was about to come down upon her by the coincidence of her name.

"Who shall read the other parts? Cassie, you must be Cassandra, your namesake."

Cassie looked positively terrified, whether of being asked to read aloud, or because she felt the doom of the seer falling on her shoulders.

"It is a beautiful name. And she is one of the most important woman in all of our literature and legends. Do you know what Cassandra stands for?"

Nobody spoke. They were watching and waiting for the new girl to be put in her place. But they were disappointed.

"Not really," mumbled Cassie. "She's just, like, a girl."

"But what does she signify, what does she bring to us across the ages?"

Squirm, blush. Then—"She knew things in a different way than everyone else."

Francesca looked delighted.

"My dear, you are absolutely right. I can see you deserve this important name you bear. Cassandra knows that it is not your brain you must trust. Not your will, either, that part of you that says 'I want.' She knows there is another way of receiving the deepest information about life. She knows how to listen to her inner wisdom. To try to pass that on to a world that would rather not believe her. Oh yes, Cassandra, I think you are well named. So: will you read the part for us?"

Cassie stuttered but could not find her tongue.

Amelia felt cold feathers of fear on her neck. It's done now, she thought. Cassie she was, Cassandra she would be. This was her naming ceremony, as engineered by Miss Morrow. The new girl would be the mad daughter, the virgin priestess who danced herself into frenzies and spoke in riddles. She would try to warn her countrymen and be reviled for her troubles. She would foresee her own death, by an axe in the hands of Clytemnestra, Agamemnon's wife. It was not a joyous fate.

"Okay," said Cassie in a small voice.

"And you, Darrin, must be Talthybius, the Greek messenger. Vida, the leader of the chorus. Shall we begin on page one hundred and ninety?" Francesca set herself up in the back corner of the room so that the students could not see her, only hear her voice fluting over their heads.

"And whose slave am I, the old woman who needs a stick to serve her as a third foot?"

This elicited sideways glances and suppressed giggles. Francesca stamped her cane.

"Ithaca's king, Odysseus, got you as his slave," said Darrin bravely.

"Ah, ah! Beat your cropped head, Hecuba, tear both cheeks with your nails! Oh, pity me, pity me..."

And they were away, swept to that sun-drenched shore. Amelia basked in Francesca's aura, the energy with which, day in and day out, she transported these unlikely children. The Headmistress rose on her toes and became seven feet tall. She was Hecuba, chief victim of the war, standing on a flat shore looking out to a bleak horizon.

"Which Greek of the Peloponnese or the north controls my fate?" challenged Vida.

"What is that glare from a pine torch burning inside?" responded Talthybius.

"It is my child Cassandra, who is rushing out here in a state of frenzy," said Francesca.

She fixed her eyes on poor Cassie. "Up girl, up," she admonished in a stage whisper. "You can't be in a state of frenzy all cramped up at that desk. Go, out the door. You are a priestess and seer about to become a bride. Gather your wits and come in at a run, brandishing a torch."

While Francesca suppressed the class by extending one long-fingered hand and moving it downward, like a conductor, Cassie lumbered out of her seat, book in hand. She brushed through the door beside Amelia. She looked about to cry, and Amelia turned to help her in the hallway. But there behind the door was a revelation. Suddenly all long arms and whipping hair, the shy girl yanked off blazer and tie and pulled her long brown curls out of their painful knot. She reached for the crocheted shawl Amelia always wore over her shoulders. Wordless, Amelia gave it.

"I need it for the seer's net," Cassie hissed, throwing it over her head. Next, Cassie-Cassandra bent to pull off her loafers and the collapsed knee socks that completed her ensemble. She would have set herself alight if necessary, to please Francesca. Oh, Amelia recognized it in her. The girl took a second to enter the role, and then burst back into the classroom.

"Raise up the torch! Bring it here, bring me light! I pay reverence to this temple—look, look!" Brandishing her shoe as the torch, she gave every appearance of being the mad bride who saw into the future. "Step high with quivering foot! Bring on, bring on the dance—evan! Evoe!"

Vida rose to her level. "My queen, seize hold of your daughter in her madness before she goes skipping off into the midst of the Greek army!"

"Oh my child," said Hecuba/Francesca, "I never thought to see your marriage celebrated amidst the spears and lances of the Greeks..."

"I will not speak of this," Cassandra shot back. She read from the text as if it had been written for her alone; gone was her feeble voice and tucked-in chin. Her eyes seemed to reflect the flame of her torch, the smoke and ashes of Troy behind them. Amelia and the students watched in awe as Cassie's voice rose and whirled in the small classroom. "I will not sing of the axe that will enter my neck and others', of the conflict that will see a mother killed thanks to my wedding, or the overthrow of Atreus' house..."

Only Francesca remained unsurprised, and completely in character. She leaned across the desktops as if casting herself on the beaches below Troy. "Let me lie where I have fallen; they merit falling, the sufferings I know...Oh my child, my Cassandra, wracked by divine ecstasy, your purity has been destroyed, and in such cruel circumstances!"

On she went, barely reading from the text, the words flowing effortlessly and building in power until—"Fortune has her favourites," rang out. "But not one should be called happy—do not think it—this side of the grave."

The bell sounded. The bell, at the Manor, was in fact an electronic doorbell programmed to play the last four notes of "Jesu, Joy of Man's Desiring." Francesca snapped shut her book where it lay in the palm of her right hand: "Enough!" she announced, instantly back to the present. "Thank you, Vida, Cassandra, Darrin. All, take up your pens. I shall give you a note."

Cassie stood tucking her shirt back into her kilt and looking embarrassed. Amelia handed her the blazer and socks she had retrieved from the hall floor. It would take a few moments for the new girl with her new name to shrink back, reluctantly, inside her own skin.

Amelia remembered being the new girl. She had been the new girl at school every year her whole life. An army brat; father's in the forces so the family moves to a new base annually. "Adjusting," as her parents called it, to new places got to be too much work and finally in grade ten she gave it up and drifted to shore sullen and friendless in British Columbia. School was restful in Burnaby; she didn't even have to try to make friends, because the black vapours that surrounded her were by then impenetrable to eye and ear and she did not care who was out there. She closed in on the end of the school year without a passing grade to her name, nor a skill to apply to a future, nor even a pleasant word to say to another living creature. A family decision was made to send her to live with her grandmother in Toronto. She resisted. But begging came to nothing. She was moved again against her will and set down even angrier and uglier than she had been the year before. Grandmother put up the money for her to attend the Manor School. Her parents had burned out by then.

She could see herself, seventeen years old and forty pounds heavier than she was today, squared off against the world, stupid, red hair frizzing angrily around her face before being drawn back to a tangled tail that hung down her back. Standing at the foot of the staircase to the second floor, white shirt with dirt inside the collar, misbuttoned; tie askew with a strangler's knot pulled sideways at the neck; kilt straining on her nonexistent waist. In front of her was the beautiful full-length portrait of a red-haired woman in a loose dress with a large bonnet, holding a basket of flowers. Its saffrons and crimsons were magnetic against the cool green walls of the house. Amelia was curious. The woman had a sulky power, a wounded, sensuous look for all her innocent trappings. What was her story? She slid over to read the writing on the bottom edge: "Lilian," it said. "1904. G. F. Watts."

The door at the top of the stairs opened; the Headmistress of the Manor School began to descend, a tricky business, as she wore some floating, fur-trimmed gown and impossibly high heels.

"My dear," she said, extending a long graceful hand. "How do you do?"

Amelia could think of no response. Miss Morrow looked at her in a kindly way. "My office is above." She took a few steps into the hall and stood before the portrait. Her hand fluttered up to her waist and paused there in a subtle, eloquent wave, halfway between a

'Hello' to a loved one and a guide's indication of a precious item in the collection.

"My mother," she said, before turning back to climb the stairs.

At the landing they turned and climbed some more, as the stairs grew narrower. Farther above, where Amelia did not dare look, were the Principals' lodgings. Small quarters, but no matter: most weekends they went to New York to visit the museums. Amelia had gleaned these scraps of sophistication from overheard locker-side conversations. Francesca opened a door.

"Please come in," she said.

The little room was stuffed with plaster busts and gold icons, the walls and windows draped with tapestries. Miss Morrow blended into its riches like a pope into a Vatican parlour. She perched on a fur pelt on a green velvet divan and gestured Amelia to a loveseat. Their talk was to begin.

"Childhood is a hoax," said Francesca.

"What?"

"A hoax," repeated Francesca firmly. She had quickly determined Amelia's exact stage of rebellion. "Life starts right in at you not caring if you are five or fifty. You may use up any number of your precious appointed years trying to understand this. Or you may simply take my word for it. There is no part of life that doesn't count."

All Amelia could do was stare. Had Francesca read her thoughts? She knew she had screwed up badly but she had assumed it didn't really *count*, not yet, because she was still a kid, and anyway tomorrow she would start trying and the whole bad record would reverse itself.

"The dose life gives you," continued the Headmistress, "is as harsh and as richly wounding to babes as it is to those in their final years. Until death, as the poet said, joins us to the great majority."

Speak for yourself, Amelia thought. How dare Miss Morrow say this? No adult was so brutal, certainly not on first meeting. But then she grew curious. Maybe Miss Morrow was speaking for herself.

Had she ever had a childhood? And, if not, who robbed her of it? Presumably that horrid woman, Lilian, hanging in the front hall.

Obviously Miss Morrow had been born, had been young once—but how and where? Had she toddled in elegant garments trimmed with fur, in narrow waists and high ruffled collars, porcelain-skinned and coiffed? When had she become posture perfect, measured as a metronome? Amelia's grandmother had heard things around town, rumours that Francesca had been on the London stage, that she was a countess, that she had a villa in Greece. It's nonsense, her grandmother had said, but looking at her Amelia wondered: Could it all be true?

Here was the point at which Francesca unfurled herself from the divan and walked around Amelia's chair thrice, in the manner of a sorceress, noting the set of Amelia's head on her shoulders and the angle and length of her neck. Here was the baptism, the naming ceremony. After the likeness to the Long-Necked Madonna had been pronounced, the Headmistress retreated to her divan, sat, and spoke on. Amelia came to understand that there would be no tolerance at this school for her lazy and rude behaviour, that she had immense gifts and was duty bound to employ them in the service of great works, greater knowledge, greater understanding of the human condition. The lecture was apparently artless, spontaneous and sincere. Amelia found herself in complete agreement. Total reform of her behaviour would be immediate. The lecture ended. A smile was bestowed. Francesca rose. Amelia rose. They walked down the stairs together, and stood in the front hall. Then, "Have you any questions?"

Amelia did have a question. But it was not about school work, it was about Lilian, who gazed discontentedly down on them. "Why do you have the painting of your mother there?"

Francesca looked up to the portrait, then down to Amelia. Did she notice the similarity of expression, the curious frizz of the red hair around both faces? Unclear. Nothing disturbed her composure.

"You show curiosity, which is the first sign of aptitude. One must never thwart curiosity. It must always be encouraged by forthright responses. Lily—my mother—was an orphan." She told Amelia the story, how Lily was invited to play in the garden at Limnerslease, home of the great painter George F. Watts and his child bride, the great actress Ellen Terry. How Lily had been adopted by Watts. "And one day he saw her in her garden hat, and the shepherdess' dress, as you see, and he painted her. Two years later she married and came to Canada. This house was built for her, and this hall alcove was designed especially to hold her portrait."

"Where is she now?"

"She is dead now; this painting is the only place where she is alive. That's why art is such a marvellous thing, Amelia Holt."

"Is that really what she looked like?"

Francesca's face, which had been luminous with the pleasure of this encounter, turned opaque. "The eyes are very much her."

Francesca would have been a marvellous actress. Perhaps what made her a good teacher was the great actress in her past, that oft-remarked link to Ellen Terry. A bit of a reach for a relation, but that had never stopped Francesca. The Ellen Terry connection was one of the myths of the Manor.

Amelia took the myth at face value for her student years. But later, when she returned to teach at the Manor, she investigated. The facts were that "the Master," G. F. Watts, painter of mythological scenes, fell in love with Ellen Terry when she was a mere fifteen, and playing on the London stage. He, forty-seven, considered adopting her but was told she was too old; he asked his friends if he might marry her, but they said she was too young. He kissed her, and she thought she was with child and told her mother they must be married. She wanted, she said, to live with his pictures.

It is unclear if the marriage was ever consummated; Ellen was found cast down the staircase on her wedding night, weeping and clinging to the banister. Watts liked to fumble around, someone said later, but he couldn't do much. When they divorced he paid her an allowance to keep her with her parents, and away from the immoral life of the theatre. She went on to have a glorious career and several more husbands.

After Ellen, Watts conceived a passion for her playmate, Lily. Having learned his lesson, he adopted her and married a woman more his age. Amelia classified it as one of those Victorian stories where unusual sexual proclivities went under the rubric of charity. Plainly put, the Master liked little girls. You could feel it in his painting of Lily. The fey presence of the young girl with her basket of flowers was infused with erotic longing. One could see her arrogance, her sense that she held the old painter in thrall; one felt too that the Master had pinioned her, a lovely butterfly on a corkboard. A fair exchange.

Under those smouldering eyes, the eyes of Lily-by-Watts, the ordinary Monday wore on. Classes changed as ever at the sound of the Bach chimes and, as ever, when Miss Morrow crossed the foyer, she allowed her left hand to rise to her waist and float for a second like a small displaced wing, acknowledging Lily. Hello, Mother; notice me, Mother; *pace* Mother. At first break, the doors opened and the kids spilled down the walk to Taddle Creek Drive. Ashley went around to the wrought-iron gates and unchained Spit, the stiff-whiskered mongrel she'd adopted. He was a squeegee dog before she had him and he'd been hit by a car. He flinched all the time at the sound of engines and she thought that was cool.

Across the street and beyond were the Wychwood Barns, once storing grounds for Toronto's streetcars, now disused. The windows were boarded over, but tracks still ran in and out of the sheds under the locked wooden doors. Grass grew through them. It was a good place to burn, to shroom, to get hammered. It was a good place to do any number of things meant to be accomplished without an audience, and most of them had been done there. Beyond the yards was St. Clair Avenue. Manor students were technically not allowed to go that far on breaks. Instead, they were to buy their meal at the truck.

Without exception, the truck appeared at break times throughout the day. And there it was on this ordinary Monday, parked in front of the school, its quilted-look aluminum sides agleam in the sun, the canteen truck in all its glory, coffee warm, grill hot, counter stacked with bags of sour-cream-flavoured potato chips. Ferdinand presided, as he did every day, swarthy, with his huge head of black curls and his stumpy arms, his awkward lurch on one lifted shoe.

"What you wanna do? You 'sposa pay me for that. You pay off that tab one day soon?" he said to Ashley. She'd taken a chocolate bar to feed to Spit, even though Roxanne kept telling her that chocolate was toxic to dogs.

"My dad's gonna come and pay."

"Yeah, you say so. Tell me when; I wanna know."

He took a toonie as downpayment and grinned. They were good for the money, these kids, and he didn't want them to go hungry. Some of the girls looked for any excuse to starve themselves.

"Like, Ferdinand, how old are these egg-salad sandwiches?"

"I pick 'em up fresh this morning! It's good enough for those guys fixing the library down at the university, it's good enough for you."

The rat girls grabbed some Diet Cokes and then ran down the sidewalk away from school, headed across the street, planning to go hack some dang on Smokers' Corner. Cassie hung back, and then bought a hot dog. She ate it standing alone. The rat girls watched her as they leaned against the shed wall; carefully she sucked the mustard off each finger in sequence.

"That girl is just weird," said Ashley.

"Look at her," muttered Maureen. "Like it's eleven o'clock in the morning, and I'm going to eat animal fat? Gross."

"You never eat anyway," said Vida.

"Have you heard, like, the way she hums? Like when she's doing math or something? Fuckin' drives me up the wall."

"You got a spliff?"

"I got rollies. I got weed." Maureen pulled a zip-lock bag out of her knee sock.

Cassie looked on in mild astonishment.

———————

After break, because it remained unseasonably warm, Dr. Laird decided to take his science 20 class outside. For this autumn's new-comers to the school it would be the first time they'd hear the omnibus Pond Lecture. For the others it was a repeat. All good lectures bore repeating.

He led the way down the terraced lawn, his faded black gown hanging from his shoulder blades like drooping bat wings. Miss Morrow was by his side, narrow and Edwardian in a fawn suede skirt as soft as chamois, her right hand holding a broad-brimmed straw hat firmly down on her head. She would never allow the sun, even reduced in its impact as it was at this time of year, to discolour her face. The student body trekked out from the basement exit.

The pond, or "our pond" as the Principals were fond of calling it, was home to birds and fish and various life forms, and was, more importantly, inspiration for the annual restatement of the theme Life is Circular. Everything from sketching to eurythmics to biology had been taught around the edges of the pond, although swimming was no longer desirable due to poisonous scum. The students arranged themselves round and about on rocks and against the trunks of trees, their binders open on their knees. The rat girls were conspicuous in their absence, and Francesca held up her hand to stop proceedings.

"They're coming," said Amelia. She could see them, scattered, giggling, all arms and legs and swinging knapsack straps, struggling out the back door of the school. Stoned again, no doubt. They headed for an open space and then, seeing that Cassie sat directly beside it, pointedly moved away.

Dugald settled himself somewhat precariously atop a large rock at the edge of the pond. He held his breath and raised one black eyebrow until the rats settled down. Then he began to speak.

"Students," he intoned, "my dear, dear students. It is such a marvellous, marvellous day." On cue, a cardinal sang in the trees. Amelia looked up and caught a glimpse of the pretty dun breast and the red tail of a female. She looked down and saw the idiot Dimitri write "marvellous day" under the date in his notebook.

"The pond is rich, diverse and the beginning of all life. We have much to learn here. A few facts before I go on. This pond was created by man. Not god. Man is a copycat, not a creator. Genius is not afraid of repetition. Nor does a true professional fear redundancy. We must imitate greatness. If not greatness, then what?"

He took this overly formal, almost coy tone when he was most enjoying himself. As if he would have liked to be meeting them for the very first time, and impressing them with his civility and wit. "Miss Morrow will in due course give you classes here in painting, and you will discuss the organization of space, framing with landscape elements, these painterly concerns, kept uppermost in mind by the Park's designers. For this, as I have pointed out to you, is a man-made nature, but nature all the same.

"How did this happen? I shall remind you. In the year 1890 the founders of Wychwood Park, Mr. Marmaduke Matthews, who was, as many of you know, my grandfather, and his partner, Mr. Alexander Jardine, owner of the Golden Sun Baking Powder Company, dammed Taddle Creek at this spot. A small digression: What do you suppose it meant to be a baking-powder millionaire in the nineteenth century? Would you make a million marketing the stuff now? Who uses it?"

"We used it to make fire extinguishers in grade ten science," said Sara helpfully. Everyone laughed.

"Look in your kitchen cupboards. One battered tin that remains for years, if you have any at all. But then—*then*—women used it several times a day. Baking bread, pies, cakes...What, I wonder, is today's equivalent?"

"Make-up?"

"What is the chemical composition of baking powder? What does it do? It causes other ingredients to change states, does it not? Is it a catalyst? I give you questions more than answers. You find the answers. What interests me about baking powder is that it causes transformations. Transformations, students, are in everything we study. Changing state or form. Ovid calls it metamorphosis. Who knows the Greek?" There were no hands. Jacob would have answered but he had forgotten his clipboard and was trudging back up to the school.

"But I digress. As I said, let us get the facts out of the way. Take a note, if you please!" He paused while the disorganized got out their pens.

"*Recall.* The Lake Iroquois Escarpment. Point form. A steep drop of approximately twelve metres. The lake itself, a great flat body of fresh water, stretching from here to Buffalo. The escarpment as shoreline. Shoreline shrinking back to leave Lake Ontario as we know it. In spring, water running over the escarpment lip to meet the lake waters. Taddle Creek as runoff. Yet you see it not. Indeed, all we see is a little pond, and the pond is stopped quite still, and appears to go nowhere."

He gestured through the light gold leaf canopy, beyond the six-foot wire fence, which had been erected by the neighbourhood council to prevent children and drunks from falling in.

"All that flows out of our pond is a very small sludgy stream of water, which disappears not far from here down a sewer grate at the corner of Davenport and Bathurst. I have taken many of you to see it: the remains of Taddle Creek slipping away, darkly away. Into the sewer system! Can you imagine? This is all that may be seen without donning a frogman suit and plunging into torrents of Toronto's waste. The lively Taddle, reduced to carrying our shit." His voice was picking up volume. Francesca took up a post to his left, facing him, watchful. He paused for a moment. "Forgive my language," he remarked, more mildly.

He was forgiven. His charm was a good part of his success as a lecturer. A titter went through the rat girls, who had taken seats on damp grass and were feeling the soft cool ground through kilts and bare legs.

"Once, the Taddle gurgled brightly in sunshine past us all, through the city and into the lake. Gaze behind you: can you see it?"

Experienced students gazed at their fingernails or their shoes. The more recent arrivals, those who had not heard this lecture before, looked nervously over their shoulders as if the creek and other figments of prehistory might rise up at Dr. Laird's call.

"It would have been right before your eyes had you sat here one hundred, or one hundred and fifteen years ago. It is now Invisible. But even though it is invisible, it is there. It is more real than MTV, more real than Thai spring rolls, more true than the *Sunday Sun*, more important than the Lastman-mayor and those bloody appliances he sells—why do you suppose that is?"

"Because you keep talking about it?" quipped Chino.

Francesca, her arms folded across her chest, threw a warning look at the boy. Satisfied that there was no mockery, only matching humour, in his remark, she cast her eyes respectfully back to her husband.

"Do you see? While our giant metropolis seems at first to have erased it, the reality is, The Creek Lives!" He gazed at skeptical faces. "You will want proof, I suppose. Very well. Its path exists. Last year we took a walk along its banks. Recall: we journeyed southward walking over the ground that hid our bygone waters, down into the Annex to the Cathedral of St. Alban, on Albany Avenue. The creek formed a swimming hole there. Then eastward, where it crossed Bloor Street and ran with gently sloping banks between the Royal Ontario

Museum and the Royal Conservatory of Music. Its dry bed is what we now call Philosophers' Walk. It pooled again in front of Hart House. It meandered down to Massey Hall. And so on and so forth."

"Dr. Laird?" Jacob the brain was waving his hand. His were the only questions Dugald ever took.

"Yes, son."

"That might be proof that it did exist. It isn't proof that it exists now."

"Right you are! I stand corrected. All right, students. What is the proof that the creek exists today? Why, the pond! The pond is the first proof. It is fed by the spring. And further proof that the creek flows invisibly underground? When they built the Park Plaza they struck the flow. After heavy rains, there is flooding in the basements of the Museum. In the basement of the Hospital for Sick Children water also rises. It is the Revenge of the Taddle."

Amelia hissed at the rat girls, who appeared about to topple into the drink.

"Allow me a digression... This is the city that once uttered the slogan Sewers not Moores! You're too young to remember. Even your parents may be too young to remember. But Francesca and I remember. That shameful time when the great British sculptor Henry Moore offered the city his sculptures if it would build a gallery for them, but the council decided to spend the money on sewers. Pipe dreams, indeed."

Vida nudged Maureen's foot with her toe. They smiled, not at each other, but at the toe of Maureen's shoe. Francesca moved to separate them.

"But to get back to science... Before us Taddle Creek was a lifeline for the Mississauga Ojibwa Indians. And before the Indians, the pine and balsam, the beavers—"

A massive gasp of suppressed laughter followed the word beaver. Francesca swooped down and pulled two boys from the ranks, shaking them by the arm.

"...swans, frogs and snapping turtles, which shared the waters. Today as you look around the pond you will see black willow, Manitoba maple, black locust. You might find beech and elm, blue spruce, a chestnut tree and even the rare Chinese gingko. You will hear the word ecosystem often enough. This is indeed one. The swans are bottom-feeders and therefore help to control the weeds. So are the goldfish, which have made scientific history. And therein lies a tale. Who has heard it?"

Oh, I have, thought Amelia. I have once or twice. She was feeling pleasantly sleepy under the sun.

"Cast yourselves back about ninety-two years. It is June, in 1908. A small boy who lives in the park is going away for the summer and will not be allowed to take his goldfish. Wanting to at least give them a chance to live, he tosses the tiny greyish specimens in the pond. He is told that they will freeze to death, over the winter. But this little boy, who is wise indeed, replies that if they die they will at least have had a glorious few months swimming in the pond first.

"But, miraculously, the goldfish survive not only all summer in the wild but all winter as well. In spring the children report it, the fishermen report it. Indeed, the fish have not only survived but multiplied, and the next summer there are more. How did they do it? We know the pond is very deep in places. Do they live under the ice? Perhaps. But some claim that a goldfish can freeze solid, and then melt and come back to life in spring. We have tested this, at the Manor. With a twelve-inch giant goldfish produced right here. Froze it solid and..."

Francesca and Amelia shared a small smile. That would be the time he lifted the great slippery frozen fish and smacked it on the counter of the science lab, where it shattered into a thousand pieces and girls ran screaming into the street.

"We were unable to bring it back to life. But—they do survive. The pond becomes a hostel for abandoned goldfish as more and more residents deposit their unwanted fish.

"Now eight years have passed. Our boy, the boy we began with, is eighteen years old. He has gone overseas to fight in the Great War, and he dies, at Amiens in France. His family, grieving, walking by the pond, look into the water and what do they see? Multitudes of gleaming orange fish beneath the surface, full of life, full of vigour. And they take some pleasure in that. They understand that the boy, with his faith that a risky existence in the larger pond was better than life in a bowl, had prefigured his own life. And death. And they knew that he was glad he had gone to war, even though he did not come back."

Here Dugald permitted himself a sentimental pause, for the boy in question had been his uncle.

"So you see. Goldfish. Transformations. Metaphors. Lovely things they are, with a tail like a froth of tulle, and gleaming scales. But they are cannibals, you know. They even eat their own young, when they can't find anything else..."

———

Amelia slipped away from the pondside lecture, back to the second floor closet that was called the administration office. Leaving the door open the crack that was required—Francesca hated to give anyone complete privacy—she sat at her desk. She did two things.

First, she called Forrest Bard and left a message on his machine asking to see his contact sheets of the commencement. She was curious, idly so, some might say, but then her curiosity was never entirely free of mischief-making. Second, she pulled her laptop computer out of her desk drawer, stealthily, as if it were contraband. It was contraband. Francesca hated computers. But as it was becoming increasingly difficult to track the payment of fees, the purchase of uniforms and the students' grades without one, Amelia had reached the point of secret defiance. She began typing in names and records, her long, expressive lips pulled back firmly, creating dimples of determination as she tapped away.

In the doorway appeared a shade, the thin form of Miss Morrow atop her platform shoes. Was the Pond Lecture over early? Amelia shut the screen and lay her arms and chest over the laptop as if she'd been napping. "Mmmm?" she said. "I'm so tired, I'm sorry."

But Francesca seemed not to notice. She was preoccupied. "The new girl, Cassandra, is going to be lovely."

"Yes."

"Some of the others are being cruel. They say they find her behaviour frightening. They tease her. I would like you to help me put a stop to this."

"Yes, Miss Morrow."

"She is immensely gifted."

Amelia had heard that before. Amelia was not so certain. Cassie frightened her as well. She was too intense, perhaps slightly mad. "She hums."

"A nervous habit," said Francesca. She stared over the desk with an absent curiosity. "Sit up, dear. I suppose it's not too soon to think of our spring trip to Greece? We must let the parents know that it will be available to the older students."

Amelia shook out her hair to distract Francesca's gaze, and slid a large brown envelope over the computer. "Yes."

"The chance of a lifetime, to accompany Dugald and me to the birthplace of the ages."

"It's a few months off but, yes, Francesca, I'll write up a notice."

"You'll write up a reminder? Thank you, Amelia darling," she said. "I did need some more Xerox copies of "La Belle Dame sans Merci" too. The little scoundrels complained that I didn't have enough when I distributed them last Friday."

"It won't be difficult to get a few more." Amelia hoped against hope that the Headmistress' glance would not come down as far as the desk. Normally the posture and elevated gaze of her leader would ensure that.

"And put that computer away."

Amelia flushed violet. It had slid halfway down to her knees. She drew the thin, charcoal-coloured machine slowly onto her lap.

"You know I do not allow them in the school. You must not *persist* in working on one. It sets a bad example to the children. They must practise their handwriting—"

"At sixteen?"

"At sixty!" Francesca snapped. "The connection is there, always, with the brain, in the fluid curves of a good cursive hand. I will not see it lost! All records and communication at the Manor School will be kept by hand!"

Amelia's heart had begun to race in her chest.

"The parents want—" she began. She could not bear being scolded. She wanted to throw the machine at Francesca's feet, or out the window. "The parents wonder about accuracy—" she tried again. But she knew it was useless. She ought to shout that she would not be ordered about any longer, that she would not be party to this insane resistance to labour-saving devices. But she merely bit her long lips until they hurt.

"Child," said Francesca, almost beseeching.

"I am not your child."

"No. You are not."

Francesca betrayed no heat. Several minutes passed, during which Amelia slowly put the computer under her desk near her feet and withdrew from a bottom drawer the old green leather ledgers where grades were recorded. Francesca stood, her face as pale and untroubled as ever, looking out the window toward the gardens where Dugald strode, gown aflutter behind him, students in his wake.

"I have no child."

Amelia fumed. Of course she had no child. Children would have been a disaster and not only for the waistline of this woman. She had imaginary children. What was that line about poetry? Real toads in imaginary gardens? Francesca had real gardens with imaginary toads. Blood children would only have muddied the definitive notions she had about intellectual dedication and passion. The students were not children but accomplishments, like the pottery vessels from Limnerslease, tempered in the same fire, glazed and deeply scored, as it were, by Manor masters and Manor principles.

"I have loved the children of others," said Francesca.

There was a silence. Amelia cocked her head on her long, sinewed neck. What was this? A moment of regret? An appeal for understanding? Then, as always, her affection for Francesca overflowed the cup of her anger.

"You have indeed, you have done it with extraordinary devotion," she mumbled, noting the past tense. "And I—" What could she say? She felt as strongly as ever the desire to help Francesca and Dugald, to be part of their noble and occasionally absurd struggle to uphold ideals of greatness in a world of disposable, thirty-second cool. But how, when the older woman so resolutely resisted?

Amelia had signed on as assistant in all matters in order to understand how the school was run, to improve the efficiency, eventually to change it for the better. But the more a change began to seem necessary, the more remote became its possibility. As easily as she could once imagine the little Eden carrying on into the next century, so now could Amelia predict the decline and fall of the Manor School for Classical Studies. Occasionally she fantasized a palace coup, although, as she was the only worker in the palace, this seemed unlikely. Might there be a rebellion led by a child, one tiny fireplug who stood up against the weight of all these years, all this authority?

A doomed rebellion it would be, of course. She and the rebel children would be the infidels cast against the Principals, who stood with the greatest masters of all time, Rembrandt, Van Gogh, "Leonardo," as Francesca called him, as if he were her dear friend, Keats, Chaucer, Picasso, Dali. And G. F. Watts. Thundering like God out of one of his Titian-puffy clouds.

The rebellion would be lost. Amelia would be thrust out of Eden.

Her heart swelled with the imagined loss. The rock garden planted each spring by the children, the crypt with its copy of the Rosetta stone, the six-foot sepia photograph of the goddess adjusting her sandal from the Temple of Athena Nike that hung in the stairwell. She mourned in advance the missed karate championships, the poetry marathons, the art-gallery field trips. She bade farewell in her mind to the deliciously odd students: the Russian girl who painted as if she'd worked in Michelangelo's studio, but whose parents were certainly black-market mafia; officious young Jacob, who stood with his hands in his pockets outside the door to the school every morning to greet them all.

It was too much to lose.

"Amelia, dear."

She raised her head from the ledger. "Yes, Francesca?"

"You are a great personal delight to me, a great personal delight, Amelia."

What was this all about?

"There they come," the Headmistress said, and her voice faltered. She suddenly turned on her heel and left the room.

It was nearly four in the afternoon before Amelia could pull out her laptop again. Then suddenly the new girl was in her office.

Stop calling her the new girl, Amelia said to herself. She has a name. Her name is Cassie. At least it was when she came here. Now it is Cassandra.

Cassandra stood in front of Amelia. She did not speak. It was obvious she wanted something. It annoyed Amelia that she had to be the one to initiate the communication.

"Yes? What can I do for you?"

"I don't know," said Cassie. "Maybe nothing."

This was added wistfully, not aggressively.

"Well then, neither do I." Really. At that hour of the day a student had to look sharp or Amelia had no time for her. And Cassie was an annoying girl. She had a touch of the British schoolgirl of the fifties, chubby and owlish with a smeary mouth all atremble. But there was a blindsided look to her: she did not meet your eye. She was humming absently and twisting bits of fabric in her fingers.

"I think I lost my English binder," she finally confessed.

Amelia braced herself.

"And my history notes."

She was breaking it to her slowly.

"Maybe French too."

Amelia sighed. She recognized the hand of James Janitor. She hated this part.

"James Janitor jettisoned them," she said. "The jackanapes." The word play did not bring a smile to Cassie's face.

"What?"

"The consignment of student work to the garbage by custodial staff is one of the Manor's more contentious policies," Amelia explained. She often became alliterative under stress. It was a habit she'd picked up from Miss Morrow. Words were crisp, various and linked by common beginnings. Difficult speeches, especially, took on this formal quality. She tried to lighten up.

"We are a very small school. If everyone left his binder—his coat, his knapsack, his artwork, whatever—out on the table, we wouldn't be able to see the desks for trash. No one could work. School policy is that the janitor collects what is left behind at the end of a school day and throws it all out, I'm afraid."

"For good?" Stark terror.

"Miss Morrow's rules." No, that was not good enough. Amelia not only had to explain the rule, but to defend it. "The students do eventually learn."

"But all my work!" Cassie looked as if she were going to cry, more from the perceived injustice than from her own hurt; Amelia recognized the look. Then Cassie went on the offensive, if somewhat pathetically.

"I'll get my mother to phone."

"Oh, don't, please," said Amelia wearily. "It's been done." In fact, only this morning a mother had called in to complain. To Amelia the mother had said, first thing this morning, "Can it possibly be true that you have thrown in the garbage Darrin's entire French binder for this term, as he claims? And that he will be required to recopy the entire course by hand from Vida?"

Amelia had explained and, after fifteen minutes, Darrin's mother had hung up the telephone, infuriated at this rigid policy but half-believing that it would work, that next time Darrin would put his books and binders in his locker immediately after class. But it rarely worked that way. In fact the students who had the greatest difficulty organizing themselves were hit again and again by the janitor's de-structive raids, were utterly destabilized, failed to find and recopy a decent set of notes, and fell further and further behind. Sometimes a kind fellow student engaged in a weekend's orgy of xeroxing to per-form a rescue, but more often bad went to worse and the kid ended up in Miss Morrow's office. After the F was given Miss Morrow would issue a dispensation; in exchange for Darrin memorizing "The Wreck of the Hesperus," he would pass history; if he wrote a one-thousand word essay on attic vases, he could advance to grade ten without having to repeat grade nine art. The benefits of this program entirely escaped Amelia.

Cassie broke down in tears. Tears upset Amelia. Besides, she was feeling rebellious. "Cassie," she said, overcoming her revulsion at the girl's lack of self-control. "Come closer." Cassie stepped a foot closer to the desk. Amelia gestured for her to shut the door.

"The truth is," Amelia said in a low voice, "I hate the garbaging policy. I picture James Janitor as Death with his scythe and his reek-ing, rolling garbage can, roving the darkened halls of the Manor after all have gone home, searching for victims. I can see him in the gloom of near night, unloading his heist behind the shed, into a sinister large green bin."

Again her attempt to make the girl laugh failed.

"Let me tell you something. Can you keep a secret? You must not tell Miss Morrow because if you do she will think I am a snake in the grass."

Cassie nodded and sniffed.

"Let me tell you this. It will save you some grief. It took me a year to learn this when I was a student here."

Cassie stopped sniffing.

Amelia whispered. "The truth is, poor James hates to throw things out as much as the students hate him for doing it."

"Huh?"

And so Amelia revealed James Janitor's secret. Under the vengeful eye of Francesca Morrow, at precisely 3:45 in the afternoon, he did indeed sweep the forgotten books and papers off the tables, and more than occasionally a purse, a knapsack, a stray glove or a sweater, swept all into his blue can on wheels with the black garbage bag inside it. Then he went behind the studio to the shed where he kept the lawn mower, the floor polisher and his antique vacuum cleaner and mops. He pulled the bag out of its blue catcher. He tied a knot in the top and placed it carefully behind the hanging mops in the corner so that it could not be seen. Garbage collection was on Tuesday and Friday mornings, so before eight a.m. on those days James Janitor was mysteriously to be found in that shed, although he did not begin work until three-thirty in the afternoon. A student could approach him and, with a potted African violet (which James' wife collected), a package of cigarettes or even a chocolate bar bought on the tab from Ferdinand, purchase back his lost items.

Thus Amelia explained both the draconian laws of the Manor and the way in which these laws could be circumvented.

Cassie asked, "Does Miss Morrow know?"

"Oh heavens no."

"Well then, it's not fair and I can't do it."

Amelia was shocked.

"Everyone does it," she said.

"But it's dishonest."

"Well, sort of." Amelia explained that there were those in the student body who believed that Miss Morrow knew and understood all of the above, that it suited her view of life: one should be punished for sloth and disorganization and forgetfulness, but that it was punishment enough to have to descend into the underworld of the shed and have to make bargains with the gatekeeper of the House of the Dead. Then again, there were others who were convinced that Miss Morrow really did intend every careless student to lose forever his or her school work, and that she would have been outraged to know of the trade in textbooks and binders that went on at the back of the property.

Cassie's pasty face worked; she sucked her lips inside her teeth and her eyes popped. "I won't tell anyone, Miss Holt," she said. "But I think you really are a snake in the grass."

3

THE MARRIAGE
RITUAL

DUGALD LAIRD OPENED the side door and stepped away from the Manor. He took the narrow brick path alongside the house, the path that led away from the park toward Taddle Creek Drive. It was the path the students used, coming and going. He listened for voices and heard only the purr of an expensive car pulling away. He listened with the other ear, behind, toward the coach house, and heard nothing. Of course this did not mean much. He heard very little.

And yet, as he insisted, rumours of his deafness were vastly exaggerated. It was not true that he couldn't hear the questions in calculus class. Not true that he didn't hear swearing in the halls between classes, nor that girls' higher voices never reached his ears. And certainly not true that he didn't hear the laughter at his ancient jokes or, rather, at the fact that he still told them. It was true, however, that what met his ear most pleasingly these days was silence.

The silence now swelling around made him conclude that the last of the students was gone for the day. It was five o'clock, after all. Even the slowest, the most reluctant to tear herself away, would have gone off to the streetcar, the pool hall, or been picked up at the curb by a mother in an Audi. Amelia, for a change, appeared to have fled the premises ahead of her charges. More luscious even than the exterior variety was the silence inside his head. The perfect, unbroken, spacious, all-embracing, even voluptuous silence of his seniority. Dugald Laird, at the age of eighty-five, at last understood that he was old.

He was a tall man, fit as a fiddle, his doctor told him. He had reached this great age, this stupendous age, effortlessly. He had been, until now, not so much old as avid. In the lines of his sharp-chinned, somehow febrile face was written a desire for life, for more life than had been granted thus far, for admiration, for adventure. His body had become harder, sharper and more pointed as years stripped the flesh from it. He could be faintly ridiculous, in the way of a line drawing; his more astute martial arts students likened him to Don Quixote, minus the horse. He did have a vaguely Latin look to him, and he did on occasion, like that Spanish jouster, set his spindly limbs against windmills thinking they were giants, but he saw nothing shameful in this. There were enemies abroad in the land, certainly. Enemies in lax principles, weak morality, a lost path to the sacred spring of human imagination, to the glories of the ages of Homo erectus. One must keep one's powers at the ready.

But Dugald was not Spanish. He was not black, native or Asian either, although the glow of some darker-skinned interloper—black Irish? Mediterranean? Native Canadian?—had always lit his features mysteriously, seductively. He was born and bred in the tidy enclave of Wychwood Park, a legitimate grandson of its English founder. Though his other features remained true to the traditional Canadian Celtic/English/Scots mix, his skin and narrow eyes had allowed him to adopt many guises. When he finished high school he grew a Fu Manchu and played mah-jong in Gastown. Then he shaved it, grew a ponytail and walked north from Horseshoe Bay with a rucksack, eventually taking a job as a cook in a lumber camp, where he was assumed to be native by all but the natives. He made his way back to Toronto at the beginning of the war only to be rejected for enlistment because of a heart murmur.

It was a point of pride, in retrospect, the young man he'd been, flailing drunkenly at police in the doorway of the Wheat Sheaf on King Street, sixty-odd years ago. The old dojo on Richmond had saved him. Dugald had discovered it by wandering out the side door of the bar, along the alley, and down a set of stairs to the basement. To this day the smell of rising damp went straight to his belly, where lay the coals of that early rage, pounded out into those bags that swung like giant lozenges from the ceiling.

The first thing he had seen in the perfectly clean and empty below-ground room was the old black master, with the ears that curled forward like cupped hands, kneeling in front of a shrine. Karate was not known then, in Toronto. The joke in the bar was that the black-skinned basement warrior known to his disciples as Sensei had come up through the Underground Railroad. But he was hybrid, as was his art—part Filipino, part Korean, a little Japanese. The old man took no notice of Dugald. Dugald watched, completely still, while Sensei went through his kata, punching and blocking and kicking in geometric patterns around himself as if he were the mechanism of some complex, humanoid clock.

Once he began to study, Dugald loved the martial arts, the grimaces on the faces of his fellows, the kiais they shouted: "Die!" "Stop!," the untranslatable guttural sound, no language at all, when a punch hit home in the solar plexus. The sheer exhaustion after a three-hour session. Dugald worked night after night for four years to get his black belt, then went longer to hear himself called Sensei. Along the way he'd picked up a little Japanese, a language that at first baffled him, written as it was in letters no one could understand. And the discipline had led him to university, to that other mysterious alphabet, Greek, the Greek to Pythagoras, and so on to the joys of science and of course to his beloved, Miss Morrow, back here where he came from, in Wychwood Park.

Clearly the stream that had carried him, irrevocably it seemed now, back to his beginnings, was anything but direct. There were pools and backwaters along the way. As a young man he had been angry. He had been violent. He did not know then, nor did he really know now, where the anger came from or how to escape its grip. He only knew that he had given it a life, a language, an expression that was both exquisite and deadly, and that in this way he had become its master. This was his gift to the Manor School. He understood rage, and those who possessed it. He understood that its origins were profound and often inexplicable. Also that rage was a habit, a haunt returned to by those who had no imagination. That the man—or woman, more often than one thought—who had rage inside had to grow another power that was greater or rage would take him over.

It was a huge task, the mastery of anger. There was an angry child at the school now, a tiny girl called Vida; she had become, through Dugald's coaching, the best karate student he'd seen in a decade. Karate was an excellent tool to help you along the way, but also a risky one. Dugald could tell Vida, and intended to soon, that he, Dr. Laird, had once been so at odds with the world that he feared his trained body would commit murder without his permission. His big toenails could slash an opponent's throat. He had had nightmares of kicking people and seeing their arteries explode into spouts of blood, as if a neck, or an arm were a fire hose. At a low point, he went to the emergency room of the Toronto Western Hospital and begged to have the nails of his big toes removed. After witnessing a quick demonstration of his side kicks, the doctors removed the nails, but consigned him to the Queen Street Mental Hospital. There, the patients wore little paper shoes and shuffled from narrow wards to lounges. In the lounge, in his sashed hospital robe, Dugald met another man. This particular man kicked off the brown paper slippers and put his bare feet up on a chair and Dugald saw: he had no nails on his big toes.

"What belt level are you?" Dugald asked, displaying his own nail-less toes.

"Black," said the other man. He had tattoos on his biceps and his back but he was gentle, and he and Dugald drank tea many afternoons, lounging in upholstered chairs like a couple of declawed cats. Dugald wondered where his friend was now. Dead, no doubt, but cured.

Karate had not cured Dugald, but it had controlled his symptoms. Francesca had cured him, he supposed. She had cured him of everything in his past life. All previous memory had been overtaken, had swirled away down a sinkhole, when he met Francesca. His bride, his baby, his partner in pleasure, his partner in the school. He adored her. She was the water in his silent marine mind; others when they appeared swam small and brief through a world of Francesca.

He drew the heavy, six-inch skeleton key out of his pocket and pulled shut the iron gate on the path leading to Taddle Creek Drive. Students and Amelia gone, the house belonged once again to him and his wife. Behind him the pathway ran past the house, alongside the terraced garden, to the coach house. The row of student lockers on its outside wall had been freshly painted brick-red, to blend with the architecture. Hands on his hips he surveyed the grounds, the garden emptied of bloom, the moist brick of the house where he had taught for fifty years now: fifty years!

But he numbered not so much the years as the students who had passed through the halls, phalanxes of them, in groups of fifty a year, fifty times fifty equals two thousand five hundred, a small army moving on to universities in Canada and the United States, to Britain. These days Dugald thought of commissioning a frieze to run around the Manor over the portico, under the roofline. A metre tall, it would recall the Parthenon's. On four sides of the house, looking to east, north, west and south, the Manor frieze, like the original, would be carved in low relief, a procession of departing scholars with books atop their mortarboards. Boys and girls with their knapsacks, their binders, their easels and sparring gear, their skateboards, their bicycles, their dogs, their guardian angels, existing in a continuous present tense, forever arriving, forever completing their studies, forever departing, heads bent as they pressed into battle after leaving the sacred precincts of the Manor. All moving onward, sometimes with quick gladness, sometimes drawn back with reluctance. And where the procession had its beginning and its end, Dugald and Francesca seated like Zeus and Hera with sceptres and shields.

Dugald was fascinated with the Parthenon frieze, as he was with many things Greek. It was the handling of time that he adored, the way the frieze galloped and then stood still, the way an onlooker could feel the great procession back up at a corner, and then stretch out to full tilt down a long side. The way time overlapped itself, and the great parade was both beginning and reaching its conclusion at the moment an onlooker's gaze took it in. And so it was with Dugald's life here at the Manor.

It was the procession that had meaning, not its goal and not the individuals. All of those students into whom he had poured his energies year in and year out. Including the worldly successes, the Connaught Borks, the Jim Byrds, those who had gone on to be cabinet ministers, sculptors, capitalists, classicists, there was not a face he cared to see again! Indeed, the major fuck-ups who'd wandered these halls and were now weaving baskets in his old haunt of Queen Street Mental Hospital, drying out at the Donwoods or doing time in jail were just as important to him. The casualties too must be in the procession. The handsome boys mounted on Harleys or smoking up on the corner, the rebel girls puking and punching each other out must follow the shuffling boys with chains hanging from the pockets of their wide carpenter's pants.

Because, Northrop Frye and the healing properties of myth notwithstanding, there was only so much you could do to repair the damage of a benign upper-middle-class Toronto childhood. Dugald ought to know. He saw it as his job to redress the smug self-righteousness that was seeded even in the best of them, fed and protected by their own mother-world. The ravages of a childhood amongst philistines were, in his view, only a little less severe than the scars left by the more usual forms of abuse. He loved to bring to a sensitive child, to a budding artist, to an intelligent, unusual adolescent the comprehension that there was a world beyond Cineplex, the Eaton Centre, SkyDome and the stock exchange. He imparted the knowledge, the humility, that would turn them into civilized persons. And yet after all this time he could not summon a single face to make him smile. And so Dugald understood that it was not to young people he had devoted his life, but to what they went through, the agony of becoming oneself. That, he was beginning to think, had no clear end in sight either in their lives or his.

There was a time when he would have insisted that he loved adolescents. They were under construction; one could take a sow's ear, as Francesca liked to say, and make a silk purse.

My heavens yes. Some students came to the Manor fit for nothing at all, the casualties of a lax and unintelligent public school system, of brutality or absence at home, of their own natures, of the times. Behaviour students, the public system called them. Public schools made a half-hearted attempt to educate them; the private system simply turfed them out. Maybe these kids pilfered field-trip fees from the teacher's drawer; maybe they stabbed another student with a geometry compass. The more enterprising organized protests against compulsory sailor suits for fourteen-year-old females. Having sex and drugs in residence rooms was a favourite trick.

Behaviour students, rebellious students, call them what you will. Francesca and he had pledged never to label. These were students whom the system had failed. Brilliant minds. Budding artists. Little adults with great souls. They were the ones they'd set out to teach. And at the end of it, what could you say? What was that song one of the rats had played for him, her earphones blaring into his good ear?

"I can make a dress out of a feed bag and I can make a man out of you!" Hah! Occasionally one was able to help a child become an adult self that he or she would not have become otherwise. For this hope he and, especially, Francesca lived.

The word "hope" made him smile. He was freed of it now, freed of despair too, and that was the best of it. Perhaps that was the measure of a life well spent.

He sauntered farther away from the house and looked back at it. Lily's house. He pictured the frieze around the top of the second storey. It would make a motley procession, to be sure, that long defile of youngsters who had crossed the threshold of the Manor. Francesca, bless her, still held that she had never met a student she didn't like. This was why, by mutual agreement, she handled all prospective students. She approached each young person with faith, hope and charity, waving aside the shamed mumbles of their parents. Dimitri had failed grade seven math three times; Roxanne had been ejected from Bishop Strachan for insolence of a high order. Cassie had her own version of Tourette's syndrome or something that made her burst out in weird humming songs, and sometimes, under pressure, twirl. Vida was supposed to suffer from attention deficit disorder, Maureen to be clinically depressed. Jacob was "gifted"; Sara had learning difficulties. Francesca did not subscribe to any of those labels, though she had learned not to annoy the parents by dismissing them out of hand.

In intake interviews Francesca allowed the parent—a mother, usually—to relay this information, at the same time waving it past her with one long elegant hand. Surely there was something at which Maureen or Cassie excelled? Yes, look at that poetry: wasn't it marvellous? And the French! Obviously a gift for language. Ordinary schools failed such talented youngsters. And the ones who had no study skills, who could not complete an assignment, who didn't know long division (although they were in grade nine!). They simply had to apply themselves. Good posture was essential as well.

Francesca would cure all ills with a course in life drawing, or perhaps ancient Greek.

So Francesca worked her magic. On Jacob, the strange young man who waited outside the school door each morning greeting his peers, sober as a funeral director. On Maureen, the beautiful one, incompetent at long division but unparalleled at cutting hash. On the silent Russian girl, whose parents were clearly gangsters, whose sketches of Renaissance madonnas brought tears to the eyes. Francesca did it with faith. Yes, they could be helped. They could be brought along. They were valuable individuals. In fact, at heart she believed that they were more valuable than their peers winning relays at Upper Canada College or at Branksome Hall only a stone's throw away. Dugald had seen the spines straightening as Francesca's footsteps came down the stairs. Heard the hallway chatter that she dreamed of in her ideal school: Was the storm scene in the Stratford performance of *King Lear* a success? Was Dali a genius or a fraud?

Oh yes, there were many times when he and Francesca walked between classrooms beaming with pride. In his memory of those times it was always April, just before the annual trip to Greece; in springtime the halls of the Manor shone with a particular golden light. The tiny purple blossoms of wisteria drooped from the pergola amidst a temple of green leaves, as if these were the slopes of Parnassus, not the hill above Toronto.

Of course, Dugald ruminated, still lost in thought behind his gate in the twilight's darkening, if the magic did not work, there would be trouble. Take Darrin! A year had gone by and this stubborn, recalcitrant son of a plastic surgeon still refused to tuck in his shirt. Furthermore, he would not rise when Miss Morrow came to a classroom door although he'd been reprimanded repeatedly. Perceptibly, Francesca's attitude to the boy had begun to alter. Dugald had seen it often enough. When the formidable energies of his bride were marshalled against a child, he would begin to feel an odd pity for the doomed student, no doubt undeserved and more to do with his own anxieties than with anything else. Darrin's days were numbered. Once Francesca had turned against a child, she was not to be deterred. Though she'd never met a child she didn't like, she might learn to dislike a child she knew.

Dugald laughed to think of it. His bride, varied and delectable as a wedding feast, was as fearsome a foe as she was enviable an ally. Dugald had emerged from his King Street years with a body hard and lethal, his will honed, and a wish to build a school to rescue troubled youths. Francesca had come along the road and offered to share his dream. Their love rivalled the loves in myth and literature. He remembered. Oh, he remembered—sex that was like gods' play. Himself tumbling amongst her curves and blessed by her liquids. How astonishing that this woman made for passion should turn out to be exactly what Dugald needed: teacher and manager, tender combatant. She had Latin and Greek, she loved the classics, and art, and poetry, and fatefully was connected to a Wychwood house. He hired her to teach. Francesca had made his dream come true. Dugald might be Headmaster, but Francesca was the power of the place; that was obvious to all but the blatantly stupid, and there were no blatantly stupid individuals at the Manor. Irresponsible, unresponsive, temporarily criminal perhaps, but not stupid.

Dugald shook his head impatiently and turned to go back inside. He remembered his early passion, how it spilled into zeal. To spend the night in Francesca's arms and the day in the classroom was heavenly. He'd known that Bunsen burners and life-size drawings of skeletons would turn into the Eternal Flame and Leonardo's drawings, that the boys—because at first he thought only of boys who'd had as much trouble as he had in finding their way in the world— would troop through the doors and be saved. Troop through the door they did. He taught them higher maths and science, martial arts. He cited the ideal structure of the Viking ship, simply crafted, ancient, streamlined, perfectly adapted for its purpose, and possessed of lasting beauty. Another example of the genius of Homo erectus. Of the good ship *Manor* Dugald was captain, chieftain. His position at the helm was a sacred covenant between Francesca and himself, for hadn't he conceived the ship, built it, laying his principles deep in all its angles, informing every bulwark? Yet it was she who had bent the timbers, softening each one so that it fit to the magnificent curves, polishing and holding high the bold prow, applying the simple elegance of their theories to the tiniest detail of deportment. And it was good.

All of this was good, and right, and as it should be.

But just then, as Dugald stood on the driveway congratulating himself on the arrival of an earned, a justified, peace of mind, just at that very second, a disturbance entered his silent mental aquarium. A new face. Or, rather, an old face newly recollected. Meryl.

He was startled. He saw the face, and then it was gone. He moved his feet in agitation. Saw it again, and went chasing after it with his mind's eye. "I know you're there! Who are you?" he said, aloud, but there was no one to hear him. He knew this face, this woman. She could not fool him! Somewhere in that tank, that circular tank where the coloured fish of memory swam and circled, finning forwards, finning backwards, sinking decades and then rising alongside a string of bubbles, was Meryl. The lost one, her face screwed up in a parody of fierceness, her black locks escaping the topknot she'd tied them in. She was white-haired now but when he had known her she had black hair. During the war or just after. Fresh from her job folding parachute silk in a munitions factory in Ajax, Ontario. Wanting to fight but, like him, having no way to get to the enemy. She swam up to confront him. Meryl.

"Oh, it's you," he said, and batted her away.

Dugald Laird was difficult to take by surprise. Even now. His reflexes were still good, his royal-blue eyes with irises lined with black were sharp; there remained some black in the small pointed beard that underlined his lower lip. His hair was more salt than pepper, but his skin was robust and putty-firm. The bored female students in senior mathematics wondered what he used on it. Was he, like his bride, an enthusiastic consumer of beauty supplies, health-food remedies, vitamins and massage services? They concluded that, more likely, it was the great love that he sustained for Miss Morrow that kept him young.

But Meryl! She took him by surprise. Where had she come from? Gone, gone, she'd been gone for more than forty years and with her the children, her noisome, messy struggle to survive without him, her garnering of sympathies that ought to be his, her tendency to damage his reputation, her infuriating persistence in living.

Meryl. She had come back to his mind after an absence of decades. Not exactly decades. Only two days ago she'd been there, that face in the crowd that stopped his breath for a few seconds. But Meryl had understood, hadn't she? She had not stood in his way.

Go, Meryl, he said, and she went. That fog had lost its soft grey fuzz, becoming black, and a chill that spoke of the winter to come had begun to eat into Dugald's tweed jacket, stiffening his limbs just when he needed to be limber. It was time to go in, to don his gi and his hakama. Francesca would be ready, in the coach house. He reached the door, walking slowly in his leather carpet slippers, and looked back, noticing a movement on the far corner of the street, Smokers' Corner. Some of the girls were standing there, in a group. At least he thought they were his girls. They were not in uniform. He recognized the frizzy orange crest on the little fast-moving body that was Vida, the angry one. Probably they were up to no good. Francesca would want to do something about it. He did not. He waved lazily in their direction.

Unnoticed by him, the corner of the tapestry in the front window dropped.

A Cheese is by definition a voyeur, keeping an eye on people who are not Cheeses, ferreting out their secrets, taking notes on who doubles up with whom, and just how it is done. On this ordinary Monday after school was out, and after Cassie took herself off, suffering, but righteous, Amelia walked to the shaded front room and lifted the corner of the tapestry that covered the window. There Dugald stood, lost in thought. If only she could hear what he was thinking. Since her unhappy days as a teenage outcast, Amelia had been a relentless and unrepentant snoop. It was not nice, she realized. But the world was full of nice people who never found out what they needed to know. Amelia needed to know what was to become of them all.

Today was the day. Today—a long day, a day in which she had received a brisk reprimand from above, a day in which a certain doubt had pervaded the atmosphere of the Manor, a day in which aspersion had been cast on her loyalty from below. Yes, today she would do what she had wanted to do from her very first week at the school. She would spy on Francesca and Dugald in their sacred marriage ritual.

Francesca switched on the lights, little flame-shaped bulbs that flickered like candles in wall sconces. As always before the end of the day she had the larger boys fold and remove the wooden stage from which she lectured, and pile the chairs and desks in the closet. The coach house was dojo, studio and lecture hall. It could hold a karate class of twenty and, minutes later, be the stage on which Francesca performed. It was older than the Manor, and had once been a communal property of the Park. When the artists of Wychwood still grew their own food it had housed pigs, cows and horses. There were marks on the pine floor where the stalls had been; the loft had a wooden door that had once been a hay window. As dusk gathered, the old studio asserted its age, its intimacy. The oak panelling creaked and the smells left by farming rose, together with the smell of oil paint. In this twilight hour it had always been Francesca and Dugald's place.

Now she drew the heavy tapestries across the studio windows, wiping the blackboard of the day, erasing her darlings and with them the outside world. She walked to a narrow closet with a curtain for a door and unzipped her dress, a frock of very fine camel hair with a high neck and flared skirt. It was not true, as some of the girls gossiped, that she bought her clothes directly off the runway in Paris. (How could she with English Grammar to teach?) But it was true she enjoyed the acquaintance of certain boutique owners around Place St. Sulpice and the Rue Royale. She favoured, now, Christian Lacroix for his sense of history and Issey Miyake because the Japanese understood fabric.

The dress unzipped and flung over the top rung of a ladder, she bent to unbuckle the platform shoes she'd had since 1930-something, shoes that were in perfect repair and, this year, had become fashionable again. Although her doctor had told her the high heels were destroying her vertebrae, she would not give them up. Someday she would trip and break one of those racehorse ankles. But not today.

Stocking-footed now, brought down to size, she sat on a high stool and pulled her tights from one long, sinewed leg and then the other, with that look of intense inner contemplation women reserve for removing hose. She shook the tights in front of her face and draped them over the neck of the hanger. Then, standing, she crossed her arms and reached behind her shoulders to pull the slip over her head, wincing ever so slightly from some arthritic pain in her shoulder. She stood revealed in her smalls.

The waist of nineteen inches, which Dugald extolled on commencement days, was perhaps mythical. But what remained was near enough to marvel at. Francesca had caused gasps when she was young and now occasioned gasps of a different order: she was so well preserved! (a phrase that revolted her). How had she held on to her figure all these years? Of course she'd never had children. But Francesca would discount that as a reason. It was all too easy to become fat, children or no: it had nothing to do with pregnancy but with a failure of discipline.

Off she trotted behind the drapery, re-emerging with her white cotton gi. It was soft with many launderings, wide cuffed at the elbow. The jacket crossed from left to right, in the men's way, over her breast, and did up inside with narrow ties. These she knotted, her fingers expert in the dark. Then she reached behind the curtain for her hakama, the long, black pleated skirt that samurai wore to disguise their foot movements and confound their enemies. She stepped into it and drew the front flap up to her waist, crossing the long ties behind her and then back to the front. Then she raised the back flap, bringing the stiffened waistband up against the small of her back. She knotted the ties firmly at her waist and made a little ceremonial bow with the loose ends. Fully dressed, she reached back into the corner to the weapons rack for the bo, the ulysees, the wooden blocks called tompha.

———

Amelia, peeking down on the ivory arc of her mentor's silk-clad back, nearly let out a nervous giggle. Why was she doing this? Perhaps she was a person who would violate a privacy simply because it was there. Perhaps she did it because she did not know herself. Such a person created havoc in the lives of her sure-footed friends.

Amelia had spied on her employers for so long she considered it part of her contract. She watched them when they strolled in the garden. She eavesdropped when they spoke in their private quarters. It was easy: Francesca had to shout because of Dugald's deafness. She felt no guilt. Was there not that actressy ambivalence in every move the Headmistress made? Francesca was performing, if not for Amelia, then for some other invisible audience.

Believing herself alone, Francesca entered the open space, dropped her weapons, kicked her skirt out from beneath her feet and knelt. She remained on her knees, eyes half-shut, hands in her lap, head erect.

A minute later, Dugald entered by the same door. He too bowed to the empty space. Then he bowed to Francesca. Principal and vice; sensei and sensei; man and wife. Dugald in his white jacket and black hakama was serene and full of dangerous grace. He padded to where Francesca knelt and with the same swift kicking motion diverted the hem of his skirt, then began to sink into a kneel, his knees splaying out smoothly, without a pause, so that the right touched the floor first, then the left, while his back remained erect.

"Sensei ni rei."

Francesca bowed; her face touched the floor.

"Sensei ni rei," repeated Francesca.

"Shomen ni rei."

They bowed together toward the shrine in the corner.

Dugald turned and faced the front of the room. "Tachi ni rei."

Amelia froze into the oak panelling.

"Eus."

"Eus," Dugald responded, bowing his head to the floor. Francesca followed, saluting him, her head skimming the wooden planks. Dugald turned back to face her.

For three full minutes they sat in Zen mudra, fingertips of opposite hands touching, resting on their upper thighs, backs straight, a plumb line from top of head to sitting bones. Amelia gazed at the neat, skirted buttocks set on the turned-up two-toned, wrinkled heels, heels that could be hands, that could be sentient objects, not simply rounded calloused skin. The soles of Dugald's feet were white, puckered white like a Chinese bun, but the skin darkened just where it changed from bottom of foot to side and top.

Francesca looked at and through her husband. The light was dim. His face was obscure. The room vibrated. Love, Amelia supposed.

The Cheese stood in the shadows and watched. She loves him

because he's been hers for so many years, Amelia thought. She loves what has given her solace and strength whatever the irritations: his *there*ness.

And he loves her qualities, admires her with every atom of his frame. Francesca was elegant, spirited, definite and funny. She was a brilliant and dedicated teacher. She knew more about literature and mythology and painting than anyone else on earth. Of course Dugald loved Francesca.

They loved each other. But differently. A partnership, a joint ownership: that was their marriage. The school was part of it, and Amelia too. Even she, in making the school run, was part of it. The love was great, but what would happen when one part changed?

Dugald and Francesca rose and stepped backward, each alone retrieving a weapon, coming to face one another holding the short bamboo ulysees.

They bowed again. "Eus," said Dugald.

"Eus," said Francesca.

"Sinawali," announced Dugald.

They raised their weapons and lunged to opposite sides, one foot forward, and began to strike them together: five long, curving blows meeting in an X over their heads, one undercutting blow at their knees, and a seventh slash overhead. They repeated the pattern and then reversed it, with five more long cuts slashing upward, a sixth above the head, a seventh to close. In the forward ulysees strokes they wrote as if on a vertical plane of glass dividing them. In the overhead ticks, the plane of glass moved to become a ceiling against which their ulysses switched, the firm wrists, the white knuckles. Their eyes locked as the bamboo clashed overhead. Then, sensing the moment in each other, they began to whirl the weapons in figure eights about their waists. Dugald allowed the tiniest drift of a smile to cross his lips as they stood, weapons whirring about their hips. Amelia imagined the tips of the sticks as swallows, a male and a female. In spring the little birds followed one another through the air, the male flying behind the female, close on its tail, looping and returning, swiftly, evenly.

Then, at an instant so precise it could only be determined by intimacy, the whirling sticks stilled. Dugald's usually pale face had begun to colour, and small beads of moisture to form on his upper lip.

"Kata, su ishi no kon," he announced. The small electric candles flickered in the wall sconces; the white of their gis magnified the rays so that they penetrated the darkening studio. They exchanged their short ulysees for the long bo, and the dance of the swords began in earnest, each partner engrossed in a calligraphy of arm, leg and weapon, each in a cube of his or her own creating, in solitude yet a solitude delicately matched by that other identically engaged figure, a painful beauty.

She was ready for him: whatever strikes he makes she will block. When she strikes, he will block. An actual blow to the temple, the ribs, the solar plexus, as opposed to their mimed, carefully blocked strokes, could fell the other. But the militant dance was not aggression so much as a fantastic and elaborate protection of the space around the self, a hieroglyph of each person's dignity. This battle to the death, never taken to the point, but always in rehearsal. The mating rituals of dear old Homo erectus.

Now Dugald returned his bo to the weapon rack and tucked a sword into his belt. Francesca chose the tompha, holding the wooden knob in her hand and using the wooden block to protect her forearm. Dugald's knees drew together in a mustering of power; the sword rose over his head and his knees split again as he brought it down, terribly, blade first, to a point straight in front of his chest where Francesca had been but was no longer, for she had danced aside and blocked his thrust with her tompha. They repeated the movement with Francesca clearing his sword from along her calf, and then punching. As she did she uttered a terrible kiai: "Die!"

The Cheese stood alone and thought of dying. Not of her own dying, not quite. But of theirs. Of one partner going first, the other dying of grief. Of Carmen, of Moira Shearer in *The Red Shoes*. Of all Miss Morrow's romantic poems, of *The Rubaiyat of Omar Khayam*, of "La Belle Dame sans Merci," "The Eve of St. Agnes." Dugald and Francesca had been married so long they could not be divided: they were two parts of one complex character, two personalities displaying their lights. Each had given the other rights of life and death. Watching the elderly couple spar—nimble, fierce and utterly engaged—she felt the most dreadful stab of envy. A lifelong love. An intertwining of minds, dreams, days. How beautiful it was. How dangerous.

A discreet honk sounded outside. It would be audible only to one who expected it. Amelia expected it. She gazed a last few seconds at Francesca and Dugald—who knew if she would have the nerve to sneak in here again? Then, still unseen, she turned and glided out the door.

He'd parked on Exeter, kitty-corner from the Manor and on the other side of Taddle Creek Drive. It was late now, after six o'clock. There were few lights on this side street, because the better part of the block was occupied by the disused streetcar barns. This was good. An astute observer would remark that the truck had no reason to be at the school at this hour for there were no students to feed.

Ferdinand eased the gearshift into neutral and gave a little gas to the motor before he turned off the key. He liked to hear it roar. The canteen truck was his love and his livelihood. Its sides and back were polished aluminum in a quilted pattern of triangles inside squares. His licence was bolted to the back: Metro Licence #17652. There was a small Canadian flag in metal above it. Clipped to the visor inside the cab was a plastic card with his picture: Ferdinand da Silva,

147 Concord Avenue, Toronto, Age 39 years, Owner/Operator. The outside and the inside he washed every week so no dust or mud dulled its shine.

He leaned across and opened the passenger door. Amelia jumped up onto the front seat. Ferdinand reached for her hand.

"I am so tired," he said. "What a day. You want a Pepsi?" Actually, he had already retrieved a cold one from his stores in the back. He passed it over, along with a straw.

She pulled off the keyhole-shaped opener and pushed the straw in the hole. She didn't want to hear about his day, but she nodded eagerly. Men love to dramatize their work.

"Okay, so it goes like this. First I gotta get to the construction site at Cottingham and Yonge at 7:45 a.m. to give the fellas coffee, and sandwiches. They've been working since six, eh? And I'm late because of that construction at College and Spadina. So the coffee's not brewed, and the steamer's not hot. After that I get later, for the whole day I'm behind the gun. Eight-thirty I'm supposed to be in front of that big library where they're moving the sewers and I'm late there, and after that more traffic. Problems! It's supposed to take me thirty minutes so when I'm done I can just about make it up Bathurst to here."

"It sounds stressful."

"Yup," he said and slid his arm over the back of the seat so that his hand dropped down onto her right shoulder. He got his left hand ready to touch her left breast when it came in range, and pulled her toward him. She resisted but not much. Mostly she sipped her Pepsi and eyed the Manor where Francesca and Dugald sparred.

"From this angle you can't even tell it's a school. Okay, maybe at eight-thirty or at four o'clock you'd see the kids coming out in their kilts and blazers. And then they just sort of scatter, so you'd have to be watching to notice," she said.

"They're waiting when I pull up," said Ferdinand. "They come running."

She stopped talking. So did he, for a minute, to kiss her.

"I gotta admit, even before I met you, the Manor was my favourite stop of the day. It's not often you get to see kids on this job, since most schools have a cafeteria. I like kids."

"I know you do," Amelia said. "And they like you." Ferdinand let the girls sit in the cab while he doled out soup and cookies; they changed the dial to 92.5, put their feet up on the dash and rocked. Miss Morrow turned a blind eye: it was off school property. "The girls especially," she added.

Ferdinand had no children. His wife still hadn't recovered from the doctor's report that said it would never happen. Portuguese people tended to believe women were failures if they didn't bear a child: she had wept for weeks. Ferdinand finally said to her, "You've got to stop crying," And she said, "Why?" This much he had told Amelia. She was struck by the story. She thought, I could tell her why—because if she doesn't, she'll lose her husband.

"But like I was saying, from the Manor I gotta boot it back down to Cottingham to all those stops I made before, and then be back here to give the kids number two lunch—"

"They don't have lunch—" said Amelia automatically. "Miss Morrow thinks it makes them pokey."

"What're you calling it? Snack? Okay. Afternoons are pure hell now, I got five stops between two and four-thirty and the traffic's backed up all over town. It makes me crazy how you rich people double-park in front of your dry cleaners and pasta restaurants, never caring if you stop an honest man from earning his living."

"I'm not rich," Amelia protested in mock horror.

"Sure you are."

"Am not."

"Are so."

They butted each other's shoulders and chests, giggling.

"Better be careful in traffic, or you'll get into an accident."

Ferdinand shook his large, troll-like head. "Kids gotta eat," he said. "Fuel their bodies."

Amelia laid her head on his broad shoulder. Food was Ferdinand's mission, and the truck his means. His truck, like others in the individually owned fleet on their errands of mercy around the constantly self-renovating city, had a stainless-steel side that dropped down, revealing a grill for hot dogs and sandwiches, and plexiglass windows behind which chocolate bars, apples, chocolate milk and root beer reclined like art objects or prizes to be won at the midway. He had driven his truck for the past three years. Before that he'd worked in a furniture factory lifting and carrying, and he got a sore back. He bought the truck with money from worker's compensation, and he loved it with his whole heart.

"Traffic," he said. "It's bad, but it's nothing. You don't know," he said, "how wonderful it is to be out on the streets, driving the truck all day in the sunshine, supposed to be your own boss, supposed to say hello to people face to face. Supposed to stand there handing out a cardboard cup of coffee or soup, a foil-wrapped steamed hot dog or a sandwich, supposed to take their money into your own hands and give back the change. And when I know my wages supposed to come out of this money, a profit to pay myself. And no bosses! Traffic, it's nothing!"

Amelia tried to imagine, for a minute, having no boss. No Francesca. Elegant and ferocious, back there in the coach house swinging her sword. If by some chance she were to materialize, and catch sight of her Madonna wrapping the famous long neck around Ferdinand's short, thick one in the cab of his truck, there would be trouble. And that would mean Ferdinand's job. It might even mean Amelia's.

"I've got a boss," she murmured.

"I got my wife," he said.

Ferdinand too felt a certain danger in what they were doing. This went beyond the obvious—that his wife would raise a ruckus that would wake the dead, that she would probably throw both Ferdinand and his truck out of the house, the garage, the community, the church and the country if she could manage it. This was a professional risk, a risk to his livelihood. Miss Morrow would not like it.

He enjoyed the danger. It was yet another of the pleasures of self-employment. He nuzzled into the soft place over Amelia's collarbone. "I remember the first time I get the job, supposed to go upstairs to speak to this ancient dolly with the big bazzoos and the tight belt around her little middle, and she supposed to give me some lecture about "her darlings" and how they supposed to have little snacks two times a day. I've got to tell them to be respectful and I've got to be respectful as well, because it's Taddle Creek Drive and all."

He'd told Amelia this before.

"And me, I go to grade eight in Portugal. That day I got the job, I stare at those white heads of the old men and see that writing around the tops of the rooms, and I think: maybe all the high schools in Canada are like this. But now I know better."

"No kidding."

"You people the only ones come out on the lawn waving sticks like swords." He put his hands on Amelia's waist and rotated her toward him in small semi-circular twists, like he was taking the lid off a jar.

Amelia was thinking of herself at this moment not as a jar or even as the Cheese, but as the Madonna with the Long Neck. She saw the Parmigianino painting in her mind, its palette of subdued teal blue, burgundy and taupe, the exposed limbs of the strange chorus of young girls gathered to the right of the Madonna, her equally over-sized and elongated baby lying heavy on her lap, her hand with its beautiful tapered fingers gesturing toward her left breast in such a way as to suggest that now, just now, she would uncover it to suckle the babe.

But Ferdinand was ahead of her. His index finger had come between the buttons and invaded the cleft between her breasts to brush her nipple. Then before her breath returned he had reached for her other cleft where a surge of wetness made everything very slippery.

Perhaps she was a bad seed. That's what her mother had thought. Despite the fact that a line down the centre of her body wanted only to press itself against his gearshift and himself, Amelia strained back and seized his wrist, pulling the thick hand with its hairy knuckles out of the waist of her skirt. He was breathing heavily and uttered a wordless protest while striking his forehead against her shoulder.

"Not now, Ferdy," she whispered. "We can't do this now. We can't do it here. You've got to get home. So do I."

Twenty minutes later Amelia waited for her bus on Bathurst Street.

At the end of the day cars streamed up from downtown, the drivers attempting to decompress after a day's work in sleek, traffic-trapped cars. They were sleek, prosperous people, the kind who could have been Manor parents, and they passed her without a glance, their children's teacher a nonentity in a bus shelter. One car, a Lincoln, turned left onto Taddle Creek Drive and slowed in front of the sidewalk that led out through the screening shrubs from the Manor. Looking for a child, perhaps. But no child appeared and the car turned right and headed out to St. Clair.

Amelia could see both ways: down the hill to the city, and westward to the disguised front of the school. Then she noticed, in the gloom, a young person sitting on the garden wall, arms folded across her chest. It was a girl, a lonely girl. She drummed her heels against the stones. Cars went by in a slow stream; one or two drivers turned, bleary behind their windshields, to see the girl.

Cassie, thought Amelia. Alone as usual. Has she no friends? And what is she doing here so late? Her heart thudded in alarm. Did she see me get out of the truck?

Cassie kicked a stone down the driveway. But it did not appear to make time pass any faster. Darkness began to fall. She stood, and looked for her stone on the gloomy sidewalk, and then gave up. She waited, blank and cold, as if willing something or someone to arrive. Suddenly, a green Volvo swerved out of the right-hand lane and stopped on a dime. Her mother, no doubt. At the same time, Amelia's bus drew up and she turned away.

4

AN AGITATION THAT WON'T GO AWAY

ENGLISH LITERATURE CLASS. Francesca mounted the wooden platform, holding in her arms the embossed leather binder from Florence in which she had collected, over the years, her favourite English poems. She paused, theatrically, and scanned the students. One can never have too much drama in the classroom. Then she pivoted gently, sweeping her gaze once more over their heads. It was her silent command that they compose themselves, breathe in through their noses and out through their mouths, and fix their eyes on her.

A hush began to fall, but not fast enough.

"Gentlemen! Ladies!" She waited until the stillness was utter and prolonged.

"Thank you."

This was when she felt most alive. When their eyes were on her. She swept her skirt from behind her back with her long, blade-like hand, the same hand that copied Rembrandt etchings and broke boards. Leaning a little on her cane she slowly lowered her hips into the leather sling chair, at a steady pace so as not to lose the students' attention. Knowing their eyes remained on her, she let her own drop down to her lap and, lifting her hands in the full knowledge of their enduring beauty, opened the leather book.

What would it be today? What to read aloud? Which loved

cadences to let her voice dance in, which words so long cherished that they made their own pathways through her brain, and became like the veins and arteries of her body, carrying the blood in, the blood out?

"I want these great works to become a part of you! Engrave them upon your soul!" This was Francesca's real work. She passed along the masterpieces and disregarded the unpleasant works of man; she gloried in Rembrandt and Matisse but held of little account the collapse of Rome, the Dark Ages, the Black Death, slavery and Hiroshima. She allowed a tiny smile to play around her lips as she spoke: there was irony here, too, for those who could see it.

And what *was* it to be today? Gilgamesh, the lament for Enkidu? "I weep for Enkidu, my friend, Bitterly moaning like a woman mourning I weep for my brother. O Enkidu, my brother,/ You were the axe at my side,/ My hand's strength, the sword in my belt—"

No.

Shelley?

Not today.

Yeats? Perhaps, although with his so recognizable rhythm he was almost candy. "O body swayed to music, O brightening glance/ How can we know the dancer from the dance?" But always a pure joy. Her binder opened to "Sailing to Byzantium" and before fully knowing she would, she was reading aloud:

"That is no country for old men. The young
In one another's arms, birds in the trees—
Those dying generations—at their song,
The salmon-falls, the mackerel-crowded seas,
Fish flesh or fowl, commend all summer long
Whatever is begotten born and dies.
Caught in that sensual music all neglect
Monuments of unageing intellect."

Although the first line alarmed her, she warmed to the poem. The silence was good; she felt her audience with her. Her voice caught when she reached "Consume my heart away; sick with desire/ And fastened to a dying animal/ It knows not what it is." Too beautiful, too sad. She breathed in deeply to restore her composure.

She had them turn to the page in their books. What is it, what does it mean? she asked. The first stanza. What is going on here? The summer, birds in the trees, the salmon-falls. What is he talking about?

Dumb looks.

"What is it like in that country? Cassandra? 'The young in one another's arms?' What kind of country is it?"

Cassie flushed. One just knew watching this girl that she understood, that she felt the poem, felt it in her sweet, passionate heart. But she could not speak.

"What is it? What is it that the poet writes of? What kind of country is it, Cassandra, where the young embrace?"

Her face flushed red.

"What are the people like, there? 'The young in one another's arms, birds in the trees...'"

"They must all be sluts," Cassie said.

And the studio rocked with the glorious laughter of twenty teenagers. Even Francesca had to smile. Then she held up her hand to stop the noise. "Oh Cassandra dear," she said, when silence was reclaimed. "You are so very judgemental. It comes with innocence— do you see that, class?" This was the joy of teaching. Innocence became the subject. With Cassandra's little gift they marched on through the poem.

But innocence such as this child's—was it not a dangerous condition? Her body daily acquired more astonishing architecture, the great carapace of shoulder, columns of leg, portico of breastbone, but the skin over this was like baby skin, mushroom-pale, bland. She knew nothing and felt everything. It was frightening to see one so undefended, someone whose face was ruffled by every notion.

Francesca moved on to "A Prayer For My Daughter."

"Have I not seen the loveliest woman born
Out of the mouth of Plenty's horn
Because of her opinionated mind,
Barter that horn and every good
By quiet natures understood
For an old bellows full of angry wind?"

She expected outrage and she got it.

"He's saying that it makes her mouth ugly to speak her mind!" Vida could be depended upon for feminist indignation.

The trouble was Francesca half agreed with Yeats. They might as well learn now that an angry woman will never achieve her aims. This is not to say a woman should not have ambitions, no indeed: it was simply a matter of comportment. Francesca set herself as an example to them.

"We speak of ceremony, of grace," she said. There was so little in their lives. One of her tasks was to find that missing grace in literature, in art. She showed them the wild rhythms of Van Gogh's landscapes, and sometimes there was a little catchlight, a gleam in the eyes, the pupil tightening black as an idea lodged. Suddenly she could no longer resist.

"'Ode on a Grecian Urn,'" she said, "page thirty-four."

And there it lay, flat upon the page, this mazed garden that she had trod faithfully, oh, thousands of times, always losing herself in delight and awe.

"Thou still unravish'd bride of quietness," she began. "Thou foster-child of silence and slow time." And time indeed did slow to a near halt as she read aloud to them.

But that was not the part of the poem she most longed to hear.

"Bold Lover, never, never canst thou kiss,/ Though winning near the goal—yet, do not grieve . . ."

The distress moved off Cassie's face and Francesca made a mental note: the idea of non-consummation reassured her. Never-never land. She wanted to think more on this but read on, finding it impossible to stop the beautiful and measured dance.

"She cannot fade, though thou hast not thy bliss,
For ever wilt thou love, and she be fair!"

Today these words brought Francesca near tears. It was as if she had never read the poem before. All her life she'd strived to live as Maiden, on a theoretical level, of course. So Dugald was cast as Bold Lover, neither wilting nor fading. And yet the poet said— "thou hast not thy bliss." Francesca was shocked, because now, today, as never before, the poem spoke to her chidingly. Was it possible that she had sacrificed her bliss in order to remain youthful, her waist as slim as ever, her thick hair as lustrous? What would bliss have been, then? For the constant and draining effort of remaining untouched by time—the surgery, the stretching, the creams and dyes—what have I missed? she asked herself. The bliss of communion and decay, of losing the colour, the shape, the distance of a work of art, over time becoming as unremarkable as a heap of clothing on the floor? Of exposing her incipient un-beauty, her worry lines, the part of her that was not made in heaven?

She moved past this troubling part in the poem.

"Who are these coming to the sacrifice?
… heifer lowing at the skies…
What little town … is emptied…
… thy streets for evermore
Will silent be—"

"We will see these heifer 'lowing' when we go to Greece together in the spring, class," said Francesca. "They are on the Parthenon frieze. The heifer, you see, were carved in Athens in 450 BC. Keats took his inspiration from the Elgin Marbles when they were brought to the British Museum."

And now to end it:
"More happy love! more happy, happy love!
For ever warm and still to be enjoy'd,
For ever panting, and for ever young."

Today these words seemed to mock her: for ever panting, indeed. The knowing ones amongst the girls were giggling again. Francesca grew indignant.

"It's no laughing matter, young ladies. Immortal words and who are you to scoff, if it's scoffing you are. Let me hear you tell us, Darrin, just how this young man feels, reaching out for his beloved, there on the curve of the urn."

Darrin smirked, mostly for the benefit of his friends. Then, his grey eyes grew serious and not at all afraid. This was how the wretched boy who would not tuck in his shirt won her over. How she loved the ones who were not intimidated! It pleased her immeasurably, but she'd rather be broken on the wheel and tortured than let any one of them know.

"He feels he's about to burst with love," he said. "But she's frozen. So he's frustrated. He can't *wilt*."

Uproarious laughter from the class.

"Ah yes, frustration is the special province of young men, isn't it?" Francesca remarked.

Darrin held her eyes a moment and then arched his brows. He was a boy with unusual sexual confidence.

"Maybe it used to be," he said. "It's not so much today."

Those who grasped the meaning of this exchange held their hands over their mouths. Sometimes Francesca became furious at impertinence and sent the offender from the room. Other days she rather enjoyed it. Today she gave Darrin one of her rare including glances, the one that was often followed by the remark, "Ah! My dear, you are one of us." It had been a lesson about youthful lust and who would have thought it? Cassandra's outrage—"They're all sluts!"—seemed now to echo rather more persuasively in Francesca's mind. And so the poem ended.

"When old age shall this generation waste—"

Ah yes, death again, there it was. She did not want to face the skeleton today, the folds of skin on haunches shrunken to resemble coat hangers. No one shall die, not on her watch. She hurried on.

"Thou shalt remain, in midst of other woe
Than ours, a friend to man, to whom thou say'st,
"Beauty is truth, truth beauty—"

Salvation. Consolation. Beautiful things will carry us through life. Such was her belief. To pass on this idea to children: that was the mission to which she had dedicated her life. It was a good place to end. In her most characteristic and imitated gesture, holding the book open in the palm of one hand, she chimed "*Enough!*" and snapped it shut with her long fingers, as the last four notes of "Jesu Joy of Man's Desiring" rang out.

A long day over, Francesca lay on her back in the iron bed with its spears rising upward to a square made of iron rods eight feet above the floor. A suggestion of canopy but no curtains. It was as if she lay on the bottom slab of a transparent cube, a cube of glass. Her husband snored softly and regularly beside her. Francesca drew her plait over her right shoulder and, in the habit that had become such a comfort over the years, began to stroke it, first with one hand, then the other, drawing the tresses down, down over her chest as if she were pulling on a rope, drawing a bucket up from some deep, narrow well.

She had in her mind an agitation that would not go away.

An agitation that wouldn't go away: she'd heard that phrase before, she'd used it; it meant, to an artist, the coming on of an obsession, of a great work perhaps. But great works were not hers to create.

Only great workers. She know who she was. Whatever else you could say about Francesca you could not accuse her of having a weak grasp of her identity. That luxury was reserved for the woman in the downstairs hallway, her mother, Lily. "Poor" Lily Watts Chapman Morrow, foster child herself, though not of silence and slow time. More of weakness and uncertainty. Exiled bride, war widow. Lily was not strong enough to stay here alone and so she ended up back in England, and then in Greece, married to Francesca's father, Mr. Morrow.

Francesca did not feel like any daughter of "poor Lily." The woman was trouble, you could tell by her face. And pathetic too! She always thought her real mother must be that other beauty, Ellen Terry. Ellen Terry who went from child marriage to divorce and back to the stage, on her own two nimble feet. It was Ellen Terry she had tried to become as she grew to womanhood. In fact she had run away from poor Lily, the first chance she got, run "home" to Canada. And here she remained. Not looking back. Maintaining a passing acquaintance with her mother, whom she was careful to acknowledge each time she crossed the hallway. Not regretting one tiny bit the loss.

What then was this disturbance of memory that took her relentlessly downward?

It was October. There were colours. The shrubs were blazing orange, and the succulents had turned to red, standing proud in the staged perennial beds. The dried hydrangea petals trembled, and the last few roses were still visible. The chrysanthemums took pride of place. The birches' brilliant yellow lay in tiny shreds on the lawn, but the glossy dark needles of pine and fir and the frosted juniper asserted that fall had not yet taken all the life away.

And there on Taddle Creek Drive stood one lissome young woman, thirty-seven, nineteen, thirty-five, in a navy frock hemmed at mid-calf and fashionable slingback shoes, her raven hair cascading down her back in a way not fashionable but irresistible. She stood like one lost, peering intently at the back of number 45 as if she expected some sign to be given, some dear one to emerge. She stood and stood, unselfconscious, not caring if she were observed, her arms hanging simply at her sides. It was Francesca, of course, waiting for destiny.

And along the road came Dugald Laird. On his way back from the greengrocer on Bathurst with bags of vegetables and fruit for his maiden aunt Alice, who was living, still living, the oldest of the Park "originals," at number 23, backing onto the loathsome streetcar storage sheds that had sprung up to the north. Alice had been old her whole life. Now she was getting frail. Dugald had given up hope that she would let him have her house to begin a school, but he was still devoted. He felt his love for the Park more with each passing year. He rejoiced in his eutukhia—good fortune—to be connected to such a place.

He saw the vision in his path.

Staring at 45 Taddle Creek Drive as if she knew the place. Walking a little up the path and positioning herself so that she could see more of the house.

"It's useless," he said, stopping within earshot. "The house was built so that you couldn't see it from the road. The garden has been maintained especially to cloak and mask the house, to enclose it in veils."

Or somesuch. Let us say he waxed poetic. It was that sort of an afternoon and the sight of a woman like Francesca put Dugald in that sort of a mood.

"Oh, I know," she said lightly, continuing to stand fetchingly on tiptoe even in her high-heeled slingbacks. She did not look at him. He was perhaps a dozen years older than she.

"How do you know?" he said. It was rude and forward but he could not help it. Was she perhaps a student of architecture? There was something foreign in the way she spoke. English but not exactly English. Canadian but not exactly Canadian. Dugald had a good ear. He felt just ever so slightly slighted by her tone. She obviously did not realize where she was.

"This is Wychwood Park," he said. "The beginnings of it. More of the house—but not a great deal more of it—may be seen from inside the park. It's a private road but you may walk on it. May I show you?"

She looked at him then full face and momentarily he could not breathe, she was that lovely. "Oh, I know. I know this is Wychwood Park. It's what I've come to see. And I would be ever so grateful if you would show me. But who might you be?"

Her conversation sounded as if it came straight out of an English novel, sort of Jane Eyre meets the Mad Hatter in mid-ramble through the countryside. Or perhaps this was only because Dugald and Francesca had both related the story, publicly and privately, so many times that the dialogue had become arch. Even in Francesca's dream she has doctored the scene.

"I might be Dugald Laird," he said picking up on her tone cleverly, he thought. "But then again I might not be."

She had been extending her hand. She drew it back. There was enough of the actress in her to instantly fall into role.

"I see," she said, Alice-like. But she didn't. She stood puzzled. He was contrite.

"No, truly, I am Dugald Laird. And if you know about Wychwood Park then you will have heard tell of my grandfather, at least. Marmaduke Matthews."

"Oh," she said. "And is Cyrilda your grandmother?" She fell in step beside him. They walked a little way along the road that wound around the pond. He was astonished; although people ought to have known his famous founder grandparents, few did. He said as much, looking at her with undisguised delight if not, already, adoration.

"Oh there's the pond! I didn't know if it would still be open. I thought someone died in there."

"No," said Dugald. "Not in the pond. In the war."

She was certainly beautiful. She knew it then; she knows it now, looking at pictures of herself. Tall, statuesque, but fragile, her strength entirely hidden by a dancer's grace, her eyes grave yet at the same time naively expecting wonders.

"But how do you know?" Dugald asked, finally.

"My mother always spoke of Wychwood." She hesitated. "Growing up in Greece I longed to see it."

"Your mother? In Greece? I don't understand."

And so the story came out. The names were the names, the dates fit, it all made perfect sense and Dugald Laird, whom Francesca had met by chance in the street outside the Manor, was perhaps the only person who would have known it. Did Dugald also know that Lily had been a model for G. F. Watts?

Dugald knew. He even knew that the front hall at 45 Taddle Creek had been especially built to hold her portrait. "Poor Lily," he added respectfully. "She didn't live here long. The Manor was built in 1910. After her husband was killed in the last year of the war, people lost track of her."

"She wished she had come back. She longed to come back. It was simply that my father—"

At some point Dugald cried, "Oh my god, it's fate," or so he says. Francesca maintains he said nothing of the sort; it would have been too corny. But Dugald claims that in extraordinary moments people say exactly what they think, and this is what he thought. They talked about her father.

"Charles Morrow. Son of the archaeologist. Also an archaeologist. A man from the Park," Francesca said. "You didn't know?'

"Charles Morrow? I knew him. He was already a man when I was growing up, always away travelling in Egypt and Greece doing excavations. His wife stayed home. Then there was one trip from which he never returned. No one spoke about it."

"That's because he was with Lily in Greece. He got a job doing excavations around Delphi, where the Oracle was, on the slopes of Parnassus. There were three daughters. I am the middle."

"So poor Lily wasn't so tragic—"

"But she was," said Francesca, gazing at the path. "Somehow even after getting someone else's husband she was lonely. She could not manage Greece, and he was so often from home."

She said it that way, the English way, "from home." Dugald was charmed. He had been charmed for half an hour but now he was further charmed.

"She used to tell us stories about the painters here, about how lovely the Park was. It was home to her. She'd been motherless and fatherless from an early age. I thought that meant she had simply been born without parents, the way people are born without arms, or sight." Francesca looked up at Dugald and smiled. She was wistful, as Lily had been. "All she had was G. F. Watts, whom she called the Master."

"Did you ever meet him?"

"No, he'd been dead a long time. But she described him, so clearly, with such reverence, that there is little more prominent in my memory than this great white-bearded man, so lauded and so erudite, allowing the children to beat him at Old Maid. I even know his motto: 'the utmost for the highest.'"

They walked along through the white oak and the sugar maple, white pine and ash. The Park was just as Francesca's mother had described it. "You see how the oaks create a series of frames for the house there? Do you see how you can never see the whole house? How the landscape runs from one lot to the other, smoothly?" The framing, the filtered views, the feeling of secrecy as well as of community that was created. It was exactly, *exactly* as Lily had said. The road rose and fell gently. To their left, the shield-shaped open space dipped into its gentle depression and the waters of the pond lay silken in the eerie fall light.

"He was the only one who ever made Lily happy. He and Ellen

Terry," said Francesca. One might accuse her of name-dropping to impress the young man, if one didn't know her better.

"Ellen Terry the actress?"

"She was a dear friend. They played together as children. You see Watts married her, but the marriage didn't last. My mother missed her terribly when Ellen left Surrey. They both sat as models for Watts. But he destroyed his sketches and paintings of Ellen when she was sent away."

"Why was she sent away?"

"Small minds, Mr. Laird. And jealousy, I should think. The brace of women who ruled him determined that the great man was so demoralized by Ellen's shenanigans that he was unable to produce. And he must produce, not only for art's sake, but because his livelihood depended on it. So Ellen was shipped back to her parents. Like being sent down from school for failing a grade. For three years she sat at home darning socks and listening to her sister play "Moonlight Sonata." Then she eloped with William Godwin and took up the stage again, where she spent a glorious lifetime." She laughed. "Unlike Lily."

"Her life was not glorious?"

"No. At first she was his second muse. In Scotland Watts painted her as a young Highland girl with a lap full of flowers. He painted her as Red Riding Hood. He painted her, she told me, simply as herself. He called her to the studio one day, she said; her eyes always shone in a peculiar way when she talked about it: 'He asked me to pose with a laurel wreath around my hair. But it felt false and we took it off. I had only my simple garden hat. He worked all day and by nightfall it was done.' That's what she said.

"I think the portrait is in that house." The Manor had just come into view.

You could hardly see it, so carefully had the oak trees and the chestnuts been massed on the terraced lawn that went up and back from the road. "She never married him and hence could not divorce him: she was no actress but merely became a young widow, and then the unhappy second wife of a man who had been hexed by antiquities and bones. So it was not a glorious life."

"But yours will be."

"Oh, yes," she said.

There was only the sound of their feet crunching on the pavement as they drew closer

"The house is there," Dugald said.

A house in itself and of itself is rarely a beautiful thing but the Manor was beautiful. Francesca looked a long time. Then she turned to Dugald as if she had just remembered his presence.

"Where do you live, Mr. Dugald Laird, that you are carrying your groceries home?"

"I don't live here. My aunt does," he said. He pointed to where the stained yellow brick and pointed gables of a late-Victorian house could just be seen through the glade.

"I didn't ask you where you didn't live," she said, "but where you do." He saw that there was no escaping her curiosity.

"In another part of the city," he said.

"Ah," she said, softly.

"And what do you do?"

"I am going to become Headmaster of a school, a very special private school," he said.

"And where is that school?"

"In my dreams."

She laughed at that, merrily. "How marvellous. And what will be so special about this school?"

"Ah!" he said. "You have asked the right question."

They stood under the leafy veil that softened the sun, shadows of which moved on the grass so that it seemed a gently tossing sea. He told her, and when he was done she started to walk up the driveway.

"I don't know if you should do that," he said, coming nervously out of his trance.

"Oh, but how else will I meet the owners?" she stopped. "Will they think me very rude? I must see the portrait. My mother said she left it there for safekeeping. I have a letter that says I can get it back."

Dugald followed her up the winding path to the house. He wondered aloud if it were the best time.

"Of course it is the best time," she said. "I've come all this way."

That was an insight into Francesca's modus operandi. Perhaps Dugald missed it. She uttered it at the same time as she moved closer to him, so close that a curve of the thirty-seven-inch cloud above her waist accidentally brushed his upper arm. He coughed to cover his gasp.

"The stones are a little uneven. Perhaps you would like to take my arm?"

"Thank you so much. I should be very grateful."

They linked elbows and approached the front door of the Manor.

Who remembers what they said to the couple who answered the door? How easy or how difficult it was to gain access to the front hall where the painting did, indeed, still hang? To remind the owners that they were custodians only of this painting, that it waited for the daughter to recover it? Suffice it to say that a little later that day, the two of them stood in front of the portrait of Lily.

The girl stood in a springtime haze, be-hatted, be-ribboned, in a shepherdess' gown, offering her basket of flowers. Francesca was shocked, seeing her mother as a girl younger than herself. Poor Lily had a sullen but mischievous face; it was the original of what Dugald called a trouble face—sweet, wayward, stubborn, passionate and irresistible.

Who remembers now how difficult it had been to persuade the owners that the house must be returned to family, and that this was the time? It was the best time, after all, because Francesca had arrived. Surely they had been ready to sell in any case. No one recalls the practical details. It didn't really matter whose money it was— both Dugald and Francesca claimed at various times to have raised the lion's share—it only mattered that they had made up their minds, for that moment and for a very long time to come, that all of this was meant to be.

Now Francesca was alert again, awake, in the dark of the night, the house humming around her. Poor Lily's house. She felt tonight more strongly than ever the pull of the portrait, the irresistible pull of the Master and his life's work, the idea that although Francesca might not make art, she might inspire it. These old men, this old man, her beloved husband Dugald, now lying beside her: she was handmaiden to genius, midwife to his dreams, the dreams of others. Francesca sighed. She tossed her plait impatiently onto the pillow, this bucket-rope, this well-pull, narrowly missing horsewhipping the snoring Dugald. Then she turned her back to him and lay on her side staring at the wall, which was painted such a deep eggplant that it was nearly black and enveloped her like night.

Farther back, she whispered to herself. And she went there, an old game she played to comfort herself.

Arachova, her birthplace, the mountain town built straight up the slope of Mount Parnassus. Snow enclosed it in winter, and flowers in spring. Each row of houses was at the level of the rooftops of the one below; the inhabitants walked uphill to pray and downhill to shop. Above the church were the alpine meadows, and below the town olive orchards spread to the sea.

The hillside was sewn with goat tracks; rocks protruded from the soil. The house walls were roughly hewn of stone and mud; the paths were of brick sloped to allow a sluice of melting snow water to escape down their centre. The white-painted cottages were topped with the curved red tiles that had adorned them since antiquity, the god Hermes standing on the corners as a waterspout. Over and under and around it all, knitting all together, grew the black vines. The people were poor, but they ate their own cheese and drank their own retsina, and—remarkably, Francesca thought, for she observed them closely when she visited—generation after generation followed the traditional way, happily, for all one could see. People dressed as one another; they did the same work as one another. The women cooked and cleaned and wore black when widowed, the men walked down to the cafés to drink at the same hour each night, dressed in their good suits.

She plunged down even further, deeper, into time.

It was 1936, the feast of St. George, and her birthday. Yes, on that very day her mother had given birth to another baby, and by the end of the week Charles Morrow had dug an enormous hole in the hillside facing the sea, her older sister had attempted to drown her and Francesca had decided to dedicate her life to art. She remembered it all in sunlight and brief, bright spurts of action between which was only glare—empty space.

It began when Francesca was alone in the stone house on the mountainside with her mother. And her father was at a dig at nearby Delphi. A long way down the slope from the house was a blue plate with frills of white: that was the Gulf of Itea, a twisted arm of the great Mediterranean Sea. Francesca rarely went down to the water; the descent was too steep for pregnant Lily. For that reason and others Francesca longed for a governess, someone who would spend the whole day taking her wherever she wanted to go—to the church to see the icons, to the high rocks above the village where she could climb in the thorny bushes, to look down and see their house rimmed, contained, neat as a cell in a beehive, the orange tile roof festooned with stones to keep the tiles in place. But there was no governess.

Lily had been distressed all morning, moving restlessly from room to room. Francesca stood in doorways watching her. "Mother? Mother?" Lily jerked her head at the girl, go, go away from here. But Francesca would not go. Finally Lily herself fled, mewling like a puppy, behind her bedroom door at the top of the stairs. Francesca followed her but felt a slicing as the bedroom door cut the air between them. She gaped: there was the door in her face, with the carved wood, the heavy iron sliding bolt, the latch. The voice was muffled.

"Call your father! My water has broken."

Francesca looked at the crack under the door and waited for the flood to appear. In her dreams she waited for it still, for the bloody viscous mess. Which waters were these? Her father liked to read the Old Testament; there was water, water everywhere. Here a woman was forced to drink the bitter water that was sprinkled over curses written out to her. There the waters of Babylon by which we sat down and wept. Somewhere else the water of jealousy?

The water—seen or unseen—made her afraid. She knew that her father had caused it, understood that he was not sorry and, since this was biblical and a matter of life or death, did not blame him. She knew the release of the water was a shaming thing because her mother felt it to be so. That it would flow out under the crack under the door, flood the stairway, gush out the front of the house, leak into all the culverts and down the staircases designed for spring runoff from the upper slopes of Mount Parnassus. There would be such a hue and cry about the water, about cleaning it up.

She ran downstairs to call for help, all the while knowing there was no one else in the house. She ran to the garden, the dry, walled-in garden with the single olive tree right in the centre. There was no one in the garden either. Her sister was gone, out for a walk, shopping in the village, who knew? She found the telephone, a cumbersome black thing stuck on a wall, solely for the purpose of calling England: no one in the village had a telephone. She picked up the receiver and banged it, rattled the hook it hung on and, suddenly, a voice came on.

The voice was from somewhere else, not in the village. Greek, but not local. Tell my father to come, she cried, it's time. It's time.

Her waters have broken. That's what my mother said: tell him my water has broken.

The voice took in this information: Francesca could tell she had made an impact with her story. An unbearable buzzing assaulted her ear. She held the receiver at arm's length and sobbed. She put it down and ran back to look up the stairs at the bedroom door, heard her father's car snorting and echoing like a bull through the narrow stone passageways, made for donkeys, for people. No one else in the village had a car. He had come.

She does not know, to this day, how it was that her father chanced to come back at that moment, in his fawn-coloured automobile, his glossy brown fedora of Italian make—a Borsalino?—and his beautiful long overcoat, also fawn. It was too soon for him to have come to her call. To this day, when she hears hurried, raised voices speaking in Greek—as she does every spring when they make their school trip to Delphi—she feels the panic. She is again staring at the crack under her mother's bedroom door, again believing that some fissure had opened in her mother from which waters would flood the house.

In visits to the village, Francesca still met people who had worked with her father in the excavations at Delphi. They were not, in fact, so much older than herself, less than a decade, some of them. It was a small community, stitched together by family and history that excluded the Morrows. But it seemed that the entire population knew the story. On that day your mother had the baby, that day her labour began and only you were there to help! Such a brave little girl. But white as a sheet when the men arrived! But at the time Francesca remembered hearing only the excited Greek voices and seeing no faces, only the swirl of her father's coat around his calves as he came out of the driver's side of the car, wedged between walls in the stone path he used as a driveway.

He moved toward the house like a man running in weighted boots. Would her mother's water come down before he reached

Francesca, making a waterfall out of the safe set of wooden steps up which she climbed at night to bed, down which she climbed in mornings to the sunny courtyard, her father finishing the soft-boiled egg he ate from a glass? Lily's muffled cries rose from under the door. Would the baby drown?

Hurry, she said but she had no breath with which to speak.

He was hurrying but the weight of his feet held him back, and the curved path was being pulled backward underneath him so that even as he moved his glued feet forward he stayed in the same place. When at last the path stopped retreating he was shot off it, through the doorway, arriving at a sudden stop at Francesca's feet.

He stood looking up at her, and try as she might she could not hear his voice for the sound of the waterfall in her ears. She felt she was up to her ankles in it but when she looked she saw that the floor and the stairs were dry.

Deliver the message. Perfectly, quickly. No deviation from the exact words. You need to take her to the nurses. Her water has broken.

The waterfall stopped.

Right, he said, unhurriedly, as if he knew something Francesca didn't, which he most assuredly did. Come and help, we may want to carry her, he said to men behind him. And Francesca withdrew to the kitchen, shut out of her mother's pains, her crisis, her flooding, by this man who took control. She watched the door open, watched her mother with the balloon stomach (still a large balloon, so it must be filled with something other than water) helped down the stairs. When they couldn't see her she ran after them. At the door there was the cold sun, the crunching steps on stone and gravel, the car doors opening. It was spring, wasn't it always spring on her birthday? The car doors slammed and the vehicle took the turn out of the driveway on two wheels. The whole caper, the arrival and rescuing of her mother, had been, now she looked back on it, only minutes long.

End.

Nothing more. The memory was blotted up by light; the two characters who were her parents flared and disappeared. Because they were gone, Francesca the child was also gone.

Later that day, she existed again. Her older sister Antonia was home. Antonia had two friends staying, from her English boarding school, and Francesca was bothering Antonia and her friends. She knew she was, and she was enjoying it. Antonia hated her but her friends thought she was cute; the kitchen was hot with laughter and the steam that rattled out from the top of the double boiler. They were making chocolate fudge. In the top of that double boiler Antonia had melted sugar with butter, a great luxury, and added chocolate. Now she was testing the drops. Francesca pushed into the centre of the crowd, right next to where the tumbler sat on the counter. As the fudge cooked it went through cluster stage, soft ball stage, hard ball stage. It was the soft ball stage they wanted, the friends repeated, soft ball.

A drop of the sauce fell off the spoon into the water. Everyone stared. The mixture did not hold together at all; it dispersed in the water like a lot of messy little hairs. "No, no, not yet," the English girls cried. Antonia dutifully poured out the water and waited for the fudge to cook more.

A man appeared, without any warning, in the doorway. He held his felt hat, not as nice a hat as Charles Morrow's but a good hat nonetheless, in both hands.

"Everyone in this house has a big, bouncing baby sister," he said. In Greek. He only spoke Greek.

Francesca understood this was cause for celebration. And all the more so because it was the feast of St. George. And her birthday! Her sister—her older sister (now she had to distinguish, because she had two, and the second one a sort of twin)—told her friends what the man had said. They all exclaimed. They all laughed at the messenger. He had told them all they had a baby sister, but he was wrong, wasn't he? Only Francesca and Antonia had one.

Then they remembered they were making chocolate fudge. They put a drop in the cup. The drop went stiff and stringy. Their fudge had gone right through the soft ball stage. The elongated drop of caramel sauce, which was nearly a string of hard caramel, trembled under the surface of the water.

Francesca stood at the edge of the gaggle of girls. She felt her whole life had changed. She was now between walls. No longer the younger, the baby. Now she was the middle: walls on both sides. Like her father's car, wedged, not able to move.

The chocolate drop was a baby floating in water. She stared at it until it grew bigger and bigger and then dissolved. Then the whole picture fell apart: the house in Greece, the girls around the stove.

Lily stayed away from home a week, at a nursing home in Thebes while Francesca and Antonia were subjected to the rough care of the neighbourhood women. Their father behaved with surpassing strangeness. Francesca could see him from her bed in the tiny second-floor room she shared with Antonia, wedging the car up the narrow path as close as he could come to the house, the local workmen following him with donkey and cart, their shovels and picks rattling. While the new baby sister got a firmer hold on life in the hospital, Charles caused these men to uproot the olive tree in the courtyard. Francesca saw them do it, the great rootball twisting into the air while the trunk and branches, roped and anchored, went down, the men yelling excitedly in Greek. Stupid donkeys being backed into the space and pawing the earth as they pulled forward. The round bottom of the tree scraping a bare place on the gravel path as it was dragged away.

The men went on digging. They dug a hole perhaps five metres across where the tree had been. This caused confusion, mud and turmoil in the village because everyone's roots and pipes and walls were dependent on, if not literally part of, neighbours' roots and pipes, not to mention walls and vines and gutters and roof tiles. This interconnectedness Charles dared to disturb with his excavations, not only at nearby Delphi, but right here in their few square metres of private space. Black-wrapped women howled at Francesca over the stone piles and she did not know what they were saying. When her father appeared they ducked their chins and cast their eyes down and said nothing: he was the foreign historian/gravedigger who believed in the greatness of their ancient history. Perhaps more importantly he was the provider of jobs for their husbands.

The walls of the hole were brown, clay-like, and shone when, astonishingly, the Mediterranean sun departed and the skies let down streams of rain. Water collected in the bottom of the hole, but only stayed there for a day before draining away into the stony soil. The next day the men returned with rolls of thick, speckled paper. They papered the hole and went away, only to return dragging a burner on a tripod with wheels. They melted tar, and with big brushes jumped down inside and painted the hole black.

The lily pond, for that is what it became, when the tar dried and it was laboriously filled with the scarce and valuable rainwater, was a gift for Lily, to surprise her when she came home with the baby. Charles Morrow even imported water lilies from France to grow in it, but that was later. Was her mother pleased when she came back from the nursing home with the baby wrapped in a crocheted shawl? Did she express joy to see the olive tree gone, and the black crater in its place? It seems to Francesca that there were tears, but there were always tears after a baby was born: women became emotional and unhappy exactly to the degree in which they were blessed.

How long was it before Antonia pushed her into the pond? Lily had not yet returned. Francesca could not remember how the fight started. She only remembered the surreptitious, violent push, the quick shove on her shoulder blades. In she went, over her head, a celebrated non-swimmer, a girl who screamed bloody murder when even wee frothy wavelets came up over her ankles at the beach. The push was certainly murderous in intent and might have succeeded, except that Francesca took this shocking moment, when she hit the chill water and her churning feet brought no contact with the bottom, to learn to float.

But the horror of Antonia's laugh, the betrayal it represented, stayed with Francesca until this night, sixty years later. Antonia hated her! She wanted to destroy her! She was jealous, dangerous, angry, not to be trusted. Francesca knew that. She also knew that Lily, for all her apparent helplessness, had kept the rest of the family from going mad, but now would no longer protect Francesca.

The pushing incident had been observed by the black-wrapped women, who didn't like Antonia in the first place because she spoke to them as if they were all servants. The women took it upon themselves to demonstrate her attempt to drown Francesca for Lily when she arrived home. Fairly soon thereafter Antonia went back to boarding school. And Francesca received, for her suffering, the gift she so desired: a governess.

And that led to everything else. With the governess, Francesca began to learn Greek in earnest. Of course the governess was not for Francesca's benefit, not entirely, in fact hardly at all. No, it was for the baby's sake, for Lily's sake. After the fright over her water breaking, Lily deemed it unsafe for Francesca to know only English. With a baby in the house there might be emergencies; Francesca must be able to speak Greek. Fortunately for her, the governess herself suffered from a broken heart and rejected all things modern, teaching her that only language, only painting, only music, only poems that had stood the centuries were worthy of attention. Ancient Greek had not helped much with the telephone operators. But it gave her Homer, and a whole new world.

Francesca snorted derisively there in her cube-of-light bed in Toronto, these many years later: it was all for the baby—the governess, the Greek, the Odyssey, the dramas, the philosophy, the laboriously acquired and ecstatically embraced new language. Her education was all for the baby, not for Francesca herself, all for the children, the children . . . and she was finally truly asleep.

5

THE OTHER
KINGDOM

YOU MIGHT IMAGINE the Manor to be Miss Morrow's and Dr. Laird's fiefdom, that the students, ruled, straightened and instructed with rigour, and punished with passion, were powerless. "Never not in anger," said Miss Morrow when she took out the strap. It was a quotation from T. S. Eliot, and she contended that it advocated only spontaneous and furious corporal punishment: calculated, dispassionate wallops would be immoral. It was difficult to square this with the karate wisdom of Dr. Laird: "When your anger goes out, your fist stays in." However, when Jacob pointed out the contradiction, Francesca told him that not everything squared in life, as opposed to in mathematics. Young logic was never to prevail.

But you would be wrong. In spite of, or perhaps even because of such inequity, there was a flourishing teenage society. In language and in law it opposed authority, emphasizing secrecy, subversion and shock value.

Cassie leaned against the trunk of the huge Norway maple. A last few yellow leaves clung to its upper branches. In the flower beds the hollow brown stems of lilies leaned together, the spaces overgrown with weeds and blanketed with soggy, decomposing leaves. The tree dominated all. The last time the science class was held down here, Amelia had kicked its trunk. "Maybe it's time to get rid of this greedy old thing," she said. "Drinking every bit of rain as it comes down. Nothing small has a chance to grow."

True, Cassie thought. The tree sucked up all the water, and the light as well. Probably small plants could not find enough soil amongst the enormous knotted tree roots that bulged up out of the earth. In autumn they got buried in fallen leaves and in summer they had to struggle in deep shade, under the giant green umbrella.

"You're very wrong!" Miss Morrow had cried. "The tree has its roots far down in the soil where Taddle Creek still runs; it does not live on surface water."

Cassie figured that the huge old maple wasn't the only problem with the garden. The problem was nobody dug in it any more. Nobody took care. Amelia had suggested they skip the planting and create a stone garden out of coloured pebbles. They could make designs using colours and shapes from Monet's garden paintings, she said, blue and purple and pink in overlapping circles, just like Giverny. By way of Japan. A stone garden you only had to rake and maybe weed now and then. But Miss Morrow was scandalized and said No, no, no. Sacrilege to do this to a garden designed after Gertrude Jekyll.

But it was just as bad to let it go to seed. The present decay showed a lapse in standards.

"Garden could use a fall cleanup," Cassie's mother had said on one drop-off. "Why don't you kids get together and do it?"

The kids didn't. The lapse in standards was evident, too, in the strange events that had begun to happen: Dr. Laird spouting off to the walls and ceilings, oblivious to the students, Miss Morrow crying and rushing out of classrooms, leaving no one to teach and the whole school having to watch *I, Claudius* over and over. And the little rats, late all the time, and always whispering, which only added to

Cassie's dread that people were going to die, or an accident would happen, and life would never be the same again. "All changed, changed utterly," as it said in that poem about Easter that Miss Morrow liked. "A terrible beauty is born."

Stories circulated, such as that Amelia was quitting, that Miss Morrow was dying, that she and Dr. Laird couldn't afford to keep running the school. Cassie loyally disbelieved all of the stories, but she was practically the last holdout; the others rolled their eyes when she shouted, "There's nothing's wrong here!"

She pushed herself away from the tree trunk. The truth was, the Manor School for Classical Studies *was* changing. But the Manor was not supposed to change! It was not allowed to change. Not the Manor, not the school, not this Garden of Eden. It had to remain, and Miss Morrow too, just like Michelangelo and Leonardo and Homer and Shakespeare and Yeats. They all had to stay the same, to keep Cassie safe. And they would. "Think positive thoughts!" she told herself. It would be disloyal to Miss Morrow to think anything else.

But the negative thoughts burst through. For instance, today Miss Morrow had gone crazy in Greek class. She swept down with her cane, a fierce, pained expression on her face, leaned over Chino's desk and seized his paper. Then, gracefully, her white neck fully exposed to the shaft of light coming in through the window, her head arching back like Hecuba when she learns she has to become a servant, Miss Morrow groaned and held the paper high over her head, ripping it from end to end.

"She *rent* the paper," Cassie whispered to Sara. Tore was too small a word.

Sara was the only girl in the school to whom Cassie felt superior. She was small for her age, suffered from pink eye and was timid. Sara nodded while they both stared mesmerized at their teacher. This howling rigid woman was not the Miss Morrow they knew, kind, patient and, unless pressed too far, adoring of her charges. She made Chino do an hour of calligraphy because his work was so messy.

So strong was Sara's faith in Miss Morrow that she knew right away what had happened. "She's not herself," she had whispered back, importantly.

Unfortunately, Sara was not a good whisperer. Vida overheard. She gave a quick, hard stare, then got up to return her books to her locker. The class was over. Sara and Cassie picked up their books. But Vida was waiting by the door.

"That's bullshit. Miss Morrow's torn up lots of work. She's torn my head off, too, enough times." Her tiny, neat cat-face came up close to Cassie's and she looked into her eyes in a penetrating way. Tension vibrated within Cassie. A silent, interior hum.

"Something's wrong. I can feel it," said Cassie.

Sara nodded miserably.

Sometimes sympathy was the hardest thing of all. The humming became audible.

"Don't," said Vida, casting a dangerous warning look.

The three of them walked out of the classroom together. Vida's small muscular body danced in the covered walkway holding the lockers. The orange spikes on the top of her head vibrated with indignation.

"You guys are fully fucked up over this. Your problem—" she said, jabbing her small index finger at Cassie, "is that you think like a fucking grown-up. You gotta think like a teenager. Here's an example, OK? That was *so cool* when Miss Morrow spazzed on Chino," said Vida. "Maybe she'll go fully ballistic. Maybe the school will have to close. Maybe the Greek trip won't come off. Then we'll get holidays." She cut some kind of hieroglyph in the air with her hand, and spun on her heel.

Miss Morrow did not spaz again that day but Cassie was wary and frightened; she could not concentrate on her reading and got a detention. She was glad of the extra forty-five minutes in the quiet coach house—underlining important words with her ruler and saying them under her breath, she could believe that somehow, underneath, her beloved Miss Morrow was still intact.

At noon the next day there was an episode in the boys' washroom.

Three boys, Chino among them, were changing for karate in the tiny washroom, which had a toilet and a shower but no cubicles. A fourth boy pushed to get in. Chino suffered from claustrophobia.

"There's too many guys in here. Fuck off!" Chino called out the door.

Amelia happened to be across the hall and heard the fracas. "Change somewhere else," she said to the boy outside the door. "You can see there are already too many." A struggle broke out over the door, with more boys joining the one outside, trying to push it inward, and the three boys inside trying to push it shut. Miss Morrow approached, her heels tapping in the hall.

"That will be enough!" she roared, pounding her cane on the floor. She claimed there was nothing wrong with either of her legs; she limped only because she grew tired, being on her feet all day long. But the rumours said that she was turning into a cripple, that she had injured herself in a kobudo fight with Dr. Laird. In any case she drove the cane three times into the floor again. The combatants outside the door scattered.

"There is room for one more in there now, I believe," Miss Morrow announced calmly.

Chino, worked into a claustrophobic frenzy, burst out the washroom door shouting. "There is not! You're a liar! You're a liar!"

He collided with Francesca, nearly knocking her to the ground. Only the cane kept her upright. Amelia saw the strain on the tendons as Francesca braced herself against this flying boy and was electrified. She waited for the explosion to come. You do not call Miss Morrow a liar. You do not bump up against her person. The consequences would be enormous.

But nothing. There was nothing.

Francesca straightened herself and walked on as if it had not happened. Step, step, thump. Step, step, thump.

It was worse than a dressing-down. The rat girls hissed at Chino from the history room, where they'd been hiding.

The student lounge was a tiny room that must have been the spare bedroom when the Manor was a house. Nobody went there except to use Miss Morrow's Xerox machine, but it did have a tattered red velvet couch. On this cold and rainy November day, Vida sat at one end and Cassie at the other, facing each other, talking.

Vida was Cassie's friend. How that began: Vida was teaching Cassie to be a kid. To laugh at adults' rules. To swear when embarrassed instead of blushing. She hadn't had much success yet, but Vida picked up Cassie's books when she dropped them outside her locker. And when one of the other girls muttered something vile, Vida stuck up for Cassie. Cassie was at first afraid to look at Vida but when she did, she thought Vida was beautiful. When she had looked at her sitting in the next desk, she almost had to reach for her hand. Better to sit like this, face to face, the old cushions with their worn nap at their backs.

Vida reminded Cassie of something. She studied her, trying to name it. A bird who had been forced from the nest too young. Cassie saw it clearly. The girl had fallen out, or had been tipped out. It might have been by accident or, knowing her, she might have jumped. Maybe Mother forgot to fly back with the worms. It had been too crowded in the nest or some threat from the outside— a cat?—had overturned it, and there was the Vida bird, on the ground before she was ready to fly. The bird/girl had been orphaned in a metaphorical way and she had been bouncing on the ground, flapping and squawking, years before her time. This would account for Vida's greasy, foamy, spotty plumage, the puny bones of her shoulders, legs and hips. Those parts you never saw, only got hints of because they were forever stashed inside baggy leggings, sweatpants (which she wore even under her kilt!) and outsized sweaters.

Vida was talking about tags, the names the kids on the street used. It was cool to have a tag and to go out and spray-paint it on a wall, under someone else's, or if you were looking for trouble, on top of that other tag. That was a terrific insult and if you did that the other person could come and find you and jump you.

Cassie listened, twirling the loose threads on the fringe of her kilt between her fingers. She felt protective of Vida, even though Vida was much tougher. Vida had been to raves and she had seen her friends go so crazy for cocaine that they were kicking walls.

"Once," she said, "I tried crystal meth, but I'll never do it again. I'm too paranoid."

"What do you mean?" Cassie could smell Vida's small, sour sweat from the two-foot distance at which she sat.

"I'm not going to get paralyzed from convulsions, am I? I like my body." Vida stretched her bird arms and legs elastically, and then drew them back in toward her.

Cassie's arms felt watery and buoyant and were alarmingly inclined on their own to reach out and grab this girl and hold her. That was really the sum total of the impulse, simply encircle Vida with her arms and draw that hunched body toward her own.

"I don't ever want to completely lose control. I'd do E, though," Vida went on.

"What's E?"

"Hello? Where have you been? Ecstasy."

"I don't know anything about drugs," Cassie said.

"Oh, dealers can be tricky. Don't let on how much of an idiot you are about this. People take advantage and rip you off. It doesn't matter if you buy it from your best friend, you never know what you're getting."

"I guess I could never buy it, anyway," Cassie said picking her fingernails. "I only get seven dollars a week allowance."

"Mostly girls don't have to buy it," said Vida, flipping her top-knot from one side of her face to the other, and then drawing it down beside her cheek so she could rebraid it. "The guys will give it to you for free. Trouble is, they always expect something in return."

Cassie held her breath and in the silence she could hear the hissing intake of Vida's small, half-open mouth. Vida looked down at her fingers and played with the nails, which showed vestiges of a coat of nail polish and much chewing. Ecstasy was one thing Cassie was afraid of and not only the drug. Mad Cassandra of Troy fell down in ecstasies, that was one kind. Perhaps this strange feeling in her arms and legs, drawing out her blood toward the girl sitting across from her, was the beginning of it. Vida was a medieval creature, like one of the figures carved into the arched entrances of Gothic cathedrals. A gargoyle of great intensity and animal strength who had come to the door of the cathedral and had been stopped there in stone, arrested by unknown sculptors. Cassie was fascinated by Vida, but she was even more fascinated by the restlessness in her own arms and legs. They kept lifting and sailing out into the air, then needing to be tucked back in as if they were inspired, and a little reckless.

"*The young in one another's arms, birds in the trees, those dying generations...*"

What it all meant was lost on her, and she was angry that she could not name it. She had never felt such a persistent and specific desire to be near, to know, another person. It was of course not the kind of thing boys felt for girls, or women for men, not at all. She just could not stay away from Vida. And Vida knew. Cassie cast her eyes down so that her eyelashes shadowed her lightly freckled cheeks.

"If only I wasn't so fat and so slow, I could go out with you," she blurted.

Vida smiled kindly, acknowledging the truth of this. She continued to stare, almost cross-eyed, at the narrow braid of dead hair she was making.

"You could come with us. If you got some baggy jeans, you wouldn't look fat," she said. "If you can get money I'll take you. And a hooded sweatshirt and some goggles. You'd look phat."

Cassie didn't know how, but she would get the money.

The chimes rang. They stood and walked to the door. Cassie pictured that medical chart in Dr. Laird's classroom, the one of the human body with the skin taken off, and all the muscles and sinews, veins and arteries coloured in red purple green and blue. Most of hers were jumping off the bone and waving out there, like fronds, like tentacles, in the air. Come here. Come here.

Vida stopped at the door. "We always hug when we say good-bye," she said. "As mean as we act to outsiders, that's how cuddly-sweet we are to each other."

"OK," Cassie said, her voice muffled by Vida's shoulder because she had tripped forward so fast, faster even than she was able to get the word out of her mouth. Her head tipped down onto the smaller girl's tiny, prominent collarbone. She felt ill, she felt agitated, as if some large tumbling ball of wind and thorns were rolling up the road toward her. She rocked back a little, surprised, and then stood, her hands closing over the smaller girl's spine, holding her steady.

The rat girls stood shivering on Smokers' Corner. It was late November and the sun was so low after school it was practically night. Around the pile of knapsacks on the sidewalk stood Vida, Maureen, Roxanne and Ashley; squatting beside them was Ashley's dog Spit. Across the road, at her usual post on the wall waiting for her mother to pick her up, sat Cassie, kicking her heels. The others had stuffed their blazers and kilts into their lockers after school and were now dressed like trailer trash, wearing jeans so tight their thighs were like sausages or so baggy you couldn't even see a leg move. Their belly buttons were exposed under shrunken T-shirts and their thrift-store leather jackets hung open.

Cassie wore her duffle coat with all the toggles done up. Her knee socks were down around her ankles and she wore mitts someone had knit for her. She stared at the rat girls when they weren't looking. Now that they were out of school uniform she could recognize them for what they were.

They were a gang. It was clear. Cigarettes dangled from their lower lips. They had perfected the angry stare to the point that other girls and even boys grew dry-mouthed at the sight of them. They spat across the tracks at subway stations and would jump any chick on College Street if they wanted her jacket. They were fifteen and sixteen but their ID said they were nineteen. They got thrown out of bars for drunkenness and aggression. The hostility fairly dripped from their black fingernails.

Vida was the smallest and seemed to be the leader, mostly because she never stood still. Her black hair was shaved tight against her head, almost all over, exposing her nape, her pointed ears and the sharp widow's peak over her pale forehead. From the crown of her head sprang those spongy, matted strands dyed fluorescent orange, which she braided, or not, in which case they flopped like the leaves of a lily. Under five feet fall and built like a child, she moved with quick menace. She had a green belt in karate. Her hairdo was inspired by Sensei's direction to live "as if your hair were on fire."

Maureen was the girl who most impressed the younger ones; even Vida idolized her. Sara and Cassie, who had little to do with the rat girls, admired the way she looked, the way she talked, and especially her clothes. Maureen looked as if she'd been built by a clutch of lusting teenage male computer animators: perhaps that's what made her so angry. For the whole month since she'd broken up with her last boyfriend she'd been swearing she'd never let another man touch her, ever, and she was sticking to it. She had peach-coloured skin and naturally blonde hair that she tried to ruin by bleaching. She had full, curving, sardonic lips and high, wide cheekbones. She was loose-limbed and rangy, broad shouldered as a rugby player, but with a delicacy she could not entirely destroy. Sixteen, she could pass for thirty. A careful row of earrings, five in all, lined the rim of her right ear. The rhinestone she'd had in her navel got torn out in a fight, leaving a large scab. Invisible was the genital piercing, which was giving her trouble. Her tongue was pierced, too, a silver barbell gleaming when she spoke; one had the impression, watching her mouth, that despite the foul words that came out, some pearl was forming inside its oyster shell.

Today Maureen was antsy. One leg jiggled so that the chains linking the front and back pockets of her jeans rattled. She picked the scab on her navel and wiped the open sore with the edge of her too-short T-shirt. Two horizontal tears in her jeans just under the swell of her buttocks opened like little lips when she stomped her foot.

"Fuckin' fuckin' fuckin' fuckin' hell. He fuckin' screwed me over, the bastard."

"Maybe he's just late."

"Bastard was meant to be at the sheds at two-thirty. And he's not. It's like, after four o'clock." She shook the dried ends of her hair, which looked as if they had been regularly chewed, out of her mouth.

"Well, were you there?"

"Course I was fuckin' there, I walked out of the studio while Miss Morrow was going on about some bloody windows—"

"The Jerusalem windows," said Roxanne. She turned her toes out and bent her knees a few times. Then she rose on her toes and balanced. There was a primness still in Roxanne, a remnant of the goody two-shoes ballerina in her bow-shaped lips, which she coated with burgundy lipstick, in the bun she wore at the back of her head. But Roxanne was not to be trusted. She had a hair-trigger temper; she scratched and bit like a fiend.

"Like, duh, who gives a fuck what kinda windows," said Maureen. Then she turned on Vida, feeling her competence threatened. "What do you think, I'm like some kind of idiot?"

"Well, no, I just wondered," said Vida. She glided around behind the group and looked up Wychwood toward the yards. "They must've got held up or something."

"Held me up is what they did. They've got my fuckin' fifty dollars. I took that money out on purpose." Maureen dropped her cigarette and ground it under the foot of her three-inch platform sole. She immediately reached in her pocket for another.

"Took it out of where?"

"My dad's wallet. Where else?"

The group stood digesting this bitter pill. Free money, lost.

"So is he gonna find out?" piped Ashley.

"Oh sure, what else?" said Maureen.

"I guess you're gonna get shit."

"Naw. He won't even fuckin' care."

"He won't? Why?"

"'Cause he's a fuckin' idiot," she snarled. It was a sore point with her. Why should she go to all that trouble to steal if her dad didn't even care? Ashley laughed. Everyone froze. "What's your problem, bitch?" Maureen said, staring Ashley down.

This was not easy to do because Ashley was five-foot-ten, intimidating even without the dog, who growled as soon as a harsh word was directed her way. She had been training to be an Olympic swimmer since she was eleven. At her first private school she beat up two girls who stole her knapsack. She was invited to leave the school, which she considered vastly unfair. "What do they teach at that place anyway, swiping?" At her new public school she fell in with the smokers, the potheads, the street kids. By the end of the first term of grade nine she was failing every course but physical education. She had a kind word for no one but Spit who she'd picked up in a tent city by the tracks. She rarely went home and ate only one meal every two days. When her mother talked curfews Ashley sent her to the hospital with two black eyes. The swim coach saw the flesh dropping off her frame and called Children's Aid. When her father brought her to the Manor she weighed only ninety-eight pounds: most of her food went to Spit. She wore torn jeans and a sleeveless T-shirt to reveal the wolf heads tattooed on her upper arms. She had a ring through her nose, and black lipstick. "Such wonderful bones," said Miss Morrow. "I can see a great sense of balance and order in her."

"Perhaps we overdid the training," her father explained. "She's a trifle too physical and she worries about being fat." He failed to mention that she'd robbed a convenience store in the company of two boys who'd been too scared to squeal on her. He did tell the headmistress that he imagined on registration at the Manor the nose ring would have to go. "Let's do one thing at a time," said Miss Morrow. For a time at the Manor Ashley got away with murder. She didn't hand in assignments and her notebooks were non-existent. But morning after morning of Ashley and Spit arriving late at school in a taxi from god knew where wore on Miss Morrow's patience. Miss Morrow chastised Ashley. Ashley treated Miss Morrow to a gusher of expletives. People gasped. Would Ashley punch her lights out?

But no. Miss Morrow was not worried. After all these years she feared none of her intransigent students; she simply had difficulty sustaining her interest. Ashley's continued presence at the school was, at the moment, in question.

"My problem is," said Ashley levelling her grey eyes at Maureen's, dropping and grinding her cigarette on top of Maureen's and returning tough for tough, "you and your shitty attitude."

"Hey, hey," said Vida darting back to the group from her position as sentinel. "Those guys were sketchy, I always thought they were."

"What the hell?" Maureen was so jumpy that her fists came up to her sides, but she knew enough to keep them in.

Spit snarled. Ashley smiled lazily. She'd made her point. Maureen wouldn't take her on, no one would. "You're shit for like stealing from your dad. Shit because you think you're a dealer and you can't even get shrooms. The guys aren't gonna get here with the stuff."

They all listened. Maureen's dad's wallet had supported many a night's burn.

"Oh, they'll get here," said Maureen lamely. She turned to Ashley with a contemptuous face. "I'm not gonna take any more money from him anyway," she said. "It's just like too boring." Then, tossing her cigarette butt, she looked back. While they were talking Cassie had got down from the wall and crossed the road. She stood ten feet away, shifting her cloddish feet.

"What the fuck's she doing here?"

Cassie flinched, but held her ground. She was unsure she wanted to stay and afraid to leave.

"Like—hello?" Maureen gave her a bitchy look.

Cassie glanced at Vida. She would definitely not be anywhere near these girls if it weren't for Vida. Vida took a long drag on her cigarette.

"She asked me," mumbled Cassie.

The rat girls all laughed.

"Yeah," said Vida. "I want her in."

Ashley put her fingers down her throat and made like she was puking on the sidewalk. Maureen scoffed.

"Vida, you're on crack. She's like pathetic. And she's a suck-up."

"No, she's not," said Vida. "She's cool."

Spit inched forward on his chain, whining and wagging his tail in Cassie's direction.

"Dog likes her," said Roxanne.

Maureen laughed and punched Roxanne's shoulder.

"Don't put words in his mouth," said Ashley. "He votes the way I vote."

"So are we voting?" said Maureen, incredulous. "Like, what the fuck?"

"I think she's kinda cool," said Roxanne. "Did you see how she kicked those guys at her locker?"

"Yeah," said Vida, admiringly. It had happened when Chino was teasing Cassie, and it was part of the pattern they could now see. First she hummed, then she spun, then, if pressed, she kicked.

The fact was, even the tough girls were a little afraid of Cassie, because she was so strange. She was unreadable, a dark cloud from which a storm or a genie might arise. No normal creature was capable of such shape-changing. She was neither large nor small. She towered or shrivelled depending on her mood. When she was sad, she sank into corners of rooms, drooped in chairs; the air seemed to come sighing out of her. Her face screwed up with suffering and she was inconsolable. When she was hurt—and she was hurt by frequent snubs—she composed a bilious scowl. She might scream or hum, she might kick or cry, you never knew. She could be smart or stupid, depending on the day. Sometimes she laughed all by herself and just didn't care if kids stared at her.

When she did laugh, which was not often, she was large and loud; bubbles of mirth came out of her mouth. That's what had attracted Vida. Vida saw her as a big pillow, wanting hugs. She had put her arms around her when Cassie was upset, and felt something very solid and resisting there. She'd become something of a project, to Vida. Innocence clung to her; no matter how Vida made up her eyes or moussed her hair, nothing changed that bland, slightly thick, unintentional doltishness. And Vida had come to admire it.

"She's a wuss," Maureen said dismissively. "She's like scared of everything."

It was true. Cassie was afraid but not, like most teenagers, of the possibility that she did not measure up, that people thought she was a freak and a ditz, or that boys didn't find her attractive. She feared greater calamities—that greenhouse gases would cause the pond in Wychwood Park to evaporate, that famines in Africa were spreading, that nuclear reactors in India would be put to bad use. The main channels of her mind were chock-full of such dark thoughts. Fear gave her a look mistaken for dullness and inattention; it made her eyes travel off to one side, as if by not meeting your glance, she might ward off danger.

"I say she's in," said Vida.

"In," said Roxanne.

Spit barked. Ashley laughed. "Who gives a shit," she said, more to spite Maureen than anything. "In."

Maureen said nothing. What was there to say? She took a few running steps and kicked a knapsack. It flew up in the air and landed in front of Cassie. "Fuck!"

Cassie politely picked up the knapsack and carried it a few steps closer. "Come on," said Vida, "in means in." She pointed to a bit of sidewalk next to her. Cassie edged nearer.

Done. The other girls smiled at Cassie. Maureen changed the subject.

"So you said you were gonna show us," Maureen challenged Ashley.

Ashley took her time getting a cigarette out of the pack. Her fingertips were cold, and they fumbled while rolling the little edged wheel of her Zippo.

"Show you what?" she asked, though she knew. She blew out the smoke and stared straight into Maureen's snapping round brown eyes. "Give me a toonie?"

Maureen snorted. She'd given the fifty to the drug dealers and she only had a toonie and a couple of quarters left, which she was saving for coffee. "OK, so who cares?" she said and turned away.

Vida stepped over the knapsacks and slid behind her, stopping her from going. "Wait," she said. "C'mon, Ashley, you promised."

Ashley inhaled deeply and let the smoke explode out of her mouth.

Vida looked back at the Manor. "She'll come out. She'll catch us. Let's move around the corner."

Ashley rolled her eyes expressively and mouthed the word "suck-up" in Vida's direction, but she did reach down with her long arm, grab the knapsack strap and begin to saunter toward the sheds. Maureen simply glanced at her knapsack; Vida seized it, throwing it over her shoulder with her own so that she walked bent like some mountain troll carrying a bundle of coal. She signalled Cassie to follow. This left Maureen free to walk on her own, unburdened, straight across the road in front of a car, making it swerve and brake and causing the driver to clutch at his chest convulsively before giving a vigorous finger out the window to her lush retreating ass. "OK, so show me," Maureen said when she arrived at the side of the abandoned shed. "I'm not waiting here forever."

"Don't make such a big deal of it," said Ashley. Then she dropped her cigarette and pulled up the sleeve of her leather jacket. There it was. Carved deep into her arm under the wolf-head tattoo, the recent knife-lines scabbed over with black, a highly legible "Help Me."

"Cool," said Vida.

"That's fucked up," said Maureen.

"Ooooh no," said Cassie, peering over shoulders.

The others exchanged looks of irritation.

"Oh, oh, oh."

"Shut up, Cassie."

"See?" snapped Maureen.

Cassie's moans spooked everyone. Miss Morrow said Cassie had a nervous condition and that she couldn't help it. She said it didn't take very much to quiet her down and this was true, it didn't. Sometimes. If Cassie trusted you. Vida held up her hand. It was a Miss Morrow gesture. "Hush," she said and put her hand on Cassie's shoulder, hoping it would calm her down. Cassie was deeply interested in Ashley's carving. "Oooooh, ooooh, oooooh," she uttered in declining whoops.

Her eyes slid over to meet Vida's. The tension began to go out of her chest. She let out her breath. The moaning stopped.

"Thank god," said Roxanne.

Maureen regarded Ashley's cuts impassively, revealing none of her admiration. "I've seen worse. I've seen it where girls have like totally criss-crossed their arms with cuts. So it's like a fishnet stocking that's way too tight? I've seen it where the cuts are so deep and spread open they can't heal any more and they, like, ooze."

"Where?" challenged Ashley.

"In a training school. On TV or something."

Cassie made as if to run away but she didn't. Instead she edged sideways to see better, over Vida's shoulder, and then sideways again to hide behind Maureen. Slow moans started to come from her mouth again. When Vida jerked her head to instruct, Cassie put her hand over her mouth. When she uncovered her mouth it was to ask: "Why did you do it, Ashley? Slash yourself like an apple strudel?"

Ashley's frame registered a jolt: she held herself in check while deciding whether or not she'd been insulted. She couldn't decide. With an effort, she elected to answer the question rather than punch Cassie in the face, regarding her arm with a mixture of pride and thoughtful revulsion. "I liked feeling the pain better than I liked what I was feeling before I did it, you know?"

Cassie clapped her hand over her mouth again to stop a moan. They all watched as she slowly unglued it from her lips. "The pain," she said, "the ever-ending pain."

"Never-ending," Vida corrected. Cassie had a way of mixing up words. Miss Morrow said Cassie had a huge vocabulary but she mixed it up. She began a small moan again. Smiling, she put her hand over her mouth and rolled her eyes at the girls.

"Hey, *friends*, hey, Cassie?" Vida said lightly, reaching out her hand and gripping the other girl's wrist. Cassie had no muscle whereas Vida had no flesh, only sinews.

Maureen was still staring at Ashley's arm. "When did you do it?" she asked.

"Just like at night when I was watching TV. Anyways..." Ashley tugged the sleeve of her jacket down over her arm. She looked back toward the Manor. "I hate this school," she said. "I know places downtown where you little shits would be toast. It's boring here. I'm gonna quit. It was just like my dad's idea that I had to go to school anyway. So that I don't kill my mum. If I don't go here she won't let me live at home. Bitch!"

"Yeah," said Maureen. "Trouble is, if you don't go to school, the day is like a million hours long. And if you don't have a place to live you've got nowhere to shower or anything." She didn't mention eating because that always got Ashley agitated. "I've done that."

"I haven't," said Vida enviously.

"You don't want to," said Maureen seriously.

"I do, sort of."

"It's no big deal living at my place," said Ashley bitterly. "Like, my parents leave these lists for me and my brother, like we're supposed to share the household chores and get dinner going. So like, nine times out of ten we don't do it, although my brother's this complete suck and if I let him he'd do all his work and half of mine too. So Spit and I tie him up—" Ashley nudged her dog with her toe so that he looked up at her, his tongue hanging over his teeth, "and torture him."

Cassie stared goggle-eyed. "Why don't you let him do the work?"

"Are you totally stupid? She already likes him better than she likes me."

Nobody said anything.

"Well, anyways," said Ashley, in a summary tone. They all fell silent, as she wished. "I'm getting out of here."

Then, "Wanna come to Futures for coffee?"

They all bent down and dragged their knapsacks toward their feet. Unconsciously synchronized, they lifted the bags with the straps crossed, swung them behind and over one shoulder so that the straps uncrossed, put one arm through and shrugged, to settle the weight. All but Ashley, who gazed with superiority at this sign of their acquiescence, their childishness. She didn't do homework. Cassie swayed from one leg to the other. As luck would have it, today she had no violin lessons, and her mum wasn't coming to pick her up for an appointment with the shrink. She had no good reason on earth not to go for coffee.

"Coming?" said Vida to Cassie.

"Yup." She looked directly into Vida's eyes.

The streetcar back door popped open with its vacuumized sigh and the five girls spilled down the stairs onto the traffic island. Cassie scrambled through the curbside lane of traffic to the sidewalk to wait for the light, while the others ran around in front of the streetcar and cut across the two westbound lanes of traffic. They were on the other corner before Vida looked back and saw Cassie waiting like a dolt for the green. She pointed north on Yonge toward Futures and Cassie nodded. Then Vida and the others cut kitty-corner across Yonge and ran on up the street.

When the light changed Cassie set out determinedly to catch up to her friends. Well, *friend*s, maybe. As close to friends as she had. What would her mother say if she saw her in the coffee shop? she wondered. What would Miss Morrow say? More important, what would Cassie say when she got there? She never had anything to talk about, and she felt stupid just sitting there. One of them might say to her, why don't you talk, are you stupid or something? The thing was, if you smoked you didn't really need to say much at all, because your time was spent getting a lighter or a match, bumming a cigarette or being bummed off, lighting it, sucking on it, puffing out the smoke. You could look cool without doing anything else but smoke. But Cassie couldn't smoke. It made her eyes water and it made her cough, and she for one believed all the handouts from Miss Morrow about your lungs turning black and you getting addicted in three cigarettes and it taking the rest of your life to get off it, that is if you didn't die of lung cancer by the age of forty.

But the rat girls would just say, cool, and who cared if you died at forty? You'd be so old then it didn't really matter. But Cassie knew her mother was already forty-five so if she'd died at forty, Cassie would have been only ten years old and that would have been pretty sad. She nearly started to cry, just thinking about it, and now she walked more slowly up Yonge Street. Vida said that teenagers didn't think anything mattered if it was going to be more than, say, two weeks from now. They just didn't think that far in advance. That was normal, Vida said.

Cassie was not normal. She had too old a head on her shoulders, as her grandmother used to say. Mind you, she didn't think it was fair to say anyone was like a fifteen-year-old. Fifteen-year-olds can be like just about anything. There are a lot of differences between kids of the same age, she said to herself, in a conversational way. Some of them smoke and sleep over in their friends' basements. Some of them just want to go home and watch TV and have dinner with their mums. Some of them moan without meaning to and have terrifying dreams about being tied up in a net. Miss Morrow said that it was Cassie's conviction that she was different more than anything else that made her different.

But Cassie knew she *was* different. She was even different each day from what she'd been the day before. Sometimes her own mother hardly recognized her. She said she had a beggar's face. Cassie recalled the exact moment when her mother told her this. They were trying on hats at Margo's Fine Hats on Rosehill Avenue. Cassie loved it. Each hat transformed her face. Pudding face became Victorian chocolate box child face became the Queen Mother. With a bowler hat she looked like a man, a chubby man but still a man.

When she looked across the street she saw that she'd walked all the way past Futures and was heading farther up Yonge Street toward

who knew what. She looked back over her shoulder and her eyes
fixed on the door of the coffee shop where a fistful of kids stood on
the sidewalk. Suddenly, the group exploded and one small figure
flew out toward the roadway, a small figure with flames coming out
the top of her head. Vida. Cassie could hear shouting, and then
someone big was going after Vida, was grabbing her in a headlock,
Vida's head disappearing under the big girl's arm.

Cassie stood panicked, arrested in what had been, let's face it,
flight from the difficult situation of having coffee when you're not
cool. But now she was drawn back by loyalty to the only one of the
rats who had ever been nice to her. She began running—a heavy,
sloppy affair, Cassie's run—coming up to the fight just as a whole
gang of girls circled Vida and the big girl. The spectators were cheer-
ing. Vida had her hands up in fighting stance. The big girl's nose
was bleeding and she was swearing. Vida wasn't wasting any energy
on taunts. Cassie could feel the tensed focus of her mind and her
body. It was just as Sensei said: try not to fight but, when you have
to, fight to kill.

"Vida," said Cassie, "careful." She was moaning although she
didn't know it; she was feeling the agitation. It was coming over her,
whatever it was.

The big girl caught sight of Cassie and saw the flicker across
Vida's face that meant she'd heard her friend. Taking advantage of
that split second of lost concentration, the big girl flew toward Vida
with her hands forward, trying to grab Vida by her neon plume. And
then the gore splashed across Cassie's inner eye. She had one horrible
mental image of the orange topknot pulling off like a carrot out of
the earth and Vida's skull bursting forth a fountain of blood.

"Ah! Ah! Ooooh!" shouted Cassie.

This mystified the big attacker, who stopped for a moment
to stare.

Cassie found herself shouting with the rest as Vida caught the big
girl's nose with the heel of her palm, following it up with a solid punch

to the solar plexus with her opposite fist, and then grabbed her by the shoulders, pulling them down to where Vida's tiny knee could crunch against her chin. Finally she shoved her away, bringing her heel down on the girl's instep as she delivered the blood-curdling kiai: "Die!"

The big girl roared and tried to limp away. But Vida hadn't let up her stance or her fierce concentration. She feinted like a matador around her victim, who was holding her nose and her stomach at the same time and making roaring noises like a bull. Her friends pulled her out of the circle yelling, "No fair, she doesn't fight fair, look at her—she's like doing kung fu or something!"

And now the big hurt bully staggered toward Cassie. Cassie had learned karate moves but half-heartedly; she knew it would all desert her the moment she was confronted with a real fight. Although she could howl when howling came on her, that was inadvertent. When she tried she had no voice at all. It had taken her six weeks to raise even a squeak of a kiai.

Cassie was so frightened she put one foot behind the other and did a limping step to spin herself around. She rotated once and when her face came back to the start the girl was still there. So she spun again, faster, and then she was twirling.

Faster and faster she went, everything blurring around the outsides of her spin. Her arms flew out and up from her thighs, her long, limp arms with the beautiful hands at the end of them. No one could come near her while those arms were clipping through the air like blades on a blender. She almost tipped over; she slid like a top from one point on the pavement to another, and the fighting girls moved away from her. She slid again in their direction. She made her hands into fists and they became heavy.

Faster and faster she spun. She felt her fists smash into someone's flesh. One of them, by the feel, connected with a chin. She was amazed at herself. She thought it was Vida who'd gone down on the ground but, no, through her dizzy wild eyes she could see the orange topknot bobbing and hear Vida's delighted screams of laughter.

"Go, Cassie!"

She couldn't stop now. If she stopped they'd get near her. They'd jump her and pummel her with their fists. It was a little tiring but she'd have to keep going.

"You better watch out," cawed one of the enemy. "You're so dead."

"She's bleeding!"

"Fuck!"

There was another heavy bash on Cassie's hand but she breathed in and out fast and kept twirling. Around the edges of her vision she could see Vida, who appeared not to hear the taunts but approached and retreated in perfect karate kata that connected with no one.

"Cops!"

"Get outta here!"

Scramble of feet, curses, promises to return, and the world began to slide off the edge of the plate of the pavement. Cassie was slowing down. Vida came up warily behind her, and Maureen and Ashley were there.

"Hey," said Vida. "Hey, hey," and put her hand on Cassie's shoulder. "You can relax now. She's gone."

Cassie shook her hands loose. She was so dizzy she staggered. She tried turning back in the other direction to steady herself. It didn't work. She bent over and began to vomit.

"Freak! She's a fuckin' freak!" yelled a departing enemy.

"Yeah, yeah, yeah," said Maureen grudgingly, patting Cassie's back. "We know. But she kicked your ass, didn't she."

But it was not over. From around the corner three of the girls came running back together at the Manor five, stupid opponents with no plan, but one of them bumped Cassie and she fell. From the sidewalk she looked up and saw Ashley and Vida in fighting stance, with Vida yelling commands. Roxanne was clawing the leader's face. Maureen, who'd never taken karate, got hold of one of the girls around the neck and began booting her hard in the legs. The other girl was trying to figure out what to do with Ashley and Vida, who were punching and rushing, kicking and letting out loud kiais. "Yaaa—eee—iii!" they shouted.

They'd all forgotten about Cassie, lying flat on the ground, her head close to where Roxanne and the gang leader were fighting. Roxanne seemed to be losing. Cassie reached out and grabbed the other girl's foot, thinking, I'd better do this fast. Rolling onto her back she twisted the leg one hundred and eighty degrees around, then kicked out like you do after a somersault and managed to use her momentum to roll upward onto her feet, the gang leader's foot in her lap. Needless to say, the girl went down like a tree.

Cool, thought Cassie, I can do it. I did it.

After that the girls ran off with scratched faces and torn clothes, with bloody knees and elbows and with sidewalk dirt stuck in their hair. Vida got busy and dusted off Cassie's kilt. "Those guys were way bigger, and look who kicked butt," she said. "Cassie, that was so cool."

I'm part of the group, thought Cassie, dazedly. I'm part of the group.

6

THE
INTERVIEW

THE FIRST DAY Cassie had stepped fearfully into her office, Miss Morrow had made a promise. "You can absolutely count on me. I will never let you down." Whatever happened, her calm would be stronger than Cassie's fear.

She promised too that the Manor would stand as long as it took for Cassie to finish high school. "You must not worry, Cassie: there is life in me yet! Dr. Laird and I will see our little rats through their graduation, without fail." She promised, implicitly, that nothing would dissolve her union with Dugald, that their love was perfect and contained all of them within its circle.

"The Manor has been here a long time. We could never close our doors and leave you all in limbo."

She made Cassie feel that "Cassandra" was magical to her, important enough to stave off her retirement, her aging, even her death. And Cassie took Miss Morrow's promises to mean that, even if her attacks became too much, even if the school were to fail (an idea that she refused to entertain long past the time the others were predicting it), even if the world as they knew it came to an end—and in a way it did—that the essential Francesca Morrow would be Cassie's friend for life. Cassie believed that their natures spoke to each other and always would. Perhaps everyone subject to the power of an idol has such fantasies.

But Miss Morrow did not come into Cassie's heart at their first interview. It was not even at the naming ceremony, when she gave her the role of Cassandra and Cassie ran through the classroom draped in the seer's net which was really Amelia's shawl. It was later than that, on the Tuesday morning of the week after the fight, when the Headmistress called Cassie to her office.

Oh, it was a morning. A morning when Cassie had to gather her courage like a discarded nightshirt from around her feet, a morning already savaged by an encounter with Chino and Darrin, both of whom had snarled and said, "Watch your step, girl, we're gonna get you again today." Even though they grinned to let her know it was a tease, and allowed her through the iron gate, it was enough. Teasing is just a reminder that someone has power over you. "Supposed to laugh," Ferdinand told her when he saw her tormented look by the truck, but she could not laugh. Teasing made her fearful and angry. The boys were the cats and she was the mouse, and she was supposed to pretend she took as much pleasure from the game as they did.

Nonetheless, onward! as her mother always said. Up the elderly (never say tattered) carpet into Miss Morrow's office, there to see her seated in the perfect centre of a green velvet cushion, which itself was set in the perfect centre of the divan. Cassie took a seat upon the stiff little loveseat. Folded her hands in her lap, gazed directly at the Headmistress. Miss Morrow was erect, and immaculately groomed, at her best at this early hour, 7:45, to be exact, her favourite time to meet students. Her handwritten notes to one side, her voice drawn and considered, she spoke.

"Good morning, Cassandra."

Miss Morrow grew out of the cushion like a tree out of a mossy forest floor. The chairs, their positions in them seemed ageless, like everything else in the room. On the tables were the plaster heads of Greek men and Egyptian women that Miss Morrow called busts, an embarrassing word that made the boys snigger. There were thick, embroidered tapestries tacked over all the windows. Did she have an allergy to sunlight, or did she believe its intrusion would damage her precious artwork? Her precious complexion was more like it: that was what Vida would say.

"Good morning, Miss Morrow." Oh, a very poor excuse for a voice, nasal and indistinct. She squirmed to find a spot on the hard loveseat. Her opponent/proponent was slim as a rail, a rake, a ramrod. Not a beanpole, nothing so rustic—slim as a Modigliani perhaps, but nothing so naked. Beside her on a table lay a file that contained Cassie's marks for this term. She quaked. A summons to Miss Morrow meant a dressing-down, a punishment, dismissal, even. It could also mean praise, expressions of enormous faith, laughter and a bathing in her pure and seductive charm, but under the circumstances this was unlikely. Who could tell by looking into Miss Morrow's smooth-powdered and apparently benign visage?

"Do you know why I have called you up to see me?" Miss Morrow's voice was drawn, hollow, theatrical always. Yet here in the small attic office it achieved a degree of intimacy; Cassie felt her heart begin to exit her chest, drawn toward the Headmistress, the Vice.

"No, I don't know," Cassie said, flushing red. In her secret heart she was guilty of such a welter of infractions she could only guess what was in Miss Morrow's mind.

Miss Morrow lifted the file and opened it.

"Dr. Laird says your math has fallen dreadfully behind. There have been two cases where homework was not completed. The in-class exam was unfinished." She flipped over a sheet. "He says you are disturbing the other children in science class and that on occasion you have simply walked out of the classroom with no explanation." She flipped a page. "Miss Holt says, on the other hand, that French is going reasonably well, although you still refuse to participate in oral exercises."

Miss Morrow allowed the last two words, oral and exercises, to drop between them as gently as a wooden ball on a lawn. The pause was perfection.

"And then there are the classes we have together, Cassandra, our English poetry, and our drama."

Cassie hung her head.

"Your oral memory work is excellent, but the written is dreadful. You failed to hand in the list of poetic forms and your essay on *King Lear* was very untidy and much, much too short."

Cassie was melting down into a puddle. Soon there would be nothing left of her.

"Sit up dear," said Miss Morrow. Cassie's spine obediently shot upward. Miss Morrow allowed another few seconds for emphasis.

"And so I am confused. We all know, I think, what you are capable of in academic terms. Simply put: great things, Cassandra, great things. But these goals, these prizes, which are within your reach, cannot be gained without an improvement in attitude."

The rigid uprightness of her carriage allowed Cassie to slump in spirit. She did not know about the goals and the prizes. They seemed to exist more in Miss Morrow's mind than in her own. Miss Morrow seemed to believe in her. But why? Maybe she had fooled Miss Morrow. No, it was not possible to fool Miss Morrow. If Miss Morrow was saying all this, she meant it. The Headmistress folded her elegant hands and gazed deep into Cassie's soul.

"You know you are a great personal pleasure to me."

Okay, but Miss Morrow was going crazy, that's what Sara said, that's what all the kids around the school hinted. Cassie shifted in her seat; Miss Morrow's eyebrows shot up.

"Laying aside your academic work, Cassandra, let us discuss the scenes."

Scenes were what they called her fits. When she began to moan or to hum, when she twirled, and when she kicked. Miss Morrow allowed herself a small smile. In fact, if the truth were known, in her secret heart the madness was an aspect of this girl—mysterious, timid child that she was—that Miss Morrow rather relished. And Cassie sensed that some undisclosed miscreant in the Headmistress did secretly approve of the fact that, when provoked, Cassie became a wild thing. Miss Morrow went on, ruminating.

"Dearest, I am so glad the humming is under control. Twirling, too, I haven't seen in some time. How I do recall when you first arrived here! How long ago was it? Just in September?"

Cassie nodded.

"From that school where they didn't know how to spell!" It was another of their little jokes: Cassie had been at an experimental school. Her student record had been sent over with spelling mistakes the likes of "redily" instead of "readily" and "elementry" instead of "elementary."

"Yes, you spun like a top then!" Miss Morrow gave a delighted laugh. In the verdant, peaceful atmosphere of the Manor, twirling was generally unnecessary. Everyone was to be congratulated. But then Miss Morrow's laughter stopped and the fond smile changed into a frown of concern.

"And now this." A soft, soft voice.

"This? What?"

"Do the words Yonge and St. Clair suggest anything?"

"Oh," said Cassie. "The fight?"

"Can you tell me what happened, Cassandra?"

Cassie heard, tantalizingly, the hint of compassion in Miss Morrow's delivery, of understanding, even of forgiveness. But it was only a hint. Overall hung the possibility of the massive disapproval that made the Headmistress' entire slim torso go stiff, and turned her mean, mean, mean. Cassie tasted bile. She thought she might throw up on the magic carpets, the green velvet pillows. She might have to run downstairs covering her mouth, but then she might barf on the needlepoint version of the fifth panel of the Unicorn tapestry with its motto "A mon seul desire."

"I went after school with the girls. They don't usually ask me so I was happy." That much was true. "And there was a boy," she added, haltingly.

Miss Morrow stirred. "A boy?"

"Yes, an older boy. A big boy, like a man." He got bigger by the second in Cassie's mind.

"There was a large boy. All right. And?"

"I've seen him before. And he always teases me. He calls me squinty or pigface or—" she didn't dare say the word 'skank'—"just anything he thinks of and it gets me so mad. And so he saw me and this time he picked me up and put me upside down in the garbage can." Her voice rose high.

"Oh he did," said Miss Morrow. "He did, did he?"

"He did!" cried Cassie. She had been sitting up straight; she sat even straighter, and her face went red. Her indignation at being thought a liar strengthened her, even though she was lying. Then, distressed at what she saw in Miss Morrow's face, she sank back against the loveseat. "My face went right in it," she muttered. "Mushy rims of buns with relish and ketchup, leftover Coke and ice cubes, Egg McMuffin." A tiny inadvertent hum started up inside her.

Miss Morrow took one long finger and swung it slowly back and forth across the space between them, as if she were running it along the strings of an invisible harp. "Remain calm," she said. "Facts would be helpful."

Cassie's voice came out loud and raw. "He did too put me upside down in the garbage can! And the can tipped over and I fell on the ground and I had ketchup and mustard in my ear. And everyone was laughing."

"Oh dear me," said Miss Morrow. "How revolting." Distaste was on her face; was it the image Cassie conjured of herself, dressed like a hot dog, or the spectacle of the girl herself before the Headmistress, telling her tale.

"I ran at him and gave him an uppercut. While he was reeling I picked up the garbage can lid and then someone gave me a tree branch. I tried to fight him like you do in kobudo and I got him once across the temple before he broke my stick," she finished. Her humming had turned into gulps and sniffles.

Miss Morrow produced a box of tissues but Cassie didn't see it; she wiped her nose on the sleeve of her blue blazer. "Here," said the Headmistress shoving the box forward and rattling it. Cassie snatched a tissue and began dabbing at her nose distractedly.

"Do you recall," said Miss Morrow slowly, "Sensei's words in the beginning of our *Journal of Japanese Sword Arts*? Which I pointed out to you at the beginning of the year?"

"No," said Cassie miserably. She had expected a more visceral response.

"He says, 'When your anger goes out, your fist stays in. When your fist goes out, your anger stays in.'"

Cassie sniffed. "I know, but it's stupid."

For the first time Miss Morrow showed her own anger. "It is not stupid, Cassandra. It is great wisdom. Do you understand? When you are angry, and you are out of control, it is the worst time to use your physical strength. Think! You are so powerful in your thoughts. Yes, the training that we give can turn your body into a lethal weapon. Although in your case, certainly not any time soon."

"The boy won, and he didn't even take martial arts."

Miss Morrow waved her long pale hand to dispel this irrelevant fact. Always destined to go overboard, Cassie could not contain herself. "How would you like it if someone put you in a garbage can?" she cried.

The image was so incongruous that Miss Morrow smiled. "Let them dare!" she said. "You see? You must become the kind of person no one would dare touch!"

"Yes," said Cassie. "But how?"

"Dignity! Posture! Pride! Courage! Never show that you are afraid, dear girl. And you never will be."

They sat for a moment in silence. Slow tears ran down Cassie's face. Miss Morrow stared straight at her. Her raven hair, her white skin, her perfect makeup before eight o'clock in the morning, her black-belt focus, all of it bore down on Cassie. And there was something else, the glimmer of a smile, a knowing. Miss Morrow saw inside her, Cassie was certain. The tears continued in their slow tracks down Cassie's cheeks. She began to wilt. Still they sat in silence for long moments. Cassie's whole face was wet. Her nose was running. Miss Morrow passed the tissues, then she spoke.

"Well, Cassandra, that was an interesting story. And you are the worst liar I have ever encountered in all my years of teaching."

Cassie burst out in sobs.

"It is totally out of character for you to lie. You are a truth teller. Think of your namesake."

Fuck my namesake, thought Cassie. What about me? She peered up at Miss Morrow from under her swollen eyelids. There was a glow of affection on the Headmistress' face.

"You are odd, Cassandra, but you are authentic. I have never met a girl like you and I have met many a girl. Obviously you are lying for a reason. But I shall sit here no longer listening to you do this shameful thing. Nothing that happened yesterday can be as bad as this lie. Shall we start over?"

Cassie nodded wordlessly.

"Would you like to tell me what happened at the Future coffee shop? Would you like to tell me why you and Vida, Ashley, Maureen and Roxanne attacked a group of girls on Yonge Street?"

Cassie drew in her breath. She straightened her spine. Her loveseat was lower, she noticed; she could not come up to the level of Miss Morrow's eyes, but she could try. "No," she said. "I would not like to tell you, and I will not."

Miss Morrow gazed at her fixedly. Seconds passed; they stretched to a minute, a minute and a half. Neither the woman nor the girl flinched. In the end it was the Headmistress who looked down. A ghost of a smile moved her lips momentarily.

"All right," she said. "Do not tell me. You are assigned to copy out the first three books of the *Odyssey* by Monday. You may go now."

Cassie stood. She felt so much better that she could have told Miss Morrow what it was she was hiding: there was no reason they had attacked the girls. There was no why. But Cassie had won the fight. She had used the twirling because it was what happened in her brain. That now Vida believed in her, instead of just feeling sorry for her. That now the rat girls thought she was a valiant fighter, although she wasn't. She was full of fear, always. But she could not give up this new admiration that surrounded her; she would not give it up even for her true self, even for this love for Miss Morrow that sprang up so painfully in her chest, as she turned and, staring at her feet, left the office.

Miss Morrow had laryngitis. She gestured dramatically that she could not speak, wheeled in the video cart and slotted in a cartridge. Then she whispered hoarsely to Darrin, who repeated her words to the class.

"I have no voice at all due to the flu. It happens, every few years. We are in an enclosed space, you see. And there is damp. Sometimes I think the viruses come from the old Taddle under the basement. You will watch the movie and take notes on it."

Miss Morrow pressed the start button on the video and waved goodbye. As soon as she was gone, most of the students put their heads down on their desks to sleep.

Roxanne did not. The movie was *The Red Shoes*. A bit high from the dope she and Ashley had smoked before school started, she settled in to watch. She could hear Chino's soft snores behind her. But it didn't matter. She was there on stage with Moira Shearer. She could feel the dancer's feet in the red shoes, and the pain in her heart. When it was over she ran out of the class in tears. No one else seemed to care, but Cassie got up and followed her. At first Roxanne hid around the side of the lockers, but then she took the paper towels Cassie found in the washroom and tried to stop crying. Cassie wet a towel to rub off the mascara that had run down Roxanne's cheeks.

"I used to be a dancer," Roxanne said, "before I, like, got old."

"I don't think you're old," said Cassie.

"Well when I was, like, twelve. I used to love that movie. It's you know, like, you can't have both your love and your art: and since you can't, you just, like die. It's so fuckin' sad."

"You think?" Cassie had thought the movie was dumb. She thought if she could be a dancer she wouldn't bother with a man.

"It makes me wish I could go back. Get into my tunic and tights, just dance and get all sweaty and exhausted and think of nothing."

Everyone knew Roxanne had done ballet. Her feet turned out so far she could plant them heel to heel along the red line that was painted on the studio floor for karate class. Her footprints looked as if she were about to split herself down the inseam and walk off in two directions at once. When adults asked why she gave up dancing, she would toss her head and say she wasn't very good. Teenagers would never ask such a stupid question: the answer was obvious. Girls gave up stuff like that because it wasn't cool.

Roxanne was fifteen. It had been two and a half years since she quit ballet, two years since she came to the Manor. When she came, Miss Morrow had said to her: "Don't you think I can see what you can be?" But Roxanne had not become anything much. Not yet. She was a bad student and she had attitude.

She had been so dutiful, once, in her opaque black tights, with hair scraped back so tightly that her eyebrows stretched and her shell-shaped ears were exposed. But one day she came home, threw her dance bag across the room and announced that she was quitting. Her father concurred. How far could she take this thing, anyway? She was no Karen Kain. Her mother fought back: threats, promises, entreaties, tears. But it was already too late. She would use her ballet body for other things. Roxanne was hanging with the neighbourhood girls whose jeans rode up between their legs and down beneath their navels.

"I don't see how you can think nothing," said Cassie enviously.

"You can if you're dancing. It's so cool."

The two girls slipped away down the hallway and into the empty lounge. Roxanne kept saying Cassie didn't know. "Seriously, Cassie, I have been so out there." She told Cassie how her curfew had always been eight o'clock. When her parents refused to extend it, she just stayed out. Once she didn't go home for a week. She slept over at a friend's. She crashed in a guy's van. Her parents never would have found her. Her new friends were from crazy families. One girl's dad was drunk all the time and lived on the main floor while her mother lived on the second floor. One night the father kissed Roxanne, slobbering into her neck. His daughter picked up a butcher knife and threatened to kill him. Another girl Roxanne met had been raped with a fork while buying drugs. They used to meet boys and have sex in an empty garage down the lane from her house.

"I thought if I found a boy to love me I'd be safe. But they only wanted to fuck me. They didn't ask me on dates. It was so gross. What I found out. I just kept getting drunk because it was too weird when I was sober."

Cassie was impressed.

Roxanne finally was kicked out of school. There was a big family conference and her parents decided to send her to the Manor. The first thing Roxanne thought was, "Maybe here I'll get a boyfriend." But the boys at the Manor were geeks, and the only girl they wanted was the beautiful Maureen. After that, Ashley. Roxanne was pretty far down the list.

Cassie was flattered that Roxanne was confiding in her. She watched Roxanne all that week. The girl did a lot of crying, so much that she had to stop wearing makeup because her skin was getting red under her eyes where she tried to rub off the smudges. Without the makeup she was very pale. That was one of the changes. There were more. Cassie thought it was one of those metamorphosis things Dr. Laird talked about.

By Friday, Roxanne was listening through an entire lecture on the Labours of Heracles. Then they did "The Lady of Shalott" in class. "'I am half sick of shadows,' said the Lady of Shalott." Roxanne burst out with enthusiasm: she *loved* the poem. Vida protested that it was old-fashioned. But Miss Morrow said, like she always did, "This is above fashion and beyond fashion. These are the great works! I want them to enter your hearts and minds!" Roxanne nodded her head and stared. When she moved along to "A loaf of bread, a jug of wine beneath the bough and thou beside me in the wilderness," Roxanne started to recite along with her. At break she repeated the phrase over and over under her breath.

"It makes the ugly pictures go out of my mind," she told Cassie: the raw bleeding scalp of the girl they'd beat up on College Street, the insane shrieking laughter coming from the dark corner of a garage where someone surely was being raped, perhaps even herself.

The next week in art history Roxanne was still paying attention.

Miss Morrow stood on her podium. "The End of the World is the myth of the twentieth century. It is present in every piece of art created. Take a note!" she commanded. "Black pens." She waited until the shuffle subsided.

"We have no optimism." In fact, Miss Morrow did not really like much of her century's art, or its thinking. Still, they had to study it. "Even the Eastern religions with their ideas of reincarnation provide only fatalism. We in Western society fear that we are facing an explosive, utter annihilation of the world, brought about by nuclear war perhaps, or the destruction of the environment." She paused for the students to catch up to her. "Or the destruction of the environment.

Because we in the West do not believe in rebirth, this end of the world we anticipate will be final."

The pens scratched over paper.

"Indent," said Miss Morrow. "Underline. Cassie, you need a ruler, you can't underline with the edge of a file folder!"

Cassie scrabbled through her pencil case.

Miss Morrow went on. "Since the beginning of the century the visual arts, literature and even music have altered so totally that we can call this change a destruction of the language of art. It appears at times that painters want to erase the entire history of their art. In fact they wish to revert to chaos."

Miss Morrow looked down at the students in the front rows. "You remember Chaos? It's what Milton wrote about. Chaos. Give me a definition."

"I can't find my ruler," said Cassie.

"Then you are excused to go and get one."

Cassie stood up. She knocked her binder off the desktop. The rings sprang open and pages broke out onto the floor. Some groaned. Others laughed. Cassie stood looking down in dismay.

"Well, go!" snapped Miss Morrow. Her eyes widened. She might have rolled them had her ethics not strictly curtailed her from mocking her students. "Cassie, you would try the patience of Job!"

Cassie went, hanging her head. Half-giggling from nerves.

"Give me a definition of Chaos," Miss Morrow said again, in her wake.

"The inside of Cassie's locker?" piped Maureen.

Miss Morrow looked horrified. "I do believe that is the pot calling the kettle!" It was one thing for her to comment, another for the students to comment on each other. Vida raised her hand. "What is it now?"

"I don't have my book."

Miss Morrow heaved a sigh. "Go then," she said. And gave up getting a serious answer to her question.

She resumed her lecture, looking straight toward the back wall of the studio. "Yet is it truly all darkness where we are going? Is this wiping out not *in itself* a new idea, a creative act? And that in itself is hopeful. It shows that our artists can be roused to answer back, to fight back, to rebuild a coherent world."

There were days when Francesca believed this. Days when the certain existence of the darkness ahead seemed to demand a response. But she saw that she would lose what audience she had left if she continued in this vein. She made the graceful segue, as if premeditated, the favourite tool of the trade of teaching. "The beloved Master understood this." She bid the class turn to their loose-leaf binders full of colour Xeroxes of art book reproductions of famous paintings, faithfully copied by Amelia and distributed to the students early in the year. Many a class was spent simply gazing at pictures while Miss Morrow lectured. Here was comfort. Here was—

"—G. F. Watts. Perhaps the greatest painter of his time! Imagine how lucky I have been to have been drawn into his aura by my mother! Although I never met the man, I have learned everything I know from him. Consider his portraits of William Morris, of Dante Gabriel Rossetti, of Tennyson, copies of which you should have in your binders. These are my links, direct links to the past, to that coherent world of which I spoke.

"Turn to the pages of Watts paintings, please. His audacious canvases of allegorical subjects captivated the people of his time. He bridged the nineteenth and twentieth centuries, moving forward but at the same time bringing us back once again as the artists of the Renaissance brought the public back, to the earliest classical forms. His *Orpheus and Eurydice.* His *Echo.* His *Aristides and the Shepherd.*

"Often have I thought of Aristides over the years. A great citizen of Athens who was ostracized by his fellow citizens. And why? Because of jealousy. 'I am tired of always hearing him called the Just,' they said, and cast the fatal disc to have him thrown outside the walls."

Somehow, today, Watts was not so comforting.

"Oh, and *Psyche*. Turn your pages. You have it there. So beautiful. So sad. You know the story, girls and boys, of Psyche? How Cupid falls in love with her and visits her at night? She knows she must not look at him, but she is overcome with curiosity, and she can't resist. Holding the lamp over his face, she lets fall a drop of oil. He wakes. Psyche is caught in the act. Therefore, Cupid is lost to her. Do you understand? To see all is to lose all. So teaches the myth. And I believe it.

"Turn the page again. His *Minotaur*. Oh, especially his *Minotaur*. This is a painting! It prefigures all the disintegration and chaos that is to come. Watch how the monster is portrayed, wistfully leaning on the wall, watching for the ships to come bearing the Athenian youths and maidens given in tribute for him to consume in his maze. You see the art of reduction, or symbolic representation, how less is more: why would we want to see the carnage itself, why would we need to see the blood of sacrifice? Better to dread its coming, and to gaze upon the half-human visage of the monster."

Roxanne understood. Artists were fed up with everything being pretty. It wasn't fun to paint that way any more and also they'd noticed that real stuff didn't look like that. Roxanne sat with one skinny leg poking out diagonally from her hip, so that she could, although she didn't really mean to, trip anyone passing. It was a ballet stance, coming back through her body's memory despite her attempts to curb it, unlearn it.

She declaimed to Cassie on the way to coffee. "I just totally *get* those guys. How they figured that life was a mess and there was no god and no order to the universe and everything was chaos? And then when Miss Morrow says once you get to chaos and you actually paint a picture of it, you're on the way back up? So even if your picture looks like hell it's an expression of hope?"

"That's so cool," Cassie said.

Ashley kicked Roxanne's ankle and slung her knapsack onto her back so that it hit Roxanne in the gut. Roxanne looked as if she could easily scratch her eyes out but at that moment it didn't seem worth it. She just muttered "bitch" under her breath and walked faster.

The next day in class Miss Morrow climbed to her podium and recited, with her eyes closed, François Villon's "Ballad of the Dead Ladies."

Tell me where, in what country,
Is Flora the beautiful Roman,
Archipiada or Thais
Who was first cousin to her once,
Echo who speaks when there's a sound
On a pond or a river
Whose beauty was more than human?
But where are the snows of yesteryear?

The queen white as a lily
Who sang with a virgin's voice,
Big-footed Bertha, Beatrice, Alice,
Haremburgis who held Mainne
And Jeanne the good maid of Lorraine
Whom the English burnt at Rouen, where,
Where are they, sovereign Virgin?
But where are the snows of yesteryear?

When she finished she opened her blue eyes; they were rimmed with water. She explained how Joan of Arc dressed as a man and led the French into battle; how she was burned at the stake for heresy.

Tied up above a pile of faggots (suppressed giggles from the boys) and simply set fire to, with a torch of burning pitch. She told them about the poet, François Villon, how he had been a scholar, as she would have them become scholars. How after leaving university he became a low-life and a scoundrel, frequenting brothels and mugging law-abiding citizens in the narrow, wet-stoned alleys of Paris. But he was an artist and he spoke for his time; he sensed that the glorious days of courtly love were dying. "Metaphor," exhorted Miss Morrow. "What did he mean, 'where are the snows of yesteryear?' What is the answer to that question?"

No one showed a hand.

"Well, where are they? Quite literally. If you wanted to find last year's snow, where would you go?"

Cassie never minded making a fool of herself. Half the time she didn't notice when she was making a fool of herself. So she put up her hand.

"The Leslie Street Spit," she said.

And the whole class broke out laughing.

She protested, "Well, that's where they take it when the snow trucks go out and they load it up and drive it down there. I've seen it all piled up in huge mountains." Then she made it worse. "When I go birdwatching with my mum."

Miss Morrow had to pound the desk to stop the laughter. She bowed her forehead into her upturned palm.

"Cassandra, dear Cassandra," she said. "You will be the death of me."

But when she lifted her head she was smiling. "Anyone?"

"It's true. The snow might last there even when it's gone everywhere else," said Vida. "They shovel the De La Salle rink for the hockey games and pile the snow outside; it lasts practically 'til April.

Thus Vida rescued Cassie and then the debaters got into it.

"He says yesteryear, not yesterday," said Darrin.

"If it fell before Christmas it's last year's snow."

"Normally it's gone, that's the point! Snow melts. What is more evanescent than snow?"

"Some snow lasts for years, like for all time. In the mountains."

"In the glaciers."

"Maybe in the Antarctic."

"Here, too, in the Arctic.

"Villon didn't know about Canada."

"They didn't even have Canada then."

"But in, like, the *Ancient Mariner*?" said Cassie slowly. "Remember when he goes into the land where there's always snow and ice and it's death? If the snow lasts all year it's a land where there is no life."

"Villon didn't read the *Ancient Mariner*. It's written in English and besides it was a couple of centuries later."

Miss Morrow stepped off the podium, her work done. She assigned the poem for memory work for the next day.

––––––––––

At break they sat on the stone wall in front of the Manor sipping Cokes from the truck. Cassie sucked mustard off her fingers. Then a long drip of ketchup on the front of her blazer caught her attention. She licked a finger and tried to rub it off. She was the only one who ever ate. She had a hot dog at every break, which meant twice a day. Vida always gave her grief and told her she should eat dried fruit because it wasn't fattening. Her mum didn't like the eating either, which she didn't witness but which she could only assume by the growth of Cassie's waistline. Ferdinand let Cassie run a tab and today he'd told her it was up to seventy dollars. She was going to have to pay it off. Then he gave her a hot dog, on the house.

Ashley examined a mole on her upper thigh through a hole in her navy tights. Spit leaned his head on her knee.

"I'm thinking of carving another message, in my leg this time," she said. "Don't know what to say, though."

Maureen stood moodily a little way off.

Roxanne chanted from the English handout, trying to get the others to chime in. "Tell me where, in what country, Is Flora the beautiful Roman—" Cassie joined in and then Ashley, mockingly, accenting the wrong syllables.

"The queen WHITE as a LIly who sang WITH a *vir*GIN'S voice BIG-footed Bertha—"

Roxanne said, "You could carve 'Ballad of the Dead Ladies.' It's such a cool title."

"The whole thing? Like my leg's only so wide, eh?"

"You could pick one name from it. Like—" she ran her eyes over the handout. "Big-footed Bertha." She giggled.

Ashley jerked her head in warning; watch what you say or I'll drill you.

Then Roxanne said, "Maybe we should all take our names from this poem." She jumped to her feet, excited.

Vida went, "Yeah!" and Cassie said, because she knew she was included, "What an excellent idea!"

Jeanne the maid of Lorraine had to be Vida, because they were both fighters and they were both like boys. Echo was Cassie, naturally, since she was kind of a fractured echo. Roxanne was Snow because she was so white. Maureen had to be the Virgin Queen, which left Ashley as Big-footed Bertha. No matter that Ashley scowled; the deed was done and Dead Ladies they were. And when they chanted the poem each one had to answer to her name.

Cassie fell in love with poetry then too. It was a visceral love, a passion felt low in the belly for an unattainable beauty. She would slump down in her chair (until Miss Morrow caught sight of her and chimed "Posture!"), listen to every word and feel it pound through her veins to her heart's core where something seemed to be happening.

Cassie was developing shoulders and hips and a rib cage, their adult shapes emerging from her formless tadpole self. She could see that baggy girl behind her; she regretted the time she had been such a loser. Where had it gone, grade seven and grade eight, she chimed to herself? Where are the snows of yesteryear?

All of Miss Morrow's poems seemed to speak directly to Cassie. Some days it was Yeats—

"The wrong of unshapely things is a wrong too great to be told;

I hunger to build them anew and sit on a green knoll apart—"
and some days it was Keats. That morning Miss Morrow entered the classroom clad in a black dress with a low scooped neck and tight bodice and a skirt that descended in points to her ankles like the down-tipped petals of a black flower.

"My heart aches, and a drowsy numbness pains

My sense, as though of hemlock I had drunk,"

Half the girls in class were chanting along.

"Darkling I listen; and, for many a time

I have been half in love with easeful Death,"

In Cassie's veins she felt the surging of the rhythm but something more, a seductive grieving.

"Now more than ever seems it rich to die,

To cease upon the midnight with no pain..."

It seemed so adult. Death was there, always there, in the background of poetry and art. Roxanne and Cassie talked about this. They approved of it greatly. Death became so real they could see him, grinning down the back reaches of the pool hall or even in the kindly face of the streetcar driver on St. Clair Avenue. Roxanne and Cassie always pointed him out to the other Dead Ladies. It's him, they'd say, and it became a joke: Miss Morrow's friend Death.

Objects of great loveliness they saw every day; beautiful music poured into their ears and marvellous tales from the classical past were spun out for them. So it was not with despair but with a kind of inspired sense of the grandeur, the squalor and the shortness of life, that the Dead Ladies set out like François Villon to be scholars, poets and artists by day and to live a life of crime by night. Cassie believed, she said she believed, that somehow this was expressing Miss Morrow's dream for them. They began by putting their tags up on the walls of the buildings behind the Beckers store, putting their tags over top of someone else's tag, asking for a fight.

But asking for a fight didn't give them a plan of action, as Vida was fond of observing.

It was afternoon break. Cassie was eating her second hot dog of the day. She hadn't been going to have one, just a Coke, but then Ferdinand had reminded her, nicely, that her tab was up to eighty dollars. Somehow that made her hungrier.

The Dead Ladies sat on the edge of the retaining wall, their knapsacks scattered at their feet. They had only been a gang officially for a few weeks but a paramilitary discipline had been imposed on the group. Vida was talking.

"We need to let people know who we are."

"The tags are up."

Big-footed Bertha, Echo, Snow and the Virgin Queen, and on top of them Jeanne the Maid of Lorraine. Every day they examined these tags on the walls of the sheds, hoping that some rival had come along to paint over them but it had not happened. Yet. So. There was trouble out there, trouble to be found, and Vida, the Maid of Lorraine, would find it.

"We need money."

"We need money?" said Cassie as Echo. "What do we need money for?"

"To pay your debt, stupid," said Ashley.

"What debt?"

"Don't call your sister stupid!"

"Eighty bucks, wasn't it?"

"He shouldn't let me keep buying hot dogs every break," Cassie said in her most practical voice. "But I can ask my mum. I don't see why we need to steal it." Although in truth, Cassie didn't know what she was more scared of, the criminal activities or her mum.

"It's what we do. Right?"

Nobody said anything.

"We could each steal some of it from home," suggested Maureen, though she found this idea boring. "I could probably get ten."

"Family doesn't count! We have to rob someone real!" said Roxanne.

"It's not even a good reason, paying Cassie's tab."

Vida fidgeted through her brown-belt kata in an understated way, fists going up and down, knees popping out below her kilt as she bent them.

"I think Ferdinand should just drop it," said Roxanne.

"We could kidnap him and torture him to make him drop it."

"He can't," Cassie protested. "It's his job. It's how he earns his money."

Roxanne got up and went scuffing through the piles of dry, dusty leaves. The piles were huge here, at the foot of the old maple trees that lined these side streets. People raked the leaves into heaps at the curb for the city truck to come and suck them up. It was an amazing sight, that city truck that hoovered the leaves away. Until they did it was fun to play. She took a few steps and threw herself down into a metre-high pile. Bits of crumbling leaf flew up into the air all around her and she sank down a foot or more, bouncing. In a minute all the other Dead Ladies were walking around, kicking the leaves into piles and then jumping in. Except for Cassie.

"I wouldn't," Cassie mumbled. "There might be dog shit in there...or broken bottles." She stood on the side, dubious, while Vida, lieutenant or corporal, paced around her soldiers, reluctantly allowing them a small break from duty.

"What can we shake down?"

"Maybe the Beckers?" said Maureen, brushing leaf dust off her legs. "There's always a lot of people around there. Like, tons."

"So?"

"We'd need a gun."

"You're psycho. What about the jerk-beef place across the street? It's really small and the guy's alone most of the time."

"Yeah, but his friends are scary. They're all huge. Like, *huge*. They work out at that weightlifting gym."

"We do karate."

"But we don't know how to fight. Remember last time? It was Cassie who got us out of there. Just by being so weird she took them totally by surprise."

They all laughed, remembering.

"We could try to get weapons."

"We could. That would be cool."

Roxanne stepped back a few metres, ran and threw herself on her side into the leaves. Then she rolled over onto her back and stared at the sky. "I don't know, guys," she said. "I don't know if it's worth it just to pay Cassie's tab. I mean, wouldn't Ferdy just like forget it if we kinda asked him?"

"Get Miss Holt to ask him."

"Amelia, oh yeah."

Everyone started to laugh. Maureen minced in the middle of the leaf pile. "'Ferdy, darling, you're so hot, I just can't wait to get my hands in your pants, how much did you say my tab was?' Can you do that, Cassie?"

Cassie turned bright red and began a very small hum.

"Don't," said Vida.

"I think we could solve Cassie's problem just by sending Miss Holt to, like, take him down. You can tell he's drooling to get up somebody's kilt."

"That's not the point!"

"Amelia doesn't wear a kilt."

"Whatever she wears, he's been up it already!"

Cassie hummed more loudly to drown this out.

"He's like so old. And he's, oh, hairy, and short, my god it would be so creepy, can you imagine?"

"Do you think he'd fall for it?"

"He'd fall for it," said Maureen, the Virgin Queen. "Oh you bet he'd fall for it. They all fall for it." Bitterly, so bitterly that the others stopped to stare.

"Anyway," said Vida, trying to regain control. "Anyway, that's not the point."

"What is the point?"

Vida sighed, exasperated. "How many times do I have to repeat it? Because we're the Dead Ladies and that's what we do. A life of poetry during the day and a life of crime at night."

"So we have to do this at night?"

"I'm scared to go to the 7-Eleven at night."

"No, Roxanne, you've got it wrong. They're supposed to be scared of you."

Maureen started to laugh, high and long, like a hyena.

"I don't think so."

"Like I said, why don't we just get Ferdy and torture him or something until he promises not to charge Cassie?" That was Ashley.

"Hey, yeah, and we could all get free stuff from now on," said Maureen.

"We could put a tax on him."

"That is like such an amazing idea," said Ashley. She stopped kicking leaves and stared at Maureen in admiration.

"But if we did he could just go away and not come back," said Cassie.

They ignored her.

"Cool," said Vida. "I like it."

"Yeah, but we like Ferdy," said Cassie.

"You do."

"I do," said Roxanne.

The others stared at them.

"And your point is?" said Maureen.

"Why would we do this to someone we like? I don't get it."

"You don't get anything," said Vida in disgust.

"I get it," said Cassie in a small voice. Because she did get it, in a sick way. "It makes it sort of worse, you know, like we're really immoral people if we even practise our crimes on people who are kind to us."

There was a short silence.

"Cool," said Vida. "She gets it."

"I'm not saying I want to do it, just that I see how it fits in a twisted way. If you wanted to do something ugly, I mean."

The Dead Ladies began to laugh and throw the yellow and brown and red leaves, fragmented by now to small, dusty bits. They pitched their armsful at each other and dodged and bent again and tossed the leaves back and forth until the air was afog with floating bits of leaf, until the air was littered and whirling and their hair and sweaters were coated. Maureen was sneezing, and Ashley was wheezing—leaf-mould allergy said Vida like a daycare supervisor. That was how she acted now that she was gang leader. Spit barked insanely.

Cassie stood in the leaf shower hunched over, not moving her feet. She waved her arms half-heartedly upward, throwing the leaves that came down on her up again and back into the whirl. Roxanne and Maureen and Ashley were killing themselves laughing, bashing into each other, pretending to be quarterbacks or front ends or some football thing. Cassie didn't want to move; she was enjoying the way the leaves took the light down, the way you could stand with your head in the cloud of them and the world seemed brown as humus, and smelled of earth, but how, when you let them drop past your ears, the leaves simply vanished and the sun came out again. Each time she lifted her hands she got her head back into the mould-smelling fog, a darker place, a place of whirling forces where she felt at home.

Some days Amelia climbed the Bathurst Street hill to school, wanting the exercise. She brought her newspaper from where it had been tossed, in a transparent orange plastic bag if the day was wet, on the front porch of her apartment house. Halfway up the hill, at Davenport, there was a little basement diner with cosy fifties-style booths with turquoise Formica tables. Today she steered eagerly into its warmth, her cheeks stinging from the slushy rain.

"Just coffee, please."

The man behind the counter, a compatriot of Ferdinand's clearly, with the same thick chest on a short body, ducked his large head in acknowledgment. She had an instant's affection for the old city cafés with their cast of thousands dishing out comfort without haste or foamed milk. She loosened her coat and removed her scarf. She pulled *The Globe and Mail* from her briefcase, and settled in for the fifteen minutes of withdrawal that preceded the normal eight hours of compulsory engagement. The owner shuffled over and placed the thick white mug of coffee before her.

She breezed through the first section, stopping briefly at the grainy photographs of refugees in Grozny. She made a mental note: there was enough tragedy in those women's faces to animate the drama classes today. She skimmed the column of an arts writer hoping for a laugh, but he was in high dudgeon, bitterly complaining about lack of government support. There was a column called "Lives Lived," about people who had died. In fact, two whole pages were obituaries; the lugubrious baby boomers who ran newspapers were obsessed with what was passing out of this world. She glanced at the column: which Holocaust survivor who taught opera in her basement and made kasha for her grandchildren would grace it today? There was a picture. It was the old woman, the once-beautiful and mysterious old woman.

Meryl Desmond Laird.

The mug slipped in her fingers, tipped, and a big splash of coffee hit her shirt front.

"Shit!"

The café owner looked up and smiled.

"Pardon me?"

Amelia shook her wet hand. Drops of coffee sprayed over the table. She put down the mug and picked up her napkin.

"No, not. I will fix it." The owner approached with a damp cloth. Amelia dabbed away at the top of her blouse as she read.

Beloved mother…ceramic artist…wisdom and wit to her grandchildren…single mother before it was common…walks in the country, knew the names of all the wildflowers…When did she die? When did she die? Amelia squinted at the italics at the top of the column. November 22. Only six weeks after Commencement.

She didn't finish the coffee, and hurried out of the café. I knew it, she thought to herself. I knew it at the time, my instincts told me she was someone key, I wonder if Francesca saw the column. But Francesca did not read the daily press. Halfway up the block Amelia realized she'd left her rather soggy newspaper in the booth, and she had to hurry back to get it, just as the owner had moved it to behind the cash register in a pile with *The Toronto Sun*.

"My paper?"

"Of course." He smiled.

The rain had stopped and the sky was beginning to clear. She was sprightly, walking toward the Manor. She would set the paper out in her office to dry.

The term wore on: now it was December. Never mind the snows of yesteryear, the snows of this year hadn't come. In history, they were studying the pantheon of the Greeks. They came to the lame one, the troublemaker on Olympus. He was the keeper of the flames, Hephaestus, and he had a smithy. He made Aphrodite's crown, and he was her husband, even though he was ugly and lame, and she was beautiful. He also made Pandora's box and put all the evils inside, but left Hope at the bottom.

Cassie thought of Hephaestus every time she went up to the truck. There was Ferdinand behind his counter with all of that reflecting metal around and above him. He was short and dark and hairy. He had a huge head; he stayed behind his grill and his steamer tray for the dogs so that you couldn't exactly tell how tall or short he was, but his head seemed out of proportion, as if he were a dwarf. Cassie had not seen him walk far but she knew he limped; one shoe was built up. He was ugly but there was something sexy about him. You could feel the vibrations even when he handed you a hot chocolate. He was ugly and Miss Holt was beautiful, and perhaps they were lovers.

The idea of sex made Cassie want to hum very loudly indeed. She found the idea of naked bodies grabbing and thrusting at each other repulsive and frightening. She was certain it was for other people and not for her. Not now or ever.

At last the snow came. It was warm out, with no wind, and the flakes came down slowly, fat and juicy, the kind that stuck together and landed like butterflies on your hat brim, your fingertip. The Dead Ladies met after school and went for a walk in the Park. They scouted the rim of the pond to see if anyone was there. It was quite solitary, and still. The girls approached the edge, picking their way over rocks.

"Okay, stop now," commanded Vida. They all stopped. "Let's sit down," she said. They were standing in front of a large fir tree. Its branches made an umbrella; the snow caught on it. The ground underneath was cold, but dry. The girls scrambled under and sat in a circle, their legs sticking into the centre.

"We should plan our project." *Project* was what they had taken to calling it, in case someone overheard. "How are we gonna do this? And when?"

Cassie sat slowly after the others had found a place. She never put herself completely inside any circle, and she never stood in any line at the appropriate distance from the others, but left twice the expected space. This had driven teachers mad throughout her school career—the phys. ed. teachers, the music teachers who had to teach square dancing, the recess supervisors who made the kids queue up to go back into the school. But Cassie had never been dissuaded from this habit; she didn't trust the other kids and wanted to be out of range if they started to push. Also, she didn't feel she *belonged* that close to her peers.

So this time she sat down a little outside the circle and apart from the other gang members who now were leaning forward over their jutting knees and passing around cigarettes. Of course the branches hung down and scratched Cassie, and the snow came down on her legs. Vida took a look at her and gestured with her hand, come under, come under. "Join," she ordered.

Cassie put her fists down into the frozen ground and shifted her buttocks a few feet closer to the tree trunk. Vida was not satisfied. "In!" she said watching until Cassie had wormed herself in so her back was against the bark.

"Okay, all present and accounted for," said Vida.

"Present?"

"This is as bad as school," complained Ashley.

"I propose that we make an example of Ferdy," said Vida, paying no attention to her critics.

"He's my friend," protested Cassie.

"Nobody's our friend who's not in the gang," said Roxanne. "Anyway, he's threatening you. He's like gonna squeal on Cassie to her mum and she's gonna be, like, dead meat."

"Oh, I doubt my mum would mind—" Cassie started. But then she thought about it. She was really not supposed to be buying those hot dogs. If she'd known the gang would go to war about it she'd never have eaten them for sure.

"Tell us what he did to you," said Vida.

Cassie said nothing. She looked into Vida's eyes. Then slowly she opened her lips. "I don't know what you mean." She looked to one side and to the other and saw the expectant faces. Vida was on the other edge of the group; she felt far from her. "He didn't do anything. Really."

"Tell them what you said to me."

Vida was getting very bossy with all this gang stuff. Cassie didn't like it. "It's just like—that when I go there to the truck I get sort of mesmerized."

"What's that?" said Maureen.

"Like hypnotized," said Cassie. "I get sort of staring at him and he's got this huge head and he's sweating half the time—"

"Yeah, and he's like, what are you having today, girls?—"

"Yeah, and his eyes are swimming, and really black underneath—"

"With huge circles under them like he's never slept for ten years—"

"He's got allergies probably," said Roxanne. No one listened.

"Go on," said Vida.

"I don't know, I just feel so nervous and then I get hungry and I can't think of anything but I need a hot dog."

"Really, he's forcing her to buy them and she shouldn't have to pay—"

"He's kind of evil, don't you think?"

"He's fucking Amelia," said Ashley flatly.

The snow continued to fall thickly against the late afternoon sky. It was dark out, and light out at the same time.

"Are you sure?" Cassie cried.

Ashley just cast her a scornful look from her side of the tree trunk. "I saw them."

"Like where?"

"In the truck, where else?"

The girls looked satisfied with this revelation. Of course Ashley had seen them. Whether or not it was true, the idea that Amelia and Ferdinand were fucking fit their notion that all grown-ups, especially those who had authority over them, were corrupt.

"When?" said Cassie. Challenging. She surprised herself.

"Late, like around five when they think we're all gone. He had his head in her lap and he was going down on her and she was all stretched out over the seat and she had her head thrown back and her mouth way open. Like she wanted him to put something in there."

"That's psycho. In the day?" cried Roxanne.

"It's, like, dark at five."

Cassie's stomach fell with a jolt and she thought she might vomit. She wanted to shout out that it could not be true, but something prevented her. It was the time months ago when she saw Amelia get out of the truck, late. It was the way Ferdinand's eyes went over her shoulder and looked behind her, at the very end of break, when the other girls had started back for the school and Cassie was still eating, or maybe buying a chocolate bar. It was that searching eager look in his eyes. He wanted Amelia; that much was true. And then Amelia always came out to have her private moment with Ferdinand. She would buy a coffee and gulp it down while the kids were just getting back to class.

"He just thinks she's nice," Cassie managed to say.

"The Cheese? She's not nice. She's hot. He wants her, and he's having her."

"No!" Cassie cried.

Vida stepped in. "Okay, so three things against him. He's putting a hex on Cassie and now he wants the $125 dollars she owes him, and he's doing it with Amelia—"

"It's all my fault," said Cassie miserably. She sobbed.

"—so I say we get him. It's only a question of how."

Roxanne stretched out her left leg and bent over it so that her forehead touched her knee. She bounced a little and pointed the toes of her left foot, and then pushed her heel out so that she stretched the bottom of her foot. Everyone watched. She slowly folded the left leg in and put the right one out.

"We can't do it in front of the school or they'll know it's us."

"He has a bunch of other stops—"

"Yes, we can, we can do it here. Look how early it gets dark now. When his truck is parked around the corner," said Ashley. "When they're having sex," she added.

"We can catch him with his pants down."

"Don't you think we might need to practise first?"

"Practise what?"

"We need some acid, that's what we need," said Maureen.

"Let's practise on a bank machine."

The snow was already melted on the streets. They tried to get money from the bank machine at St. Clair and Yonge. They had a plastic card that Vida said would activate the dispenser. Cassie got to stand on the street and watch out, so at least her face didn't show up on the video cameras. But the others' faces did. They all looked stretched out, sketchy in grey and white, huge faces they were, on towering heads and shoulders with little dwindled feet way down below. The card just kept getting spat out and finally a buzzer went and they all ran. Cassie felt the future coming on and knew that this was leading nowhere good; the humming started inside her. Only Vida's calming arm on her shoulder as they walked up to the street-car kept her from gnashing her teeth and yelling out loud.

7

DUGALD'S
DRIVE

DUGALD WAS SUPERVISING the Christmas physics exam. It was one of those days that felt like twilight all day. Amelia came to the open classroom door, wearing a long skirt made of a slippery fabric that clung to her hips, hugged her knees and then feathered out around her calves. Her bosom was tightly bound by a navy satin vest buttoned smartly down the front. She asked to speak to Dugald. He could not hear what she was saying, but he could smell her shampoo, wafting off the spray of long hair down her back, Lily of the valley. He thought his heart would stop. The scent carried him out of the school, away, to a corner of a garden by a kitchen door. In spring the little plants with their sharply pointed leaves crept under the fence and spread amongst Meryl's herbs. They grew to a height of about six inches, and then the tiny white pendulous bells appeared within the leaves' folds, shedding their beautiful, intimate scent. The scent of his young wife, his babies, his youth.

No sooner had the last student left than Dugald pulled a checked cashmere muffler from the dark cupboard in the front hall. He put on his Burberry and turned the doorknob silently. He would not have admitted to anyone that he was sneaking out, so ingrained were his habits of resistance, but he was in fact attempting to slip the coils of his bride's attention for an hour before kobudo.

Within seconds, he was behind the wheel of his hunter green BMW. A delicious sentiment rose within him, which he sought to name. What was this adventure? Escape or escapade, dalliance, deceit, innocent excursion? It hardly mattered. He was free.

He was not supposed to drive the car alone. He was only allowed to drive it with Francesca in the front seat calling his attention to every stoplight and rival automobile on the road. His failing eyesight caused her to twitter nervously when he was behind the wheel, but the fact that she herself had never learned to pilot a motor vehicle (as she liked to put it) meant that he was still their driver. On occasion Francesca suggested they hire someone, Ferdinand, perhaps, but Dugald found the very notion humiliating. He loved to drive.

Down Taddle Creek Drive to Bathurst Street, an easy right turn, and south over the crest of the hill to Davenport. The left turn at Davenport required more concentration, but he knew what he was doing: one had simply to watch for the light to turn orange and then go. If a car coming from the other direction collided with you it was the other guy's fault. From here, Davenport sloped off eastward. It was on one of these little streets running off it, Howland or some other name. There had been a dairy next door, something with Silver in the name. This side of the railroad track and too near it to be pleasant. It had been a poor little house, but they loved it. For a moment he thought he'd missed his turn, the way seemed so long, but no, there was the dip, the turn southward, here the wee triangular park where they'd pushed the perambulator.

Dugald drew in to the little nexus of streets, for three byways came together here, not two. He was jolted by the blast of a horn: surely it was not intended for him? But he did not remove his foot from the gas pedal. Continuing the slow pressure that made his engine throb slightly beneath him, Dugald pressed on into the traffic and managed the left turn. It would have been a shame to damage the car; his view was that most other drivers recognized the superiority of the BMW's frame and would retreat rather than collide. Isn't that why people drove expensive cars?

He drove along to number 183. There was a narrow drive—he didn't remember it being that narrow—banked by low stone walls. He drew in, and stopped the engine. The silence like sleep that accompanied his every waking moment now deepened. This was the house. There was no car, and it appeared there was no one at home.

And why might he imagine she would be here? It had been fifty years. Why would Meryl still live here? Because she was fixed here, in his memory, in the kitchen, the living room, the sloping back garden where the lilies of the valley crept under the fence? He had not even considered that she might have moved.

He used to come here, even after he left them. He was sure he had, that there had been cordiality; it seemed to Dugald that he had sat by the hearth after the fire that burned within it was no longer his, after it had become her fire. That he had not minded. After first imagining and then hoping she would vanish from the earth, he began to view Meryl's continuing existence as a small miracle. He observed her getting along without him with detached good humour: he was glad she was not drowning in sorrow (or did not appear to be, more accurately), glad that she was able to float and to care for the children. He did not have enough feeling for her at the time to wish her dead. That came later.

What he told Meryl, in those first years after he had left her, when he was called in to hear a music recital or discipline a rebellious teen, when they had a late-night brandy by the fire, was that he did not love her any more. He did not love her, and it was obvious that he should move on, to another woman he did love, who, coincidentally, shared his passion for the school. Meryl was not enthusiastic about matters pedagogical. She remained stubbornly fascinated with the infants she'd brought forth from her own womb, as if they represented all infants. While he was dedicating himself to the youth of the city, to Youth with a capital Y, she toiled dully and domestically with her own. Clearly his interest—which he regarded as experimental, intellectual, even philanthropic, as opposed to hers, which was hormonal and egocentric—must predominate.

Now this clarity was fogged. Dugald sat in his cooling car in a driveway he hadn't entered for some thirty-five years that in all likelihood did not lead to his ex–wife's house. He had forgotten about the lily of the valley. In any case it was winter. And yet he continued to sit. He was baffled by the way his past had looped around to be so close to him. He did not understand any more how it was he had left Meryl. She was a good woman. They had much in common. And he had started out with her. It would have been fitting, he now thought, to finish off with her as well. Perhaps with a long rest from each other in the middle. But that would not be possible as she was quite utterly gone from this earth. Or was she? He had seen her face, in a crowd. He had seen her, not so very long ago.

No, he did not recall why he had to break with her so radically. An observer would have said it was Francesca. Francesca and the school. But had Francesca insisted? He didn't think so. Francesca had been too proud to insist. She steadfastly did not mention his wife: mentioning her would have given her an existence where she had none. Dugald had barely mentioned her himself. It was only after a month or two of passion and planning with Francesca that he let her know of his entanglement. He knew he couldn't keep Francesca if he stayed with Meryl. The choice was his. And he had made it in a defiant fury.

"I love Francesca," he raged to the quiet and watchful Meryl. "She supports my work."

"It's one thing to support your work," she replied. "It's another to support an obsession."

He remembered few of Meryl's actual words but these. They had distanced him further when she uttered them: he looked at her as if down the long lens of a telescope, a woman receding to some other place not here, not with him, a woman whose life he imagined would be hugely diminished once he had left her. She was deluded, and selfish, and probably incapable of love. She spoke, from time to time, of her own needs, which had struck him as fantastical, opaque and irrelevant. She was likely a narcissist and certainly not fit to be his partner.

She surprised him, however, in being a very well-behaved ex–wife. She had been a good sport about being left, that was the main thing. They had tried to be friends and if this failed it had not been her fault. He could see this now. After however many years the visits dwindled to nothing. There was no more reason for them. He had no interest in her. The children, also needy, self-centred and insufficiently devoted to Dugald's pursuits, eventually ceased to call. At this point Dugald could not summon up their names, although during certain of his afternoon naps the names pranced on the roof of his mind like so many reindeer. "On Comet on Cupid on Donner and Blitzen." For all practical purposes, Meryl and her brood were gone. And he did not regret it. He was on to his real life, the life of the school, enraptured with his bride, and fulfilled by the important mission of bringing the classics to unshaped Toronto minds.

So the years went by and then it was a decade, two. Once or twice, Dugald was filled with a longing to call Meryl, to hear her astringent tones. Strange as it was, these desires came when his ambitions were excited, or thwarted, one or the other, when the highs of emotion swept him. When he had won, or lost. At moments of reckoning. Then it seemed he needed more than Francesca's warm breath between his shoulder blades at night. More than Francesca's intelligent, passionate partnership. At those times while wanting Meryl he hugged Francesca to himself and thought of his ex-wife with the rage of disappointed desire, and even hatred. She seemed to represent some failure in him, now. And he hoped that Meryl and her memory of another Dugald had been wiped out.

And yet here it was, and here he was, searching for his wife of so long ago. Dugald scolded himself inwardly. How could one require more than the emotional rewards offered by the beautiful, ir-reproachable Francesca? Was there anything Francesca failed to pro-vide? But even as this impossible thought occurred, its answer rang in his temples. Yes, there was. Francesca gave, indeed she could only give, Francesca's love. What he needed now at this long remove in time, in the mad perverse way of humans, was Meryl's love. Meryl's approval. Meryl's forgiveness.

"You know, Meryl, we never went to Greece together," he said, speaking aloud in the closed cabinet of his car. He spoke as if it were then, not now. "You would love it. And the children too. We must get over there before too long. You would be fascinated by it all!" His face became animated as he looked at the wooden door of 183 Alice Street. "I'm sure you would understand my passion to save the temple."

The temple! That too came back to mind from a long long burial. Here was a moment where Francesca had actually let him down. She had never truly supported his plans for preserving the Parthenon. Oh, she had not gone against him, not exactly; she had simply, in her subtle way, steered events or perhaps steered him so that the school, which had been his dream but had somehow turned into her dream, took precedence, and Dugald was unable to follow his own dream.

Which had been?

Even his dreams were now blurred by time. But surely he had had them. They had to do with restoration, preservation. It was so nearly his, once: when they went to Greece, and he had in his hand the means to save the Parthenon from destruction and it seemed, for a few weeks, that he might actually have the opportunity, when the newspapers were calling and heads of state sending emissaries. That was marvellous, the high point of his life. His heyday. Francesca had been with him: he needed her unquestioning adoration. And yet at the same time, was it not then he most longed for Meryl? It seemed to Dugald now that he had only wanted to stand for one moment in the cool splash of Meryl's regard: do you see what I have become? As if she had slighted him. As if she had become the cool disapproving phantom of his youth and childhood, the source of his rage, she whom he could not impress.

But Meryl would understand. Would she not? Understand, but not flatter. Support, but not at the cost of the rest of her life. Or his. The Parthenon project, in moderation.

In Dugald's eagerness to revive Meryl he thought, now, that he might revive that long-forgotten ambition. If he could revive it! Why ever not? The need was even greater than it had been in the fifties. Automobile exhaust and travelling air pollutants were destroying the honeyed stones of the glorious temple overlooking Athens. Left unchecked, this subtle, relentless erosion would whittle the columns, dissolve the friezes and bring the stones tumbling down to the ground. Too late the Greeks, indeed all the citizens of the world, would realize what they had lost: priceless monuments to the classical period of Greece, priceless links to the sacred spring of the Western imagination.

A little-known fact was that this relentless decay could be arrested. The ruins could be protected with a spray coating of silicone. The means were within Dugald's hands. Back in the fifties, a fellow resident of Wychwood Park, a certain Mr. Brentwood, president of Silicone Coatings Canada, had offered to supply the silicone, the truck-mounted spray guns, to mastermind the project. It was only left to Dugald to be intermediary.

And he had served that function well. He had been in touch with the consul general, the ambassador, the newspapers. It had all been underway when, mysteriously, silence had fallen. Someone had grown ill, someone had been replaced, priorities had shifted; disaster. Nothing. Never had Dugald been so disappointed. And that too he wanted to bring to Meryl at this late date. As if she could comfort him. Why had he never imagined when he left her that he might, one day, hunger for her compassion?

The Parthenon, Meryl! He pounded on the steering wheel. Built by Callicrates under the rule of Pericles, with the great sculptor

Phidias, and given to us all. Preserved by Dugald Laird with the help of Budge Brentwood, both of Wychwood Park, Toronto. I could give it to the next millennia of mankind. A structure of such grace anyone with a shred of humanity in his being would be brought to tears at the sight of it.

Love for Greece had been the foundation of his new life with Francesca. For that's what the last fifty years had become in this shifting of mental perspective, this rolling of the cylinders of his memory that had overtaken him—a new life featuring Francesca and Dugald as Principals of the Manor, journeying year after year with bands of young people to the shrines of this ancient culture. But that foundation had not born fruit in this, Dugald's very particular desire. It would have been his own achievement, whereas the school was shared, and if one were perfectly honest, the school was mostly Francesca's. But Meryl! Meryl would somehow have stood beside him (not *in*side him) and he might have preserved the Parthenon.

He found that his forehead was resting on the steering wheel. "Excuse me," he said, lifting it. Was Meryl here? He wanted the chance to present himself, dreams and all, to her. To return the whole life and its passions, its accomplishments, and hold this one, its failure, to Meryl as display: this is what I became, after you. This—in complicated, painful, mazed ways—is what I became because of you. And, even, for you.

But of course it was he who had slighted her. No one doubted it. It was a deep wound he had inflicted, abandoning the mother of his children, the woman who had put her life in his hands. And he had done it lightly, expecting that she would bless his going, sympathize with his need. How ridiculous he had been. How heroic she. He could perceive it now, in a place that had been curtained before. He was not alone. Men frequently left their families, more frequently now; he had done this in 1949, after all. He had done it thinking there was nothing much wrong with it. People were allowed to change their minds. She was an adult. She would manage. And she had managed, he gathered, because she had never, after that first decade of child-related calls, communicated with him.

But how sad. To have lost that part of his life. He looked at the house. No lights were on. Had she moved away? Whoever lived there would laugh at him, would consider him a foolish old geezer, chasing some phantom of memory. That would be intolerable. Perhaps he should retreat. His hand went to the key in the ignition. His intuition told him that Meryl was not there. She might not even be alive, he suddenly thought: but no, not possible. Were she to die the children would have called. Would they not? His children whom he did not even know? If she'd died, he'd have seen the obituary anyway. He read them assiduously. Still, best to withdraw.

Get a grip on yourself, Dugald, he said.

Now it was Francesca's voice that had taken over in his head.

It was downright frightening how, after decades and decades of loving a woman, a man was not himself.

Get a grip on yourself, he repeated in his own voice.

I have a grip on myself, came the reply from within. So tight a grip that I have not been able to speak for all these years.

The thought that he was a foolish old man and must appear so appalled him.

Oh Meryl, he thought. Oh my life. Where have you gone?

He placed his palm on the windshield; the glass was cool. He was no doubt mad. That was fine; he was accustomed to thinking of himself as mad, to being thought of as mad. It was a significant part of his charm. Reassured by the cool glass against his palm that, indeed, he was in his car, that he was awake and seeing, if not hearing, Dugald turned the key and felt the engine leap to life. The car waited only for the pressure of his foot to find its freedom. He backed down the driveway without looking and narrowly escaped hitting a vehicle that had swung at that instant around the curve at the bottom.

On the way home a klatch of girls walking down Bathurst Street caught his eye. Flaxen hair, orange hair, lank brown hair, kilts hiked up, thick-soled boots like blocks of concrete on their feet, the girls from the Manor. Hands deep in pockets, heads jutting forward belligerently, boots scuffing the pavement—they left much to be desired. One hardly recognized them. Fortunately Francesca was not with him. The girls did not look at one another but with heads down and eyes on the pavement seemed to mutter conspiratorially amongst themselves. Looking for all the world like a nasty gang of thieves.

There was much going on here. Much going on that he—and likely the other adults at the school—was too preoccupied to notice. These were trouble girls. Trouble was coming, was perhaps already on them. Really, he must speak to Francesca about it.

Instead he went to Amelia. If only to smell the perfume again. It worked but this time brought only pain.

"Those girls," he said, "are trouble."

"Oh, yes, I know the ones you mean," said Amelia.

She reflected a moment. What to say to Dugald. How far to go?

Amelia, the Cheese, alert to the semaphored meanings of eye-wink and head-jerk, was on to the Dead Ladies. She watched after class to see them stuffing their Manor blazers in their lockers after Miss Morrow had stalked upstairs to her napping husband. She saw their outfits—sometimes the minuscule tight skirts and platform shoes, with blackened eyes and fake hair pinned on under their own, falling in flat sheets down their backs, sometimes the huge jeans and hooded sweatshirts so they looked like boys. Amelia heard them whisper behind locker doors and knew about the shrooming. She had even heard of "the Project" and wondered what it meant. She saw the Dead Ladies skulk off after school and noted that Cassie, shape-changed by a pair of bell-bottomed jeans and a plaid lumberjack shirt with the collar pulled up to half-hide her ears, and a pair of swimming goggles over her eyes, went along with them.

"I know what you do—" she began to Cassie one day, but Cassie only opened her eyes wide and said, "I don't do anything."

"I saw you on Friday night by the bank."

"The bank? It wasn't me." She went white as a sheet.

"The pond, the bank of the pond," said Amelia, looking at her strangely.

"Oh," said Cassie. She leaned on the washroom door with her back and disappeared inside.

Amelia tried another tack.

"Does your mother allow you to wear those ridiculous shoes?" she asked as Ashley strapped on a pair of three-inch platforms that made her mince like a six-and-a-half-foot geisha.

"My *mother*?" Ashley shot back. "Like, Miss *Morrow* wears them."

If Amelia hoped to get into a conversation this way, she was disappointed.

And, truthfully, once they were off school property, she rarely thought of the rat girls. She had other things on her mind, escapades of her own.

"I think you're right, Dugald," she said, shaking her head. "If only I knew what to do."

She moved her hand on the desk, spreading out the pile of photographs that lay there.

Dugald looked down, as he was meant to. There were the glossy eight-by-eleven-inch photographs.

"What are these? Of Commencement Day?"

"Forrest Bard sent them. Have a look."

He picked them up and leafed through.

Meryl.

His knees felt weak. He blanched, and gripped the edge of the table.

"Dugald, can I do something for you?" Amelia took his arm, her eyes round and innocent between the two mahogany curtains of hair. She sat him down in her chair and ran for a glass of water. *Meryl Desmond Laird,* she thought. Who had been written out of the myth. Who now, curiously, and in a way almost Greek, had reappeared.

Satisfied was how Amelia felt, returning with the glass of water. Satisfied with her mischief: it was enough. How cruel. Why did you do that? Miss Morrow might say. And the answer, the true answer, was that there was no reason.

8

LIGHTS
OUT

I T WAS NIGHT. Everyone had gone home. The Principals had gone home, too, to Mount Olympus, overhead on the third floor. Amelia sat in the little second-floor landing office as she often did, surreptitiously tapping the student records into her laptop. She had decided to include the alumni, in a separate file, because it was fun to see names like Connaught Bork and Jim Byrd, and because then she could throw out their old files, or perhaps send them their old files, asking for a contribution in exchange for their destruction. Miss Morrow would never allow it but one day it would be up to Amelia to decide.

At this moment the house gave a small shudder. The golden threads of light that had been spun down the stairs from the third floor were snapped, abruptly. The office where Amelia sat fell into a black well. Instantly, two voices, one male, one female, called out in alarm. Amelia felt under the desk for her purse where she carried a miniature flashlight, in case of power failure. The power failed often at the Manor.

"Oh no!" cried Francesca, from the top of the third-floor staircase. "Dugald, is that you?"

Dugald's response was muffled.

"Did you plug in that electric blanket again? You know you can't—"

The electric blanket was chief among the appliances that, when used in conjunction with anything at all, blew fuses. The Manor had its original wiring. It was strung with extension cords like an old Christmas tree, and when one bulb expired the whole network gave out. Now the house was as dark as the day before creation.

"You know you can't do that, darling, while the light is on in the bathroom," Francesca cried. "I can't see a thing! And now I'll have to go down to the Vaults."

"I'm here," Amelia said. She switched on her flashlight, pointing it at her own face. She looked up the staircase at Francesca in the black hole of the third floor.

And Francesca looked down. There was Amelia, on the second-floor landing, illumined in the gloom, the Mannerist Madonna of Parmigianino—swan-necked, peering out of one of those canvases that has reverted almost entirely to darkness.

"Oh, my dear. How you frightened me."

"Sorry. I was in the office."

"You were! Working on the accounts so late? I thought you'd gone home."

"No. In fact I may have made the fuse go myself! I just turned on the—ah, the, I moved the lamp over the desk. Don't worry, Francesca. I'll go down."

"Thank you, thank you, my dear. You're so kind. No, of course, it was Dugald. You know. Shall we just—wait?"

"Don't go anywhere. I wouldn't want you to fall. Tell Dugald."

"You have the flashlight?"

"I have it."

"You're marvellous. We'll just sit tight, shall we?"

"Tell Dugald to unplug that blanket!"

And down she went to the underworld, her piercing little beam ahead of her. She took the carpeted stairs to the back door, and then descended a flight past the chapel with its curved Gothic ceiling. She went down another half-flight of stairs, ducked her head and directed her steps into the utter black of the sub-basement, the "Vaults" as this level was fondly named. Here was the smell of drains and sump, of sewers that might back up at any moment. The floor was covered with a slick of water that gleamed under her flashlight. The Taddle, rising unbidden after rains. Dugald would be pleased to know.

The flashlight beam caught the dull metal of the fuse box. She opened the door on rows of the stub ends of fuses and peered inside, flashing her sharp white beam into the mysterious glass cells to find which little connecting metal strip had broken. She hated this part. It frightened her. She searched the rows, found the broken one, unscrewed it and pulled it out. There was a little cloth bag on the shelf beside the box. This she picked up and undid the drawstring. She put the flashlight on the shelf and wriggled her hand inside, feeling all the knobs with their ridged edges.

For a moment, she ran her fingers amongst these cool, smooth, round, hard plugs imagining them as—what?—great smoothed gems buried in the Sphinx as some ruler's best possessions. Or petrified testicles perhaps. Yes, here were the balls of all the Manor men, fossilized. She fingered them, naming the ones she knew. Connaught Bork (two), Dugald (two), Jim Byrd (possibly only one, it would suit him), Ferdy. Not Ferdy. He still had his balls.

She couldn't see, in the dark, the power of each. Was it a 30, a 20, or a 10? She needed a 20.

Amusing herself, she rolled them between her fingers in the dark, trying to guess which one would be a 20. Dugald? 10 maximum. He was over eighty after all. Darrin, 30, 50 even, if such a thing existed, big strapping Darrin. Hard to tell about those jocks, though. He could be possessed of a wild sexual energy, he could be a frenzied tiger or he could black out in a few seconds, overwhelmed by the stimulation.

She thought 20 for Chino, possibly one of those defective 20s that blew right away. She needed a good solid 20 that would last. No one wanted too much power; it was as bad as too little and could lead to overloading of the wires, even to a house fire. No, for a good solid 20 she'd choose Ferdy. He had to be in there. For the moment, she put him in there.

"Give me Ferdy's balls," she said aloud, reaching blindly into the bag and pulling out one fuse. Setting down the bag, she shone her flashlight on the little metal strip under the glass. It was a 20. She brought it to her lips and kissed it, then screwed it into the empty socket. There was an immediate hum and the house, somewhere above her, came to life again. Power. Terrifying to think that most of the top two floors were on that one fuse. It couldn't be right. Yet that was how it had been as long as she'd been here.

Amelia headed for the stairs. There were no lights on between the Vaults and the second floor, hadn't been when the power was off and wouldn't be now. She walked up, white flashlight like a probe before her, and when she reached the second-floor landing heard Miss Morrow's dulcet tones.

"Wonderful job, my dear. How marvellous that you chanced to be here at this late hour!"

"No problem," muttered Amelia.

Francesca leaned over the banister, her hair in its plait at the side of her head, black, lustrous, young hair, glimmering like a rope in the light that now shone from behind her. If it were let loose it would cloak her entirely.

"It is indeed marvellous to know we can count on you, Madonna of the Long Neck!" she said. No matter what tensions the day brought, by evening it was back to the pet name. To Francesca all was forgiven, all would go on as usual; Amelia would be there to serve and protect, like the Toronto constabulary. "But you mustn't work *all* night. Isn't it time you went off to find some friends and have some fun?"

"I was just leaving," smiled Amelia, feeling more Cheese than Madonna, very cheesy indeed as a matter of fact, put out and sharp and not to be trusted. "I'll put away what I was doing, is all. As long as you and Dugald are all right up there?"

"Of course we are, my dear." The silken tones and tresses withdrew simultaneously.

All was silent. Amelia stood a few more minutes in the dark, in the tiny office, looking down on the courtyard. She saw the past of the school, the snippets of medieval passion plays, the recitations of the Prologue to *The Canterbury Tales*, the singing of madrigals and the acting of scenes from *Henry IV, Part One*. Karate gradings, when the big black belts arrived from all over Toronto. It had been a marvellous place. Had been. Would be. The school would all come to Amelia one day, if it survived its founders. But while they presided, Amelia was held in abeyance, waiting to begin.

Francesca strode up the stairs past the office with a white bag labelled CAREFUL HAND LAUNDRY bobbing over one shoulder. She was dreaming, no doubt, of the chef's quenelles at the Pierre or the stroll arm in arm with Dugald through the Egyptian tombs at the Met: they were leaving for New York in short order. Meanwhile, here was Amelia, back at the ranch sending out invoices for next term's deposit.

"Francesca, have you got a minute?" she ventured.

There was a dramatic pause as Francesca deliberately and with intent slowed her forward, upward momentum.

Would there be a next term? wondered Amelia. The gradual but steady departure of students made it seem all but impossible. Today it was Chino. Not destined for brain surgery, but a lad with a future, as Dugald always said. In grade eight, on admission to the school, he'd read at a grade-three level. Now nearing the completion of grade thirteen, he did Latin, music and calculus with *elan*, if not total accuracy. Miss Morrow regarded Chino as a boy she had rescued from certain illiteracy: she therefore expected that he and his parents would maintain a posture of extreme gratitude at all times.

The exchange had been honoured, but Miss Morrow grew overly ambitious. For her own sake, or for his (who knew?), she was determined to push Chino's seventy-ish grades a notch higher before he went out into the world. Her method was to give him zero on every assignment that did not represent a quantum leap forward. Chino for his part was restive. Last week Miss Morrow had rejected his English assignment on the basis that he had no right to question Milton. Yesterday, Chino had dared to submit a written suggestion that the science laboratory was antiquated. Miss Morrow expelled him on the spot. Chino's parents had finally had enough. Hence the parental note that Amelia waved up the stairwell.

"Shall I read it?" Barely pausing for permission, Amelia forged ahead. "'Dear Miss Morrow: As much as we admire your methods, we feel that, at this moment, we must take issue. The F in English you gave Chino does seem a little severe. Now he tells us he will not be allowed to write the mid-term because he criticized the Bunsen burners? And that he has in fact been expelled. We trust there has been some misunderstanding...'" Amelia looked quizzically at Francesca.

Francesca grimaced down upon her acolyte. They knew each other so well there was no need for words. Amelia understood that Chino smote Francesca's very heart when he passed comment on anything about the school, particularly its age. Amelia understood Francesca's expectation that as the goddess who had saved him she deserved worship. Was that unreasonable? Francesca asked. (Of course, she uttered none of this, nor did Amelia.) How would you feel if it were you? If it were not for me that boy would be digging sewers. If he were lucky. Is not a little respect due?

"I presume you would like me to write back that there is no misunderstanding. That it is never wise for parents to involve themselves in the assessment process."

"Quite," said Francesca.

"But that the boy is not *expelled*, per se... Not permanently. We shall allow him back in a few days or a week. When he has learned his lesson." This was a great concession.

"But can we—can you, I mean, guarantee that he will get good enough marks to get into the university of his choice?" In fact Francesca had this power. The Manor was her school. The ministry had inspected her for years and never once found a flaw in the students, though the marking system was entirely arbitrary, and there was no court of appeal.

"Of course he will! Manor students are above reproach! Amongst the finest scholars in all Ontario universities. I personally am aware of what each student is capable of, and of what he or she actually achieves. What I say will be on the record; he must simply do as I say. He must simply have faith in my method. I spent hundreds of hours with that boy..."

"Privately, may I reassure the parents?" Amelia said, "Something like, of course, he'll graduate, he'll have the marks. Because as you know, those first-term report cards have to be sent off to universities."

"Do you imagine I would have the boy dangle over the abyss, suffering torments of insecurity?"

Amelia averted her eyes. Yes.

And Francesca thought, Amelia, you are a coward. If you were brave you'd lodge your complaint before you knew I was backing down, not afterwards. A most infuriating trait. She flared her elegant nostrils. "Oh, don't worry, I'll be good. You can promise the parents I'll grade him realistically according to his work."

"I wonder," persisted Amelia, "if we may not be a little beyond that point."

Francesca lengthened her own exceedingly long neck, and proceeded up the stairs with that white laundry bag like an angel's wing folded over her shoulder.

"Would you allow me to read the rest of the letter aloud?"

Without Francesca's permission, she skipped to the pertinent last sentences: "'Much as we love the school. Blah blah blah...we feel we can no longer tolerate'....and so on until the end. 'Without a very deliberate change in attitude from the school we shall be forced to withdraw him.'"

Francesca halted on the stairs. "Have they pulled him out?"

"No. Not yet. They are giving us a chance to be 'reasonable.'" If they were not reasonable, Amelia surmised, the parents would come in Monday morning, and that would be the end of Chino, pulled out of the Manor and put, for the last part of the year, into Oakwood or Northern where he would be "reduced to a number" but could get regular evaluations and regular credits, and move on from this magical mystery tour.

One could not put Francesca on sufferance in her own school. She drew up her long back and faced resolutely toward the heavens.

"Well, then. I fail to see what can be done about that, if they choose to be so foolish. I shan't *apologize*."

Amelia's face fell. "An explanation is not an apology," she began. She was trying to protect Francesca. She did not want to let her imperiousness, her increasing pique, the mad whimsy of her responses, jeopardize the boy's future. And the school's future. They could not afford to lose another student. "There is the matter of the Greek trip as well. We were counting on him to bring the number up to ten."

Francesca took in a troubled breath. "Yes. It would be a great pity if he were to miss it. You might point that out. And, if you must, *explain*. We do not apologize to students." Then she began to climb again, continuing around the turn of the next landing; directly over Amelia's head her footfalls could be felt.

Amelia sat down to write an apology on Francesca's behalf.

Half an hour later, descending the stairs, his weekend bag in hand, Dugald stopped by the office to ask Amelia how the numbers were for the Greek trip.

"We have just enough now: ten students will be joining us," she said. She was counting on Chino.

"And we have reservations, at the Acropolis View?" he asked, looking searchingly past his approaching spouse as if there were something beyond her presence that he could not quite make out.

"I'll call the hotel on Monday."

"Ah, yes!" he said. His eyes were unusually bright. "It will not be long now."

Francesca appeared beside him. She had a habit of doing that, as if his every conversation with Amelia might be dangerous. "You're not giving Amelia weekend work, are you?" she enjoined with a playful scolding face. "You know the dear girl must get out and have some fun while we're away. Very likely there's a suitor awaiting her."

"Very likely," said Amelia.

Francesca took his elbow and led him away.

When at last they left, Dugald behind the wheel, Francesca beside him, finger waving, announcing the route, Amelia was at the door to wave goodbye. She could imagine every word, though Francesca's voice was subtracted by the glass enclosure of the car. She felt instead her diagonal glance, a lowered, steely gaze, and was struck by the strongest enmity radiating from the Headmistress to herself. It was a shock that bathed her in cold sweat. Hatred—the word was not too strong—was conveyed in the line of that beautiful neck, in the set of those shoulders, in a sexual competitiveness that was impossible to miss.

If I had to guess, Amelia thought, I'd say that woman hated me simply because I am young. Well, young in comparison. (Never mind that Francesca was young once, and had never allowed herself to age.) And what is to resent in my dull little life? Here I am, after all, standing in the doorway like a governess waving them off to their romantic weekend in New York.

But Francesca was the only one allowed to have a lover in this Olympus; Amelia was meant to burn with unsatisfied desire.

Amelia worked for an hour, another hour. The office was an uncomfortable spot no matter what the weather, and frigid, now that winter had come. She crossed her arms over her chest and rubbed her hands over her elbows—she wouldn't stay much longer. Ferdinand was coming at eight. Though her little window looked over the back, she would hear his horn in the driveway.

She twisted in her chair, anticipating its sound. The Portuguese troll, the older girls called him. She'd been wounded on his behalf. True, Ferdinand was short, with a limp and a huge head thick with curls; true, he did not display the social graces of Manor boys, accustomed as they were to the pallid dining rooms of Toronto's racquet clubs. But they could not guess his secret gentleness. His lips had fantastic contours that skimmed hers with the lightest tickle, or attached in a wet clamp that took no prisoners, skewering her up against the backrest of the passenger seat of the canteen truck. The heavenly truck, even a glimpse of whose gleaming metal sides now made her breath come short.

The horn sounded, a sweet, silvery toot. Amelia shut the notebook in front of her and reached for her coat. She ran down the red-carpeted stairs, under the curved plaster ceiling of the foyer, and opened the oak door. She reached back to turn out the lights, then twisted the knob and stepped out onto the flagstone porch. There it was, the truck, shining like a spaceship that had just touched down. A smile of pure delight lit her face.

She stood, framed, she knew, by the solid round pillars, the overhanging roof of the Manor. There was a creak in the still night and then the sound of the truck door shutting, and he appeared, rounding the front fenders, his cloth cap in his hand.

Ferdinand: dark, short-legged, short-armed, his chest like a bellows. He looked up toward her, humble but fierce, passionate. Hephaestus, blacksmith to the gods, keeper of the forge, a solemn man with a simple destiny: to love Amelia. To attend to her physical needs. He was nourisher, caretaker—as Virginia Woolf would have it, the poet with the butcher's face. He stood with dignity, important to himself, if not in the grand scheme of things, and Amelia was delighted with him. The cap was like an offering, a suggestion of manners taught by his mother, of his childhood home in that other world where he originated. Amelia liked to think there was some long-left gleam of Mediterranean light in his face, in his eyes. She tripped down the steps toward him conscious of her legginess, of her lesser gravity.

"Before we leave," Ferdinand began, "I want to ask—"

"You want to ask?" She stopped as he spoke, one last foot on the stairs.

"Can we go inside?"

"Inside? Why?" Amelia eyed the silver chariot that had featured in her fantasies all week. How she bared herself in it, feeling the cool leather against her thighs. How Ferdinand clambered over the gearshift, lowered himself over her lap, somehow, contorting, pulling at clothing, his hand on that long black stick with the large knob on the end, swearing when he bumped his head on the roof. Down on his knees in the leg space he so conveniently fit, dwarfish as he was. Then that magnificent head, the misplaced head of some ancient king, wedged between her thighs.

"Inside?" she repeated.

He took two steps forward. "Are they gone?"

"Yes, they're gone. I told you they'd be gone." Irritated, just a touch, at having her authority questioned.

"Then take me inside. I want to see."

He stepped up to the foot of the stairs. Her desire hit her in the chest, rising from the smell of him, her breath catching, her belly sucking inward. There was a chestnut odour to the man, a wood-roasted, sweet-sour warmth that radiated from his whole body. She heard a throaty bird hoot: the barn owl from the trees around the pond. Wise Athena, high up in those maples, on the watch for careless mice. A portent. Was Amelia bewitched by this creature, this tender of flames?

But he was the more bewitched.

"I've never been inside the Manor," he insisted.

"Really?" All those years of bringing food and drink, rolling up outside as classes ended, his tires popping gravel at the edge of the road. All those years of jumping down from the high driver's seat and smiling, his natural gloom banished at the sight of Manorites in their sloppy blazers and side-yanked ties, and he had never been inside?

"Well, only the first time when I met your boss. But I never saw anything."

"Okay," Amelia said, reaching down and taking his hand, "I'll show you."

"I'll move the truck."

She watched as he backed out of the drive and parked on the side street, so as not to raise suspicions. A thoughtful man. And practised in intrigue?

She unlocked the door with a silent thrill: this was forbidden. "It's dark," she whispered in the hall. She took his hat out of his hands while his eyes adjusted. She moved to turn on the lights.

"Don't," he said, "I can see."

And in the gloom of the wood-trimmed halls, the rooms with windows stopped up by tapestries, he could see. He examined the portrait of Lily, the blackboard diagrams of molecules, the tacked-up posters of skeletal structure and food rules.

"Do you want to see the coach house?"

He did. She took his hand again, and went down the narrow side stairs and into the driveway, leading him: his square truck gleamed like a block of ice at the street's end. They walked under the pergola to the coach house. Amelia felt at her waist for the chain, modelled after Miss Morrow's chain, of course, which held her keys. She opened the door with a slash of pride in ownership. False ownership, borrowed pride. Ferdinand stepped in the door looking awed, and Amelia found the light switch.

The students' art hallowed the place, made it magical.

"Who does this?" He'd stopped to gaze at a copy of Michelangelo's *David*. He admired the Jerusalem windows. He marvelled over the Madonnas of the silent Russian, the spirals by Cassie.

"The tubby one who runs a tab? That Cassie?" He whistled.

The sparring equipment, hanging in the cupboard, was white and haggard and seemed half-alive. It made him jump back, teeth bared, his dukes up.

Amelia felt his admiration like another wooing; she could see him loving her for her knowledge, for her association with great and beautiful things. She preened as he whistled through the gap in his teeth. She showed him the handwritten copies of the first two pages of *The Rime of the Ancient Mariner*. His hand, relieved of the hat, came around to touch the small of her back and he rubbed her there, letting his hand drift lower over the firm bulge of her buttocks. She felt a small readying twitch between her legs.

"Come," she said, turning out the light. "There's one more place."

Why did Amelia decide to show him the sanctum sanctorum, the chapel? The tiny chamber in the lower reaches of the house was reserved for objects of worship: museum reproductions of a Renaissance pieta, a copy of the Rosetta stone, black and red amphorae. No one from outside the school was allowed in. The students themselves only entered on special occasions and they were required to stand in reverence.

Amelia put her hand on the door. She signalled for Ferdinand to bend his head as she did, so as not to bump it on the low ceiling. But as it was he was so short he did not need to. They entered in silent awe, half-ironic on Amelia's part: it was after all a simple basement room in Wychwood Park. But its power was palpable. Whispering, she reached out her hand to point. This is a real bit of a pyramid, she said, and that is a mask from Africa. Ferdinand appeared to listen but his eyes lingered on her arm, her fingers, instead of travelling outward to the objects of beauty. Then he lifted his own stubby, dark-skinned hand and wrapped it around her wrist.

"Stop," he said.

She stopped.

He wound her arm around behind her back, which pressed her chest up against his. "Kiss me."

She obliged.

He placed his free hand on the small of her back and delicately pressed her pelvis toward his.

Pursuing her lips with his own he slowly edged her back toward the wall. Amelia could not see where she was going and feared she would trip on an Egyptian bust. Her breath came more quickly than before, loud in the small, enclosed space. Her lips explored the texture of his, thick and foreign, shaped by the sounds of a different tongue. She put her hands on his buttocks. They were lower than hers, and hard, chiselled. He was very strong. Even his lips were strong. They stood, exploring familiar, and yet still new territory, sensations. He edged her farther back.

"Watch out for the Rosetta stone."

"What's that?"

Amelia laughed. Miss Morrow would die a thousand times if she knew that he was stumbling about amongst her treasures. Ferdy laughed too and moved her backward again. It was a dance, this one; he set the direction. She was off balance. There was only one place she was going to end up: the floor. She narrowly missed capsizing a statue of Aphrodite. She stumbled over a low wooden chest on which was displayed a Japanese go set, and the little black and white stones went flying onto the carpet.

"Whoops," she muttered, freeing her lips for a moment from Ferdy's. By this time she was leaning sideways against one of the two small chairs that graced the chapel. She had no choice but to put out one hand and slide, gracefully, she hoped, to the floor. In a second he was on top of her. He was a thickset, heavy man, but when he lay on her he was light, seeming to weigh no more than a large muscular fish, a cod no doubt.

She let herself sink into the rug. As he rocked between her legs, the rug turned to sand beneath her. It seemed to have no hardness but to be a beach where she and he had been carried by small persistent waves. He moved up and down, hiking her skirt up her legs. Slowly, his lips closed over a piece of her neck. Fish, waves, water, beach, she thought. He began to buck, and then to thrash. She felt the urge to laugh: he snuffled at her collarbone and she knew he was laughing, too. It was such a relief. Only a grown man could laugh while making love. Boys thought you were laughing at them. And well you might be: the whole procedure, if viewed from the ceiling for instance, was comical.

"Not here! You absolute silly," she said.

"Not supposed to do this here?" he teased.

Amelia allowed him to press her thighs apart with his thighs. He pulled at the buttons of her sweater; she, in turn, pulled his shirt out of his pants at the waist. The small of his back was hairy and concave. Hairy male backs had made her feel nauseous until she met Ferdinand. But now, since he'd given her such pleasure, she had acquired a taste, a taste for the short darkness of him, his hirsute torso; the mass of curls on his head brought tears of tenderness to her eyes. No more the elegant, blond Greeks with their measured proportion, their arrested grace and demure downcast eyes. Now the dark interloper, the crude foreigner, the natural one. She was mad for this man, truly mad for him.

His pants were down, exposing his hairy buttocks. Her skirt was up. She put her hands on the thatch that covered his thighs, pressing him up, away from her, only to let him bear down again so she could groan again. She moaned into his hairy ear and was rewarded with more bites. She imagined herself, again, on the ceiling, looking down. Amelia was happy, happy. Then he stopped.

"What are you doing?" she whispered.

"They come back," he said.

"They don't," she whispered, but even as she did, he sat back on his heels, pulling his pants into place, doing up the zipper.

"Yes," he said, "they do."

"They've gone to New York."

"Well I think it was a short trip," he said, dusting off his legs. "How are you gonna get me out of here?"

Amelia was simultaneously trying to button her shirt and crawl to find the shoes she'd kicked off (under the pedestal of the Roman bust). She tried one more giggle but nothing came but a strangulated moan. She was mortified.

"You're crazy," she said. "They wouldn't come back. Why would they come back?" But her heart was racing, and not in the way it raced while he was on top of her; in quite another, unpleasant way, knocking angrily against the inside of her rib cage as if it might break the bars. They could not possibly be home and yet there were the steps in the hallway above. She'd left the light on outside and now it was off. The tall clacking of those unmistakable platform heels came down the stairs followed by, immediately, a figure in the doorway.

"Amelia? Is that you? Amelia?"

The dressing-down was horrific, quite the most vicious Amelia had ever received or ever heard anyone receive, and it would have been worse had Miss Morrow not finally broken out in a rasping sob and turned her back on them. Ferdinand, his morose head drooping over his chest, used this moment to escape, scooping up his hat from the floor where Amelia had dropped it.

"Excuse me, Madam," he said, and edged past Francesca in the doorway with a sidelong salutation to Amelia. Then he trudged up the wooden stairs with surprising dignity: how he managed, Amelia did not know, although she looked after him, even in her panic and humiliation, and thought to herself, there goes a good man; his wife is a lucky woman. He took the turn above the landing and opened the side door to the lane: he was gone.

"Francesca," began Amelia.

"Don't even speak."

"I—this is most embarrassing—"

"Never fear. It shall be dealt with," uttered Francesca in steely tones. Then she raised an eloquent hand and laid it across her brow, as if taking her temperature. She even sobbed a little.

"Oh, Francesca, I am so terribly sorry—"

"Enough!" Yet there Francesca stood. She did not walk away.

Amelia wondered if there might be something else wrong. Surely, Francesca had nothing more to say. This moment *in flagrante* must lead to so encompassing a rupture in their relations that the thought of further communication between the two women was anathema. And yet Francesca remained, swaying a little. Since she did not leave, and since she appeared so broken in spirit, there must be more. And Amelia, so practised in understanding her employer, so educated in the soothing arts, understood. It could mean only one thing.

"You've come back early," Amelia said, in a low voice. "Is Dugald—?"

Francesca sobbed again. This time it was a true sob.

"Oh, Dugald," she said.

It was all she needed to say.

Amelia moved toward her. "Oh dear, I am so sorry."

Francesca shifted herself away. Amelia could see that the Headmistress did not want consoling from her, defiler of the sanctum sanctorum that she was, but unfortunately Amelia was all there was. Resistance fought need. Need won, for once. She leaned, almost imperceptibly, closer. Amelia put out a long, strong arm and took the older woman by the shoulder.

"Don't tell me, let me guess. Dugald got into a rant..."

Francesca, face in hands, nodded.

Dugald did this sort of thing. He got working on one of his theories, his lectures, and it simply took over his mind. He would forget, or appear to forget, where he was, and who might be listening, and would abandon himself to the argumentative mode of discourse. He would become rhetorical and unreachably so.

"About the Parthenon?"

Francesca had her face in her hands. She nodded. It was the one she liked the least, clearly. Another rant would have been preferable.

"But you couldn't just let him go through it, let him wear himself out with it?"

"I couldn't," said Francesca. And did not say the reason. She could not because now his rants were not simply scientific inspirations and wild notions. They included reference to that other life, that long-buried and long-dead past that was no more except, it appeared, in Dugald's mind. And complaints of specific failures on Francesca's part, which were terribly unfair. "He is not himself. He's getting old."

"Eighty something," said Amelia.

Never before would Francesca have admitted it aloud but indeed today it did seem so; Dugald was a thin, frail elderly man on an airplane, talking excitedly of a scientific innovation made obsolete years before. Amelia began to blush, whether from shame or from pity she did not know. Francesca backed away and stood staring at the statue of Aphrodite as if in its lines she could discover a verse to act as balm.

"This is most painful to relate. I hate even to think of what happened next, it's so appalling. The end of the story, if I may tell it before I begin, is that although my dear husband is physically at my side at every moment, I see now that he is not able to help me. If we are to survive I must have my wits about me. I must see life steadily and see it whole."

"Yes, Francesca," said Amelia.

Her familiar, submissive tone steadied Francesca.

"To go back. We arrived at the airport for this beautiful weekend escape to which I had so looked forward. As always Dugald parked the car. We got through to the ticket agent, then the customs officer with his rude inquiries. He demanded, 'Are you related?' I said, 'Yes.' Dugald said, 'No.' I said, 'He is joking. I am his wife.' Dugald looked at me as if he did not even know me and said, 'You are not my wife. My wife is—Meryl.'"

Meryl. Yes, Amelia thought.

Francesca broke off, and put one hand over her eyes as if to shield herself from too much light. "Fortunately, I managed to persuade the customs officer we were who I said we were, and we went along. Dugald was shuffling. I do hate it when he shuffles because it makes him look old. And it is only a matter of inattention. So I reminded him to pick up his feet and for a time he did. We always fly executive class and in very short order we were seated in the cabin with a stewardess leaning over us.

"And then it started. He began to rave. About Greece. He forgot, or appeared to forget, where he was, or who might be listening, and abandoned himself to the argument. I can normally keep it under control. He accepts my eye signals and at the very worst a quick verbal command wakes him to reality. But he kept saying he wanted to see this Meryl, and others, his family, he said—some names I didn't know—and insisted I was not his wife. He called the stewardess.

'Miss, how many hours is it to Athens?' he said. 'About ten hours,' she answered. 'But we are not going to Athens.'

"'You may not be. But we are,' he said.

"'No, sir, we are not.' She thought again. 'Sir, may I check your ticket?'

"'Oh, that won't be necessary,' I said. I always carry the tickets.

"The stewardess now appealed to me. 'Miss Morrow?' She obviously had our names on her printout in the kitchen. 'You understand that this flight is going to New York?'

"'Yes of course,' I said. 'Dugald?' I patted his arm. 'He knows. He's only joking. That will be our next trip.'

"'Oh,' she said dubiously and walked away.

"'Darling,' I said, 'You're so forgetful! We're going to New York for the weekend. Athens is two months from now!'

"But he was not listening to me. I decided to let him wear himself out. It used to work. But the preservation of the Parthenon had taken over his mind. Dugald believed that we were on the way to see this dream achieved. The stewardess returned with our glasses of champagne. She appeared to tolerate his chatter, even to believe it. I should have recognized this as a danger sign. I put on my white gloves and stood up and walked down the aisle as if to go to the ladies' room. I always wear white gloves to go to the lavatory on airplanes because studies have shown that the handles to the washroom doors are absolutely crawling with germs. This is why people become ill after flying. In the aisle I spoke to the stewardess.

"'Please pardon my husband. He's a little overstimulated,' I said. When this kind of thing happened in the past there was never any further problem. People recognized Dugald's exceptional qualities and enjoyed his flights of scientific fancy. As did I.

"The stewardess nodded, kindly, I thought, glanced at my gloves and moved on.

"When I returned to my seat the head steward was beside my husband. Dugald was describing the spray guns that would be aimed at the columns from the area in front of the monument. To spray the silicone of course. But they are not terribly intelligent, these people, and I wonder if they thought he was speaking about gunfire and took him for a terrorist. Dugald! In any case, the steward drew me aside.

"'I am sorry to tell you that we have had to ask that your husband be removed from the flight,' he said. 'I am presuming you will want to leave as well?'"

Now Francesca's eyes were circled with white, and staring. Like Hecuba, Amelia thought. Her king, her city, was crumbling.

"I am simply devastated. We had to leave the car and take a taxi home. I did not trust him to drive and I cannot. All the way, Dugald ranted on as if he were living in that long dead and buried past. It was dreadful, dreadful. Only now, as I led him into the Manor, did he realize that our weekend trip to New York was cancelled. I took him up to our nest, our love nest above the schoolrooms, and sat him on the edge of the bed. He pulled off his socks. Ah, home! I thought." She began to laugh—or was she about to cry? "But when my back was turned he leaned over and plugged in that electric blanket. And there was a hum and a shudder and suddenly we were in darkness. That fuse again!"

Now the ironic razor-edge came into Francesca's voice, and her words became arch. So Amelia was not to be forgiven (how could she be?). Even though she could be used.

"And so. Amelia, my trusted assistant, is of course not here, for it is night. I must attend to the breakdown myself. Down I come, down, down into the basement. And on my way to the Vaults, I hear the most dreadful sounds, pig-like squeals of delight. You!"

"Oh, Francesca, I am so terribly sorry—"

"Enough!" she said.

9

THE
ATTACK

THAT SAME FRIDAY night, Cassie was late at school. The Dead Ladies had gone off without her and she was glad. They'd had a short, business-like meeting at the sheds after class. Ashley was upset because Spit was whining and puking. Everyone else was quiet.

"Okay, all present and accounted for," said Vida. "Agreed that we make an example of Ferdy."

"Agreed," they all said, except for Cassie.

"Cassie, you have to speak when everyone else speaks. Agreed?" Vida tried again.

Cassie looked into Vida's eyes. "An example of what?"

Everybody laughed. Vida ignored the question.

"We can do it right here. Sometimes his truck is parked around the corner here late," said Ashley. "Like about seven-thirty or eight. They get in the truck and have sex. We can get him in the dark." She knelt and began to pick bits of grit out of the pads of Spit's paws. She murmured to him, "You don't feel well. Poor puppy..."

"When he's weakened after the act."

"So we'll go play pool and come back later."

"And you better get rid of that dog," said Vida to Ashley. "We're not having the stupid dog with us."

"Well, what am I supposed to do with him?"

"Tie him up somewhere."

"He's sick!"

"I can't come," said Cassie. "I've got to go find my English binder."

Vida glared at her. "You better be here when we get back."

"I will, I will," Cassie had said.

Cassie went back to look in James Janitor's shed, but he waved her away. He was crumpling papers into a garbage bin. She stood a long way away from him and asked about her binder. He just shook his head. He never did business until the morning after. Cassie went back to the coach house. She really wanted to escape and go home and tell her mother about the Project, but she couldn't. If she didn't show up, she could never come back to school again. The Dead Ladies would definitely kill her, even if she was Vida's favourite. Besides, if they attacked Ferdinand, Cassie had to be there. Perhaps she could help him.

She felt grand and tragic, with everyone gone, waiting for the end to come. She had this time to put in. She thought she would just sit in the coach house and read. She went inside and in the quiet read three chapters of *The Moonstone*. She put her head on the desk and slept awhile. But she wasn't supposed to be in school this late, and she got nervous that Miss Morrow would find her.

She came out the door and began to cross the lawn, stealthily, in shadow, so as not to be seen. She saw the cab's light in the circular drive and remembered: Miss Morrow and Dr. Laird had gone away for the weekend. Then who was arriving in the cab? She hung back until the lights went away. She did not see if anyone went into the Manor or not. It was frightening, like a murder mystery.

She stepped onto the grass. The chill twilight air with its crystals of frost caught her like a hand on the throat. She looked south; the skeletal trees afforded a view down the hill to the city. It was all grey, pierced only by yellow lights. A small fog rippled up toward the Manor from the sunken pond. The whole park looked haunted, suddenly, the pond below shimmering in twilight, the Manor behind Cassie looming ghostly amongst the dark evergreens. She crept around to the front. The Manor's windows were curtained; they always were. The school had a shut-away face. But little cracks of a warm yellow light showed in the gaps; Amelia must be in there tidying up.

She went down the path into the pool of light thrown by the coach lamp mounted on the side of the house. The tall wrought-iron gate rose in curlicues from the driveway. Its shadow drew circles on the paving stones, like the great circles in illuminated script. She slipped between the gate's half-opened wings. Descending the path, she stepped in and out of the shadow circles as if they were hopscotch squares. At the bottom, she veered to take her accustomed seat on the flagstone wall that ran across the garden. Her feet dangled over the few stiffened sprigs of ivy that clustered around the base of the maple tree.

She was terrified.

She got up and tried doing hopscotch down the path. The Dead Ladies would have scoffed. It was one of those childish games she was supposed to leave behind. There were certain drawbacks to being in the group. Cassie felt nostalgic for being a loser.

She saw, parked on the side street facing the streetcar sheds, Ferdinand's shiny metal truck.

Her humming began, loud and insistent and completely on its own. It sounded like the noise you make blowing waxed paper over a comb.

She saw figures flit through the shadows.

It was too dark for hopscotch. Cassie decided at the last minute to go home, and take the consequences. She had started to lope toward Bathurst and her streetcar when she heard Vida's voice.

"Echo!"

Cassie saw them in the long shadows beside the empty sheds, where they'd been waiting. The disused streetcar tracks, which had taken the cars in and out of these garages, gleamed like snakes under their feet. One by one they stepped out from the wall. Big Bertha and the Virgin Queen, slouching and smoking, taller than most boys; tense, jittery, delicate Snow; little power-packed Maid of Lorraine doing her weird semaphore. Even though she was one of this gang, they scared her. Vida called again.

"Echo! Where are you going?"

Ferdinand emerged from the side door of the Manor with his cap in his hand. He had been transported to another world and then abruptly, brutally, his transport had failed him and he was back in this one. Dark had fallen while he was inside the house: or rather the dark of that cellar had followed him out. He felt as if he'd had his ears boxed. They burned. He did not know what time it was.

Still, he was a man of substance. He came out of the narrow path that led from the Manor to Taddle Creek Drive and stopped to dust his pant legs with his cap. He set back his shoulders, firmly, to displace the disturbing images. Ferdinand's nieces and nephews read fairy tales. His wife, who could not read English, took them to the library, where they sat on cushions and looked at picture books and had stories read to them, about giants and dragons and fair damsels and lost princes. When they borrowed the books and brought them home they recited the stories back to him. Ferdinand liked fairy tales. And now he was in one himself. He was the Beast in *Beauty and the Beast*, or he was the village simpleton who had been tricked by a stepsister to enter the castle. He rocked side to side as he strode down the pathway; his built-up shoe threw off his gait. He brushed again at his pant legs and squared his shoulders. Heading for the truck, parked around the corner, he felt in his pocket for his keys. He didn't seem to be able to find them. He didn't seem to be thinking straight.

Cassie wanted to shout: "Watch out! Something's coming!" She could feel it, see it, hear it, but she could not stop it. She began to hum, high and loud. Vida seized her hand and dug into her palm with her nails, but the humming did not stop.

"Oh sweet Mary mother of Jesus," Ferdinand said to himself. "Don't tell me they fell out there in that underground museum. What in God's name am I going to do now?"

He had his head down, and both hands in his back pockets. He had just found the lump of keys when the first clout hit him on the back of the head. The blow didn't do any damage because his chin was tucked into his chest; the stick caught the very hardest part of his head and bounced off. He stepped away from his truck, protecting his face with his fists and ready to punch somebody. He took two more steps away from the vehicle. (He didn't want the side dinted.) He looked up and all around, peered out into the gloaming. There was nothing but darkness, deeper here on this side of the street; not enough houses, and the streetlights by the barns were out, most of them.

"What the f—" he said.

Two fast-moving bodies came at him from behind the truck. Vida twirled a stick of wood and screeched karate instructions in her bastard Japanese. With her baton she whipped the enemy behind the ear and then across the opposite temple. As he went down she kneed him under the chin cracking his head up; his teeth clamped on his tongue and blood spurted. Roxanne threw side kicks and forward kicks and punches, at first connecting with his gut as he went down, and then with his face. He covered it with one arm and rolled over. The rest of the Dead Ladies ran out of the shadows and danced around him.

Like a bunch of little devils, is what he thought. Sticks and kicks rained over his head and his upper back. He flattened himself, as being less in the way of the hurricane. Cassie did nothing, just stood and moaned. Ferdinand had uttered not a single howl, but when he realized who they were he was so indignant he could not remain silent.

"Girls!" he shouted thickly—his tongue was swollen already. "You're nice girls! What do you want from me? I'm Ferdinand—"

Too late Cassie let out her piercing cry. "Watch out! Watch out! Watch out!"

It was well and truly dark by the time he was tied up with belts (long padded belts of various colours stolen from the karate box at the school) and lying on the cold floor of his own truck. Vida and Maureen presided over him while Ashley and Roxanne sat smoking in the cab. They were chanting. The poem went around in Cassie's head viciously, like a headache.

Tell me where, in what country,
Is Flora the beautiful Roman,
Archipiada or Thais
Who was first cousin to her once,
Echo who speaks when there's a sound
On a pond or a river...

Until finally she did not know if these lines were inside her head or outside. She did not know if she was dreaming or if she had tuned into some weird radio station. "He doesn't like smoke in his cab," she said.

Maureen hooted. "Look at you in your uniform," she said. The others had of course changed their clothes before the action. "Sitting there wagging your finger like a bloody nanny. You should be on *America's Funniest Home Videos*."

But Cassie insisted, with such a hysterical edge, that the Ladies were forced to listen to her. "Ferdinand doesn't like the smoke near his upholstery." Roxanne butted hers; Ashley sucked hers down to the filter and threw it out the window. Vida and Maureen got out to smoke. Cassie went back to Ferdinand, and leaned over him with her scarf in her hand. "It's me," she said, softly into his ear. "Cassie, the strange, chubby one."

He did not seem to have heard. Outside, voices went up in a roar—

"The queen white as a lily

Who sang with a virgin's voice,

Big-footed Bertha, Beatrice, Alice,

Haremburgis who held Mainne

And Jeanne the good maid of Lorraine—

At this point the whole truck shook with a great cheer as the girls lifted their voices and shouted. Ferdinand moaned.

"Shhhh!" Cassie said.

"Whom the English burnt at Rouen, where,—

Where are they, sovereign Virgin?

But where are the snows of yesteryear?—"

There was laughter when the poem finished. Ferdinand used the noise as a cover for another big groan. Cassie put her hand on his shoulder. All those hot dogs—this was all because he had let her run up a tab of one hundred and twenty-five dollars.

"The Leslie Street Spit!" yelled someone and they all hooted with laughter.

"Let's take him down to the Leslie Street Spit!"

"Who's driving?"

"Ashley, you've got your G-2!"

"No! Not my truck!" Ferdinand grunted through the belt that ran across his mouth. "You can't drive my truck."

"Wanna bet?"

He began thrusting himself about on the floor, which must have been very painful, but the girls just laughed like demons. They were completely fucked up, Cassie realized. When did they get the drugs. They had let her get away with staying at school when they went to the pool hall because they recognized that she was too weird to do drugs. Drugs might make her even weirder. The fact that they were fucked up made Cassie feel better and worse. Better because at least it was some kind of explanation, like this wasn't a personal thing against Ferdinand. And worse because it meant they really didn't know what the hell they were doing and now they had control of his truck.

They had already got his keys out of his pocket. Now Ashley was behind the wheel. The motor jumped into action and the truck jerked forward. Ferdinand swore violently into the belt that was now soaked with blood and spit, and jerked around so hard it seemed he might knock the others over in the back.

"Fucking sit on him, Cassie," said Vida.

"She's gotta be good for something," said Maureen.

"Ooooh," Cassie said like she might refuse but Vida melted her with a look.

"Why do we have to have that freak with us anyway?" said Ashley. "Do you know how fuckin' annoying she is? And you can't trust her—"

"Yes, you can," said Vida.

Cassie sat like a soft still weight on Ferdinand's shoulder. He thrashed a couple of times but she braced herself and he couldn't get free. The truck began to move. She felt like crying and in fact a couple of sobs escaped; Ferdinand was crying, too, underneath her. It must have been the shock of the whole thing, and who knew what he'd been up to in the Manor with Amelia? Cassie hoped he could feel her blessing even though she was sitting on him. Old Ferdinand, king of his own little house at Dupont and Dufferin, his wife, his brothers-in-law, nieces, nephews, sisters, mother and father, and, most of all, king of his truck, his hearth. He probably wondered what he'd done to deserve this. For sure at this moment he was thinking seriously of moving back to Portugal, considering that this was how kids turned out in Toronto, Canada.

He provided Cassie a certain comfort, the warmth of his body, as they coasted down the Bathurst Street hill toward the lake. How were they going to get to the Leslie Street Spit? Take University to Lake Shore and go east. God forbid they might drive the truck into the bloody lake with him tied up inside. And Cassie on top like a dead weight. Ferdinand gagged. He would have vomited if Cassie hadn't reached down and pulled the belt out of his mouth, at the same time gripping his chin with her hand in a gesture that said to him, "Don't scream and don't say one word or they'll gag you again for sure."

The truck lurched to a stop and a huge cheer went up.

"Where are we?" said Cassie, nearly falling off her perch.

"Tell me where, in what country—" someone began.

"Leslie Street Spit, your favourite place—"

"We are?"

"No. It's Cherry Beach, in fact. Isn't this what you wanted, Cassie?" Someone was turning nasty.

"I did not want any of this," Cassie said, and was ashamed at how her voice trembled. "This is not a safe place to be. Not at night. Not ever, really."

More peals of laughter came from the cab. They were all four of them jammed in there. Psychotic, thought Cassie. Remind me to never—

"Who says it should be safe?"

"We're the people you're supposed to be scared of in the dark."

"Except we have no idea what we're doing," Cassie said.

A little silence fell. As usual Vida rescued her. "She's right, you know."

"Well what the fuckin' bitch-ass crap are we doing it for anyway?"

"She's the one who ran up the tab—"

It was turning into a fight. To stop it someone started the chant.

"Is Flora the beautiful Roman—"

"Oh, shut the fuck up."

"I think we should untie him. What if he's hurt?"

"Oh, he's hurt, what do you think, you jerk? He's just pretending? I'm a green belt remember," said Vida.

"—Echo who speaks when there's a sound

On a pond or a river

Whose beauty was more than human?"

"Cut the crap."

"Shall I untie him?" Cassie's voice was high and tremulous.

There was a screeching chorus of "No"s.

"He's too strong for us. If we let him go he'll get away!"

"What, are you fuckin' crazy?"

"You're fuckin' cowards! Chicken shits!" Said Vida. "I mean, this is all supposed to be about the money, isn't it? Like, we know what we want—"

"Well, Ferdy doesn't know what we want."

Again they all had to listen because Cassie was being sensible.

"He has no idea what we want, or if we even want anything except to make trouble. And how are we going to get what we want if we don't untie him? I don't think he's going to talk to us with me sitting on him."

Now a little gallery of faces was peering down at Ferdinand. He tried to open his eyes.

"Jesus, he's swollen isn't he and like sort of turning colours—" said Roxanne dubiously. "What's with you and those logs anyway, Vida?"

She still had one in her hand, a bamboo stick about two feet long, which she wielded with terrific style. "It's not a log, it's Miss Morrow's ulysees."

"Okay, well, let's sit him up then and ask him."

They decided they couldn't make their demands in the closed back of the truck so someone went outside and fooled around with the key trying to open the side to the servery. Ferdinand swore and kicked. Finally the side was open and the girls stood outside on the level ground of the beach looking in, in a bizarre parody of the usual set-up, while Ferdinand was propped up behind with Vida holding one elbow and Cassie the other. He looked at their faces and all he could do was shake his head. He spit out a clot of blood.

"Oh, yuck, did you see that," said Maureen with cool fascination as she rubbed out her cigarette butt with her toe.

Maureen, with the body and face of an angel, was the worst of them. It frightened Cassie, that her sweetness was so vile. She looked away. She could see the lake water from here. It was calm, very smooth, and held a certain pale light that seemed to come up from under the water. Maybe it swallowed the reflections of the city lights, evening after evening, and then gave them back when all around the harbour became truly dark. She found the light in the water a little soothing. She started thinking about harbours, like the ones in the Greek myths, where all the great news came in on fabulous sailing vessels propelled by good winds or bad. Ferdinand was probably used to harbours like that, full of fishing boats and cargo ships from all over the world. No sailing nation was as great as Portugal. He had told Cassie that often. She could feel him sagging on her arm so she held him up higher.

It was a funny harbour here, with not very many boats, mostly only those little ferries that chugged back and forth to the islands and a few hotel-sized ships full of sugar. Cassie thought perhaps it was good luck, a symbol, that had brought them down here, her silly mistake about where they take the old snow.

"Hey, do you think maybe this is, like, the mouth of Taddle Creek? Where it goes into Lake Ontario?" asked Roxanne.

"And Ferdy's up the Taddle without a paddle."

Everyone laughed.

"No, seriously, like isn't that what Dr. Laird said? It flowed down near Parliament Street and made this little hook around and into the lake right around Cherry Beach? 'Cause that's like cool. It's like symbolic or something. We're still on the track of the magic water or something, I don't know..." Roxanne's voice began to trail off. There were people walking around on the beach. "Like, who are all these guys?" she whispered.

"I don't know, but they might do something—"

"Yeah—"

"Let's get it over with."

"He's like so messed up maybe we should just put him in the lake."

"You're a fuckin' psycho—!"

"I think that's called, like, murder?"

"No it isn't, it's some drunk driving down here and falling in the water."

"He's not drunk."

"Can they tell that?"

"They're not stupid, eh?"

"Well, then, what is a life of crime? You tell me."

"You guys are on crack. Get a grip. We had a Project here."

"Yeah we, did. It was—"

"What was it?"

"Ferdinand?"

Ferdinand raised his large head wearily and gazed under his swollen eyelids at Vida.

"You know that tab Cassie ran up? Like, what was it, Cassie?"

"A hundred and twenty-five dollars? I can't remember."

"Yeah, like we want you to forget it. Just wipe it out. She can't pay it. We can't pay it. And you're like harassing her for it."

"She never wanted to buy that stuff anyway. You sorta made her."

"He didn't," Cassie whimpered. "He was just nice to me."

"You got it?"

"God's teeth," said Ferdinand. "You did this because of her tab?" His voice sounded unreal. The beach was wide and dark, and the low light that shimmered over the water had no explanation. "Are you nuts or what?"

Vida raised her stick as if to hit him. Cassie screamed, so Vida put it down again.

"Just gimme my truck," Ferdinand said.

"What's that?"

"He wants his truck."

"Well, yeah, we'll give him his truck. But he's got to say, like, the tab is gone."

Ferdinand raised his hands with a gesture of great weariness.

"Gone," he said.

Cassie hung her head and sobbed.

"How are we gonna trust him?"

"No more tab," he said louder. "Gimme my truck."

"Yeah, well okay then," said Vida. "It's a deal. Let's give him the truck."

"Sure we'll give him the truck." Ashley had the keys in her hand and she dangled them in front of Ferdinand over the counter. Little bitch. He wasn't going to grab them from her. He couldn't if he tried.

"Give them to him," Cassie said.

"Oh sure, we'll give them to him. Then what? He's gonna drive home? And what about us, we're down here on the beach."

"Well, *I* don't know how this is supposed to end," complained Vida. "You tell me."

"Just get back in the truck and we'll drive up to Yonge Street and then get out."

"Someone'll see us. Someone'll catch us."

"Someone might catch us right here."

"I think we should drive the truck into the water."

"What for?"

"Life of crime, isn't it supposed to be? That's not much of a crime, just getting the guy to forget your hot-dog debts. Like, what kind of criminals are we anyway?"

"This is stupid," said Vida. She was losing steam. They were all losing interest.

"It's like really late, isn't it? My mum is going to be really worried," said Cassie.

Roxanne and Ashley started to laugh. Laughing and squealing, Maureen grabbed the keys from Ashley and ran for the truck door. She got herself inside the cab and behind the wheel. Vida and Ferdinand and Cassie held on to the inside walls of the servery. The side awning was still open.

Maureen locked the cab and started the truck, leaving Roxanne and Ashley scratching at the door. One of them tried to jump up on the counter in front of Cassie but Maureen had the truck in gear and was moving fast, straight down to the water.

"You don't drive it like that!" screamed Ferdinand.

This was all landfill; the original lakeshore was farther back and had been extended with dumping. Whenever the city dug up a block of road or took down an old warehouse, this was where the materials ended up, a parts graveyard for city buildings. Huge, jagged, blocks of cement had been thrown in at the edge of the water. But nobody cared what was there, at that moment.

Maureen gunned the truck without knowing how to steer. Ferdinand held his bound wrists up at the sides of his head in an agony that was not physical, though his physical injuries were significant, as would be noted by his wife in only a few hours. His pain seemed to be entirely related to the truck, the damage to his truck, his freedom, his livelihood, the love of his life, truly, the gleaming metal-sided truck with the diagonal quilted pattern on the side panels.

Maureen drove off the pavement and over a curb, and the truck crashed down several feet onto a landscape of concrete cubes tumbled at odds with one another. It tipped forward, falling to one side. There was a hideous grind as the undercarriage was ripped out. The three in the back were hurled from one side to the other, landing on the floor in a heap. Maureen went forward bumping her head on the windshield but not hard enough to crack either. The truck stalled. Everyone screamed.

The night was quiet, stunned.

The waves lapped on the rocks. The moon quavered through a rift of cloud.

And then the beach came to life. Suddenly it was clear there had been people there all the time, sitting by the banks, walking their dogs, behind the wheels of parked cars having lovers' quarrels. Car doors opened and voices called out and they began to run toward the truck. The city is full of good-hearted citizens when there's an accident.

Cassie had been thrown over the serving counter. It was easy for her to swing her legs over and step out onto a large block. She scrambled a few feet away and then turned and looked back at the truck that sat, crooked, gleaming in the moonlight at the edge of the water.

BOOK TWO

ACROPOLIS

T HE PLANE BOUNCED twice as it landed on the runway in Athens; it seemed the wheels had come off. But, miraculously, no. As the pilot applied the brakes they were all thrust forward with that horrible lurch, the obligatory seatbelts across stomachs squeezing indigestible dinners up throats. Cassie reached for the airsick bag and filled it. The rest of her vomit went over her knees.

"Nice aim," muttered Vida, commiserating.

Maureen gave a disgusted groan. Then everyone started passing her their Handiwipes.

Dr. Laird and Miss Morrow had flown first class. It was left to Miss Holt to muster the students from the tail of the plane, to make sure they had their knapsacks and their passports. The younger ones were half-asleep. The older ones were half-drunk.

The flight had been hideous: they were all shuffled between the members of a hockey team. The hockey boys had been bad enough, jumping up and down to the bathroom every twenty minutes, but their mothers were worse, partying all night long. Amelia got stuck beside a hockey mum with frizzy brown hair, the kind that gets up your nose, and a smug made-up smile. She stood over Amelia's seat half the night, drinking the bar dry, her laughter growing louder and louder. Sometime during this endless night Amelia slept, waking when the plane swooped out of the clouds in a jubilant arc over the most amazing flat turquoise sea interrupted by great motionless rocky islands. Greece! Although school trips had brought her here before, this moment was never less than magical.

To Amelia, the islands were the crowns of rock-gods, standing up to their foreheads in the sea, majestic and isolated. Just looking down on them she could feel the impulse of all those ancient navigators, including Odysseus himself, to thread the peaks together. Stories must come from islands. A place of islands is disjointed to begin with, without narrative; man makes a beginning, which must be arrival from another world, and an end, which is departure, a winding path through water. In between is the invention.

She tried to remember this bright thought for Francesca while she scrubbed the upchuck off Cassie's knees.

They all straggled into a circle at the baggage claim, except one.

"Where's Cassie?" asked Vida.

"Gone to get a hot dog."

The boys laughed.

"She fell behind during deboarding," said Amelia. "She wasn't well."

"She should have ordered the vegetarian plate," said Maureen.

Cassie appeared, the last to emerge from the gate. Amid the blazing yellow Olympic Air signs, a frieze of billboards in Greek and wafting cigar smoke, she looked for a seat. She chose the edge of the conveyor belt. It caught her kilt and tugged her over sideways.

"Psycho klutz," Maureen groaned.

When at last they'd each collected their bags, they milled about while Amelia counted heads.

"Stand still for a debriefing," she called. Deboarding, debriefing, disbanding, they were lucky she didn't defenestrate them. But, no, there would be no getting away from Vida with her orange plume, Maureen wearing her deceptively angelic face seemingly untouched by a sleepless night, Ashley, Roxanne, Cassie, pathetic Sara and the boys for the next ten days. It was a frightening thought.

We're all here, thought Cassie. We made it this far. All present and accounted for.

They had four boys—Dim-Dimitri as Dr. Laird called him, Chino miraculously still in the school, dreamboat Darrin and Jacob, the ever ob-nauseous (as Cassie called him) child genius—plus Sara and the full complement of Dead Ladies, who were at this moment threatening to pull out their cigarettes and light up.

You weren't supposed to say the name "Dead Ladies"; they had gone underground since their escapade with Ferdinand and his truck. Miraculously, they hadn't been caught. The onlookers let them pass for a group of friends on a joyride; the truck was towed out of the water. Ferdinand had simply and conveniently disappeared. The truck never came back to the Manor, and what was most eerie was the fact that neither Francesca nor Amelia mentioned its absence. The boys simply shrugged and walked north to the Real Jerk on St. Clair during break. All but Jacob: Jacob had a nose for conspiracy. He asked pressing questions and, each time he did, Cassie became nervous. She tapped her feet and sometimes hummed, and Vida glared at her. Miss Morrow complained that Cassie was going back to her old ways but she had not called her into the office to ask what the problem was.

Dr. Laird and Miss Morrow were already at customs waiting.

"Yoohoo!" called Miss Morrow to Cassie. "How did you manage?" She always checked in with her to make the girl feel safe.

"Good," said Cassie. She didn't mention the puke.

At last they were outside and on Greek soil. The Greek sun hit in huge white blocks painful to the eyes: it was the middle of the night at home but here it was two in the afternoon. In the taxi line the

Dead Ladies of one accord (except for Cassie) reached for their makeup kits and set to work with brushes and pastes.

"Girls!" scolded Miss Morrow. "We don't apply our lipstick in public!" Hers was of course perfect. In that wide and comfortable first-class seat she'd been able to repair her chignon, perhaps even to iron her gown. Amelia was a mess, hair full of static, skin dry as a leaf.

At least there was no security check on exit. In Toronto as they were going to the gate, Maureen's genital jewellery had set off the metal detector. An intransigent Asian woman had requested she remove it while Maureen had insisted that it was a piercing and could not be removed. It had taken Francesca's high-hatted intervention, and a growing queue behind, to get them through. Had Maureen been a terrorist with explosive devices between her legs she would right now be stepping into an Athens taxi unmolested.

Stuffed into a series of broken-down little cabs, they headed for the Acropolis View Hotel. Amelia allowed her head to fall back against the headrest. The air was still and poisonous, clouded with a white haze Miss Morrow called *nefos*. The buildings alongside the road were white concrete, jerry-built, cluttered with half-broken billboards and incomprehensible Greek lettering. Jacob the Greek scholar was in his element, reading aloud and laughing to himself to see a truck with METAPHORES on its side.

"It means transportation," said Dugald.

"I thought it meant truck."

"A truck *is* a metaphor. It transfers meaning," Dugald said, and chuckled.

Then a sign with COSMOS. ASSOS were matches all linked up, their little red heads like helmeted hoplites.

"It's too funny," Jacob kept saying, "too funny to see these ancient words attached to this trashy place."

"It is not trashy," Amelia corrected, but without great conviction. They jolted along in abominable traffic, the sounding of tinny horns on all sides as lanes of little cars converged and diverged. Cassie held on to the door handle and prayed for safe arrival at the hotel. A second's inattention on the part of the driver would bring them to ruin.

The boys leapt out ahead leaving no one but Cassie to help Amelia schlep the duffles out of the trunk of the rattletrap car. The fare was something astronomical in drachmas. They tried to do the mathematics: they were to divide by 218 or was it multiply by 2.8? They could not remember: either the trip cost fifteen dollars or it cost three hundred. Whatever, said Vida, hopping from foot to foot.

Jacob was paying off the other three cars from a waist-pouch bulging with paper money as they spilled into the narrow Athens street, a sorry lot in the kilts and blazers and grey flannels Miss Morrow had insisted they wear. It's *so* not cool! The students had protested, but got nowhere. Why go to Greece if you have to wear a friggin' kilt, Ashley had said, thereby occasioning Miss Morrow to launch into a mini-dissertation on how the kilt was actually Greek, having descended from the chiton (or was it peplos?) and been carried by conquering Romans all the way to Scotland. Men in skirts, men in skirts, someone chanted.

After the others were out, Francesca arose magnificent from the sagging back seat of the rusted little Vauxhall that was her chariot. "Scholars!" she cried. "Scholars, attention!" Dugald slumped beside her. Amelia put two fingers between her teeth and gave a whistle that could have launched three fire engines. They froze while searching through knapsacks.

"There it is! The Acropolis! City on the Hill!"

Francesca raised a long arm and trained her bony finger on the Parthenon visible atop its honeyed walls directly at the end of the street. All heads turned. A silence fell, the silence of due respect, the silence when imagination, kindled by years of dry books and classroom lectures, met with the actual stones under the fabled Greek sun. You could hear the intake of breath. Francesca's eyes filled with tears. It was a teacher's dream. For this she endured it all. All, for all these years.

"There it is, the most perfect structure ever built. The thing itself."

A rectangle of columns, a ragged roofline, held up to the sky like some kind of offering. That's what it was, thought Cassie, an offering to the gods. She felt the perfect peace of it, the way it sunk inside, so much larger than oneself.

Sara broke the silence. "It's *so* falling down," she said.

The rest broke out in helpless laughter. Giddy with the change in atmosphere, not sure of their footing on the rough cobbled street, they fell about into each others' arms, up against the fenders of the car, the plate glass windows of the hotel front. Miss Morrow stood, half-annoyed, half-indulgent. Her babies. The rats. It was fun every year to take ones who were so young they didn't understand, and watch the light finally dawn. She held up her hand.

"More than any other manifestation of human genius, the Parthenon expresses that understanding that put man at the centre of the world, that made beauty and proportion divine. It was built by free men twenty-five hundred years ago. What does it say to us today? Scholars?" Silence. She didn't mind. She answered herself.

"That simplicity is greatness. That beauty more than all of life is what we love. It has stood, all these years, protected by the goddess Pallas Athena. Marble. The stone that comes directly from our souls. Gaze. You will see when you get closer. Everywhere you look, gaze. Let it sink inside you. Let it enter your soul."

The hotel owner stood solemnly at attention between the glass doors, propped open, of his little establishment. "Come in, come in," he said to the students. They trooped inside. He had a name pinned on his chest: Paulus Vouzas. He shook Miss Morrow's hand, and then Dr. Laird's, with appropriate gravitas. "How many years? How many years do you come with the spring?"

"Many years," said Miss Morrow firmly. "Since I was a mere girl. How is your father? He was just married, then."

"You have not changed since I was a small boy," Paulus uttered bravely in slow English. His eyes swept, perhaps inadvertently, over the hourglass, up the long slender frame. "I look forward every spring to you to bring the flowers."

"Surely not with monkeys like these along," said Miss Morrow sharply. In the tiny lounge, Chino was shoving Darrin, who might at any moment awaken from his jet-lagged doze and pound the smaller boy into the carpet. As it was his hair stood straight up at the back of his head where it had rubbed on the airplane seat and his eyes were full of a sticky white substance. Francesca could not restrain a disgusted hiss. "Children! Attention: hear your instructions!"

They dragged their knapsacks into a semicircle around her. The Headmaster, meanwhile, sat exhausted on the sofa by the window, his eyes attracted to the tabloid-sized English newspaper. Francesca's eye fell on him. "Excuse me," she said. Instead of delivering the marching orders she stepped over to her tired husband and put her hand on his shoulder: he did not lift his head. "You do it," she said to Amelia.

"Instructions!" Amelia stepped in as smoothly as an understudy. "I trust you can remember this without pen and paper. Your room keys will be provided by Mr. Vouzas here. Stay in the chambers to which you have been assigned. There will be no switching of rooms. You now have four hours in which to unpack your luggage, shower if you wish, and sleep. We meet again at five o'clock for a walk to the Acropolis, where we will see the sun go down."

"Who shares with me?" cried Sara.

Amelia consulted the list.

"Maureen."

"Ah, like, no way?" said Maureen. "You're like, joking, right?"

"Ah, like, no, miss," said Amelia. "I am deadly serious."

Vida and Cassie were sharing. Cassie was practically swooning. Vida was so neat and small: she hung her knapsack on a hook, took her folded skirts and the jeans they all hoped to be allowed to wear out of her suitcase and laid them in a pile on the bottom cupboard shelf. Then she lay on her back on the single bed, one of a pair which, pushed together, still took up most of the room. Cassie wandered around, wondering where her other shoes were, if she still had her purse, what to do with her blazer. She took it off and threw it over the back of a chair and then lay down, awkwardly, on her back, on the other bed.

"Greece," Vida said moodily. "Fucking Greece."

"We're here."

"At least Miss Morrow's happy."

"We can see the Acropolis. That's pretty good. I bet you can't do that from every hotel in Athens."

"Fucking pile of stones."

"I think it's beautiful."

"Sure. If she'd stop telling us then I might notice."

"It's supposed to be magical when the sun goes down."

"Did you actually read all that stuff she gave us?" asked Vida.

"I did," Cassie admitted.

"Well, you can tell me," allowed Vida. Her hand drifted out and touched Cassie, who was happy. Okay. She would tell Vida. It would make the trip more fun. She squeezed Vida's hand in return. Together they lay still.

"We should sleep," said Vida.

Workers on a low roof across the street were pounding, sawing and calling out, even singing. Cassie dreamt of Helios the sun god completing his chariot ride across the dome of the sky. She knew she was dreaming; as she dreamt she heard Miss Morrow's voice telling her, "This is how the gods communicate with us, through dreams and through oracles." Helios' son wanted to drive the chariot; Helios let him, but the boy could not control the horses; by the time his ride was ended he had scorched the earth and everything was turning black.

The sun retreated from the room, turning a soft blue-grey. The workers across the street laid down their tools and headed home. Car horns retreated and grew muted; shoppers on foot went by below the window. Athens softened and gelled after the fractious energy of midday.

A telephone rang. Vida jolted off her back. "Fuck!" She scanned the room for the source of the noise. "What's ringing? Where are telephones in these holes?" She saw a brown thing on the side table and lunged for it.

"Five o'clock," said Amelia. "Time to meet us in the lobby for a walk."

"Oh, fuck," said Vida, replacing the receiver.

"Is that your favourite word?" said Cassie.

Vida glared. Then she smiled. "Think like a teenager," she said. "Remember. Fuck's a great word. Means everything."

Now it was quiet outside, the streets half-empty. The twilight was a misty violet infiltrating everywhere, the little shops they peered into, the café tables on the streets, the ice cream vendor's cart. The Dead Ladies had pale, chalky skin, and they walked along calmly, slowly, all together, peaceful, for once. Miss Morrow's cane tapped gently on the uneven ground; her heels clicked but without the military precision they attained in the wood-floored hallways of the Manor.

At the corner of Dionysus Street and the Acropolis, Francesca waved her cane and they sat. Frappés for all came to thousands of drachma: it was as if they were millionaires, dealing in such sums.

The students were large-eyed, sipping; eyes peeked over the wide-rimmed soda glasses, asking a thousand questions. But it was too late in the day for facts, too strange an hour—approaching night of Europe, morning of home—to think, to recall, to do anything but feel.

An air of joy settled over Francesca's face as she rested against the metal scroll of her chair. Here I am at home in Greece, it seemed to say, with all my charges, my children, my husband, my young assistant. They are under my command, as we come to visit the ancient civilization. Her lips rested together and turned slightly upward at the corners; her eyes drifted over the heads of the students and travelled fondly along the Acropolis walls, seeming to go from tree to tree, as if each cedar of Lebanon framing the ancient walls were a soldier and a friend to her cause.

"We shall wait here," she said.

And they did, for a long time. For what were they waiting? Until the sun's last peach-coloured beams left the clouds? Until they died of hunger? Miss Morrow sat with her hand draped over the knob of her cane, which was stuck like a divining rod into the hard packed earth under the tables, and fit her elegant profile in amongst the ruins. She began to talk about how Athens had been the home of Socrates, and also the home of the sophists. There were two kinds of men, said the sophists: Homo rhetoricus and Homo seriosus.

"Rhetoricus," she said, with an eye on her husband, "is an actor needing attention every minute of his life."

"Speak for yourself," said Dugald.

The students laughed.

"He lives on the surface where mastering the rules and winning the game matter above all. *Seriosus* is just the way he sounds. Sincere and centred, committed to being his own irreducible self. Or herself," she said, a glimmer of irony on her lips. She tapped her cane. "He, or she, does not pay attention to his lines as if he were on a stage, but only to his meaning."

Cassie watched this byplay. She tried to understand. No one knew what the right answer was, so no one spoke. Eventually it was Dugald who raised his voice.

"Perhaps, my darling bride, the problem with this marriage, if there is a problem with this marriage, is that we are both rhetoricus."

This was not the comment Francesca had wished for.

"To ground us in life," he said, almost pleadingly.

"Dugald, really, not now," said Francesca, tapping her cane once more on the ground.

Amelia got up.

"I'm afraid they're hungry."

Miss Morrow sat staring at the Acropolis. It wasn't until Ashley started to fall out of her chair and Cassie piped up, "Remember, Miss Morrow? Ashley's a hydroponic. She needs to keep her blood sugar up," that there was action.

"Hypoglycemic, but it's true," said Amelia, eyeing Ashley, thinking, anorexic is more like it. At last Miss Morrow gave a small nod. Amelia went across the street to get the souvlaki she had been raving about. "It's hunks of meat rolled in pita with onions and yogourt and tomatoes." They would have eaten rolled newspaper by then.

Cassie went to help. The lamb was turning on a spike over a fire, all stacked, layer after greasy layer of meat oozing red and white with fat. "Oh, yuck."

"You'll like it," said Amelia.

"It reminds me of whoever it was, that revolutionary hero who was roasted alive by the Turks. They love roasting things alive here, don't they?" observed Cassie.

Amelia thought for a minute. "Well, they like roasting, but not alive."

"Probably they skinned him, that hero, and his body spat like that."

The food-seller took his knife and slashed away at it.

"It's sick-making," said Cassie. "Anyway, the Dead—the girls are all vegetarians. Can you do some without the meat?"

Cassie brought them back two at a time and they were delicious. Now night came, suddenly. And then the floodlights went on.

"Look," Francesca commanded.

The Acropolis was magically enormous, the Parthenon, up on its honey-coloured pedestal, thrusting to the starless sky. The columns were so white they were like bones, or teeth.

"Ohmigod," said Ashley, "it's so amazing."

"Ohmigod, Ohmigod!" said the others.

"Can't you come up with something better than that?" Francesca asked.

"I wonder how they've got that lit," said Jacob. "Where do you suppose the floodlights are?" He got up to peer at it from one corner, then the other, of the street.

But Cassie was thinking, how did those old Greeks get the stones up there? They must have been so hard to carry. People had to really believe. They had to have passion, fervour, all those high notions Miss Morrow trumpeted.

"You know," said Dr. Laird, "the reason the Parthenon's marble is so ghostly white is that it is actually decomposing because it has been neglected all this time. They're working on its reconstruction. Look carefully and you can see the cranes."

They walked home then. A cool ovoid moon had risen. Local kids on motorbikes went by, making them feel rotten in their stupid kilts. Everyone was silent, exhausted at last.

In their room Vida and Cassie fell into bed. At some point in the night Cassie woke. The room had filled with a yellow-white glow from the window. She thought it was the moon working its way around to look in. She slid open the balcony door and went out. It wasn't the moon; it was the monument. More huge, more potent than ever. Taking the city captive in the dead of night. From this angle she could see the crane right in the middle of it. She heard an alarm sound; a searchlight moved around the base; the shadows of the trees moved restlessly across the brick face. Her view was obstructed by certain concrete roofs and gardens, and an extra-bright streetlight, but now that slowly collapsing, supercharged white temple above the soft tawny base looked as if it were being built, not like it was falling down. The cropped leafless arms of playground trees, a limp flag, the bulging rock of the hill itself, then it, this god-structure.

Cassie looked from ground to sky, following time backwards to all that time ago, when people wore sandals and gauzy tunics.

Vida was asleep, unmoved. A Dead Lady dead to the world and immune to the glories of Greece. Dead also, it seemed, to the guilt and fear that had plagued Cassie ever since they'd beaten up Ferdinand and driven his truck into the lake. Guilt because they'd hurt him badly and abused his kindness, because he loved his truck so much and they had damaged it, maybe wrecked it. Guilt because, after, nothing happened. Cassie wanted to ask someone how you got a truck to start after its innards are scraped out and dunked in water, but the only person she knew who might be able to answer was Jacob and Jacob would figure out why she was asking. Fear because she thought she might tell, without thinking, the biggest secret she'd ever had. She might blurt, she might burble, she might mix up her words and let it out, hum it, or twirl it. There were so many ways to tell. And then for sure the Dead Ladies would kill her.

Cassie couldn't sleep at all. This happened more and more: the secret did not go away with time but became a heavier burden. What had become of Ferdinand? Cassie dragged a chair and a blanket out onto the balcony. The air was colder and she could hear a hum, a low rumble like an approaching army. Was it the sea pounding? Maybe, because it wasn't very far away. She sat staring at the gleaming crown of this Acropolis, which she knew from history lectures, willing it to carry her away from her troubles, to bring her peace. She thought after a long time that it might be working. Miss Morrow would be happy: Greece had begun to enter her soul.

The next morning she was not so sure. By eight a.m. they stood at the foot of the hill; Miss Morrow insisted they see the Acropolis before the tour buses took over. However a dozen were there already, belching out grey smoke to add to the *nefos*.

Everyone said it was hotter than normal for this time of year. Cassie did not feel well. She gazed up at a hill of grey and white rubble in piles, steep staircases, falling down pillars way up on top and thought, do I have to climb this?

"*Acro* is high. *Polis* is city. Remember? Tell me, why would a tribe chose to live on a hill?"

"To see all around?"

"To keep in shape climbing up?"

"To make your slaves work hard carrying everything up the stairs?" said Jacob. He was panting and sweating already.

"As punishment?"

"Yeah."

"Because the air is better," said Vida. "You get a breeze."

Dr. Laird lost patience with their guessing.

"Tribe! Think! Primitive people, despite their lovely statues! With enemies all around. Because it was a fortress!"

"Jesus, man," whispered Vida under her breath. "Don't have a coronary."

"To have a refuge from enemy attack!" Dugald roared again only slightly less loudly. "The kings lived up there. Commoners lived below. When they were attacked they all ran up the hill."

As they walked up the dry rubble-strewn hillside, Cassie tripped and went down on one knee. She heard Miss Morrow say that the entrance was named for some French guy who found it under a Turkish rampart.

Dr. Laird said this was the culmination of Greek architecture.

Maureen said it was total bullshit and Ashley said she was tired.

Dr. Laird sprang on to a small set of steps above them. His thin arms flapped. "'For Athens alone of her contemporaries,'" he sang out, "'is found when tested to be greater than her reputation.' What am I quoting? What am I quoting? Boys? Girls?"

"Pericles' funeral speech by Thucydides," said Jacob.

Everyone stared at him, eyes hooded with hatred.

"Yes!" shouted Dugald. "'We have forced every sea and land to be the highway of our daring and everywhere whether for evil or good have left imperishable monuments behind us.' Remember that, imperishable monuments. But are they? I think not!

"There are three kinds of stones. You'll see limestone and un-baked bricks. Ancient Athens was built of unbaked bricks. And the third is of course marble. As Miss Morrow has told you, marble comes directly from our souls. You will see when you get closer. Everywhere you look, let it sink inside you. Marble. Long-lasting, lustrous. As hard as any stone anywhere. But not eternal. Take note."

They climbed some more. Dugald paused so that they could re-group around him. The steps were dusty and crowded; it was grow-ing hotter by the minute. They had had too much or too little sleep. They had eaten too many eggs at breakfast, or not enough.

"Cecrops was the first king of Athens. He was part-man, part-myth. We will see how the cult of Athena displaced that of Poseidon in the time of Cecrops.

"There are two stories. One is that Poseidon offered a horse, for war, while Athena offered an olive tree, for peace. The people pre-ferred peace. What do you think? I doubt it. The other story is that there was one more woman than man to vote, so the women, who all voted for Athena and her olive tree, won. That was too much for the Greeks so they took away the vote from women and they were never equal citizens again until this century."

"Oh, *right,*" said Vida.

"Yes, it was right."

Dr. Laird liked to tease Vida. It was a flirtation. She didn't like men but men liked her. He continued to toil uphill.

"How many times? How many times was the Acropolis stormed and overtaken? Let's count. Xerxes sacked Athens in 480 BC and he was only the first one they wrote about. The Romans took it in 146 BC. It was taken again 400 years later. In this millennium the Franks, the Catalans, the Venetians, the Florentines and finally the Turks took it. That's seven times conquered, the high city—"

"So much for living on a hill," said Maureen. "I guess that didn't work!"

The Dead Ladies laughed. They always laughed when Maureen made a joke. All except Cassie. She was excused because she was slow on the uptake and usually the joke was over long before she got it.

"It's not a laughing matter. In the seventeenth century the Turks built a mosque right in the middle of the Parthenon. They were using the Propylaia as an ammunition warehouse. And the Venetians shot at them, just as they were about to shoot their cannons at a church. The cannon fire hit the ammunition stores and the whole thing exploded: gone, the Parthenon, gone—the precious sculpture. When we get to the top, I'll show you." He walked more slowly upward, his steps dogged by the puffing and excited Jacob, who loved a good explosion more than anything.

"How do they know?" said Jacob. "It was so long ago."

Fleeter of foot, the rest of the Dead Ladies charged off after Miss Morrow. Cassie hung back with Jacob and Dr. Laird.

"There are an awful lot of catastrophes in this place," she said shyly.

"How did they blow it up?"

"They didn't exactly intend to, Jacob."

"They'd have to have quite a lot of explosives. Marble is very heavy—"

"I'm sure the Turks had all they needed..."

"Boom Ka boom. Rat-a-tat tat."

Jacob began to dance around as if he were holding an Uzi and it were the funniest imaginable toy—ratta tat tat ha ha ha hee hee hee.

Dr. Laird looked ruffled but not particularly put out. Then Dimitri and Darrin and Chino came running over to join the fun. They went wild, spazzing and gyrating all over the hill, laughing all the while. Cassie's humming began. People told her to stop making a noise but she wasn't actually making a noise; the noise was emerging of its own accord. It was a vibration in the core of her; that vibration, its potential to erupt, was lodged inside as surely as a baby was lodged in a mother's womb. Making orders to control it was vain, utterly vain. Cassie stopped walking, frightened, not knowing what to do. Suddenly Vida was there.

"Crazy boys," she said, casting a killing look at them. "Jerking off all over the place like a bunch of freaks. What are you, a firing squad? Oh, that's cool." The sarcasm slowed them down a bit, and Cassie's humming slowed at the same time; she squeezed Vida's hand.

Cassie tried to listen but she did not hear. She saw Dr. Laird's words float over her head like the seagulls, cackling, screaming, leaving no impression, no meaning. She was numbed by the Greek sun, by the ancient rocks, by the importance of it all. She felt the unaccustomed lick of warmth on her neck, her face, her arms and bare legs under the kilt. She saw Vida give a little kick at Dimitri and mouth a few words of hostility. Dr Laird's mouth opened and closed, on a sweeping gesture of his hand.

At once Miss Morrow stepped in front of him to lead them on up the steps between the crumbling columns. The stone looked like sponge, like those orange/beige lumps that hung outside all the Greek grocery stores. Cassie felt sick, as if she were seeing all this from a long way above: the Manor on its famous Field Trip to Greece. Only ten does not make a school. They were more like some greatly diminished tribe returning from forty years in the wilderness. Over the side of the hill Miss Morrow pointed out the Sacred Way through the Agora. On the great feast of Athens a procession came here to offer the *peplos* to the goddess Athena. A woolen dress, made to be worn by her statue in the middle of the Acropolis, it took a priestess and her helpers nine months to weave and was yellow with pictures of the Greek gods doing battle with giants.

It seemed amazing to Cassie that such a parade would be conducted, and that it was all to do with women. Goddesses, priestesses, dresses. The whole idea was faintly embarrassing: why would grownup men even bother to march around with a special dress in their hands, for presentation? Of course there were queens. The Queen of England for instance had a long ermine cloak. But even queens just got there by accident it seemed, when for some reason a king hadn't worked out. Women must have been more important in the old days.

She stilled the thought, because she knew that Miss Morrow would pooh-pooh and cluck-cluck her; Vida would snarl and hork and spit into the gutter telling her she was full of shit; her mother would say, Oh, Cassie, dear, you mustn't say that, your cousin has just graduated first in her medical class and even your mother has a perfectly good job... But did any of this matter? Something there is that doesn't love a wall, she remembered. Something there is that doesn't love a woman would be more like it. Tell that to Robert Frost. She scared herself: she was starting to sound like Vida. But it was true. You could tell, you could tell, you could tell. From the ugly way boys laughed at you when you had your period. From the number of times the sexy girl was killed in movies. It got so bad she could predict: if they had big tits and wore tight dresses they'd be dead by halfway through, or if not dead then tied up with a strip of cloth stuffed in their mouth, eyeballs rolling up in wordless terror.

The group was now trailing over to the tower. Except it didn't look at all like a tower.

Miss Morrow was gaining amplitude.

"This spot is dedicated to Nike, goddess of victory. It has served as a lookout from the west in ancient times. Look all around you—" the long, eloquent hand came out—"Do you see the Saronic Gulf, the Peloponnese over to your right, and down there the port of Piraeus? Who recalls the myth of Theseus and the Minotaur? Theseus freed Athens from paying tribute in blood to the Minoans. Every year seven men and seven maidens went off under black sail to die under the hooves of the Cretan bull."

Cassie shivered, hot and cold at the same time.

"It was on this spot Theseus' father Aegeus stood watching for his son, the hero, to return." Miss Morrow looked out expectantly. The pause was so long someone had to speak.

"There's a bit about the black sails," muttered Maureen.

"Yes, black sails if?"

"If he was dead."

"And Theseus did what?"

"He forgot to change the sails."

"So Aegeus thought?"

"His son was dead."

"Dead, and so what did Aegeus do?"

Chills ran up and down Cassie's back. Here, she thought, right here. It happened. She'd loved the story when she'd learned it, how Ariadne had given her young suitor a ball of yarn and how Theseus killed the Minotaur who was eating the seven maidens and seven youths each year. And then they escaped to Naxos where Theseus, she recalled, did something nasty to Ariadne.

"Aegeus threw himself off the rocks," said Miss Morrow. "Believing what was not true, and that was the tragedy. Because Theseus was returning alive, a hero."

"Why didn't he just check it out?" Vida blurted. "It makes no sense. Like, wait and see. You know what I mean?"

"Why didn't he?" cried Miss Morrow, offended on behalf of the Greeks that anyone would question their myths. "Because then it wouldn't be tragic, it wouldn't be Greek, and we wouldn't even know about it!" She walked away.

Somewhere along the way on this long morning, Cassie looked back and saw that Dr. Laird had gone off on his own. It looked as if he were lecturing to a crowd of perfect strangers. They just milled around and past him; a couple stopped and seemed to be taking in his remarks. Cassie felt an awful pain, watching him. He was becoming a joke, someone to laugh at. And it was only going to get worse. It would get worse in some utter, monostrophic way. She knew.

But how did she know? It was just there inside her; and now—why? Because she was away from home? Because Vida helped her be calm enough to think? Because she was on Greek soil and like Miss Morrow felt it was her home? She realized, for the first time, that others did not know all she did. This was astonishing, and made her blush. Did she have a special gift? She didn't think so. It was very simple. It came from watching and listening. She had eyes and ears and they both trembled like the antennae of an insect. Maybe others did not pay attention. But Cassie, for so long, when she was a loser, had had nothing better to do. It was powerful, to know. Vida, who was the most powerful person Cassie knew, did not see what Cassie saw. And she did not have her blind certainty about what was to come.

But there arose the question of what to do with her knowledge. She was unaccustomed to power. She had to tell, but there was nobody to listen. She attracted no followers. She had no *charisma*. A Greek word? Probably. She was not like other people. She had this totally fucked-up tongue, as Maureen called it. She picked the wrong word and mixed up the meanings, sometimes. And when she could not explain what she knew, when it became very bad, she had no recourse but to spin. To make a spiral of herself. A spiral was stronger than just the line of a body; twirling made her own space into a den, a refuge. The spinning was her own solution. Well, maybe not a solution exactly, but a response. She tried hard to keep it under control. For now it was frightening enough to know: Miss Morrow was worried that Dr. Laird would do something really crazy. And she was justified. Just look at him.

II

THE
FRIEZE

DUGALD WAS THINKING of the epithet "scholar," which he had chosen many years ago, an epithet he had given not only himself but many Manor students. It was a better label than underachiever, delinquent or, the term favoured by the kids, "loser," which had also beckoned. But it was a label nonetheless, diminishing. The adoption of the label, and all that desperate drive to learn, to teach, had found him at the library for five hours most nights when his working day was done. He would walk away alone afterwards into the darkness and home. To Meryl who supported him, while he studied mathematics, history. After meeting Francesca he travelled and fell in love with Athens, with ancient Greece, its heroes, its draped and undraped figures, its alphabet traced back to Linear B.

Dugald to himself was a similar cipher, a sign meaning scholar, and an angry man subdued, not legible without a break in the code. He stood now at the foot of the Acropolis waving at the students who ought to follow him. In the heat of the Greek morning his own epochs floated behind him, blurry, columns of text inscribed on tablets of stone, *logos*, which he could only now decode.

At home in Toronto he could drive by a certain apartment block on Dundas Street East and realize that one of his tablets, one of his versions, if you will, was inside on the third floor, at the end of the long hall. The first of his marital homes: he'd left himself there, laughing with a woman in a yellow room with big windows. What he feared, suddenly, heart-stoppingly, was that somewhere in this set of selves—Dugald 3.1 or 6.0; Dugald uxorious or Dugald horribilus—he had misplaced the master.

Here they were, his charges, or some of them.

"See over there?" he said. "Those are the steps that lead to the Clepsydra, the ancient spring that supplied the Acropolis with water." But he did not know if the students, particular individuals of a genus and species he'd spent his life herding about, heard him. He turned and began to climb, the students behind him. They plodded upward as if history had drained the marrow out of their young bones. "Further to the left is the hill dedicated to Ares, god of war. It was there on that rock where Orestes was brought to trial for the murder of his mother Clytemnestra and her lover Aegisthus. Do you recall, incipient lawyers? The first court of law. Come, let's climb it."

Vida and the boys looked but Dugald could not tell if they saw. He imagined himself on trial, on trial for somehow avoiding his correct destiny. Or perhaps he had been tried, found guilty, and was enduring his punishment, the punishment being exile from his own past.

To climb the Areopagus was difficult, more so than he recalled. The old marble was worn so smooth and slick it was like cakes of well-used soap. Nevertheless, as he clambered on, the steps became the stairs of the little apartment on Dundas Street East. There he could see himself propped up in bed against a cold wall, coverlet on his knees, drinking milky tea and watching a woman bathe through the open door of a bathroom. Another day in the same life he was aproned, frying fish for dinner. Or sleeping with the deep abandon of youth, the woman's arms around him. He could see himself also in a high-rise on Spadina, a walk-up on Baldwin, the small two-storey house on Alice. Past selves, real selves were living there, always a few flights off the ground.

Now he saw himself on another climb, up the rock and grass slopes of the Park behind the Manor, visiting Aunt Alice with the family. He was trailed by two dark-coated children as they trudged through bronze leaves toward the pond. He was telling them about its hidden source, Taddle Creek, about the stream that was the birthing waters of their town. A woman dawdled behind. Her face was shadowed but it was Meryl, of course, the mother. And he was not, in that self, Dr. Laird, Headmaster. He was the father of his children. Known in the vernacular as Dad.

Dad! So unaccustomed was he to the nomenclature that he laughed aloud with merriment. He sprang confidently, forgetting his age, from one bulge of slippery rock to the next. "Come along, group," he called. They straggled up the rock face in his wake. He had thrived, these many years, on the more elevated but no less passionate relations of schoolmaster and student. His blood children had vanished somewhere along the way and he was conscious of little regret, for their place had been filled by a thousand others. But father he had been, and his vision today was proof. He looked more closely at the man he saw strolling on that other, softer slope. A kind enough young man but hiding restless, ruthless energy. The energy of anger. The incarnation was so bleached with time there was little pain left in the vision. Perhaps what he was feeling now was a desire to enfold this past, to bring it forward to today. But it would be impossible. Loyalties conflicted. He had, before, worshipped at another temple. Simply put, women divided him from his old self. *Women.* Well, one woman. And thus hived off, the former selves eroded, subsided, became silent. The man he once was resigned to being history. Angry once, gesticulating, fornicating, time had settled him down.

Raising his eyes, he searched for the rest of the group. He was father to the students of the Manor, the several thousand or more of them on whom he'd lavished his attentions year in and year out. He was patient, amused, distanced by Francesca's fanfare, occasionally dangerous: all the things a paterfamilias wished to be. He was Head/Master, a force to be contended with, anger ever at the ready under a surface of genial tolerance. A man not to be messed with, despite the missing toenails. In fact, their removal was a sign that he was his own lethal weapon. To those other children, seeded in the hapless, untidy Meryl with her ignorant passions, he had been only a shadow, a wound, at best a refuge in dreams and delusions.

To think they were both over fifty now. And strangers. All this time their mother had been singular, devoted, he supposed. Meryl there in her shapeless cloth coat amongst the fallen leaves of 1947 was a woman who had once done him a favour, no more. So he had thought. Women's favours obliged no one to any form of repayment. They were given out of nature and necessity, and their granting could not be seen as an act of virtue for that reason.

"So: we stand on the Areopagus. Where Orestes was tried for matricide. It's quite a crime, that, killing your mother. The tragedians—Euripides, for instance—attempted to justify it. But no one ever succeeded. They called Euripides a misogynist, but they were wrong, weren't they? His women were real. They suffered."

Dugald wondered why the lecture kept swaying into these waters. What made the relations between man and woman the topic here? Was it simply his musings, or were there messages embedded in these rocks that begged new interpretation? Underfoot, the marble shone as if it had been polished by hand. Little plants lived in the cracks as did discarded boxes of Kodak film. He braced himself against losing his balance. There was a lovely breeze up here, Vida was right. "To the south we see the Pnyx. This was where the Athenians voted, after there were too many of them to use the Agora for the purpose." The view was superb: the water was visible through the *nefos* and, out in it, rippling hilly islands like castles diminishing into the distance. The students were pushing each other, trying to make their friends fall.

"The people, the citizens, who as you know were only the free males, voted to spend the money to build these extravagant structures. They persevered, they laboured, they made the brick from local mud and mined the marble. Pericles had his overseer. Thucydides was against the spending, did you know? How would you like to go down in history as having been against the building of the Parthenon? He said that Athenians were 'dressing their city like a harlot.' That's sexist, isn't it Vida?"

She took the bait.

"This is your famous democracy? Only men were citizens? That sucks." Vida walked beside him, her plume of orangey hair making her look like a cockatiel.

Dugald smiled and continued. "Men were citizens; women were their chattel. *Given* in marriage. Do you know that Socrates gives thanks for not being born a woman, a beast or a foreigner? And yet, observe," he said. "Athens is named for a goddess, Athena. How do we explain this?"

The breeze stopped for a moment. The sun was going to be hot. The air was going to be foul. Dugald felt slightly light-headed already, but that could have been anything, disorientation due to the time change. "I shall tell you. The oracle at Delphi told the Athenians that they had to choose between the olive tree, gift of Athena, goddess of wisdom and war, and the salt-spring or the horse—depending on whom you listen to—which was the gift of Poseidon, god of the sea."

"You told us this already," said Vida, but of course he did not hear her. Nor did he remember saying all this before.

"Those who voted for Athena's gifts outnumbered Poseidon's supporters. Poseidon was angry to have been defeated. In order to placate him the city decided to punish women in three ways. First, they would never be allowed to vote again. Second, no child could take its mother's name. And third, no one could call women Athenians."

"Greeks!" said Vida. She hissed and got all her cohorts hissing as well. She was a bit dogged, that girl, he thought, but charming. At least her anger had a focus: men. Dugald thought it wise to change the subject.

"And over there—the church of Ayios Loumbaradiaris. Can you see? Look there across the road to the rounded red roof tiles. You'll like this, Jacob. The church is named for the cannons that saved it."

Another story?

"Yes, indeed. The Turks, as I may have said, had a garrison inside the Parthenon. And on this day they had trained the cannons of the Propylaia on the church, because it was a Christian church and the Turks were Muslim. As the people in the church began to sing the Turks prepared their fire. But just as they went to light the cannons a thunderbolt came down and blew up the garrison!"

"I thought it was the Venetians," objected someone, in vain.

"But look. We are in danger of losing our fearless leader and must press on." Dugald clapped a hand on Jacob's shoulder more for balance than out of affection and began to climb down.

At a point in life one's history begins to count, to matter, deeds and goods to accrue. We never know this point except on looking backwards. Dugald had always thought his moment had been when he first met Francesca on Taddle Creek Drive. He had willed it to be that day. For what is a man but the expression of his will; what is his life but the story he tells himself? There is no editor to check the rewriting of personal histories, no rival historians to point out the errors. The other tale—that which he has decided will not count, and will be forgotten—is nothing. One cannot expect a man to hang on to recollections in which he figures badly, or to wish to be confronted with self-evident failure.

No, Dugald was not unsatisfied with his choices. It was only— but nothing. Nothing came to mind to finish that sentence, nothing but an airy vacancy in the poisoned atmosphere, filled in a trice by a breeze across a fresh field of long grass. Some ancient, forgotten scent, what was that? A wildflower native to Greece, or was it Ontario? Orange blossom? Or some plant favoured by the gods? He regretted that they could not relive the olfactory experiences of antiquity. Of course with little washing or refrigeration the whole place stank to high heaven. But there were also flowers, wine and the sweat of maidens. What scent was now on the wind? Tantalizing, erotic, even—the perfume of remorse. There was, at its source, the possibility of another way of being, a dreamt-of door to a place long unvisited. He turned his face to follow it but the scent was gone, replaced by noxious diesel fumes.

One was all you got. One life, one story. He had made his choice, although—he hated to consider it now—he had been thirty-five when he made it. All of his adult life that had gone before that choice was to be discounted, erased. Exeunt. Omnis. He had met Francesca; he had fallen in love with Francesca. Immediately, easily, Meryl and the children had faded. They had gone limp like marionettes on a stage, the performance over, the lights out; they had been eviscerated, dried out, mummified. If he thought of them at all it was as heaps of clothing on a dusty floor. Of course he knew, he had to know, that they continued on, that they had grown, shouted, failed, thrived, even loved without him. But he did not choose to revive them in his mind by thinking of it. It was a good thing too, because Francesca would never have stood for anything else. *For the Lord our god is a jealous God.* Or goddess, as the case may be.

They had not risen up, that is, until these last few months.

And today a new idea came to him, as he achieved the foot of the Areopagus, leaning heavily on Jacob. It was that his refusal to see his wife and his children as existing outside his memory arose not from strength of will, but from fear of pain. The idea shocked him. A martial artist learned to tolerate, even to welcome bodily pain; he could rise above it. Dugald knew himself to be a master of his nerve endings and his deep gut aches. But perhaps he was a coward about damage to the heart?

It was a shocking realization. But—weakened by travel? inspired by the sacred site?—one he instantly knew to be true. Heaven help me, he protested inwardly. I am too old to learn such a thing about myself. He caught sight of the crowd of students. They stood at the base of the Propylaia. This was the place where he always began to lecture in earnest.

"Pelasgian wall," he said, speeding up and pointing to the south, over the edge of the staircase. "Made of quarried stone from a chasm northwest of the Hill of Nymphs. That way." He pointed off into the foggy reaches of the city where it could just be made out. "You'll notice the stone is bluish-grey with a tinge of red-brown in the broken places. Wall dates from the Mycenaean period. Was the fortification of Athens. Stood for seven centuries up to 480 BC and did the job. It made an ellipse around the Acropolis. Ancient, ancient," muttered Dugald, "one thousand years before the birth of Christ. Imagine that."

But the enormous span of time, rather than putting his misdemeanours in perspective, served only to make it seem like yesterday that Dugald had walked away from the people with whom he had mingled his blood. And all because he did not want to feel! It was alarming. His heart begin to pound.

"I told you the Persians came and sacked Athens. Everything you see on the Acropolis has been rebuilt on top of what was here before the invasion. For instance, the Parthenon. A completely new temple. Begun in 447 BC on the ruins of the older one. Do you know what Pericles said? He said, 'Of the shrines burnt and overthrown by the barbarians I will rebuild none, but I will allow them to remain as a memorial to those who come after, of the impiety of the barbarians.'"

This was marvellously meaningful to Dugald, and had been for as long as he could remember. And yet, he saw the kids beginning to stare around to the north, to the east, from the hill, wondering what was out there in the modern city. He was losing his audience. Of course, there are no barbarians, to the young, Dugald thought. Or rather, they are all barbarians. Who is it we must keep out?

"It was necessary to build a new wall," he began again. "The second one was called the Themistoclean wall and enclosed a much bigger area than the Pelasgian. Why do you think that was?" He waited the obligatory few seconds but no hands were forthcoming. He had the sense he was racing through his guided tour but he didn't exactly care. "Why? Because the methods of warfare had become more sophisticated and the city needed greater protection. You can see the Themistoclean wall from many places in Athens. All the people participated in its erection. They threw in whatever they had, including old bricks, uncut stones, funeral monuments. Mortared it all together. Nothing carved to fit. No time. And now we must follow our leader. Who can see Miss Morrow in the throng? We're off to the Erechtheion," he explained to his audience, "where the Kings lived."

"The *erection*," Vida repeated to Cassie in a stage whisper. They began to giggle. One of the boys heard them and passed it on. "*Erection, erection*. Ha, ha, ha."

Dugald heard, his old fuzzy ears expert at getting the under-the-breath comment while missing what was shouted out loud. Some sex madness was invading these children. He lifted his hand and pointed.

They regrouped in front of the Erechtheion.

"Notice that this temple is feminine, as compared with the masculine feel of the Parthenon, which we will be coming to. Here were worshipped Gaia, Mother Earth, and, after her, Athena. Erectheus was a mythical king of Athens, thought to be a son of Gaia. Both Erectheus and Cecrops were serpents, from the waist down. The snake was the female symbol, you know that don't you?" The girls looked blank. "Athena, you will recall, was the daughter of Zeus. She was born when Zeus had a headache. He asked Hephaestus to hit him on the head with an axe. Hephaestus did, and Athena sprang fully grown and armed from the slash in his forehead."

"Did they actually believe in this stuff?" asked Maureen, kilt low on her hips, which she thrust forward insolently.

"Believe?" said Francesca. "Please remove that dreadful gum from your mouth. I wonder what that means, in fact. *Need* is a better word. The Greeks needed their myths. And so do we. Reality is too complicated, and there is too much of it." A magnificent glare silenced Maureen. "We will hear more of Hephaestus. He was the god of metal workers and his temple stands in the Agora below.

The top of the Acropolis hill was growing crowded as the sun rose in the sky. Other school groups were scattered over the rough terrain; other students equally were being instructed in the grandeurs of the monuments.

"A second part of the temple was dedicated to Poseidon," Miss Morrow continued. "There was a crypt underneath, and an opening that led to underground water. This was a spring that was said to have been created out of rock when Poseidon struck it with his trident. The sound of the sea could be heard whenever the south wind blew."

Underground water; that was the part of Francesca's speech that Dugald picked up.

"The Clepsydra, of course, was dry."

Had all the springs of the earth gone dry? He wondered. It felt so. Or gone into sewers. Never mind. Dugald had begun to rather like repugnant constructions like sewers. It was, however, heresy to say so. As he had done before countless times in his marriage he rejoiced in the privacy of thoughts: he was grateful beyond saying that Francesca could not read his mind. Because a further heretical thought occurred to him: rather than the Taddle having been swallowed into filth and thus removed from the bright shining light of day, perhaps the filth and sewage, which was after all man's natural product, had been wrongly, unjustly, stolen from the day.

Hidden springs. He had been habituated to the belief in their powers from his boyhood by the Taddle. He had set out in the world with the belief in a community of mutually dependent men living on a hill, elevated above the beasts, approaching the gods. Indeed he had founded one. Marvellous. Except that living there had diverted him from that other underground stream, which he might now call his real life.

A laughable concept, *real life*; certainly Francesca would laugh at it. And yet. As swiftly as a night cloudbank could obliterate the most resplendent moon, this notion had overtaken him and thrown him into confusion. There *was* another life he might have lived, another mould into which he might have poured his molten passions. This other life was most un-Greek and not at all mythical. There was nothing idealized about it. It featured no savage divinities, no transformations. It had to do with messy blood relations and failed endeavours, with anger and nonsense, with living in the fetid pool of one's mistakes and even the mistakes of others, of "hanging in"—horrid phrase—to see what nature, in taking its course, made of this rich compost.

He tried to see himself in that life, but he could not.

Francesca allowed time for the students to regroup in view of the six beauties who held up the porch roof.

"And now we come to the magnificent porch of the Caryatids. Do you see how they look proudly down on the Parthenon and on the sacred route of the procession? And how effortlessly they bear the weight upon their heads?"

How effortlessly they bear the weight, indeed. If he didn't know her better he'd have thought Francesca was a feminist, Dugald remarked to Dimitri, at least he imagined that he had remarked on this to Dimitri, but Dimitri's puzzled face looking back at him through a haze or cloud of some kind gave no hint. He was a dim boy, always had been, Dugald thought. He was certain he'd had this conversation with Francesca, at one point. She had defended the boy. The problem with the system at the Manor, the problem with being the kind of teachers he and his inamorata had been, was that they could make a good student out of any diligent soul, of any idiot in fact and this in itself at the end of the day deflated all that they stood for in scholasticism, excellence, merit. In any case, he continued, this time not bothering to open his mouth and make the remarks out loud to anyone, his point was that no one with a figure like Francesca's could have dreamt of being a feminist—37-19-35 it was, or close.

At the end of our exertions we discover that we have been working against ourselves. Something like that—he watched his wife. She was magnificent. However, it did not matter, he realized. He'd come to the realization that he could no longer take her seriously.

It is possible, thought Dugald, to live thirty or even fifty years in a dream.

"The Caryatids have lost their hands and their arms," said Cassie.

"Indeed," said Francesca. "What would you have?"

"They'd look a lot better if they were complete—"

"Do you think so? I disagree. I think if they had their hands they'd be tacky," Francesca said, and the unfortunate girl shut her mouth recognizing that she'd been squashed.

They approached the Parthenon. Dugald never failed to marvel at the temple. Under his arm, he felt Francesca's tremor, and he knew that the same feeling was invading her. He thought of the glorious works of man he and Francesca had taken in together, through eyes, ears, intelligence. Together they had wept at the beauties passed down to them. Beauty without extravagance, so said Pericles, and that had been Dugald and Francesca's ideal. Although perhaps, in the last twenty years, they had overspent on luxury items, car for him, clothing for her, hotels, bedsheets, meals. It hardly mattered. Their hearts were in the right place.

The temple was slightly tipped, on an angle to appear more imposing from this direction, the direction of general approach. Not only that but the base was tilted: the west facade was nearly half a metre higher than the east, to enhance the view of those who approached from the Propylaia. All of this had been demonstrated. Pericles. Phidias, the *episkopos*. Ictinus. Callicrates. Their geometry impeccable and their generosity extraordinary.

Oh, yes, Dugald had much to tell about the structure. How the vertical lines were not exact, in either the columns, nor the walls or colonnades; the columns inclined inward. How, if extended, they would actually meet, a mile and a half overhead. The columns thickened in the middle as well, at angles of the peristyle, by 1/40 of their diameter. And why was that? Because otherwise, seen against the bright sky—instead of against the cella walls like the others—they would have seemed lighter, and in the corners weaker. It was no accident but deliberate, produced by mathematical calculations.

"Speak, darling," said Francesca, as if he had been delaying. He looked in her direction, puzzled: had she been addressing him while his mind was elsewhere? It hardly mattered, he said to himself, and although the phrase had a ring of familiarity he did not recall that he had said it to himself several minutes earlier. Time for his lecture on the Parthenon. He must give it, since they'd brought these little monsters all the way to Greece.

Words of the roar of Dugald's mind spilled out into the still, hot air. It was as if the words were escaping, not just for once, but forever, as if they wanted to flee his head to make way for other, more savage utterances. He tried.

"The Parthenon is a temple of the Doric order with certain Ionic touches," he began. "The steps are of Pentelic marble. It has all the refinements of Doric architecture..." He slowed. Even as they rushed forth, he felt within himself an utterly novel reluctance to part with the ideas that he had been caressing in the privacy of his mind. But a teacher does not stint in expressing what he knew, he scolded himself, and pushed onward. "These include tiny deviations from the straight, the vertical, the horizontal and from normal dimensions, all of which gave greater beauty, anticipated optical illusions and served a practical purpose." Was this where he and Francesca had gone wrong? he suddenly thought. They sought perfection. There had been no room for the endearing deviations that enhanced beauty by *anticipating* irregularities in human perceptions. The idea seized hold of him, and his mind began to run on two tracks simultaneously.

"Above the massive architraves all ninety-two metopes were carved in high relief," he said. "Above the triglyph metope frieze was beaded astragal…the marble acroteria crowning the pediments were not in the form of figures but of great floral ornaments…"

He knew he was talking mumbo-jumbo. Neither Vida nor Dimitri, Maureen nor even Jacob could understand. He thought he might tell the students that by looking up between the columns on the inside of the colonnade they could peek at the remnants of the frieze. This was Dugald's favourite thing to do, but of course much of the frieze had been carted away by the Brits. You had to be in London, at the British Museum. Still, you could imagine it, marvel that it had been carved in position high upon the wall. He realized that he had stopped speaking. He heard Francesca's voice trill out and circle round the students, like a yapping sheepdog or a lariat, hauling them in. For a moment his mind lifted and seemed to watch the scene, so familiar, after all these years, of himself and his wife and a group of students approaching the greatest temple of them all. He was confused.

Cassie, the strange one, sidled up to him.

"It's wonderful here, Dr. Laird," she said. "You make it so special. I know we're lucky to be here with you."

His eyes met hers. He had noticed her, moving warily through the crowds, as if she expected an assassin to burst out of the clusters of tourists with dangling camera bags. Alarmingly, his eyes filled up with tears; it was as if he could see directly into her eyes. There was pain at the bottom of the deep grey pool. *Cistern*, he thought.

"Sister?" she said.

"Cistern, it's the word I'm giving you today."

"You've given me so many."

"But you never use them correctly, my dear," he said, laughing. He put his white gnarled hand on hers for a moment. "But thank you."

He loved it here. He loved the stories; the heroes and the envious gods—"They did not love people," he would thunder there in the airless classrooms of the Manor—were so close to his heart. Had he managed to pass on his love to his students? And why, he wondered now, if we can have reverence for the most beautiful, the highest places in a city, why can we not have reverence for the low? What about those sewers? Is it really respect for the Greeks we have here or a tourists' opportunism? Why not just have it all blown up by the Turks again?"

He must have spoken aloud.

"Yeah," said Jacob. "Right on."

Dugald's thoughts took an unexpected jog. This boy became animated only and specifically by the idea of blowing things up. Yet Dugald sympathized with him. If there was no will to preserve it, why not have it blown up? Before the Acropolis turned into a Disneyfication of itself.

"Jacob, for you I have a special expedition. You want to know about blowing it up? I can show you. And you, too, Cassie; we shall make a special trip."

Miss Morrow saw him lose track of his lecture, and, waving her arm, drew the students away.

And now the three of them stood, a day later, in the cool, white, ground-floor rooms of the Centre for Acropolis Studies. "You don't get much of a crowd here," Dugald said. Only a few dogged guides and schoolmasters, as well as the odd classical scholar with that mad gleam in his eye. Still it was bustling with jean-clad young Greeks all engaged in the reconstruction. Dugald stood with his head tilted upward. Jacob and Cassie tilted their heads upward, too.

"This is the frieze. The best remaining copy of it."

How he loved the frieze and the procession that was pictured there. Loved it so well he could imagine himself inside it, partaking of its ongoing, frozen present tense.

"What is it?"

"A parade, that's all. Can you tell?"

He loved the stilled excitement of it all, the tossing heads of horses, the charioteers jumping down or up from their position. The oxen straining against their yokes. Surrounded this way, in peace and harmony, by the massive bodies of the gods.

At the end of the parade, the people had arrived at the Temple. The gods were waiting, seated, in order that their superhuman size would fit into the tableau, which was only one metre high. The Olympians were easy to recognize, like famous actors, he thought, with their trademark clothing or props. Zeus was on his throne with his sceptre. Athena was off to the right, and winged Nike was having a wreath placed on her head. "That's Demeter, downcast, mourning her daughter Persephone.

"You see the Athenians are presenting the *peplos* to Athena. How secure, how safe the Athenians must have felt, looking up at this rendering of their activities. They could see this homage had been performed over and over. They could see the invincible participants, believe in them, year in and year out."

He was growing tearful again. There was something here about veils. The mortals of the frieze were embraced by the immortals of the pediments and the heroes of the metopes. In such a way the city was bracketed, enclosed, in rings, the *kredemna*, the veils, which divide civilization and order from the pressing chaos of the uncivilized world that lay beyond. Think of what was out there: barbarians, giants, Amazons. Athena perfectly represented the city then, an armed maiden, never to be unveiled, to have her protection loosened; she was unassailable.

He had always imagined Francesca as Athena. Majestic, and—it astonished Dugald to realize this—a maiden. Miss Morrow, after all. Never Mrs. Laird. That had been someone else. It was Francesca's very unassailable maidenliness that had kept him enthralled for five decades.

"This is the only place you can see the whole long frieze," he said to the two of them. "The whole 110 metres of it—do you see? It was hung this way, above your heads, and you could see the story of the Panathenaic Procession if you walked along it. There they were, the people and the animals of Athens: boys driving cattle to sacrifice, the water carriers, *hydrophoroi*, as they were called, with jugs on their shoulders. And here, a group of elderly men carrying olive branches, at least they're supposed to be carrying olive branches, but the branches were painted on, so they have disappeared."

"How do you know they're older?"

"Look, they've stopped quite still. They're chatting, the way old people do. And they're a little thicker in the body."

"How do you know they had olive branches?"

"Oh, people know. They study these things, spend a lifetime doing it. There are musicians, too, with guitars and flutes. And look at this part—a four-horse chariot with a marshal trying to get the horse behind to stop before he crashes into someone. Here's where you can feel the excitement of the parade. Look, how high the horse's hooves go—"

"He's rearing up—"

"That man is naked—did they go in parades that way?" asked Cassie, shocked.

The light came in from the windows and struck the frieze. It was a good copy, cut from the original moulds and now in better shape than the original, over there in London.

"You know what's weird? The carvings aren't so deep. It's really more like pictures than anything, I mean like pictures with bumps, but when the shadows fall on it the figures fill out just like sculpture."

"That's very good, Jacob. The relief does that. It gives the impression these people are fully rounded. Do you see how clever the carvers were? They've made the horses overlap one another, and the riders overlap too. If you count you can see; they are in ranks of seven, and yet the carved stone is never more than seven inches deep.

"They look so real."

"No, they don't. They're too perfect," objected Cassie.

Jacob nodded. "No parade was ever this perfect."

"No, but perhaps the people wanted to remember it this way. They wanted to feel that it was immediate, and alive—see how much action there is! The hooves dancing up and down, the horse's heads in waves. Look, these young men are wonderful. The apobates. Do you know what they are? Hoplites—soldiers with helmets and round shields—see? That circle there? It was a game. They had to leap on and off the chariot while the charioteer made it go full speed. Sometimes they had to leap off and run a race with the horses."

"Poor things," said Cassie. "Did they lose?"

"Sometimes they must have won." He walked ahead a little. "This is all from the North Frieze. You see, it went all around the walls. The others are here, East and West and South."

"You know what's weird? They all have different speeds. Like the winds. East has a different speed to west. How did they keep together?"

"Very good, Jacob. But in a parade it's always that way, isn't it? Some sections go faster and then others have to rush to catch up. Look at the marshal, how he has to restrain those overeager horses or they'll trample the ones in front."

"Look at that guy, he's like not holding the bridle because he's fixing that band in his hair."

"It's a laurel wreath. Apollo's tree, remember?"

"You can tell the frieze was carved to go exactly in place, because the marshal makes them all slow down to turn the corner!"

Their voices fell innocently into the silence of the great white room. It was so still now, where the procession rode, like a morgue with vaulted windows beyond it, the city under its also-white haze at one remove, the floor of white tiles echoing the youthful cheer.

Dugald was happy.

"I am happy," he thought. Here under the flying torsos, the seated thighs and legs. The waists draped and undraped, folded cloth revealing one breast or another rib cage stretched to perform some task.

"The south one, here, is very busy. There's a marshal and six horsemen in cavalcade. These are eroded badly."

"How did they get ruined?"

"We're coming to that, Jacob. You'll be entranced, I promise you."

"They're blurred to almost nothing. It looks like they're just going faster, but it's just that they're wearing out. I think Miss Morrow is right," said Cassie. "This stuff actually gets better as it gets wrecked."

Dugald smiled; it was true teaching if you couldn't be sure who said what, teacher or student.

"Look at this guy, he can't be walking at all; his legs are wrapped tight in cloth right to his ankles—"

"He can like move his arm and let the fabric loose if he wants to walk, I guess."

"Look at this guy, he's stepping up on a chest to reach up to his horse."

"And here the horse is scratching its nose with its hoof."

"Where are the girls? There's got to be girls. I thought it was all about giving that dress to the goddess," said Cassie.

"Are you going to be Vida now?" asked Dugald, laughing at her. Cassie looked startled, and blushed, so that he felt sorry. "Look," he said, "here are three girls, with discs in their hands."

"Yeah, like they're bringing their CDs to play."

"Yeah, right."

Jacob and Cassie moved off together, talking.

So Dugald had done one good thing, bringing these two out-casts together.

How to explain the peace here?

Something again to do with the life not lived. How Dugald would have loved to have been a part of the work! To be one of these casual professionals listening to their radios while drawing on graph paper a dissolving 2,500-year-old masterpiece. He turned away, smiling. Each year on returning to the Acropolis he fell in love again. Then he grew indignant that this perfect beauty should be in the condition it was. Decaying, eroding, "falling down," as Sara had observed. That these monumental creations should all end up as dust underfoot had enraged him as a young man. They could be saved! He could put himself in mind of all that now, simply by pressing a switch.

This was the song he once sang. The hope of his life, not so many years ago. His proudest plan. He, Dugald Laird of Taddle Creek Drive in Toronto, had a solution to the collapse of the Parthenon and its marble. But there had been such resistance! He could hear himself selling the idea: "Take a moment to consider, if you will. Silicone spray is resistant to water, to time, to cold, to heat. It is easily applied to large surfaces with spray guns mounted on a rolling vehicle. They could move in the trucks and spray it tomorrow." It was reasonable. It was possible. Permanence for this beauteous structure was within the grasp of all humans. But it was too simple for people. He had offered once, and had been rebuffed. The Greeks—one hardly wished to call them Greeks, they were so obdurate and backward—had refused it.

Unbidden before his eyes rose the image of a cartoon that had appeared in the newspaper at the time. Mr. Brentwood and Dr. Laird had been mocked, cruelly represented as yokels with water guns.

He realized the students were gone. They reappeared in a door-way down the hall.

"Dr. Laird, look! We found it. About the blowing up."

"Didn't I promise you?"

Jacob was ecstatic: a whole room full of drawings of the catastrophe—the lightning bolt, the explosion of ammunition after which blocks of marble flew in all directions, how fifty metres of frieze fell off.

"Oh man, can you see it? Like, splinters of marble flying through the air that would shave your head off. Those Turks. I bet the Parthenon killed them, not the gunpowder. And stuff just dropping. Like these huge blocks. Can you imagine if one fell on you? Oh man, you'd be pounded so thin, you'd be spread out like three times your size. The blood would fly out. And then it would be so dusty, no one could see? And man, the fire!"

Jacob started to dance.

"Oh man, this is how I'll do it. I'll take the camera back a long way—pan across—show the figures so tiny and helpless one minute then zoom in on a mother and her baby the next, to make it all the more terrifying."

He slid sideways into the display room, his pretend movie camera on his shoulder, back to the walls like an armed robber trying to get out with the goods, and panned across the engravings of the Acropolis in various stages of eruption.

"Like a volcano it goes, spewing rock and flame. And the Turks go running, oh yeah, I can show their faces up close, the sweat on their lips, their hands trembling as they try to scoop up their belongings—"

"Jacob, you're scaring me," said Cassie. "Do you hear it?"

"Hear what?"

The tiny cries of agony, as if they came from a toy-sized city: children wailing, timbers splitting, colonnades crashing, feet running.

"I don't, my dear," Dugald said kindly. "But then I'm deaf, you know."

"I don't like this, Jacob," Cassie insisted, her voice high. "You're too good." She started to hum and shift her feet. She started to look dangerous.

"Get Vida," said Jacob absently to Dr. Laird with his eye stuck to the tiny eyepiece of his imagined camera.

"Vida?"

"She helps her."

"I see."

"He's just making a movie," said Dugald, and ventured a little laugh. Sometimes you could get Cassie out of her fits that way.

Cassie turned her head. "Do you hear it?"

"Yes, my dear," he said, kindly. "I do hear it."

"They're warning us. Our own city, our little lives, or maybe this city, might vomit us up and we're like little fingers of life, little Tom Thumbs of human flesh. We have to scamper off to the four corners to escape the roar, the heat, the flames, the rumbling underfoot—"

She was humming loudly now.

"Towers will topple—chasms will open; people will fall in."

Jacob turned his head and nudged her. "I'll put you in it. You can be—"

"I don't want to be in it," said Cassie. "No, Jacob." Her lips were dry. Her body was shaking.

"It's only a movie. It's only even a pretend movie."

"And the walls will start to crack—these frieze things up by the ceilings will break off in pieces—"

"Yeah," said Jacob, training his camera on the ceiling. "And that's neat because they're like images of the life that's about to end.

"And the girls will come running from their flower-picking or their spinning or weaving, whatever they're doing. The stairs will start to crumble—that's cutting off escape," said Jacob, and he began to back up, the camera they could almost see trained on his feet. "And you know they're all going to die—"

"Why do they have to die?" said Dugald. "Maybe they all got away and the city was just buried in ash."

"Aw, come on," said Jacob. "That's no good. Right now they're running in circles trying to figure out where the hell to go and meanwhile the fire is shooting into the sky and the ground is rippling up and down like a wavy sea and the air is going dark—"

Dugald and Cassie stood watching the chubby boy as he swept his camera over them.

"Don't make them die."

Jacob suddenly dropped the camera. His small eyes, which were further diminished by his glasses and which rarely met another's for more than a fleeting instant, fixed on Cassie in her distress.

"Don't make them die," Dugald repeated.

"If they don't die, there'll be no box office."

Cassie stared at him. She forgot to hum.

Jacob lifted his imaginary camera and shrugged with it, then dropped it again. "All right. Nobody dies this time."

Dugald laughed. "Here I am dreaming about saving it and you're dreaming about blowing it up. I think we're both crazy."

Jacob laughed.

Cassie laughed.

The tension died. Peace returned. Dugald had fixed it somehow, he felt, or helped them fix it. He would like to tell this to Francesca.

"Jacob," said Cassie. "Jacob Finkelstein. You are going to be famous. It's all going to happen just like that. You'll be making horror films. The kind of horror films that make people vomit in the theatres, and run out screaming; parents will protest, people will picket."

"Oh *yeah*," said Jacob. "I guess. She's right, eh, Dr. Laird? Have you noticed, Cassie's usually right?" He slid by them and out the door.

12

THE GOD OF
SUBTRACTION

———————————

A THENS: A MAD golden and violet light, spreading at dusk over the city. The Dead Ladies sitting at a café in the Plaka. They had had a grand walk, looking at T-shirts and plaster busts of Alexander the Great, at postcards of that green satyr with his huge bobbing erection that made everyone giggle. Somewhere in front of them was Diogenes' lantern.

"Who was he?"

"The guy who went around in a tub."

"Yeah, right."

"No, he did. And he said something famous. Alexander the Great came up to him and asked him what he wanted, and he said, 'I would like you to get out of my sunlight.'"

"That's so cool."

The frappés were being borne their way over the troubled sea of heads by a swarthy young man. People were selling little laser lights that threw a red heat on the ground, and copies of black-and-white figure vases. The glow over the old market was eerie and dangerous in aspect, as if a pagan god were brewing a nasty temper tantrum. As if the great wild white bull were going to come, nostrils smoking, out of the clouds and rampage through all the little tables set here, his sharp curved white horns picking up the T-shirts that said Olympics 2004 or Athens, Greece, with gold-painted antiquities on them, trampling the vendors' barrows and finally screeching to a halt, hooves cracking the pavement, in front of them. The gypsy who was begging with her little girl, both of them in kerchief-skirts with fringe as if dressed for the movie by a wardrobe mistress, would run. This bull, raging, its white hide damp with pungent sweat, would roar for Cassie to mount it, mount it, or more damage would be done.

It was a *rape*, Miss Morrow had insisted, when they were looking at friezes of Europa and the bull. Not a pony ride at the fair.

And the other girls would rise from their feeble little table, which flew off in the bull-generated whirlwind like a potato chip, as did all the tables around them. The great beast would paw, breathing fire, a Sikorski helicopter landing, the vibration of air through his damp, burgundy-coloured nostrils like the insistent thunder of the motor. The bull would paw and toss his majestic head and moan Cassie, Cassie. And the Dead Ladies, her friends, would run for cover, but what did friendship count when the life of every tourist was at stake?

Put her on, put her on, Amelia would say and Cassie would be mounted on its neck clinging to the horns, her kilt spread, her damp thighs clamped on the wrinkles of the bull's thick neck.

Go! they'd say and the bull would toss and roar and then kick up its heels under the massive body and begin to run, run for the sea.

You need a thousand drachmas, someone said, poking Cassie.

They had been to the Acropolis Museum.

"More crap," said Vida.

Cassie pondered again the fact that the Caryatids had no hands. Of course, most of the significant works of Greek art had lost the loose ends of limbs. The tips of noses were favourites of the God of Subtraction, chins too, particularly the jutting male variety, toes certainly, feet often, hands with a striking violence, sometimes entire arms up to mid-bicep, or even shoulder. Ankles were sometimes gone, with the feet of course, and legs, right up to the calf. And that was to say nothing of what these loppers-off of body parts did to a penis. Barely a penis, circumcised or not, had survived the general holocaust of the extraneous.

Yes, extraneous. That was the word Francesca used. Take the Caryatids—not an arm in the bunch, all grace in the torso and legs, the draped fabric, the inclined knee, necks thickened ever so slightly and heads tilted forward to bear the weight of their baskets and on top of that as an afterthought the roof of the porch. They were lovely. But their hands had been extraneous, apparently, because their arms now ended at the elbow.

"They don't need them, do they?" Francesca had declared airily. "They're much better-looking without them. And they get the job done with their heads!"

Further along in the museum, heads, too, had been knocked off with a brutal *coup de foudre*. Never a slow erosion of lines and bulges, no, the God of Subtraction had passed through on a storm cloud, a jealous rage: what were all these idols doing with a full range of appendages anyway?

Cassie flipped through her catalogue, fascinated by the amputees. The Kritios Boy, minus both arms from above the elbow, one foot and the other leg from just below the knee. The Moschophoros, the famous calf-bearer, like a man who had walked into a land mine, no legs from the knee down, no hands, and no chin. In reliefs from the proscenium in the Theatre of Dionysus, entire congregations of folk went handless, as if it were a fashion. Gods like Dionysus, Zeus and Athena stood gracefully at ease with less than a full set, as if they had never expected more.

Maureen imitated the stance. One knee bent, the pelvis tipped ever so slightly, the little bag of sexual organs resting modest yet proud below a V of pelvic muscles. And it looked best, Miss Morrow asserted, if you had no head! Perhaps the Dead Ladies had got to her with their sick humour. But now, as Cassie turned the heavy, glossy pages, the missing parts were all she could think of. Where were they? How had they come to grief? When was the damage done? That calf-bearer was made in 565 BC; the Romans came in 146 BC. How long had the poor fellow's legs, the hands that gripped the feet of that little calf he wore over the back of his neck like a fox stole, survived into Roman times? Why the calm repose of the body when all the sentient, sensitive parts had been so violently amputated? And through what weird process of seeing, and feeling, what unconscious disturbances were the statues and reliefs thought better to look at thus violated?

She examined the Hydrophoroi so patiently lined up, their vases on their left shoulders, their calm, almost stunned gazes downward, in an elegant and layered fall—the first ahead, the second to the left, the third farther to the left and down even more. Nothing had disturbed this pose, not even the blow that removed a half of the third man's skull and his elbow, nor some other accident that had cruelly shaved off the bottoms of each of their feet. That was poise. That was concentration.

But who did the damage? Turks, Venetians, British lords, plunderers, rapists, Christians with their violent beliefs, their one god? Maybe the pagan gods themselves—or, more likely, Romans usurping the pagan magic, throwing off the questions that had no answers, ousting the lovely double-edged divinities with their excessive sexuality.

Gone. This much Cassie understood. Although she did not feel very smart, and she did not do well in school, this much she understood. The Greeks with their wild stories and their love of everything balanced were all broken up. Perhaps they could only maintain their balance by what amounted to an insane neglect of the facts.

Then they had all been taxied to the National Archaeological Museum, through streets clogged with small, rattletrap vehicles weaving in and out of lanes like so many hand shuttles on a great loom, seeking advantage, honking and jerking and abruptly swerving to avoid one another. Somehow the last taxi, carrying Miss Morrow and Dr. Laird, got lost. Arriving first, the students delightedly cast themselves down on the wide staircase in front of the building. Columns everywhere, wide and white, marble no doubt, with figures on the pediment, the blue and white Greek flag hanging listless as a cloak with no loins to cover, the front of the building a rich, dark red. The Dead Ladies were dying for fags: Ashley and Roxanne had managed to get out of their rooms the night before to buy cigarettes, which in Greece were legendary. Now the packages (two) lingered in Roxanne's pockets begging to be smoked.

"We're so just under everybody's nose."

"That's the whole idea. Like we might get up to something on our own."

"That sucks."

"I hate waiting. Amelia, how long do we have to wait?"

"What's the rush? I thought you hated museums."

"I do, but I hate waiting more."

"Just think, more reliefs. Is it high or is it low?"

"How do you spell relief?"

"C-i-g-a-r-e-t-t-e."

"I wonder where they are?"

Just then a taxi careened into the waiting space in front of the museum. Out of the rear seat the graceful, black-coiffed figure of Miss Morrow unfolded. She reached down and inside the door as if she were about to withdraw an enormous basket. But what emerged was a husband. Dugald took forever to get his legs out; it was clear he couldn't control them with their own muscles, but had to get his arms to do the job. First one, then the other, he picked up the limb with his hands and placed it outside the cab.

From the distance, across the rubbery green grass and flower beds, he looked frail, elderly, *ancient*, in fact, not at all the way he appeared in the darkened, close hallways of the Manor. Amelia stood, arrested, as Dugald pulled himself up and took the arm of his wife. Amelia didn't remember that. She didn't remember ever seeing Francesca having to help him that way. But no sooner had it come, than it was gone, the impression of immense age. They banished it. They looked brightly ahead and, seeing the students, Francesca raised her long graceful arm.

"There they are."

"I guess they went back for a nooner at the hotel," said Dimitri.

"He's too old."

"Bet he's not."

"That's disrespectful!" said Amelia.

The slender figure of Miss Morrow led them forth. Her voice trilled above the everyday repressed murmur of museum visitors, their occasional purrs of contentment, the shuffle of their sore feet on marble floors. The Dead Ladies dragged themselves disconsolately behind.

"Frieze after frieze," said Vida. "Amphora after attic-fucking, bitch-ass amphora."

"Have you noticed," said Ashley to Sara, "that not one of those boys has his thing?"

"What do you mean?" Sara looked askance at the little mess of stuff between their legs. What did Sara know? She didn't dare look too closely in case someone saw her staring.

"They're all broken."

"They're not."

"They are. Look at that guy. It's snapped off."

"Well, so are his hands."

"Yeah, okay. But some of them do have hands. Take a look. Not a single one of them has a penis."

"Well, maybe that was just how they were," said Sara.

Vida roared. "Yeah, *right*. Look. This guy. 'Iadonmenos.' Standing beside this twig-thing? See? He's perfect except somebody's chopped off his hands. And his dick!"

Sara looked puzzled. Vida hopped up and down on one leg. An elderly couple passed by her and scowled at the nearest authority figure, Miss Morrow, several dozen metres ahead gesturing with her cane at a cabinet full of vases.

"That's why Greek civilization died out, don't you know?" said Vida. "The men all lost their dicks."

The Dead Ladies began to giggle. Sara knew it was funny but she also knew that she was part of why it was so funny. She looked hurt.

"Let's count," said Vida. "Go back to the start of the room and look at every single statue of a guy. We'll keep track of how many have lost their dicks."

Maureen and Ashley busily went back while Vida, Sara and Cassie went forward, and could be seen eagerly, earnestly, examining every male figure, god or mortal.

"The whole—stuff—always looks the same," said Sara, "on every guy. Is it?"

"I guess they figured there was an ideal set of balls just like everything else. Here—no dick, no dick, no dick." Vida was counting on her fingers.

"I don't know why they designed it that way. It's a kind of sticking-out thing, which is sort of dangerous," said Sara. Her face was twisted in thought. "Especially since it's important."

"Who do you figure designed it?" laughed Roxanne. "Like, God?"

Dimitri hovered nearby pretending to read the labels on broken pottery in a glass case.

"Who do you suppose got it? It says the statue started out in 800 BC in Ephesus. And it stayed there for maybe—do the math, will you?"

"Six hundred and fifty years," said Jacob.

"Until the Romans came—"

"But they moved it on feast days."

"The janitors came in and dusted."

"Yeah, James Janitor. That's who's got their dicks."

"The women haven't lost any of *their* strength," said Vida.

"Only their heads and arms."

"Still—"

"Yeah, I know. Their bodies are okay. They're still *women*."

"That's the good thing about not having a dick. You can't knock it off."

"Guys aren't really men without them."

"Miss Morrow says it's an improvement."

"She does, does she?" said Dimitri.

Outside the hotel window the yellow light flashed on and off, a golden wink in the darkness: Acropolis View, Acropolis View. They had eaten dinner somewhere out there in the confusing city, vine leaves, calamari (deep fried, in rings), breaded zucchini slices and lamb squishy with oil. On the balcony of their room, Vida butted a spliff.

"That was good stuff, wasn't it?"

"I don't know. I never tried it before."

"I don't think you were getting any. You didn't inhale."

"I can't. My throat kept closing."

"But you must have."

Then Cassie was on her back on the bed but she seemed to be spinning around on a disc, no, a discus, like the athletes held in their giant hands as they knelt, ready to throw. She wanted to tell Vida what she knew—what she feared—about Dr. Laird, but she couldn't. Instead she said,

"I am seriously glad I didn't live in ancient Athens. All those athletic competitions must have been such a drag."

"It didn't seem like the girls had to do it. They just had to be virgins all the time, to get in those big parades, presenting *peplos* to the statues or whatever."

"I would have been good at the virgin part. I'll be one all my life," Cassie said.

Vida had removed her kilt and was walking across the windowed end of the room, a small black figure who came and went, jerkily appearing, then disappearing, then appearing again farther on.

"You won't find very many now."

"Very many what?"

"Virgins." Cassie said, erupting into a giggle.

Vida made no reply. The light flashed in the street. There was the sound of running water from the bathroom. Then came her voice.

"You're hot. Why don't you take this?"

A damp washcloth. She drew it across Cassie's forehead. The room aligned itself once more, and was still for a few seconds, then longer. The washcloth steamed on her forehead. Cassie giggled.

"You should take off your kilt, too."

Vida was astride her now, her narrow parted knees digging into Cassie's sides. She tugged at the waistband. One button on the long crossed over flap, the other inside.

"It's tight around your waist. No wonder you feel dizzy—"

Vida's hands opened the scratchy wool envelope. The cooler air of the room hit Cassie's legs. Her boxer shorts filled with the air from the room; the damp cotton lifted slightly off her skin.

"And these," said Vida. She slid herself backwards down Cassie's legs, which now seemed glued together. No longer visible in the darkness, Vida became a pair of hands peeling off the damp, thick knee socks that were collapsed in rings around Cassie's ankles. Now her feet were free, except for wiry Vida's weight on them.

Cassie's head began to swim again, so that she seemed to reawaken when Vida, a live, warm, thing, lay on top of her. It was a comfort; it satisfied a longing she did not know she had. She lay content, her friend stretched the length of her, tender but strong, fierce but sad, still at first, still, still, while her body took the measure of her, accepted the pressure of that other being. It was a shock and an honour. For someone to put their body up against yours. A way of talking. A gesture of friendship.

"Vida," Cassie said.

Vida wasn't talking.

In the room Vida and Cassie were both on their backs, covered by only a sheet, their limbs splayed in the airless heat of the Athens night. They were talking about the torsos from Ephesus—fifth-century, strong, healthy, in a constant headwind that pressed the pleats of their chitons against waist, breast, hips, thighs, the tucked in Y-shape at the top of their legs visible.

"It must have been okay, in Greece, to be fat," said Cassie. Her thighs had been sweating and squeaking against each other all day in the heat. She wished she had Vida's thin limbs.

"You're not fat," said Vida. Her listless hand strayed over the gap between the two single beds and brushed Cassie's side, below the waist. The hand went flat, moved a little up and down. "See, there's your pelvis bone. If you were fat, I wouldn't be able to feel it."

Cassie maintained an acquiescent silence. Vida's hand lay warmly on the hollow—well it was almost a hollow, at least it wasn't a bulge—above her pelvis bone.

"At least I wouldn't have been considered fat in 500 BC." Cassie was losing consciousness. In her mind she was striding across a hill, a wildflower meadow, in the lightest, airiest white chiton, with a gold ribbon tied under her breasts. The breeze was coming up her legs in gusts: sometimes the cloth puffed out around her, sometimes, as the wind sucked at her, the cloth was drawn tight against her body, clinging to her belly, her breasts, her thighs.

"Hey." She opened her eyes. Vida's warm, small hand was lying flat and unmoving on top of her mound. Her fingers would be touching her pubic hair if it were not for the fact that she was still in her boxer shorts. She looked over at Vida. She had her eyes closed but Cassie didn't think Vida was sleeping. She would have liked to have asked Vida to move her hand because it was making her hot and a little itchy. However, she wasn't sure she had the right. She shut her eyes again and waited for something to happen. Surely something would happen.

The night air sat in the room. Athens, beyond the open balcony doors, rattled and honked and slammed. There was no music. Voices rose and fell and rose again in that contemporary version of the language that neither of them understood, but which their teachers assured them contained all that was beautiful and balanced, as well as all that was mad and obsessive and sex-crazed. A door slammed. They both stirred and were awake.

"Hey," said Vida suddenly, "I know. Let's dress you up."

"Huh?" Cassie did not want to be roused from her dream of lightness.

"No, really." Vida jumped up and tore the sheet off her bed. "Let's dress you up in a chiton. Take off your boxers."

Cassie stood up, tousle-headed and dizzy. "Why?"

"Because that's not what they wore, was it?" Vida was scrabbling furiously in her knapsack. "I know I've got one," she muttered. She turned and looked over her shoulder at Cassie, who stood looking stupidly at her friend. Vida, crouched, bent over the knapsack. The knobs of every vertebra stood out in the dim city light that made its way through the glass doors. Her skin was blue and white, the muscles of her haunches pulled like belts over protruding joints, the end of her sharp and wedge-shaped, like the end of a chicken. The parson's nose, Cassie's mother called it. Vida's face, now in profile as she ordered Cassie to stand, wait, step, while she got the costume ready, was at that instant beautiful and mature, sad as Dietrich's face, hollow-cheeked, the way a siren should have looked, not like that pouter pigeon-shaped statue they'd seen in the museum.

They went out onto the balcony, dragging a chair and the mirror off the dresser. Cassie wore the bedsheet artfully draped across one shoulder, spread over her chest (just the right size, Vida had said admiringly of her breasts) and tied underneath the bust-line with a band made of two Manor school ties knotted together. The front was short, coming to just over her knees. The back was of necessity longer, because they had deemed it wise not to tear the end off the sheet, particularly because Vida had to sleep in the bed, but the long end was tucked away behind a chair so it could not be seen. Cassie's brown hair was let loose and had curled up around her face: it too was held down by a band, this time around the forehead, a white ribbon that she kept in her suitcase, a going-away present from her mother. She had bare legs and feet, and the light breeze that had finally arrived to free the city from its chain of heat held the light cotton firmly against her thighs.

"You look wonderful, you see," Vida said, and made her sit, crouch, stride, in order to look the same as the statues they'd seen in the museum. "You could take off your arms and it would be just as good."

She made little karate chops on Cassie's forearms. Cassie giggled.

"You could chop off your legs too. Same thing." Vida chopped at her just above the knee. She stood back against the aluminum railings and narrowed her eyes. "Spread your legs. Sit on the edge of the chair." Cassie obliged. "Yes," said Vida. "You could cut off—" she came nearer and put her hands on Cassie's ears. She put her face against Cassie's and spoke so softly that only the breath lasted in the air, "Cut off your head and, still, you'd be beautiful."

Cassie saw Vida absorbing her lines and locations, memorizing, unselfconscious for once, adoring. And this time she did not fear the feeling as it rose up from inside of her, too.

"Look," said Vida, turning her to the mirror.

"I don't need to. I can see." Cassie smiled at her friend.

"No, look at yourself."

"I'm looking at you. I'm looking at something that will come. You can't see," she said to Vida. "You're good but you can't see in the same way that I can."

"I don't know what you mean."

"I can see you now the way I saw Jacob with his camera. I can see you when you are grown up."

"Oh, can you? And what can you see?"

"You are going to be even more famous than him. You are going to be a famous lesbian," Cassie said.

Vida's face went blank for a minute, then she pretended that nothing had happened.

13

THE ROAD
TO DELPHI

THE FUSCHIA MINIBUS that drew up on Wemster Street in front of the Acropolis View Hotel was, in the judgement of the Dead Ladies, over the top. It was large, it was the colour of a really bad tube of lipstick, and it had strange bent proboscises on either side of its front windshield like an animation bug. But it was air-conditioned, and the thirteen who were waiting, bags in a sorry hump, quickly climbed in. The Manor had to go in style.

The Headmistress stepped up gamely to the throbbing minibus and gestured to the boys to toss the bags in the back. They loaded Dugald into the rear seat, his legs buckling at awkward moments beneath him; he was like a bag of sticks. The students fanned out amongst the three rows of seats and Francesca hung onto the ceiling strap, intending to ride the centre hump. The driver gave her some papers to sign and then got out of his seat and climbed down the stairs.

"Where's he going?" Amelia asked.

"Back to the office, I suppose. I thought you'd drive."

"I can't drive in Athens."

"Oh, it's not as bad as they say."

I don't know how you'd know, Amelia silently fumed, you've never driven here. You've never driven anywhere unless you count your relentless passenger-seat piloting. "You can't be serious," she said to Francesca but not to Francesca: what was the point? "God damn it to bloody hell!"

Then Amelia stepped into the driver's seat. She turned the key. She checked out the pedals; she put her hand on the gearshift and only then did it dawn on her that this was a standard. Not only was the vehicle roughly three times the size of anything she'd seen on the roads in this city, but she had to change gears. Francesca stood nearby, looking sporty, her feet planted a foot apart to absorb the checks and starts of the bus. Stooping, she peered through the tinted windscreen down Wemster Street, now shrunk to a goat track.

Fucking hell, thought Amelia. Well—she'll get her money's worth from me. They rolled forward and just about crushed a little bug-shaped car. She slammed on the brake and killed the motor. She practised the step dance required to control motion: brake, clutch, gas, right left right, and they rolled, jerked, stalled, rolled again and finally got going. The street was so skinny she couldn't pass the parked cars. Scooters buzzed her. She wanted to cry.

Meanwhile, everyone ignored her. The Cheese was driving. She would manage. Well then, damn the torpedoes, thought Amelia, I'll go for it. She gunned the motor and geared down instead of up. There was a monumental roar and they all fell forward out of their seats. She smiled brightly in her rear mirror, turned into the main street and roared into third. Little tin horns blasted in outrage all around her. A policeman waved, blowing his whistle. Too late! The students noticed her now: they cheered. Settling into the traffic was like joining a rally track, with cars constantly criss-crossing in front of her, honking to add insult. But they were on the road.

"On your right, we're about to pass Hadrian's Arch," Francesca called out. "See where it says this is the city of Hadrian, not Theseus? You see how the Romans had to put their names on everything?"

The students leaned back in their seats, listless, as if there were nothing beyond the glass. They'd been to Athens, they'd done that, and regarded the time in between this and their destination of Delphi as a vacuum. But nature abhorred a vacuum, as Dr. Laird might have said, and Francesca would miss no opportunity to instruct.

"Attention scholars, look out; we'll not pass by here again."

The remark was lost, all but its ominous ring. The boys and the Dead Ladies merely glowered. But Cassie never missed an ominous note.

"I have a sense of impending doom," she said to Vida.

Vida laughed. "Like Miss Morrow says, you have a way with words. It's so cute."

"No, seriously," said Cassie. Vida patted her arm. Amelia saw it in her rear-view mirror. They were seated side by side, sprawling and slumping as for once Miss Morrow was not on their case about sitting up. They were an odd duo, but a devoted one; that was good for Cassie. Vida was tough as nails. She'd make sure that the only person who gave Cassie trouble from now on would be herself.

At the wheel, Amelia felt a heady sense of power. A pilgrimage to Delphi it was, then. Pilgrimage to Delphi. What would they ask of the oracle? Dugald's future looked to be so short his only question would be—when do I die? Unless, of course, he was curious about the old woman in the photograph. But the function of the oracle had never been to predict the future. No, the function of the oracle was to give advice. Oscar Wilde said that all advice is bad advice. Why then to Delphi? For Francesca, strap-hanging, in the ascendant, Delphi—or at least nearby Arachova—was home. She had no questions to put to the sibyl. More likely the sibyl—a smoke-breathing "old woman" of fifty—would want to query her: How do you do it, Miss Morrow?

How about herself, Amelia? A woman of thirty-three whose life was still unshaped? What to do with herself? Follow Miss Morrow? But how to do that when Miss Morrow did not want her any more? Flee the teaching, live in Europe? Snag one of those married men she entangled herself with? What would she have then? A man who had demonstrated he could walk out on you. She thought of Ferdinand the Portuguese as a Roman, with his stove-like chest, striding through a recumbent Athens, shouting orders in Latin to the slaves. No. He was too short. She mustn't glamorize him, simply because he was gone, vanished entirely since the night in the sanctum sanctorum. She must remember that he was nothing but a middle-aged hot-dog seller with a jealous wife. Had Miss Morrow dismissed him? They were all under threat of dismissal—all but Jacob. No one lived up to Francesca's standards, except Dugald—and he looked as if he was about to dismiss himself.

What would the students ask? What to do with a life that had just begun but already seemed to career toward trouble? Will Homer and Euripides, Milton, Pope, Shakespeare, Cézanne or Van Gogh truly bend your imaginations into shapes that would contain that furious energy? Amelia glared down from the high window, scattering people and cars. She almost enjoyed the chaos and cacophony of the city, the block-like homes, concrete cubes with leaning crosses of TV antennae on top, giving her perverse pleasure.

"Go straight, go straight," charged Francesca. "See the arrow? National Road. To Lamia."

As if there were anything "straight" in Athens. The National Road curved and coiled, and was cut at every second intersection by traffic lights. Wee cars darted from lane to lane, trying to make time. The Madonna with the Long Neck hunched tight-fisted over her steering wheel, devil-may-care, laughing at the erratic rushes of traffic like spurts of water beetles that went on all around her. Slowly, the fuschia minibus fought its way out of the city. It was twenty-five degrees, too hot for April. The air was white and poisonous. The notion of a bypass was one that, obviously, did not have its origins in Greece. Possibly the only one.

"Are you certain this is right?"

"Yes."

"But there are no signs."

"Straight, straight. In ten miles, we'll see another sign."

They passed billboards for the United Colors of Benetton and Replay jeans. Advertisements for fifty different kinds of running shoes. Amelia decided she'd ask the Pythia how a thirty-three-year-old woman could make a life without a man. Should she be a Miss Morrow *manquée* with no Dr. Laird? Must she be the headmistress of her own lonesome heart?

"Well, little rats," said Francesca, making her way to the back, pausing beside Cassie and Vida. Behind them were Roxanne, Maureen, Ashley and Sara. "You travel off to Delphi like the Thyiads. Do you know who they were? No, you don't. Therefore, I shall tell you. The Thyiads were young women, about your age, who set off from Athens to dance their way to the slopes of Parnassus, where they would disport themselves in frenzies, possessed by the spirit of Dionysus. When they discovered an unsuspecting young man they might tear him to pieces."

The Dead Ladies looked suitably impressed.

"The spirit of Dionysus, do you know what that is? It is wild abandon, the celebration of wine and loss of oneself in ceremony."

Amelia thought the city would never end. Just when the National Road threatened to stretch out and let them move, up would come another set of traffic lights, another klatch of Athenian lads double-parking their BMWs in front of coffee shops. She shifted the gearshift up and down, to third, second and first, the motor revving and dropping, the gears grinding and protesting.

"Clutch," said Francesca.

Amelia thought she might kill her.

Dugald was unusually quiet, the triangle of his face, small eyes, narrow chin, vaguely fox-like. He was unwell, or thinking unpleasant thoughts. His eyes did not rest on Francesca with their customary delight.

But never mind. Suddenly, a left-turn arrow directed them down a bumpy extension that looked like someone's driveway and then they were on a highway. Finally out of the grip of the city, they followed the flat modern four-lane toward Thebes, and then Levadia.

"This plain was once filled with water. But Hercules stopped the river, by pushing a great boulder into a chasm in the mountain," Miss Morrow said. The students craned their necks to see the rocks in the crack, but it was covered with low bushes and swampland. By the time they were on the lower slopes of Parnassus, where Dionysus romped, the boys were punching each other over the seat backs; the girls braided and unbraided each other's hair too many times and were now reduced to playing Scissors, Paper, Rock with exaggerated hand slapping.

"Behave," said Francesca. "Or I shall give one of you as payment of my tax to the Turks. One in five children, that's what it was. That makes two of you, sent off to become soldiers for Islam. And I shall pick the noisiest ones."

These endearments always made the students laugh.

"Recall, in the play *Oedipus Rex*, where Oedipus killed his father Laius? It was at a crossroads, where three roads met—the road from Thebes to Delphi crossing with the road from Daulis. And there," she pointed dramatically down the slope, "there it is—Stop a moment, if you please, driver!"

Amelia pulled off to the side of the road.

"There is the spot! Think of it."

Cassie's eyes bulged in her pale face. "Are you serious? It actually happened?"

"We know it is written. But is it myth, or history? Where is that other intersection, the crossing of two pathways, fact and imagination? Where is that place? Does it exist? I cannot give you the answers. But you are asking the right questions.

"Oedipus was running away, trying to avoid his destiny, when he met, accosted and killed a stranger here, believing it meant nothing. A casual, violent gesture that locked him into the story that had been laid down for him since birth. It's a very modern story, in fact."

"Drive-by shooting," muttered Jacob.

"Indeed. But if Oedipus had remained in Corinth, would he

have escaped? Did all the paths he invented, no matter how ingenious, or how eccentric, lead to the same fate?"

"Well," sniffed Vida, "why kill a man at all if you know you're in danger of killing your father? It doesn't make any sense."

"Oh, Vida, you always say that," said Amelia. "It never makes sense. But you do not get to negotiate a better deal around fate." Fate was fate.

The town of Levadia looked closed-up, asleep, and jerry-built. They barrelled on through it. The countryside was suddenly pretty, with a coppery dry earth, trees in yellow, white and purple blooms and cedars of Lebanon spiky in dark green at the side of the road. There were little huts belonging no doubt to shepherds. Mount Parnassus above had veins of snow on its peak.

Skiing went on up there, said the guidebooks.

Francesca disapproved.

The antics of modern-day Greeks, approximating the lives of North Americans, were distasteful to her. She expected them, perhaps, to be cooped up in museums making reproductions of the great works.

They pulled into Arachova in the early afternoon. The town had to take a deep breath and relax its walls to let the fuschia minibus down the main thoroughfare. The narrow road was clogged with tour buses. The sidewalks spilled over with skiers with their curious burdens, moon-sized boots and sharp poles. The villagers, immediately distinguishable from the visitors by their short stature and the way their bodies drew back to the stone walls or sank into possession of the chairs in the tavernas in the square, exerted a presence of declension: we have lived here, we live here, we will live here.

And right they were. Buses came, buses went. They were mostly going now, pulling noisily from the angle parking they'd found halfway up a slope, belching as they swerved from beside a curb into traffic. All this because of the long-inactive oracle, all these visitors only a fraction of what had been, twenty-five hundred years ago.

Partway along the main street Francesca asked Amelia to stop. This was where the headmasterly couple always alighted. The students went down the road to a cheap hotel.

"Amelia, you take the children and go on to Delphi to the Dolphin. You know it, they're expecting you. Dr. Laird and I will walk up the steps from here; you can't drive it." She reached over the seats, tapping the heads of the students on either side.

"When can we see your house?"

"Later, children, of course. Later you'll see it."

Amelia doubted it.

Dugald looked around in his seat. He couldn't rise, from the looks of it, couldn't think how to rise. Francesca paused.

"Dimitri, could you pull our bags from the compartment? The Vuitton," she added. "Yes, Sara dear, what is it?"

As she gave her attention to the girl, Francesca took two steps backward and surreptitiously gave an elbow to her husband. He clutched it; her face gave no sign of the effort in her biceps to hold the elbow in place as Dugald used it to lever himself upright.

"I didn't say anything, Miss Morrow."

"You didn't need to, my dear, what is the problem?"

"How far away is the place where we're staying?"

"Just ahead, just a few minutes ahead. Look down the valley. If it's not too misty you might be able to see the Gulf of Corinth. Look in the cleft in the rocks. See if you can spot the 'vaporous fumes' the ancients saw. You're not to worry. Miss Holt is terribly competent." She passed Amelia a half-smile.

Sara did not appear mollified by this answer. She observed anxiously as the Headmistress descended the steps of the bus and, shielding her eyes from the sun with her palm, directed Dimitri to carry the Vuitton up a steep stone staircase. He did not look as if he wanted to do this particular chore, but he knew better than to hesitate. Dugald followed him; then Francesca too was out of sight. The buzz in the vehicle instantly doubled in volume. Amelia noticed they were holding up several giant German buses.

"Wait for Dimitri!"

"Let's stop for a frappé."

"Better get on down to Delphi first."

Dimitri emerged from the stairs. All the kids cheered. Behind him appeared, once again, the figure of Miss Morrow, freed of her long thin shadow. She came to the door of the minibus, watched the big boy climb back to his seat and stood dramatically holding the rail at the top of the steps with both hands.

"Recall," she said. "The Greeks thought Delphi was the navel of the world. Delphi, the name, may have come from the word for 'dolphin.' It was the dolphins who led the Cretan merchants to this sacred spot. On the other hand, the name may also have come from the word for womb. You must think of that on your first viewing of the site. Remember it was Gaia, the goddess, who was the first domestic deity—before Apollo. You may think of these things as you enter Delphi." She turned to leave.

"Miss Morrow?"

It was Vida, importunate in the aisle. "Do you believe in the goddess?"

Francesca smiled. "More and more," she said.

By the time they had checked into the Dolphin and had dinner, Amelia was exhausted and wanted only to fall into bed. But first, "terribly competent" ringing in her ears, she did a house inspection. The students were all in their rooms, thumping the pillows, pitching their knapsacks into corners, preparing for bed. They would never admit it, but they wanted nothing more than sleep either: the transatlantic flight, the three days of marching over the Acropolis and around Athens, the constant forced company of their school-mates—it was all very strenuous. But first there were a few problems to solve. One, Ashley.

Ashley sat on the end of her narrow bed with the white sheets stretched flat and tight, a scratchy brown blanket folded across the bottom, and lifted her arm to stare at her carved message. "God that's ugly," she said. Then, brightening: "Look, Miss Holt, the whole town's out and about at eleven o'clock."

"I know you've cadged cigarettes on the street and you've got plans to sneak out later. Don't think you fool me for a second," Amelia said. "The answer is no."

Ashley fell on her back theatrically, intending to mime uncon-sciousness.

Two, Maureen.

Maureen stood on tiptoe in the tiny bathroom, trying to get up high enough to see her navel piercing in the mirror. The ring through her skin there was sticking: she couldn't turn it. "It's in-fected," she said.

"How do you know?"

"I've had it before. It crunches when I turn it."

"That is so disgusting."

"Just be glad it's not the one down there," said Roxanne.

"I'm, like, seriously considering having that one taken out. I'm so mad that I ever got it done."

"Why did you?" asked Amelia.

"The girl who was with me said it made sex more fun, but duh-uh!" Here Maureen made a dumb face in imitation of herself. "I'm like never having sex again so that's not a valid reason."

"Not until the next guy," muttered Roxanne.

Three, Roxanne herself, in confidential tones.

"I need some tampons. Can I like go to the store?"

"Smokes, more likely."

"Not really, I'm like totally bleeding like mad."

"Can't someone lend you a maxi-pad? The pharmacies are closed, I'm sure."

"They're not; the whole town is open."

"No, Roxanne."

"Well, what the hell do you want me to do?"

"Borrow!"

Amelia left her open-mouthed in the door of her room.

Finally, Sara. "I'm homesick, Miss Holt. Can I phone my mum?"

"I thought we agreed calls just make it worse."

"But I need to."

"Tomorrow, Sara."

Amelia backed into the hallway. The boys were easier. Dimitri, Darrin and Chino were playing cards. Jacob was poring over plans of the Acropolis, which Dugald had given him.

"Figuring out how to blow it up?" Amelia asked.

He looked annoyed. "Who told you?"

She shrugged.

"Well, don't say anything. It's too good an idea to have floating around. Someone will steal it for sure." He mused over the papers, spread out over his bed. A fussy professor. "I've got to get it to an agent."

Amelia felt a twinge of affection for the boy, something entirely new to her.

She went to her little, stale-smelling, orange-draped bedroom (why do they love that colour in cheap hotels?). And flopped. She lay on her bed, neither awake nor asleep, for she didn't know how long. Then she was alert. She heard voices: they came from a balcony directly beneath her, which she could not see. One voice was low and earnest. The other was higher and feeble. She listened carefully, carefully. She could not make out what was being said but she could tell it was important to the girls who were saying it. She got out of her chair and went out on the skinny balcony. Cheese-like, she lay down on the concrete floor and wormed her face up between the twisted iron posts that made a railing. Her head just barely fit between them. She looked down. It was Vida and Cassie.

"Don't worry," Vida was saying. She held Cassie's hand in her lap. "It's not wrong. There's nothing wrong about it. We're not hurting anyone. We're just having fun."

"Does it mean I'm weird?" asked Cassie.

"You're not weird but maybe I am," said Vida. She lifted Cassie's hand to her lips and kissed it.

This much could just be Vida making Cassie feel better. Fine. But Vida held Cassie's hand at her lips making little popping kisses on the back of it. Amelia tried to pull her head back but her ears got stuck between the posts. She made a strangling noise that would have given her away, but just at that moment a car honked on the street. She twisted her neck and got her head out. A lesbian outbreak. That's all she needed.

But even that couldn't keep her awake. She lay down and knew nothing until morning.

14

FRANCESCA
AT HOME

MISS FRANCESCA MORROW woke in a field of snow-white bed linen. She opened the shutters and then the glass doors onto the balcony. She looked over the town rooftops with their curved terra-cotta tiles held down with local rocks, down to the Gulf of Itea, masked in low cloud but there nonetheless. Between her house and the gulf the road folded back and forth like a dropped ribbon. The terraces lay between the bands, silver-leaved olive trees tier on tier. It was heavenly. So peaceful. So quiet. So still. She turned to look back into the room. Dugald lay under the sheets, almost annihilated by the pallor of his skin in all that bleached linen.

How long had she slept? What day was it? Slowly she remembered and humiliation returned to her. They had arrived at the house earlier this afternoon. They had sent the students to the Dolphin with Amelia, as was their habit on these tours. They had been helped into the house by Maria in her black dress with her matching black teeth. The teeth showed when she smiled, which was perhaps once a visit. The bedroom had been so fresh, so cool after the air of Athens, and the diesel smell of the bus. The bed so inviting. She and Dugald had stripped off their outer clothes, lifted the heavy woven coverlet and slid under. They had laid hands on each other's shoulders, backs, waists, in their traditional, fond way, and made as if to sleep.

But they did not sleep.

Francesca did not know which of them made the first gesture. No, that was not true. She did know. It was she. But she had not done it without some encouragement. There had been an insistence in one of his caresses, a pressure in his hand, or in the way his lips met her neck, she didn't exactly know which, but she had read it as an invitation. She had responded. As a good wife would. And as a woman who feels herself to be admirable, and wishes to be admired, would. She had reached for him and massaged the flesh of his back and his buttocks, stroked the hairs of his chest and his thighs, as was her wont.

These were practised motions, but not empty ones. They had worked for years and worked well. There had been no slackening in response, no suggestion that she lacked skill in the arts of love, that she was so dull as to cause her husband to lose interest. And he, last night, had responded. He had begun the murmuring praises that for her amounted to foreplay. His hands, always cold these days, had warmed themselves in her warmest places. The murmuring became incantatory and urgent. They were ready.

And then, something had gone dreadfully wrong. Just how, Francesca did not know. It was as if some god of disorder and mischief interfered. What should have been shifts in weight and position as graceful and as familiar as those of a pair of expert ballroom dancers became clumsy. He caught her hair under his arm and she shrieked. He shifted and then fell rather heavily on her. She pushed him away so that she could breathe, but pushed too hard. He lost his balance and nearly went off the bed, which would have been catastrophic given his fragile state. And suddenly he was angry.

"You cannot always have it your way!" he shouted, erupting, spittle coming from his mouth, his face turning a most unhealthy purplish red. "I will not keep my head down all the time!"

She'd only been holding on around his neck. She let go, but he did not calm down.

"You manage everything we do!"

"I don't. Whatever do you mean?"

Suddenly his face was in hers, distorted. "You don't get it, do you?"

He never spoke that crudely. She took the high road, declined to argue, shook her head with fingers on her eyelids holding them shut. But—

"You think you're the boss! But you're wrong! I am the Headmaster."

"Of course you are, dear."

"No, I'm not!"

Then Dugald did the most astonishing thing. He laughed. "If I am no longer the Headmaster of the school, then at least may I be the Headmaster of this FUCK?!" The last word was said with such vile energy that Francesca shrank away from him in the bed.

"But of course you may be—you are." Her mock submissiveness deflated him. He rolled away.

"What on earth is wrong, Dugald?"

"I'm tired, Francesca. Tired of it all. You make kings for your vanity."

It was astonishing how petulant he sounded. Francesca was nearly crying. "I don't know what you mean!"

"I am not and I never was the Headmaster." Sighing, rolling away.

"You are."

"I am not."

"You are. Of the school, certainly. Of me? It is as you wish. And of this—" she tried to follow him there "—of this 'fuck.'"

"Well, if I am, the fuck is officially off," he said with a raw laugh.

"Darling!"

"Francesca, you are so manipulative; you've had me exactly where you want me for how many years? And you do that at your peril! At your peril! You'll see what happens: love goes, love goes!"

"Dugald! All this from one clumsy shift on the bedsheets?"

She began, as her fear subsided, to become indignant. Never had she been treated with such a lack of respect! No one spoke to her that way. How hurtful it was to be scolded while wearing no clothes, the worse if one was not as lovely, unclad, as one might wish.

But Dugald had nodded off, leaving her to toss unhappily until at last sleep claimed her.

She took out her blue silk robe, Chinese silk, the colour a peacock ought to be but never quite was. She went down into the tiny garden to sit under the net of vines that Maria's husband tied from the second storey across to the neighbour's wall. Here was the lily pond her father had dug, uprooting the olive tree, utterly empty of water. What had all that been about, the summer she was seven, when her sister was born, and her father dug an ugly hole in the ground, and she was at last allowed to have a governess? It seemed unbearably sad to her now. If she could make Dugald understand that, perhaps he would forgive her. But what was to be forgiven, after all? She was a magnificent woman; everyone said so.

Before allowing herself to sit she did her exercises; bending, curling, pressing her arms together and apart. Her legs were not as pliant as usual; her back creaked from the long hours of travel; her lungs felt clogged with the dirty air of Athens. Never mind: a brisk walk up the slope of Parnassus later would refill them with mountain air.

She forced herself to go back inside. She found coffee beans in a tin in the kitchen cupboard (bless Maria: she'd shopped for "the doctor and the lady"). She took the old wooden hand-grinder, which had been there since Lily's day, and slowly, working her biceps into a good burn, ground the beans to a fine powder. As the water boiled she measured the grounds into the bottom of a French press. She stood at the stove as she had stood in the dream she'd had months ago back at the Manor. Behind the little gaggle of her sister and her friends, making fudge on the day of the birth of her baby sister. It was as if she moved into that past moment, the girls standing around the pot of boiling candy, the drip of thick brown batter off the spoon into the water; the oohs and aahs as it formed a ball but not, alas, a soft ball. It had become a hard ball, the fudge spoiled. She recalled herself standing at the top of the stairs watching the crack under her mother's bedroom door: would blood and water flow out, and cascade down to flood the house, sweep her feet out from under her?

How good it was to be back in the house of her childhood, its terrors subsided. Of course it had seemed so much larger then. And the village, the hive of pathways and stone cottages fixed helter-skelter against each other and the mountainside: a comfort. There was silence from upstairs where Dugald slept. Francesca thought that perhaps soon there would be silence from him wherever he was, at whatever hour. And it came to her now—that she might prefer silence to an irrational anger. She could live undiminished in his silence, but not in the torrent of his words.

She poured the rich, black, foamed coffee into a yellow china cup. The long Greek day would be a bath of colour, changing hues by the hour, each phase lovelier than the last. She counted her childhood here as the start of her love for art. She had never understood why the country had not produced its own Matisse. Apparently it had spent its allotment of genius before the birth of Christ.

She took the coffee out to sit in the garden. The house was on one of the top levels of the village, nearly as high as the church, presiding over the red-tile roofs, the gulf. The sun hung over the village and the slopes of Parnassus as it had for Francesca's lifetime and countless lifetimes before her. And so it would set. It was wise to recall that. It was time to call herself in for a meeting with the Headmistress.

Miss Morrow, she began. Francesca. She did not call herself dear. She was not, in fact, dear to herself today, although self-loathing was not in her vocabulary. Usually Francesca found herself highly satisfactory, her mind, her body—and the feeling of control she gained by keeping it in shape; her devoted husband, her charges. But she was shaken, shaken to the core. She had not permitted herself to know, when in the thick of her pedagogical duties, that Dugald was drifting away. Now she had to admit that it was true. Look at the man, desiccated as a leaf. He could not hear, he could not see, unless one was twenty paces away (in which case he saw, and sometimes overheard, extremely well). He was declining. So be it. And yet—Francesca forced her mind farther into this frightful territory—that was not the worst of it. How could one put this?

He was revealing his rage. He was allowing that old anger to surface. She saw this as a betrayal of all he'd been. He was, in fact, not himself. The Dugald she knew and loved had left her.

What did one do? What did one do, when a marriage, when the postures of a marriage that had so defined one's life, collapsed, whether from infirmity, age or betrayal? Her instinct thus far had been to cover for him. To carry on as if this were not happening. Yet to stand together was surely to be dragged down by this dying thing, this tattered coat upon a stick. What did one do, what did one do? She could distance herself. But distance would only expose both of them, each of them, to the harsh weather of life. It would batter and break their extremities, and it would weaken, perhaps bring down the school they had created together. Even worse, it would destroy the myth.

She turned to her oldest and most constant friends, the poets. Yeats knew about growing old. "Soul clap its hands and sing, and louder sing," she announced to herself. She stood, and she did clap her hands. A neighbour peered out of a shuttered window. *Kale mare*, she nodded.

But it was not morning. She must move. She could not stay here.

She dressed in a long cotton skirt and grabbed the great embroidered black piano shawl she kept here for just such moments. She even pulled out the Nike training shoes she'd bought under duress from Amelia. One could not wear platform shoes on uneven ground without a husband to lean on.

It was growing late, and dark. Francesca walked down the stone steps from the main road into the houses of Arachova, narrow steps that sagged in the middle as if they'd been made of old boards rather than concrete. The edges were painted white to be visible at night. The walls too were white. Under the stucco they showed themselves to be made of crumbling stone with holes so big you could put your hand in. The gnarled stems of vines yet to bloom for the season ran like ancient bulging veins up the sides to the roofs, with their curved red tiles laid in careless, chipped rows. The old wooden shutters snapped in the mountain breeze, iron balconies here and there overhanging the walkway. There was a gutter down the centre. There had been rain in her youth: she could almost hear the sound it made in a rainstorm. A cat crossed over her head on a wire lattice strung to support a vine. Precarious. Precarious. She caught, as the passageway turned outward, a view across the lumpy hillside to other roofs, a little tower, a decorated eavestrough. She passed terrace upon terrace of little houses shut up against the night. The passageway tipped downhill; she came to the main road again. The men in their suit jackets and good trousers moved, all of a shared impulse, at precisely half-past eight, to the cafés. It hurt to look at them: other people's husbands. She climbed back up the straight staircase to the church. She was panting when she reached it. Dugald could not have managed.

The empty square at the top of the steps was illuminated by floodlights so brilliant even the full moon paled in comparison. This was a famous square, a historic square. Turkish heads had oozed out their blood here impaled on spikes. The Greeks had routed the Turks on the plains of Livadia just above. Such victories were still celebrated at the feast of St. George, which was soon to come.

But it was Francesca's own history that concerned her now. A priest with his stiff black hat appeared to carry a sign inside: he nodded briskly, mistaking her for a tourist. The sound of rushing water came but from where? She recalled, from all those years ago, that there was a pipe that emerged from an old wall at the back across the path; the spring runoff from above gushed out and filled the gutters beside the descending road, really only a paved path. It pleased Francesca that she could remember this. The sound underlay all the other sensory gifts of this place, the silent, stealthy cats and far-off motorcycles, a mother hustling her child home through the dark, struggling geraniums in pots, and the overwhelming scent of the almond trees.

And in that square, dwarfed by the great blocks of darkness and light that turned the top of the town into a hilltop stage, a Greek theatre pushed inside out, Francesca paced. And as she paced she cried. Fat salt tears sprang from the corners of her eyes. Anyone would have thought she'd have expected it, marrying a man over a decade her senior. She ought to have been prepared for his loss of potency, of desire, of the keen witty interest in all that went on around him. She might have dreamt it; she had no control of her dreams. She might even have wished for it, secretly, without admitting to herself that she, too, was tired of the mythic love affair. Had candour been allowed, even in their quarrels, she might have threatened him with it: "I'm younger than you. You're old. I'll win this, simply by outliving you."

But she did not want it. She paced and the tears washed over her creaseless cheeks, her damask cheeks, as Dugald had always said. "Oh, Enkidu, my brother, you were the axe at my side, my hand's strength, the sword in my belt, the shield before me, a glorious robe, my fairest ornament." The words of the world's first poem began to calm her.

And after she had paced the deck of this ship, this platform of grief, many times, Francesca came up with one word: alone. She was alone. But if Dugald could betray her this way, she had been alone for a long time—and was it not a betrayal, this moving away, this withering of spirit and the rage that was attached to it? Had he never been the axe at her side, the sword in her belt, the shield before her? The Dugald she had worn as armour and fairest ornament was only her idea. Had she been, as he claimed, the Headmaster all along? Was he merely a foil for her ambitions? No! He was the man she loved, the other side of her coin, the strike to her block, the poise to her counterpoise. Headmaster, headmistress: what did it matter? They had divided the territory, stayed within the lines, made of their characters one character, FrancescaDugald, Dr.Laird/MissMorrow. Who was she to become if he truly was going away? She looked down over the dilapidated rooftops to the little house, her childhood house, where he slept. "What is this sleep which holds you now? You are lost in the dark and cannot hear me."

15

A JOURNEY
THROUGH BEES

I T WAS AN exquisite morning. Amelia had hopped into the fuschia minibus before breakfast and had roared back to Arachova, picked up a tired-looking Francesca and Dugald and delivered them to the oracle site. Then she went back for the students. They all met outside the ticket office as planned at eight-thirty. The hillside was adrift in red poppies, mimosa and bushes of yellow flowers that Francesca said were St. John's Wort.

"Hey, I heard that's an upper," said Dimitri. Darrin and Chino started tearing off clumps of leaf and flower and stuffing them in their mouths.

"Careful, boys," said Dugald, oddly glassy-eyed himself. "Herbs are simply drugs that have never been tested. You don't know which part you're supposed to ingest."

"That's why they like them," said Cassie.

There was a growing line of buses panting against the curb, school groups, some of them. The idea in coming this early had been to climb up the hill to the monuments before it got crowded but the gates were locked. There were two signs giving the hours. According to one sign it would be open at eight-thirty, according to the other it would open at ten.

"It was always open at eight-thirty before," Francesca said, a new, plaintive tone in her voice. It would never do to let the troops hear that. "Shall we walk over to the temple and come back later? You're going to do your talk, of course."

Dugald smiled, absently and without changing the faraway focus of his eyes. His skin was white as a newborn's and his hair lay so fine on his scalp it seemed to be the silk of a spider. Yet he was walking with a certain *ballon*, as the French said, a bounce, as if the earth were about to release him, as if the paltry strength of its gravity could not hold him. Today he had spoken not a word to Francesca.

"That settles it," she said, as if he'd ruled. "Dugald, you sit in the shade and rest. Amelia, you and I will take the students to the Sanctuary of Athena."

It was quiet as they climbed down the path from the road. The birds twittered; the sea air blew fragrance into their nostrils. Giant purple and yellow wildflowers, thistle and clover were in bloom below the shield of red rock spiked with tall, dark cedars. Francesca began her talk beside the stone walls of the ruined Tholos. Sara was conscripted to hold the umbrella over Francesca's head to prevent any rays of sun falling on the damask cheeks. She carried out her task absent-mindedly, letting the circle of shade slip away from Francesca as the umbrella itself slid down Sara's back while she gazed off into the middle distance with her homesick eyes.

Francesca stood beside the graceful structure with its three remaining columns towering over the crumbled circle of stone. "Feel it. Just feel. How ancient. How sacred. This temple is older than any other monument in Delphi, dating from when Athena ruled here, before she was replaced by Apollo.

"Circles mean women. Wherever there are circles, there were goddesses. Later, as Delphi grew, this sanctuary became the entry point. Visitors had to come and worship, and wash, before they visited the oracle. They had to pay, as well."

Already the boys had run ahead. On the path were little smashed black things.

"Dog shit!" someone cried.

"Olives," Amelia said.

"Seriously?"

"Look, they're dropping off the trees."

"I hate olives on pizza."

"Thanks for sharing that."

A few bees were about but otherwise a lovely silence lured them on, disturbed on and off by the intermittent rush of car tires on the pavement above. They all spread out along the path past crumpled columns and careless great lumps of marble.

"The Gymnasium is this way," Francesca cried over her shoulder.

But the path she wanted was closed off by a thin loop of chain.

"Why should it be closed? It can't be. I've been coming here for fifty years; it's never been closed before." She muttered to herself. "Open to the public twenty-five hundred years! What can they mean by roping this off? Sara, can you lift the chain?"

Sara could and did lift the chain, first folding up the umbrella. Francesca slid under with apparent ease.

The rest of them followed, but slowly, single file. The stony path was overgrown and crowded on both sides with banks of wildflowers. Bees were suddenly everywhere. They were huge, fuzzy ones, like toys, like Easter chicks made of cotton fluff, great thumb-sized black bees with two yellow stripes, one around their front and the other around their rear. Cartoonish bees with round, black transparent wings and a loud indignant buzz. There were butter-flies, too. Amelia reminded Vida that the butterfly and the double axe was the Amazons' symbol. "See how a butterfly when its wings are spread looks like a double axe?" Vida loved to hear about Amazons.

But the butterflies were no distraction from the bees. Their drone filled Amelia's ears.

She had become almost drowsy with the floral scent when Maureen tugged her elbow and made her stop so she could whisper. Another menstrual emergency, Amelia figured. But not.

"Uh, Amelia, I've like, got to tell you something?" She rolled the ring in her ear. "I'm allergic to bees?"

"Oh, really, Maureen," said Amelia. "That's interesting. How allergic?"

"Like, you know, I can die if I get stung?" Her voice trailed upward.

The morning had started out so well. "Oh, great. Now you tell me." Amelia felt her vocabulary stiffen up like Francesca's. "And just what would you like me to do if this eventuates?"

"Oh, like I have my EpiPen," the girl burbled. "Right in my purse." She could see Amelia's eyes bulging. "Like my mum gave me a note but I lost it? And I meant to tell you before but I forgot?"

Amelia lost it. She had seen Francesca do it, and she had judged her for it. Now it was happening to her. "What the fuck?" she yelled. The file of kids, nine of them, since Sara had gone ahead with Francesca, stopped in its tracks. "Jesus fucking Christ! What on earth else is going to go wrong?" They all looked at her as if they could think of a few things.

"You could trip and sprain your—"

"No, don't tell me."

Voice raw, words rushing, a pent up stream of abuse inside Amelia came out as she turned on Maureen. "Are you for real, young lady?" she shrieked. "The sheer audacity! The irresponsibility! You could lose your life! You've put us all in a terrible spot!" She began kicking the stones at her feet.

There was silence for a half a minute. The bees droned.

"You should calm down," said Vida cannily. "You don't want to upset the bees." The yellow-jacketed insects zoomed around and about, touching the flower bushes, dive-bombing their ears. "I think they're very sensitive to emotional currents."

"Very funny."

Vida shrugged. "It wasn't meant to be." She stared at Amelia. "I guess this is like a test of your leadership ability."

Amelia wanted nothing more than to paste her in the mouth. But she thought better of it. In a fight, Vida would win. It was important that Amelia get the upper hand, now. She took a deep breath.

"All right, Maureen. This EpiPen. What are we to do with it? In the event you are stung?"

She surprised herself with her resemblance to Francesca, sometimes, the voice, the vocabulary, words, words, words. How long after we lose our own words do we lose ourselves?

"You have to give me a shot. But the trouble is—"

"The trouble is?"

"Well, it doesn't always work like if I get stung in a sensitive area?"

The single file had bunched up and everyone was within earshot.

"I know how to give shots," said Dimitri. "We did first aid at camp."

"Fine, then," Amelia said, more calmly than she felt. "You are assigned to follow Maureen everywhere she goes and be ready for action, just in case."

"We'll swat the bees away," said Ashley.

"No, don't," said Cassie. "You'll only get them angry. You'll only attract their attention."

They looked ahead. The bushes swelled on either side of the path. The bees hovered inches above the flowers, a spotted, buzzing net thrown over. A hundred metres ahead, nearly swallowed in foliage, floated Miss Morrow's umbrella.

"I wonder why nobody ever comes here?" said Vida.

"Maybe we should go back."

They turned their heads and looked back. The bushes swelled

behind them just as they did in front. The bees formed just as thick a cloud.

"How far have we come?"

"Not that far. But it's just as bad back there."

Small beads of perspiration were forming on Maureen's upper lip and in the hair at her temples. "We can't go backwards. We'll get lost."

"I don't think these bees are very interested in us," said Cassie. "They're more interested in the flowers."

Sometimes these kids can surprise you, Amelia thought.

"We shouldn't go back," said Vida. "Miss Morrow says you should never go back, that you should always go forward. It might be just as bad and then we'd have to catch up with the others."

"I'll go first," said Cassie. "They don't bother me. They can sting me."

Amelia thought of her namesake Cassandra. Was she not imprisoned in a beehive tomb in Troy for predicting its downfall? It made one believe in past lives. Somewhere this fearful girl had learned not to fear the sting. Cassie pushed ahead between two bouffant bushes. Then she craned her head backwards, and gave them a crooked, brave-ish smile. And they all filed after her, Maureen in the middle, Dimitri, eagle-eyed, behind her, Amelia bringing up the rear.

"Nobody has perfume on, I hope," said Vida.

"I have this wildflower gel in my hair."

"Don't go too fast. We'll sweat and that will attract them."

The bees droned obsessively over the little yellow flowers. The path deepened into the obscurity of the growth around it. Delphi had been swallowed by lime-green and sweet lemon yellow, the sky, ahead and above, narrowed, made pale. Their path cut though an old olive orchard, existing from the days when the village of Castri had grown up over ancient Delphi. The olive trees and the grass were being sawed at by men they couldn't see. In places the meadow grass had been cut; piles of branches lay at the foot of the trees.

"Should we call for help?" Amelia said.

A unanimous cry of No arose.

The flowers multiplied around them; there were tiny white and purple asters, blue blooming vines, honeysuckle and great lolling yellow heads on stalks. The olive trees had been pruned so often that their bases were like giant knuckled fists, as big as a clutch of kids together. Above the distant chainsaw buzz was birdsong. And bee buzz. The bees mobbed them in a giant cluster, at once enveloping them and seeming not to know they were there. Maureen began to whimper and wave her hands around her head.

"Whatever you do, don't hit out at them."

"I have to!" Her voice was raw with panic.

"Don't," said Dimitri, catching her hands at her shoulders. He tried to hold them still, walking close behind her, and when that didn't work he raised both of their left hands above her head, moved up to her left side and, holding her right hand at her right shoulder, with his arm around her neck, he walked beside her in a skater's waltz position. Maureen giggled once and then relaxed, her back pressed against his side.

Water rushed down on them here and there from above: melted snow, they thought, but it smelled of sewage. The earth was a crumbly clay that turned slippery when wet. Low-flying white butterflies brushed Amelia's cheeks and she had that crawly feeling of insects everywhere—in the toes of her shoes, all over her neck. Sweat started on her, too. Now all of them but Cassie were whimpering. She plodded on in apparent calm.

Through a break in the bushes Amelia saw a backpacker eating his breakfast on a rock. He looked quizzical but she shook her head. It was as if they were enchanted: they inhabited another, precarious reality and could not be reached. They had to continue; they were in a trance and if it broke the bees would go berserk. The breeze stirred everything from the trees on down. Thistles so tall they topped the boys' heads threatened them and a cold leaf touched Amelia's arm.

"Voices ahead!" cried Vida, several minutes later. "We're catching up."

"Don't run," Amelia cautioned but realized she had no need to with stolid Cassie in front. I don't believe I've ever seen that child run, she thought.

And now just as it seemed they might escape this nightmare, the bees got angry. They began to dive-bomb Amelia's face; she raised an arm to shield her brow and shook from the effort not to swat.

"Oh god oh god oh god," sobbed Maureen.

"Just stay. Just stay with it."

"I can't."

"You can."

"Argh!" It was Vida who broke ranks, cursing, screaming, crashing off into the underground with a cloud of furious insects over her head. Cassie faltered. "Go!" said Vida. She had completely lost her cool and was all flailing and flying orange hair. She tore off a branch and swung it wildly in the air. More and more bees went her way. "Go!" she yelled at Cassie. "You idiot! Get them all out of here!"

And so Cassie plodded on, humming now, and the rest all hummed along. "Tell me where, in what country, is Flora the beautiful Roman..."

And the others answered. "But where are the snows of yesteryear?"

"Is that your anthem?" said Amelia.

"Shut up!" said Roxanne and Ashley simultaneously. "You can't sing that."

"We can't leave Vida," Amelia said to one of the boys.

"She's coming, she's coming."

They could hear her crashing through the underbrush on a parallel route beside them. "God damn these fuckin' monsters!" Amelia did not know what was holding them together except for the fact that they knew the path had to come to an end.

"If we get out of here alive I'll pray to the goddess every fuckin' day," said Chino.

"Yeah, right."

Plod plod. Was it her imagination or were the bees thinning out? Amelia could hear Vida panting and gasping off to the right.

"Hey! Manor! We're gaining on you!" cried Dimitri. Just as Miss Morrow's fluted black hemline flipped into view between the bushes ahead of a small turn, they came out to a bare spot on the ground, a fragment of wall, the outlined ruins of some ancient workout room, swimming pool or lecture hall. Amelia could barely restrain herself from pushing Dimitri and Maureen out of the narrow pathway onto the open ground. As they stepped away from the fragrant, effusive bushes, the buzzing of bees diminished, diminished and died.

The kids had gathered around Maureen, who was crying softly into her hands.

"You did amazing," Dimitri said, over and over. "You were great."

And Amelia took to the sun, stretching, suddenly indolent in the heat. She breathed. She was dripping with sweat, and worried about Vida. Her heart had been in a vice; now it expanded with a timorous gratitude. Any little upset would blow her away. "Gang," she said. "Get over here." They were standing in a semicircle as a welcoming committee when Vida smashed through the last barrier of bushes and ran screaming into the clearing. Her face was swollen and she was hugging her upper arms. She'd been stung half a dozen times but she didn't care. "Is Maureen okay?" she said. They all embraced. The Dead Ladies were sobbing out loud, and Amelia shed a few tears herself.

Then Maureen seated herself on the stone remains of something, her face shiny with tears. Dimitri stood behind her looking as proud as if he were a press agent, the whole tour of kids surrounding her. She's here, they said, she's fine.

"I've never been so scared in my whole entire life. I thought I was going to die for sure. There were so many of them; I've never seen so many bees all at once. Or such big ones."

"Huge," corroborated Dimitri.

"But these guys were so great," said Maureen. "I never could have made it without you." She smiled at Cassie, Vida and Dimitri in turn. "And Amelia, of course."

"I didn't do anything," Amelia grumbled.

"You let us do it," uttered Cassie.

Maureen smiled again, utterly composed now as if she'd been born to this notoriety, this moment in time, the apex of her own special adolescent curve. Of course they knew all about these dramas from television and the newspapers. They understood the structure, the composition, even the blocking. We try to teach them Greek tragedy, thought Amelia, we restage *The Trojan Women* and they have their own references, imbibed with mother's milk: the victim/survivor flanked by spokesman/handler, surrounded by supportive crowd of witnesses, all addressing themselves to some camera somewhere, and yet to themselves. Heroes, not villains this time, but anything was possible. They could have been discussing the axe murder that no one foresaw in the next street over, or the teenage runaway who stole a car and ran down a priest walking his dog late at night, but this time it was a close escape, a victory by committee.

"That was like so amazing. We're good. Oh, we are good."

"How do you feel?" asked Chino.

"I feel," said Maureen, tilting her face upward as she consulted the little-heard inner voice of her feelings. This was foul-tempered Maureen of multiple body piercings, raver Maureen of the rumoured cocaine habit who ran drugs at night at Bloor and Bathurst for her boyfriends, this was I've-been-thrown-out-of-every-private-school-in-town-and-some-public (which was more impressive as the public schools just weren't allowed to kick you out except for violence) Maureen. Beautiful, blonde-haired Virgin sovereign who hated this world. Recall, as Francesca would say, this was that Maureen.

"I feel," she said, "fully altered. I feel like one of those yogis or something who walks through fire. I mean, it's like a life-changing thing, right?"

Jacob dared to snicker but was silenced by the glares of his classmates.

"I came here Maureen. And I will leave here someone else."

"Who will you be then?" piped Cassie, who always took things literally. But nobody laughed this time.

"I'll be..." said Maureen, looking over her shoulder at Dimitri. He gave her no hint. She looked the other way up the red rocks, to the left of Delphi.

"Delphi," said Cassie. "Delphine."

"Oh perfect, yes, I'll be Delphine."

The kids sighed. It was too perfect.

"I'm serious," she said. "It's real. I have now officially changed my name. I am Delphine."

The first thing Amelia had to do was drive Vida back to the Dolphin and get her some antihistamines for her stings. She was remarkably cheery about them, wearing them as little war medallions in the battle to save Maureen from death. "So did you do it on purpose to divert the bees?" Amelia asked. But perhaps she was giving her a little too much credit.

"I cannot tell a lie," Vida said.

"Oh yes you can."

"Well, I will not tell one then. I just sort of—lost it."

"Spazzed?"

"Yeah. But then I figured it could be useful."

"I know what you mean."

Sometimes I really love these kids, said Amelia to herself. "Hop up," she said opening the minibus door to Vida. "Let's go back and see what's next."

"Amelia! Amelia!" Jacob with his high-pitched voice, his squat, short-legged body, edged into line beside her. "Here's the big question of the day. Will Dr. Laird give his talk?"

Dugald's talk had been built up by Miss Morrow to be the highlight of the tour. "Dr. Laird will introduce you to the wonders of Greece," she'd say. "You are very lucky to be able to hear him speak while you are standing on the soil of Delphi."

"Oh, I suspect so."

Though Amelia did wonder, looking over at him. He was dusting his trousers with nervous hands, his eyes on Francesca.

There were guides here gathering their groups together. Only one spoke English, gnarled, bandy-legged and chewing on a toothpick.

"Somebody has the extra ticket of the young man. Are we sure there are not two tickets for one person? OK. I'm going to buy another one.

"See the two steep rocks? You can see fifty-foot columns. There were some here too. Any questions before starting? No questions? Let's go up."

"Dugald, are you ready?"

"Yes, Francesca," he said, his voice pulled up deep as from a well.

"Oh, darling," she said. She stepped lightly across the stones in her little pointy suede boots with the skate laces and the three-inch heels and took his arm. "I'm so looking forward to it."

Amelia's heart, newly softened by bees, broke for her. Dugald was gone somewhere else, the marrow of him, and these were his empty bones she held beside her.

As the group milled about at the base of the site, Amelia slipped away. She'd seen, rounding the hairpin turn in the mountain road, a little café beneath an arbour spilling over with wisteria vines. She turned her back on the clustering, chattering tourists at the gate and set out down the road. There was duty, twenty-four-hours-a-day duty, but there was also self-preservation. She needed a break.

Seating herself at a tiny white table under great drooping funnels of purple flowers, she felt terribly pleased. The elderly man who came her way on long springy legs with his kindly creased face looked like an ancient, or so it seemed to her, some precursor of the mountain gods, before they learned that stubby legs were better for scrambling. He returned quickly with her coffee and after setting it on the table turned to go, then turned back.

"First time, Delphi?"

"No, fifth time."

He smiled, either accustomed to peoples' return, or not understanding. The "vaporous fumes" rose from the hillside, mysteriously, as they always had. There was nothing further to say. Amelia sat, sipped her coffee, and breathed deeply. Relax. It had been a near-death experience, but it had ended brilliantly. This was a good omen. Perhaps the trip was not doomed after all.

She tried to feel the history. To sense the pilgrims, walking here over these mountains, burning with questions. To feel the frenzy of the Pythia, taken from her nearby shepherd husband, her children grown, her grandchildren, too. Seated over the steaming pot of laurel leaves and breathing the fumes, finally exploding into a dance, a rage, a performance, uttering the words out of sequence, perhaps not even in a language known to the onlookers. Then the calculating priests who took the words and moulded them, interpreted them, gave them out to the seeker of answers. Spin doctors, Dugald called them.

And their clientele, hungry for a solution or a word of guidance, who had been kept for three days, a week perhaps, in the Sanctuary of Athena being cleansed and prepared for this moment. This was the time during which the attendants of the oracle, the temple workers, could suss them out and determine what it was they needed to hear, what answer would fall rightly though obliquely on their ears and would serve the cause, the cause being preserving the power of the oracle.

As the coffee cooled in the bottom of her cup Amelia played the tricks she liked to play with history. She imagined herself as living here, then. She was one of the people: she saw this sea of olive trees, she breathed this air, she walked with this earth beneath her feet hundreds of years ago. And bit by bit the grandeur faded, despite the clever minds who ran the joint, despite the awe and the fervour of the Greeks and others who were served by the oracle—it ran down, it lost favour, it was forgotten. And an entire little village grew up over the ruins, a village in which no one knew that underfoot was the navel of the world. For this colossal ignorance they were up-rooted, these inhabitants, and moved along the road so that others, these worshippers of history, these people like Francesca and Dugald and even herself, could come and see, so that this oracle could be rediscovered and entered, laid bare for examination, revisitation, reinterpretation.

She pulled out the postcard she'd bought from the waiter.

"Dear Ferdinand," she wrote. She had promised herself she would give him up but vacillated. Never mind. People did. Maureen/Delphine's life-altering ephiphany notwithstanding, Amelia's observation was that people faltered toward renewal, toward good behaviour, toward self-improvement, and then fell back. Change was hard.

"Exquisite day. Red poppies, mimosa, huge bushes of yellow flowers, lilies…" did he care about flowers? She realized she didn't know. The background hum of the orange-juicer broke into her consciousness. She looked up. The young man of the family, con-scripted without his permission but also it would seem without protest into waiting tables in the taverna, possibly until the death of his parents necessitated that he take over the business, was staring at her fixedly. A dull but unmistakable sensation began on the back of her neck. She squirmed on her chair and was suddenly conscious of sweat forming between her breasts. She could smell herself, a not unpleasant experience. They didn't call her the Cheese for nothing.

But no. Her fantasies had settled on the Portuguese troll, the little dark man with his canteen truck full of goodies, hot soups on cold days, coffees to wake her up, chocolate bars to get her through that last period. The man whose hands were ever so much more dextrous than one would think: her Hephaestus with his furnace, her Pan with his furry thighs and cloven hooves. How Francesca hated and despised that! Amelia was supposed to package her sexual appetite, attach it to some appropriate creature so that it would go unnoticed. She would never forget the dressing-down she'd received at her hands that night in the chapel. "Not some prancing sweat-flocked steed, or some well-hung donkey, that's not what you want. Or if you do want it, get over it. Want what is appropriate, Amelia. You'll find it makes life a great deal easier." It wouldn't matter to Francesca if Amelia led her little tribe through a dozen plagues of killer bees, she would have none of her now.

"I miss you," Amelia wrote defiantly. "I miss my hot chocolate and everything else." (Underline everything else). "I think about you in every way." She seemed to recall that his wife did not read English. "I wish you would come back to the school. It's not you who should have been fired, but me."

She could hear water running. Behind her the Castalian spring, which other years had dried to a soiled trickle, was flowing out of the rock. The cleft, the redness of the rocks and a small cascade of water down the cliffs, with here, below, the veil of little buttercups, blue and purple violets, together created a blush of new life like that which came over a burn, a grave, a landslide, some catastrophe.

Cat-a-strophe: a Greek word. Yes, indeed, and didn't they just invent the concept? You couldn't get much greater catastrophes than Agave tearing her son Pentheus to bits in her Dionysian ecstasy. He'd left his mark on this place, too, that troublesome wild god. The wind stirred and off came hundreds of little petals of wisteria, pale purple, darker purple, with yellow eye-shapes inside. They fell like a shower around her and lay on the white enamelled tabletop. There was fragrance everywhere and with it the drone of the huge, fuzzy bees, which now held no terrors.

And she knew she would not mail the postcard, even if she had Ferdinand's address. But she would remember this. The zigzagged red bands of little roads going down the hillsides across the valley, the spokes of cedar and spots of blood-red poppies, amongst them near and far the strange, violent eruptions of silver cacti and tall thistles with purplish stars atop. She would remember this. She pushed out her chair and waved goodbye to the gentlemen whose good luck it was to have this concession. "I will be back," she said.

After the bees and the frappé to regain her composure, after the postcard she would not send, Amelia found the students still in disarray around the entrance to the oracle site. It seemed that Dugald was not ready to give his talk and that Francesca was occupied in trying to coax him. A quick trip around the Museum with Amelia was what was needed here. The boys protested, and were permitted to wait outside.

And so in they went, Amelia and the girls, obedient, still slightly shell-shocked. Francesca and Dugald had unfortunately not been in the mood to hear about their ordeal, but Amelia said it was definitely proof of the theory of why Homo erectus had outlasted the others. Dugald would have been proud. Amelia was proud and it cheered her on what looked to become a very tough day.

She did not know the half of it yet.

In the Museum they tripped lightly past the Omphalos, navel of the world, because she thought they'd be more impressed seeing the reproduction on the hillside. They paused a moment before a bronze tripod and she explained how it was placed over the open chasm and how the vapours rose around the Pythia as she sat over it. Then they were inside and looking at the friezes from the Treasury of the Athenians, that storehouse of the trophies of the victory over the Persians at the Battle of Marathon. Amelia found herself surrounded by the girls as they gazed at scenes from the Amazonomachy. She explained that the Amazons were like mirror images of civilization, a reversed ideal, and thus terrifying to the Greeks. "They were enormous, fierce women warriors. So determined they actually cut off their breasts to make room to draw their bows. Don't get any ideas," she said to Vida.

Indeed, Vida had gathered the girls around her and appeared to be asserting her command. Cassie escaped the group and came, strangely, nervously, to Amelia's side.

"Miss Holt," said Cassie, "we have an army, too. It's just a little army. But we have done some damage. You knew about it, didn't you?"

For some reason Amelia did not turn her head, did not indicate outwardly that Cassie was speaking. They walked a little farther from the group.

"I knew a little."

"We were called the Dead Ladies and we did something very, very bad."

"Yes," said Amelia. "I believe you did." She turned and looked the girl square in the face. "Why are you telling me this?"

"So that I can stop being afraid that I *will* tell. Do you understand?"

Amelia laughed. "You are all backwards and inside out, Cassie, but you do make sense."

"I am not supposed to tell anyone but keeping this secret is making me sick."

"Are you saying you want to tell?"

"I can't," said Cassie. Her face was white with fear.

"Try. One word of it."

"Ferdinand," said Cassie.

That was all.

Amelia tried to stop the shock that went through her, head to toe, from becoming visible. Vida strolled into earshot.

"Greek against Amazon, a Dead Amazon," read Amelia ostentatiously. "Note that the Amazons are mostly portrayed on their knees though I imagine it wasn't easy to get one there."

Vida strolled away. Amelia looked at Cassie.

"What did you 'Dead Ladies' do to Ferdinand?"

But Cassie only clapped her hand over her mouth, flushed violet and dodged behind a group of French tourists.

Amelia tried to calm down. What could they have done to Ferdinand, after all? They were just girls and god knows Amelia had been one and god knew as well what a confused set of instructions lay out there for them all. She could only applaud them for attempting to take control. Call me a corrupter of youth but that is my attitude, thought Amelia. Unless. Unless they did something really vile—she felt cold, shocked, to her marrow.

But she had a job to do. So she walked on, and they all laughed at how the Greeks invented these giant warrior women and then made certain their short little warriors clobbered them in every battle. They were still laughing when they moved on to the frieze portraying the Labours of Heracles.

"Recall: Hercules was the hero of Athens before Theseus usurped him. There is our Hercules winning his fights with the Nemean Lion and Three-Bodied Geryon. Here he is about to slay Geryon's cattle, and Geryon's dog as well."

But the girls had the giggles. Amelia had to admit the labelling in Greek museums was always amusing. Explanations were random and English was sometimes fanciful. Here was a good caption: "Two Horiefied Cows."

"I *guess* they're horrified, they've got no legs," said Cassie.

The girls fell all over each other laughing and trying to smother their laughter while serious elderly French couples who had been disgorged from a bus as cruelly green as theirs was pink looked annoyed.

"I think I need to find another vocation," Amelia muttered. "This one is very stressful."

"You can move to Greece and get a job doing translations," said Roxanne. "You can't do any worse."

There was the Homeric *Hymn to Apollo* inscribed on blocks of marble. That stopped them dead and took their breath away. Written twenty-five hundred years ago, it stood as neat as any child's notebook: something about the way a hand crosses a page or, here, a bit of wall that once passed for a page, is intensely moving even centuries after to anyone who loved words.

And there was a lovely headless statue of Apollo.

"I can't tell him from Athena."

"They all wear those peplos dresses."

The Sanctuary of Athena relics occupied an entire room. There was a gorgeous winged Nike and three female masks. The masks were long, with no eyeholes, and the female figures had their fingers on their nipples to squirt any comer in the eye with milk.

There was a circular altar with "young maidens draping ribbons" on it and various running, dancing female forms. The sway of those hips, the languorous folds of drapery, the eyes all downcast: it was quite persuasive. Amelia could see that the little lovebirds, Vida and Cassie, were rather affected by all this woman-positive energy, sometimes touching and even linking their fingertips. Well, more power to them, Amelia said to herself. It hasn't worked for me at all the other way.

"You may be beginning to get a sense of what it really means to worship a female deity," said Amelia. "It does seem like more action for the girls all around."

When they reached the beautiful Naxian sphinx—half-woman, half-lion, they simply stared, in awe; it was so full of power. But it was the Charioteer that stopped them dead. He had a room all to himself, and he stood taller than life, cold and green, in the centre of it. He held the remnant of a rein in his hand, but if he were driving horses he could never have been made of flesh and blood, for nothing on him moved, at all. He was more beautiful than anything alive; he was clearly no ordinary human.

"Freaky," said Vida, the first to turn away.

"Wait," said Cassie. She felt the cold inside. The future was bearing down on her. The Charioteer seemed to want to speak.

Vida stopped.

"Don't you see? He's like one of those mortals that the gods punished. He's been turned to stone. He probably stole a nymph that Zeus was in love with, maybe that was it. And Zeus transformed him into a statue. And took away his horses."

But Vida only said, "I hope he doesn't do it to me," and skipped off.

Cassie lingered, trapped, it seemed, in the Charioteer's stony gaze. What? she said. Coming, he answered. She froze.

The others spilled out into the sunshine. Dugald and Francesca and the four boys were looking rather bored, seated on large marble blocks. The principal and his vice huddled under the umbrella, which was quickly ceded back to Sara. Amelia purchased the tickets and at last they began to climb.

16

DR. LAIRD'S
LECTURE

"THERE WERE THREE GREEK civilizations," Dugald began. "The Cycladic, with lions, remember? The Mycenaean, that's around 2000 BC and—" The third was lost, apparently, in the translation. Dugald took a deep breath and wavered in the thin air. He caught Francesca's eye.

"See this wreath? It's the symbol of Apollo. See it? Say yes, even if you don't," he muttered under his breath. "At first it was a peasant place; peasants were coming here regularly with their goats. They must have found the sulphurous vapours, and they began to feel that the site was sacred. They made it a shrine to Gaia, the earth mother. This was before Apollo. What do we think of when we think of Delphi? The vapours, the mist, the cleft in the rocks, the hot water of the Castalian springs, female, female—this was her mouthpiece."

He gave the group a moment to nod. He couldn't hear them talking, couldn't hear them at all. The roaring in his ears could have been altitude; it could have been wind.

"The snake was her son. Just remember: Prehistory is a time for women. History is a time for men." He looked over at Francesca to see how he was doing. She was smiling, erect, her slim waist an archaeological marvel in itself; it was the waist of her own history, of fifty years ago; it was the waist of a twenty-year-old. Her face looked tense. Perhaps he should hurry on. Some kid in a sweatshirt with Wu-Tang Clan written on it moved into place beside him and for an instant he couldn't be sure if he was one of theirs or not.

"There came a time when they no longer liked Mother Earth. They preferred Apollo instead. Don't ask me why. It's too complicated. They say the gods are fickle. But we humans are fickle too, even in our choice of gods. So here's the story. Once upon a time Apollo arrived here. He was a young man. Python—snake, son of Gaia—was guarding the oracle and Apollo killed it. So he swept away the matriarchy, just like that."

He had their attention now. The best way to captivate a teenager? Talk about sweeping away mothers. Oh yes, oh boy. When he was not so much older than a boy himself, he'd swept away his wife instead, a fatal move; his children had ended up in the dustpan with her.

"Apollo had to go to the north of Greece after that. Because he had slain the son of Gaia, he had to do nine years of servitude to purify himself. He returned as a dolphin. The Cretan people saw and followed the dolphin here, first to Delphi. Delphi: Dolphin. Or, another interpretation is that Delphi means woman/ancient mother. This was the centre of the world, the omphalos. The belly button. Everybody has a belly button. It's where you were attached to your mother, correct? It's where, now that we look at it this way, you were cut off from your mother."

He turned and began to walk up the hill. And one of the boys came to walk beside him, taking his elbow. Aware that he was rattling on like a guide tape on high speed, Dugald looked again at his wife. Her face under the umbrella held by Sara was paler than normal. Was she worried? Could it be himself that she was worried about?

"We are now approaching the Omphalos, the navel, the oldest stone at Delphi."

"Is it the real one?"

Real? What did that mean, in this context? The original? The one that is now barely recognizable for what it was, that looks less like itself than the copy? "No, it has been replaced. This is a copy, a good one. The real one is in the museum." The Greeks were not above planting a reconstruction when they thought they could get away with it.

The boys began to climb on it. Dugald leaned against a wall. He watched Francesca as she watched him, with a wariness fifty years of marriage would belie. Dugald's glance gave way first. It bounced down on the heads of his charges, and he forgot what was bothering him.

"The navel of the world! The centre of the universe! That is where you are. Think about it." He appeared to be excited as if this were his first time here. He waved his arms to the students who, noticing his animation as a definite change of pace, crowded in on him. "Did you study Greek, Mr Finkelstein?"

"No, sir."

"But you did, Dimitri."

"I am Greek, sir. At least my parents are."

"Can you read the signs then, and tell us all what they say?"

Dimitri peered and Dimitri tried but Dimitri remained silent.

"The letters are absolutely the same as in Ancient Greek. But the language has changed. When we read we can just about understand what was said."

"It hasn't changed an iota."

"Very good, Jacob. A joke is a sign of intelligence."

"Do you know who invented the flush toilet?"

"No."

"People from Crete. And we call them Cretans!"

There was an appreciative laugh from certain elderly English travellers near enough to hear.

Dugald waved the heat away from his head irritably. "This was a very grand place, once. Socrates came here. They all did, to get advice. We see nothing now but the ruins of the temple and the treasures. Come, let's step along."

He began up the uneven stone path again. He was not steady.

Francesca was better on her feet in her little witch shoes than he was in his walking boots. She slid in beside him and put her arm through his. Everyone seemed awfully keen to walk with him.

"Do you think his speech is supposed to be like this?" whispered Cassie to Vida. Vida shook her head.

"You recall that Apollo had to go away as a punishment. That was re-enacted every year. For three months the people worshipped Dionysus. In winter when the oracle was silent, they had a festival of dancing, singing and drinking wine. You know what happens then? Remember Agave, who tore her own child to bits?"

He had a sense he wasn't doing well with the lecture, not that Francesca would ever let on. They climbed on. Dugald was seriously winded: Francesca had retreated. Where was the boy who had been holding his arm? He looked around; his bride was under full sail with Sara keeping the umbrella aloft. She did not look in his direction. Not looking, he tripped. His weight fell forward hard on one foot, but the knee held, thank goodness. And then there was a hand under his elbow. It was Cassie. He cleared his throat.

"My dear," he said. "How do you like the place?"

She looked at him, her guileless grey eyes, somehow deeper, darker than he'd noticed before. Cisterns, he'd called them once. Now they were like the night sky. How they do grow up, he thought, even the rats, and acquire their own mysteries. He stopped, shook off her helping arm, and shouted over what he perceived to be a din of voices on the hot dusty hillside.

"We are now in front of the temple. This is a column, that is a pillar, recall: the column is always round, the pillar is square. Any questions, ladies and gentlemen? No questions. Yes, my dear."

Vida spoke, the wild girl with the persimmon plume on her head, and he heard not a word. Then came the voice from beside him, strong in his good ear. "Tripod? It is not what you put your camera on. It is a three-legged stool. There was only one tripod and it was called the tripod of the plateau. We'll get to it."

They turned. Cassie stayed with him and he was glad of it. "To go up is very easy," he said, more to convince himself than anything. "To come down we'll have to be careful."

"It will be different when you come down," said Cassie. Dugald heard her, but had no idea what she meant. He raised his voice again, as if his listeners, and not he, were deaf; as if they, not he, were hearing a roaring in the ears.

"This is unique among the temples of Apollo," he said. "Here at Delphi, people were allowed to enter. Nowhere else. After the sacrifices, they would take a seat and ask their questions—"

People were eavesdropping. They were just tourists, they weren't even students, and they were listening to Dr. Laird.

"You are most privileged to be able to overhear," Francesca said to an American couple. "My husband has lectured at Harvard and at New York University."

"What sacrifices?" said Jacob.

Dugald saw the question but didn't get it. He turned to Cassie.

"What sacrifices?" she shouted in his ear. "He means animals, or people?"

"Oh no, no people. A sheep, or a goat, something four-legged. No dolphins, either: sacred, recall? Remember, mythology is oral. It is the belief of the people at a particular time. And there are many versions, many variations on the myths, as you see; they changed over time. About human sacrifice the Greeks were ambivalent. There are many cases in the myths of a mother or father destroying a child—Procne's Itys. Agave's Pentheus. Agamemnon sacrificed Iphigenia to get favourable winds: recall."

"Iphigenia was only my age," said Cassie.

"And a virgin. How could she be expected to make the wind rise, just by dying?" scoffed Vida.

"Agamemnon broke the law when he sacrificed his daughter, even though the seers had advised him to do it. It was known by that time, understood by that time, to be the old way, and a bad thing.

And he paid for it, with his life; for his wife, Clytemnestra, would murder him to avenge the sacrifice. And, incidentally, murder your namesake too, Miss Cassandra McVey. Yes?"

Cassie shrugged.

"Of course it was not incidental at all, Cassandra being a slave and Clytemnestra's husband's whore, brought back from the fall of Troy."

He saw the eyes of the students going dull, turning down to examine, no doubt, the notes written on the palms of their colleagues, the cigarettes being palmed.

"Sacrifices! Yes, no. They were animals. Thank you for your question."

The line of students paused while another tourist took a photograph. It never ceased to amaze Dugald that they all wanted to take pictures when you could buy perfectly good postcards better than any picture any of them was going to get, at the kiosk. There were flashes going, light meters acting up perhaps: who needed flashbulbs under the Greek sun? If a place could disappear under constant light flares as its image was reproduced, this place would fade fade fade down into light and the white bedsheets of Francesca's home. Bedsheets: an unfortunate memory crossed his mind. He felt his cheeks go crimson. What had that been about, with his bride? Had they struggled? Had they quarrelled? Had he taken her in his arms and felt nothing?

"All right, class," he continued, "I shall tell you exactly what happens to the enquirer at the oracle. First, he arrives. He must stay five days at the Sanctuary of Athena. His date has been given to him, always the seventh of the month: it was the only day the Pythia was open for business. Early that morning he would cleanse himself in the springs, below, anticipating his meeting with the Pythia at some hour later in the day. He would come to wait in the shade of the columns of the Temple of Apollo until she was led in, in her white robes. The priests sacrificed a goat. The enquirer had bought the goat in town for the purpose: goat husbandry was the local industry.

He, our enquirer, possibly from Athens, possibly from farther afield, continued to cool his heels. When it was his turn he was taken in to the Temple, with his goat. The Pythia sits over her tripod; the fumes from the laurel and bay leaves permeate the air. In the Temple of Apollo was a statue of Homer. There were written the maxims: Know thyself, and also, Nothing in Excess." Dugald braced himself athletically, feet apart, feeling the energy, the old energy, come back, feeling as if he were astride a horse, a young man again, a vital force.

"This is how it went. The priest stood guarding the door to the sacred room, where only the Pythia could enter. In that secret chamber was a golden statue of Apollo, the Omphalos, a laurel bush, the tripod. Incidentally, the sibyls did not live for many years. Inhalation of the smoke and going into frenzies were not good for them— what am I talking about?" he shouted.

The kids jumped, guiltily, most of them. Others, the ones who had been listening, jumped out of fear. What *was* he talking about? "I'm telling you this was a very important place, where top secrets were held, and sometimes not held. Think of the Pentagon."

He caught his wife in an undisguised look of consternation. She would have been open-mouthed if such an ungainly expression were possible for a person of her dignity. Dugald was rushing through his famous lecture, it appeared. Were those little flecks of white foam that flew from his lips? He laughed to himself. The divine fit, perhaps? Not he, surely.

"So let's say you have a question." He hopped like a bird with his stick to a higher position on the stony ground. "You come here and you expect five days' hospitality at least. You see, the Greeks knew that your future, which is what you can only guess at, is composed of your past and your present. The prophecy was always right for two reasons. One reason: they knew what you wished to hear. How did they know? Because the priests and the attendants found out all about you while you were being made ready during the days of purification. Second reason: everything the oracle said was ambiguous. It could be interpreted in at least two ways. I'll get to that. But now, I want you to become an Applicant. You are a king, you are a warrior, you are Socrates, or perhaps you are a local woman wanting to know which of two suitors you should marry. So you come to Delphi. Perhaps the year is 457 BC.

"And what have you seen so far? You have seen about two tons of gold. It is incredible. There was a forest of two thousand statues, many of them gold. You have seen the Sacred Way with treasuries displaying the wealth of cities, kingdoms, individuals. You are now within the temple of Apollo: it is eighteen metres by twenty-four, by the way. Inside are inscribed the two maxims I mentioned, and upon these two maxims your entire philosophy will depend. The room is like a library, there is writing all over the walls. Pindar the great poet is there, his statue, sitting on an iron throne. There is a great flame. What does the flame mean? Do you know? Anybody? It represents the spirit.

"And we must keep on with this vision. Beyond the flame is the room, the oracle. There are volcanic fumes. The kings, the commoners, whoever you are, each and every one of you is an Applicant. You cannot see the sibyl, the Priestess, but you can hear the voices.

"And you stand. Or perhaps you kneel here in the flame room. And hear the Pythia getting inspired."

Dr. Laird's feet danced, his cane tapped, the spittle on his lips gathered like the foam at the edge of a wind-tossed sea.

"She's heaving those leaves of laurel on the flame. And gobbledy gook yakkety yakkety, blah, blah, blah, comes out. Apollo—the god of inspiration—is solving all your problems. Will the oracle be wrong?"

"No!" This was vintage Dugald. The students loved it.

"No, of course not. Will you disbelieve? Will you question the oracle? No. You will not." Dugald calmed, suddenly. He turned to his spouse. She produced a white handkerchief from her bag. He mopped his brow. Vintage Dr. Laird. You could almost hear him say as much to himself—Dr. Laird imitating Dr. Laird imitating—Who had he moulded himself on, at the start? There must have been someone. Someone now lost in the mists of time. Likely he had had an inspired teacher once. He did not remember.

"So you, sir"—pointing to Chino—"you are Croesus. You are rich, recall, rich as Croesus, you are the richest man in the world. You have come to Delphi with your question; it is about your army: should you cross the river? Okay, so you ask. And the answer: if you cross the River Alys, you will destroy a great empire. So, good, this is what Croesus wants to hear. He wants to destroy the empire of his enemy. So he crosses the river. But the empire he destroys is his own. Ha! The oracle was not wrong. The oracle could not be wrong. The oracle had protected itself with ambiguity. This is what power can do and will do. Well to remember this.

"Example? Here the oracle gave Croesus another bit of double advice. 'Watch out for the mule.' And he did not. Who was the mule? Cyrus, his enemy. Cyrus was half-royal, and half-commoner, hence a mule. You see, good advice was given but it was so complicated, it was so enigmatic, who knew until it was too late? That's the business of prediction, do you understand? It was not, in fact, prediction. It was advice, offered so that it could be interpreted as the Applicant wished. See how they play the game?"

The students were beginning to smile and shift their feet on the hard pebble-strewn ground. Dr. Laird made them feel wise, made them feel special, that they were included in an inner circle of those understanding the tricks.

"It's all in the punctuation. Recall that you must remember the punctuation of a poem because the punctuation is the meaning? And those of you who've done a little philosophy with me may recall how Plato felt that oral communication was superior to written, hence, his dialogues: there was less chance for the meaning to change with the insertion of punctuation. Well, this was exactly what the oracle turned on its head. There was no punctuation! Here's what the oracle said to Pyrrhus, who was fighting the Romans. He had three great victories. At Herclia, at Lydia, and at—"

The third great victory was lost. Dugald's brain felt as if it were on fire. He was terribly hot. The noise in his ears was frightful. He had to admit to himself at this moment something he had rarely admitted before: he did not feel well. It must be the altitude, he thought, or the sea air, or the heat, the crowds, the excitement, perhaps, of seeing this most beautiful spot on earth again.

Personally, he did not believe Apollo had ever truly won over Delphi. This was still Gaia's place; the goddess of Mother Earth was still here. You could feel her heat in the crevices, feel her rage and her compassion, in equal measure. All the strategy and manipulation of male power was there, but it was only on the surface. Delphi belonged to woman. He pulled himself back (with great effort) to where he'd been in the lecture. He must finish it, but he couldn't remember what it was he thought would come next. Pyrrhus.

"The oracle said to Pyrrhus, 'Go come not in war be killed.'"

He let this pronouncement fall on the students' ears. It didn't make much of an impression. Was anything left between the ears? Or had their brains dried up in the sun, as his seemed to be doing.

"Now see for yourself how many ways that could be interpreted. 'Go, come not, in war be killed.' Or 'Go come, not in war be killed.' So the oracle has stated to Pyrrhus that he will be killed in war and also that he will not be killed in war. You see?"

They saw.

Why did he have to hurry? He stopped lecturing, suddenly, and turned to Cassie. Her face was red with sunburn.

"Cassandra, what is going to happen?"

Her face screwed up like a twisted cloth and tears squeezed out onto her cheeks.

"Don't ask me that, Dr. Laird," she said. "I don't know why you are asking me that."

Francesca stepped forward and put out a hand toward Dugald, to stop him, he thought, from embarrassing the girl.

"I don't know," Cassie insisted, almost crying. "I don't ever know!"

"I didn't mean anything profound by the question." He tried to reassure her. "I only meant what were the plans." But Cassie stepped away and did a little twirl, then another and another. Odd girl, he thought. The turmoil in his head was calming down. The noise was subsiding. He took off his Tilley hat and fanned himself. Then he put it back on again, as no sooner was his scalp exposed to the sun than he felt it prickle unpleasantly. He was losing his audience, he could see, with all this byplay.

"Do you know what the oracle told pregnant women who wanted to know which sex their baby would be? 'Boy no girl.' That's what the oracle said. Now what do you make of that? You see, it depends on where you put the comma. 'Boy, no girl' surely means she will have a boy, not a girl. But 'boy no, girl' means the opposite."

A low belly laugh began to erupt in Dugald. It worked its way up his abdomen and into his throat, loosening his bowels alarmingly on its way. But the laugh escaped, upward, while nothing escaped downward as far as he could tell, thanks to those sphincter muscles he'd worked on all those years in martial arts. He had one more point to make, and he made it with a shriek of hilarity, bringing the children along with him. He was laughing and they were laughing, too.

"Heads I win, tails you lose—that's Delphi." He roared and his huge amusement escaped upward like a balloon and rose, rose toward the stadium at the top of the hill that he would never see again, he knew, the expansive classical theatre, which sat five thousand and was mathematically engineered for acoustics so that the human voice expanded and travelled upwards on the sea air.

His legs were not good enough any more. He would never stand above it and look down to the bull's eye at the centre and imagine the owner of the voice, the human voice. Nor would he walk above to the stadium, on that roadway he remembered so clearly, closed in as it was these days by big pines and wildflowers. There was always a dizzy feeling, being on that road down on one side to the sea, and up on the other to the top of the valley. And on that road—which was the road of his life, he now understood—toward the stadium of competitions, of jumping and javelin-throwing, wrestling and chariot races, yes, chariot races, that was it, the bronze Charioteer with his obsidian eyes was coming, on that road he would consider, each year, a new possibility. A possibility other than victory, defeat, retention or loss of power. It was the possibility of forgiveness.

Now his feet gave out from under him and Cassie began to scream "Watch out! Watch out!"—the kind of blood-curdling terror-struck screams she'd uttered when she first came to the school. I thought she'd got over that by now, an irritated part of his brain said. He recalled this notion of forgiveness and how he imagined that fifty years had disappeared. And he saw Meryl's face, the old woman in the crowd at the commencement ceremony, Meryl, Sibyl, and he realized that it was not only this year Meryl's face had come to him. She had come before, annually, at Delphi; he had conceived her as mythological, not familial. And now he knew. He imagined that he could wake up as if from a dream to discover that his real life had not taken that abrupt turn all those years ago when he had left Meryl, mother of his children, bride of his youth, and found true love with Francesca and the Manorites.

He saw this as he went down clutching his heart, falling into the stones without the grace of the sensei, but jerkily and heavily like a marionette whose strings have been cut. Imagined he was waking from an epic dream that had entranced him momentarily or rather for five decades of his life and hence could not be erased. There was after all Francesca, there were the rows of "scholars" in their mortarboards, and there was himself, this second self, the other self, he had become. In fact his life did not have the qualities of reality at all but of a trial of reality. You couldn't trust it. It was full of cracks and fissures. His own self-styled Dr. Laird's famous fifty-seven-variety cynicism had taken over. The cynicism had crawled over the foundations, toppled the columns and carried away the two thousand golden statues. The gods were sneaking about behind the bushes doing mischief and one was never safe, neither from tumbling edifices nor false predictions nor manipulations nor the motives of your nearest and dearest, who promised to love you only for yourself.

This was real life, the road taken, not idealized life, untried life, the road not taken. And now he could not for the life of him decide which was the greater illusion. Perhaps there was no forgiveness anywhere, just as there is nothing that lasted, not even Greece. Perhaps this life he had been leading was nothing but the hectic aftermath of the first life he'd created and then destroyed. Perhaps in leaving Meryl and his children he had destroyed himself. Everything since had been a reconstruction, full of self-loathing, and yet so satisfying to the onlooker. A perfect restoration recreates that initial innocence, although it is perhaps a little too perfect. If you settled for a reconstruction, it would never do to look too deeply. Perhaps that was how Francesca had managed.

She was there, leaning over him. Francesca, his muse, his darling one, his amour. But he must be careful not to say, because it would hurt her so, that he was seeing Meryl and mourning the loss of her and the loss of his blood children, along with the loss of beautiful Francesca.

"And so, is it true, that the bronze Charioteer has arrived to collect me, his chiton belted against the breeze, but the pleats hanging still as stone before his hidden loins. If he has arrived today, holding the reins loose in his hands, one can only rise and greet him." These words he formed in his mind to say to her. But he did not think he had said them. She was peering at him now, her beautiful features blurred with fear, or was it his own eyes that were blurred? He thought the whole hillside was moving, the throbbing of a thousand fuschia tour buses had taken over his head and his ears were not admitting a thing. He grasped her hand, the long and elegant hand that could, turned on its side, crack a one-by-six of pine.

And what were the betrayals in her past, his darling? She had been very young, only twenty (she said) but one is never too young to have had a past life. Or indeed perhaps there had been missteps in their years together, indiscretions, although it was difficult to imagine. He thought perhaps, now kindly, affectionately, that we all come to each other scarred and undermined by our own misadventures, that each passion is an effort to escape. In Francesca he had discovered a woman whose efforts in that regard were defiant and whose achievements exquisite.

And this was what was behind Francesca and her idea of beauty. "Beauty is truth, truth beauty. That is all you'll ever know and all you need to know." So she thought, Homo rhetoricus that she was. But perhaps this was not so. He was a false thing, a reconstruction, and yet the stronger for it. He understood, he understood it now. And she? What would become of Francesca now? Francesca darling, he said or thought he said. I'm not well. I'm afraid you'll have to carry on without me.

___

For a shocked moment they simply left him there, lying on the hot and dusty stone.

His wife knelt beside him. The cell phone of an American in khakis had been handed to a well-dressed blonde woman who could speak Greek.

Ambulance... Apparent heart attack... stretcher... she was saying. Advice—

"I knew it I knew it I knew it," Cassie howled, and tore off her blazer to trample underfoot along with her tie. Her sun-streaked brown curls escaped their clip and frizzed around her face. She stamped and for good measure gave a kick to her jacket.

"Not now!" said Francesca to her through gritted teeth. She had undone Dugald's tie and loosened his shirt, her long hands tender.

Amelia sweated. She paced. She could see, down the slope, the little black-and-white police car working its way through the buses clogging both sides of the road, the siren angrily scattering tourists. The helpful American waved his hat in the air. How would help ever get here?

But at length it came, as it had to come, no matter how inefficient the country, how isolated the scene of the accident, help came because it always does come. And the paramedics with fluorescent vests climbed the hill, unfurled their stretcher and loaded him on. By this time Maureen/Delphine and even a boy or two were crying. Miss Morrow held firmly to Sara's hand, and Vida held firmly to Cassie's, as down the hill they trailed. At the bottom, a noisy argument broke out.

"It does not fit."

"How can it not fit?"

"The stretcher does not fit in the little police car."

"But it is your stretcher. It *came from* the police car."

"Of course. But it has not been used before."

"Then why have they put him on it?" Francesca demanded of Amelia, of anyone who would listen.

Oh, rational bride! Why indeed? Amelia rode in to the rescue, offering herself in the fuschia van under police escort as driver. And her offer was accepted. She had begun to believe it was her destiny to drive it. They were taking him to a hospital in Thebes. She was high up in the smoked windshield of the minibus, a comatose Dugald spread over turned-down seats behind her and a semi-hysterical Francesca telling her how to drive. It seemed the moment to say her piece.

"Jesus Fucking H. Christ! If you want me to do this, shut the fuck up," she said.

Francesca did and she looked only slightly offended, which made Amelia realize she ought to have said that long before. But it was not a time to congratulate herself. She now had to start the vehicle, let out the clutch without rolling forward over the cliff and falling about ten thousand metres down, then get the van into reverse, back up and turn without hitting the cars on either side. This on a slope in the reverse direction! She must clutch again without backsliding and go forward.

She managed all that without any major jolts and set off with the engine roaring in protest. The road had been notched out of the slope in tight switchbacks measured out by the length of a herd of goats on the trot, she thought. And there were shrines every few hundred metres to the departed soul of the last unlucky driver who had failed to brake. The turns were so tight she had to gear down to first or take it on the fly in third. She opted for the latter: she held onto the wheel and leaned away from the turn as you would on a motorcycle, then righted herself just in time to lean the other way. Under certain conditions this might have been fun. But the honking and flailing of arms at dawdling folk in Arachova, and the herd of goats that cantered down the rock face and then picked its way across the highway took its toll. She couldn't find the horn, an essential Greek driving tool, so she opened the window and yelled. It provided a useful emotional outlet and drowned out the sound of Francesca, who was keening in the rear.

In what seemed like hours but was in fact a record time of fifty-two minutes they were at the emergency entrance of the Thebes hospital. Here the police magically appeared to pave the way. She let them unload the stretcher and went to Francesca, holding her hand, dabbing her cheeks, insisting over and over that Dugald would be all right. Francesca said she wished her father was there. Her father was long-dead. Dugald's wheeled stretcher was disappearing down the corridor when she turned to Amelia.

"You must get back to the children."

"I don't like to leave you, Francesca."

"But the children—"

"I put Vida in charge."

Francesca snorted. "Vida?" she said. "That's putting a fireplug in charge of a powder keg."

17

IN THE BAR OF THE DOLPHIN HOTEL

"**B**ELIEVE ME NOT, what matter? 'Tis all one, the future comes, and when your eyes have seen, you shall cry out in pity, 'She spoke true.'"

"Cassie, stop," said Vida. "Enough already."

Amelia had put Vida in charge because she could at least karate-chop people if they misbehaved. Amelia said that after dinner they should all go to bed. It was only nine o'clock, however, and putting them to bed would be a mistake; outside the thin and rattling windows of the Dolphin Hotel the town was just beginning to stir. The students were nerved up and full of the buzz of the day's disaster on the hill. Word had it that Amelia Parmigianino, Commander-in-Cheese, had returned from her emergency hospital run so tired that she simply could not bear to utter one word and now sat in the tiny, dark Dolphin bar with a telephone at her elbow.

They didn't know if Dr. Laird was alive, or what hospital he was in. What if he was dead? Would the school collapse? Much as they loved Dr. Laird they knew that Miss Morrow really ran the Manor. But would she be too heartbroken to carry on? They could not imagine the Manor without Dr. Laird.

"I love him," said Cassie.

"We all do, just shut up."

Cassie loved Dr. Laird, but she had begun to have doubts about
Francesca. She saw today that the Headmistress was fed up with her.
They were barely halfway through their trip and everyone was fed up
with her. And Cassie had been brave, during the bee adventure. It
was easy for her, that day, that danger. She led the line, plodding
forward, dimly aware of a fragment of dream in which she'd seen this
ragtag line of people, school ties askew, blazers hooked on fingertips
and hung down the back, shirts untucked, despite the fact that one
boy had been expelled from the Manor for shirt infractions. She
hadn't seen herself in the dream, hadn't known that she would be at
the head of the line. She simply knew, from the heart's ease that
came along with this vision, that there would be no catastrophe. Not
here, not now.

But later, in the Museum, she was filled with fear when she saw
the Charioteer. He looked like Death and he probably was. Maybe it
was his job to cart away the athletes who died in the games. Or the
people who tore their sons to pieces in the Dionysian revels. She
went vacant before him, her mouth gaping, as he spoke.

"Move up, Cassie, we're next," Amelia had said, when Cassie
came back to herself in the ticket line-up. There was kindness, even a
touch of respect in her voice. And Cassie reminded herself that she
had broken her way through bushes full of bees thinking of someone
else's fear not her own. She would not let the Charioteer throw her
into a panic. What could he do to her, after all? He could not bite.

On the hillside Dr. Laird had asked her what was going to happen. "I don't know what is going to happen," she'd said. "I don't
ever know."

But in fact she did know. She knew that Dr. Laird was going to
fall down clutching his heart, that Miss Morrow would pace tragi-
cally on the parapets or whatever these walls were called until soldiers came to take him away. She saw that in a flash and she tried to
blaze it off her mental screen, to move the figures around in the
tableau, to put Dr. Laird back on his feet and tuck Miss Morrow's

hand through his elbow, with Sara alongside holding the umbrella over their heads, remarking, "Isn't the sun hot?" She tried to see them picking their way down the stones past the Temple of Apollo and out beyond the ticket kiosk, smiling, then looking up the road for the fuschia bus. She squeezed her eyes tight to make this vision work. But it did not work.

Maureen/Delphine and Roxanne had a couple of caps of crystal meth tucked into a tube of Tampax. Darrin and Dimitri were rolling a blunt, which involved cutting a Frilled Blunt cigar down the centre with an Exacto knife and filling it with weed. They were looking for the right place to smoke it. The balcony of their room was right out over the main street and the odour, they thought, was likely to drift. Sara was in Vida and Cassie's room on a cot because Maureen/Delphine, even reformed, could not stand to hear her crying for her mum in the night.

"I'm just so scared," Sara said. "I want to be asleep, but I don't know how to get there." She climbed between the heavy, coarse white sheets. Surreptitiously she pulled her teddy bear out from under the pillow.

Vida was planning their escape.

"Amelia," said Darrin.

Amelia sometimes allowed the students to address her by her first name, if they were off school property. This counted: the bar of the Dolphin Hotel, in Delphi, Greece.

The boy slid onto the fake-leather stool and looked at her in the mirror, black and marbled. Her famous neck was sunburnt, obvious even in the dim light. The pink, slightly swollen look extended down into the scooped neckline of her dress, where the swellings of her breasts began. She wanted to put out her finger and push the flesh, to see it whiten under her touch and then to see the blood flow into it again.

"Darrin," she said, looking straight back, but through the mirror, her glance like a perfect pool shot angled into the pocket of his eye. She was tired, and tired of boys. Girls, too, but boys especially, somehow, given that the chief male amongst them had chosen this awkward time to perish—in transit, in a strange country, in mid-performance. Midstream. Amidst a dream. Dugald loved that pun.

"Do you want some company?" Darrin asked. A handsome line from a handsome young man. Amelia eased her grip on her glass of retsina.

"Sure. I wish she'd call."

"It's a good sign, don't you think? I mean if—if anything like—total—happened, then she would call."

"Who knows? If he's well enough, they may move him to Athens."

The two heads were suspended above the smooth black reflecting surface; outside was the glow of lights from the crowded Delphi street, voices, too, and far off, a certain Greek singer's hit song, which had been everywhere these past few days.

"Would you like another one of those?"

Darrin lifted his arm for the bartender, who was sunk in a trance at the other end of the counter. The arm motion was sufficient. The guy had terrific peripheral vision. He'd been looking down Amelia's shirt without turning his head for the past half-hour.

"We were talking about how this must be tough on you."

Where did men get these lines? Even as lads they had a repertoire. She wondered how she seemed to Darrin, whether impossibly old or just enticingly so. Did he sit in his desk and fantasize about her while she rambled on about parallel structure?

"Yeah," she said. The new glass was delivered into her hands. "However, we can't do anything about that, can we? Darrin, are you old enough to be in here?" She still hadn't looked him in the eye. They were communicating through the glass darkly.

"Nineteen in two weeks," he said. "Anyway, it's Europe, right?"

She smiled into the mirror. They looked rather good together, their bright heads, hers the burnished auburn with side curtains, his the dark blond, with chiselled chin and shadowed cheek, the type you might have called a Greek god until you came here and saw how soft and female the male faces actually were. He intends to seduce me, I suppose. And then, no, it can't be. Why would he want to? I'm nearly twice his age! Because they like that, she thought. As I ought to know, there is no accounting for tastes. Amelia put her fingers up against the three small lines she could see around her neck in the mirror. The sunburn accentuated them: they were white. She stretched her neck and made them disappear.

"Swan," he said. "I don't know where Cheese came from."

"The Madonna with the Long Neck, that was how it began, but you wouldn't have known that. It was before your time. I was supposed to look like her."

"Swan is better."

Darrin's hand came up and covered hers on the bar. She looked down at it. His hand was exactly as expected: chiselled, blond-haired, of course, tender. A not-having-worked-a-day-in-his-life hand. She compared it with Ferdy's, the last male hand to have made contact. Ferdy's were burn-scarred and thick-palmed, dark, stubby hands that appeared insensitive but which, in fact, were as skilled as a concert pianist's.

She missed him. He must hate me, she thought.

She wondered what the girls did to him to make him go away. Maybe in a moment of madness he had confided in his wife and was under house arrest? Who knew? She longed to see him, smell him, touch him. But she had renounced him. She had renounced what he stood for. Time to find someone suitable. Although suitability had always seemed so dull. Falling in love with someone suitable was like playing golf as her parents had advised her, because it was useful. She hadn't taken up golf yet. Perhaps she had to come to terms with the fact that she was never ever going to choose a pastime for its social utility, nor a lover for his suitability.

"Where are they all?" she idly asked.

"Didn't you tell them to stay in their rooms?" Carefully he used the third person, excluding himself. "I know Jacob's there." Then he looked down at her hand. "I was wondering," he murmured.

"You were?"

"Uh humm. I was wondering—oh!" Darrin looked into the mirror and sucked in his breath. "I can't believe I'm saying this, Miss Holt—"

"Amelia, please." It irritated her now to be spoken to with that respectful prefix, "Miss." Even just plain Holt would be better.

"Right, I said that already, didn't I? But I was wondering what you would say if—what you would say if—"

Was this false modesty, was he only pretend-shy? She looked in the mirror. Her eye carried out beyond the bar door and into the foyer. The concierge was not at her post. Was it her imagination, or did she notice dark shapes gliding along the other side of the desk? Surely the switchboard was still operating, so if the call from Thebes, or more likely Athens, came, she could be summoned. Everyone here knew about Dugald. The crisis, catastrophe, *monostrophe*, as Cassie said, had excited the sympathies of all the staff and half the guests. The old gentleman? Oh my god! Francesca and Dugald had been sending students here for years, not that they ever stayed here themselves but that was understood. "Doctor and the lady" were intended for finer, rarer pastures and the staff here was more than willing to mother the students just to indulge their refined masters. Amelia let her head tip a little more toward Darrin's so that his hair brushed her temple.

"You were wondering?"

She was suddenly past the posing and conjecture. A velvety rub of his head on hers. And it was as if all her skin were velvet and his hand—the hand that now travelled lightly over the skin of her forearm—was all over her, raising the nap.

How bad is this? she asked herself. What risks? The kids walking in, the Headmaster even, miraculously resuscitated, the boy himself boasting, myself being made a fool of? She could not, at this moment, calculate. None of it—the parents' ire if this came out, the reputation of the school, Francesca's furthered lowered opinion of her and, in fact, firing—none of it mattered at all. Had she not already lost her job? The old order was falling. Death was in the air, the scent of it, like lilies, awakening, stirring loins everywhere. The need for a life excitement to counter the awful nearness of mortality. The need for more danger to balance the danger that had tripped her heart all day. What was a calculation but the mind stepping back in fear from instinct? She could not, would not calculate.

"I was wondering—" By now his lips had opened and shut, opened and shut as if he were snacking on her hair.

"If you could kiss me?"

He blushed. She could feel the heat of his face. Even so she felt it was a fake blush. Just how innocent was this boy? The idea that he was pretending, acting the overawed schoolboy, excited her.

"Is that what you were wondering?"

He nodded, soundlessly.

"Say it."

He said nothing. She put her hand under his chin, and lifted it. She withdrew her eyes from her own reflection in the mirror and gazed at him. He spoke.

"What would you say if I kissed you?"

18

ESCAPE

N O ONE AT the desk: that was good. Darrin and Amelia at the bar, leaning, heads together. Such an uninviting lobby. Full of ugly black leatherette and a floor flecked with gold. Vida went first. She was dressed in black, as planned—a sweatshirt and her usual baggy leggings. She'd wrapped her kilt over her shoulders and pinned it under her chin so that it hung like a swashbuckler's cape down her back.

Dim-Dimitri was next. He let Vida get across the dangerous open space between the desk and freedom, and watched her silently open the front door a foot and slip through. Then he followed, a much larger figure in blue jeans and a hooded Gap sweatshirt worn inside out so the big white letters did not show in the dark. His jeans were wide and the crotch drooped: he had to hold the chains that hung from pocket to pocket so they didn't rattle. The rapid shuffle of his feet, invisible under the piled up length of pant, made him appear to be on wheels, in the manner of dancers of the Beijing Opera, a videotaped performance of which the students had been forced to watch in Miss Morrow's drama class. He was noiseless; the apparent ball bearings on the soles of his feet gave the impression of a well-oiled shopping cart being pushed along. In the centre of the floor he took an abrupt, shopping-cartish right turn and ducked through the opening where Vida held the door.

Next was Maureen/Delphine. Her white-blonde hair, on which she had spent a good hour with brushes and gels, burst up from her scalp as if she'd stood for a few seconds with her finger in a socket. Her right ear was freighted with studs and hoops, all up the lobe and well into the cartilage at the top. She wore a long skirt of Indian cotton that, when she passed the single table light in the lobby, revealed the scissoring of her long legs right up to her crotch. Her bony shoulders stood up like the handlebars of a bicycle, through a sleeveless black T-shirt, her long arms she held straight down and pinned to her buttocks as if they were handcuffed behind her back. Between her hands rode the tiny leather backpack containing the stash. Though reborn as the goddess-worshipping, pure-bodied Delphine, she was not averse to smoking a little cannabis on the slopes of Mount Parnassus to acknowledge the spirit of Dionysus.

Sara hung back, watching Maureen/Delphine's feet. She was half-asleep; she did not want to be here. She had been trying all night to get through to her mother in Toronto but the front desk would not let her make a long-distance call, and Amelia had not been around. Over her school kilt she wore the voluminous lemon-yellow sweatshirt her mother had packed in her bag with the idea that it would make Sara easy to find in a crowd. Obediently, like a sleepwalker, Sara plugged along trusting the girls; she trusted anyone who was nice to her, and even those who weren't, if they had an air of authority.

Past Sara came Chino. Fourth in line, he was, and holding his breath. He was all in black like Vida, his sweatshirt hood pulled up over his head. His thick black hair, scorched with gold from the centre part, was cropped against his neck and shingled upward so that it stuck out horizontally from the top of his head. He affected the slouching, foot-dragging Toronto adaptation of an LA-ghetto walk. But he was surprisingly nimble; he slid into the lobby like a cat burglar or Fred Astaire, making a full revolution to scope each corner of the lobby, smiling his belief that they would make their escape good. His glance lingered on Darrin busy at the bar seducing Amelia. He would have liked that job. Although it was not so shabby to be heading out with the Dead Ladies where he hoped, in the shadows of the old shrine, to get some play. He disappeared through the doorway once and then reappeared, hissing and waving his hand urgently to make the rest follow quickly, before it was too late. Half of them were out now. But Sara shivered at the edge of the open door, stopped, and said in a loud whisper, "Maybe I need my coat."

Swift and dark Chino closed the gap between them, putting his black-shirted arm around Sara's shoulder, a hand across her mouth, pulling her blonde head into his chest and gliding across the marble tiles to the door. "Out!" As he spun, he hissed at her, "Quiet!" Then he pushed her into the fresh air, under the black and hollow dome of stars. He twirled around once more to check. Yes, Miss Holt and Darrin were getting it on at the bar. Yes, the rest were waiting, a silent clump at the foot of the stairs. He jerked his arm upward: go for it.

They emerged together from the staircase, giggling explosively, causing Amelia to turn around on her bar stool. Ashley and Roxanne had both tied up their hair with dark bandanas, Ashley's navy with white dots, Roxanne's burgundy with the same. Cassie had a black scarf tied across her mouth at her own request. Ashley and Roxanne were on either side of her, holding her arms. She did not want to call out or make a noise that would cause them to be discovered. It gave something of the prisoner to her appearance, which had at first pleased her and then, when she looked in the mirror, frightened her.

In the centre of the lobby, Cassie went stiff with fear, so the others elected to pull her rather than take the risk of her twirling like a top. In fact, at that moment Amelia turned again. Chino held up his hand. They froze, holding their captive steady. Amelia scanned the lobby but saw nothing.

"Did I just hear something out there?" they heard her ask.

"Naw," said Darrin. "It's like, they've got cats or something."

Amelia turned back to her own image in the mirror.

Chino scooped his arm again. Come on, come on. They skated across the floor, Ashley and Roxanne, holding Cassie nearly rigid up on her feet. Not another sound escaped their lips as they went determinedly about the task of getting her out the door. Outside, Roxanne set her long fingernails into the tight knot at the back of Cassie's head. "You want this off? You want this off now?" Cassie nodded. Yet when the cloth came loose the sound came out. They took her arms again and ran.

"Where's Jacob?" Chino gasped through his teeth, loping.

"Not coming."

The parking lot was deserted. The street, only a few metres distant, was partially lit; tourists rambled along it looking into windows at coffee mugs and T-shirts emblazoned with images of Apollo. The rest of the group was waiting in the darkness around the corner from the hotel's lit facade. Once free of the building they could mingle. There was, after all, nothing illegal about being out on the street at eleven o'clock at night.

"People will say they've seen us," said Vida, fidgeting. She had some notion that they might escape Delphi, escape Greece altogether, hitchhike across Europe. She was counting on a clear getaway and a long head start.

"It doesn't matter," said Chino. "No one cares."

Sara let out a modest bleat of protest.

"Of course they care. Miss Morrow would fuckin' kill us," said Vida with satisfaction.

"She's like forgotten we're even here."

Cassie looked back over her shoulder in the direction of Amelia. She liked Amelia, now the lone guardian of the school. But she was off duty. Absent Without Leave, as Dr. Laird would say about students who failed to show up at class.

"Amelia's gettin' it on with Darrin, eh?" said Dimitri.

Cassie shifted uneasily, her light cotton trousers blowing against her legs.

"Does Darrin have a crush on Miss Holt?" Sara whispered.

The others laughed.

"He does," said Maureen/Delphine and this time she put her arm over Sara's shoulder, enveloping her in a cloud of the wildflower hair gel she'd borrowed from Roxanne, who had shoplifted it especially just before they left Toronto. But what did it matter? Now all that was in the past. Destiny was driving the bus.

"Let's head," hissed Vida. She sprang off the curb and strode on ahead with the complete assurance of a military leader whose platoon was right on her heels. "Just don't catch anyone's eyes," she charged them, looking back over her shoulder only once.

<hr>

In this way the eight exited the tourist village of Delphi at 11:30 p.m., under a tiny crescent moon and a sky that shone in its blackness like patent leather. There were eight, not ten, because Darrin was with Amelia at the bar, and Jacob had refused: he was writing up his script to send it to an agent. Each trod with eyes on the heels of the one who walked before, that is, all but Vida, who with her short-legged jog had set her gaze on the middle distance. That they had a mission was plain to everyone who noticed them. And some did, the observant ones, asking themselves: what is this, a band of teenagers going to their hostel? to a waiting tour bus round the next bend in the road? to a party in the bushes? Camping out of town, one thought. Someone even recognized the group as members of the school tour he'd seen on the slopes of the oracle, the group from which the old man had been taken away in an ambulance. But no one questioned their going.

They plodded on and in several minutes reached beyond the lights of town to where the blackness of the mountainside was nearly

total. On the roads that zigzagged down to the gulf and up to Arachova an occasional car toiled, its lights wiping across the landscape
as it pulled through a hairpin turn, its revving motor, as the walkers
further distanced themselves from the talk and clatter of downtown,
adding mystery to the night. Cassie was less afraid, now. She had
weathered her terror in the afternoon simply by pretending it wasn't
there, hadn't she? Fake it till you make it, Vida said.

Roxanne and Ashley still had Cassie by the hands. It was dark at the
entrance gates to the Delphic Oracle. There was no security, no
night watchmen, no alarms to set off, nothing but a loose, low chain
across the path. Vida dove over it and rolled onto the grass. The rest
stepped over.

The shrine lay mysterious, huge and ancient in the darkness, all
theirs. As they stood, awed in spite of themselves, the stones seemed
to emit a faint gold and ivory light, and the darkness to shrink
back. As their eyes adjusted, the more like the day night became, a
day without people, without noise. A day that belonged to them,
where history was not be mediated by old people, by the burden
of knowledge.

They stood at the foot of the Sacred Way.

"Go," said someone.

"Yeah, go."

Vida had to hop from step to step because her legs were short and
the steps were so tall and so broad. "We're going right to the top,"
she said, "because we didn't get a chance today."

"Where do you want to do the stuff?" said Roxanne to Maureen/
Delphine, who was smiling in a blissful way and did not answer.

Up they went, higher and higher, past the Treasuries, past the
Omphalos. Sara in her yellow sweatshirt was the only one who stood
out in the darkness.

"She's going to get us busted," said Chino. "In that shirt." And she was cold. Chino took off his black sweatshirt and made her wear it over her own. Only her thin legs from mid-thigh down stuck out of the bottom of the balloon it made of her torso.

They came to the Rock of the Sibyl. Vida scrambled on top of it.

"I shall make a prediction," she said.

"Don't. It's sacrilegious."

Vida threw back her head, opened her throat, and ululated. Ooo-oo-oo-ooo-oo. The sound crashed into the quiet and made the rest of them shrink against the foundation walls.

"Fuck, Vida, they'll hear you and we'll get caught."

"No we won't." She jumped down, eyes glittering. "You don't know what I just said, do you?"

They didn't.

"And you're not going to know."

Who started it, the chant they'd promised to abandon, from the gang they said no longer existed?

"Tell me where, in what country, is Flora the beautiful Roman..."

"Echo who speaks when there's a sound on a pond or a river..."

"But where are the snows of yesteryear?"

"Don't," said Cassie. "The Dead Ladies are bad luck."

"We're not doing any more crime," said Maureen/Delphine. "We made it through the bees. We can be born again, like the opposite of the first Dead Ladies."

"We are through with school; Dr. Laird is dead!" Chino shouted into the night.

Cassie got sad and quiet thinking of Dr. Laird. If he was dead he had joined the heroes from the past, like Homo erectus. She was silent as they toiled uphill. They passed the Temple of Apollo. There was a long traverse, then, across the bottom of the theatre. They fanned out onto the flat half circle that had been the stage. Roxanne threw her arms wide and did some grands jetés on the diagonal. Dimitri began to declaim, some speech he'd been forced to memorize about a sceptred isle coming back to him in a fragmented way.

Chino jeered experimentally. His voice was huge in the darkness. Behind the fan of seat rows on their right rose a steep cliff. "Hey, this is the place he talked about where it was built to magnify your voice."

They smoked their blunts. They drank from Dimitri's flask of retsina.

"School's fucked, drink up; Laird's gone, party on." The others picked it up. They walked back and forth like picketers on the stage.

Cassie coughed on a cigarette. "Echo-echo, echo, echo, echo," Vida called. "Echo who speaks when there's a sound on a pond or a river."

"It's not me!" Cassie cried.

Not me, not me, not me.

They walked and they sang out their silly rhymes and their rhymes rose into the hillside. Slowly to the walking they added little slaps; as each student passed another he would put out his hand and tap him or her on the shoulder or the back. Soon they were walking and slapping, walking and touching, and then they were all holding arms over shoulders and moving together, pushing and pulling each other this way and that so that the line staggered and nearly pulled itself apart, or one end went down on its knees. It was just something they were doing, like some kind of tribal dance.

"Let's go up farther," Vida yelled. She bolted into the pitch blackness.

"Watch out!"

There was a small half-fence that Vida hadn't seen. She was moving so fast it caught her at the knees and pitched her forward onto her hands. Her head went down and caught the first tier of seats. Old marble may look soft, with the corners worn away, but it is not a cake of soap. Vida was dazed for a moment and lay where she had fallen. In the dark, she was hard to see.

"Where did she go?"

"She's there, she's on the ground!"

"Vida's down! Vida's down!" The girls came running. Ashley, too, tripped on the fence and went down on her hands and knees on the far side of it.

Chino knelt beside Vida. "Are you all right?" He spoke loudly, as if her fall might have made her deaf.

"Of course I am," she said. She spoke into the earth; her voice was muffled. She did not lift her head. "I'm wet. Who poured water on me?

"Nobody."

"My face is all wet."

Cassie lifted Vida's head. Her forehead was wet. Even in the darkness you could see; her face was running with blood.

"You cut yourself."

Vida put her hand up to her forehead, then to her crown, then to the back of her head. "No I didn't. I can't feel a thing."

"That's 'cause your head really bleeds a lot even if it isn't deep." Cassie put her hand on Vida's face, and moved it slowly up above her nose and onto her forehead. The whole area was slick with blood, which even now, so soon, was starting to go sticky. "Let's go back," she whispered in her friend's ear.

Vida shrugged her off. "It's okay; it'll stop," she said, scrambling to her feet. "I actually can't feel a thing."

First Dr. Laird, then Miss Morrow. Now Vida was deserting Cassie. She stiffened, and a moan forced its way through her lips.

"Don't worry, I'm okay," Vida said putting her arm on Cassie's shoulder. "Okay? Be still."

Cassie was still.

"Cassie listens to you," said Chino, suspicious of something he could not name.

"Let's go up farther."

Chino took the lead and as they climbed reached back to take Vida's hand and Vida took Cassie's until all eight of them were stretched out in a snakey line climbing the steps of the theatre where they were not supposed to be.

"We're not supposed to walk here," whispered Sara.

"I guess that was why the fence was there."

"This is, like, ancient, and if everyone did it there wouldn't be any stairs any more so people couldn't see what the theatre was even like."

"So what if they couldn't?" said Ashley. "Ancient is just old and falling down. Most people who come here and go oooh and aaaah are totally faking it. It doesn't mean anything to them. They just think it's supposed to."

At the top of the theatre a long path led off to the left. Stadium, it said on the sign. They had not made it up this high today. It was darker up there. The moon got stuck behind the big cliffs, which took away the light.

"Let's go."

"We don't know what's there."

"Just the stadium, remember, where they had the games?"

They walked along the track.

"Have you got more stuff?"

"Yeah."

"Cool."

Cassie looked at Vida. But Vida's face seemed to be blacked out. It was a long walk to the stadium. Uphill.

"How did they ever get up there?"

"You'd be in some procession."

"Yeah, and carrying a fuckin' calf on your shoulders."

"You mean a horrified cow."

Crazy laughing rippled up and down the line making it hard for them to walk. The path flattened then and suddenly a new angle of the rock face above allowed the moonlight in, and the stadium was visible, a huge flat oval of pale earth. Around the far side rose a tier of stone bleachers. There were trees beyond that, bringing darkness in their branches, a wooded slope perfect for Thyiads to run loose in. The boys went out into the flat area and lay down. The heat of the day was still in the stones.

"They had all the games here didn't they? The chariot races."

"Yeah. The Charioteer. People fell off and got trampled to death."

"They did not."

"Sure they did. Where's the stuff?"

They all gathered in the centre of the oval.

Cassie lay on her back. She could hear the beat of horses' hooves on the earth. She could hear the Charioteer's whip cracking the air above their necks and the excited neighing as their heads pitched and tossed like waves in a stormy sea at the Charioteer's feet. Somewhere beyond, at a remove from this central contest of man and beast, of piston legs and spinning wheels, she heard the voices of a great crowd. The people roared, in their diminished way, in the distance, their voices indistinguishable from each other. A gust of wind carried the scent of pine across her nostrils.

And she thought, this place feels like home. The stones are warm with the past under my hand. If I touch them I am transported. She thought of Dr. Laird then in the cool white museum in Athens, showing Jacob and her the beautiful frieze; she thought of the apobates with their round shields jumping on and off the chariots.

How clever of Miss Morrow to know. So what if I am reincarnated from some Greek maiden, she thought. Does it have to be Cassandra? That seems a little too obvious and, anyway, Cassandra wasn't even Greek. Yes, I see things before other people do. But it's only because I am watching and listening. And no, no one listens to me when I warn them. That much is okay. But I don't like the part about being raped, lying across a shrine. And I would hate to be a spoil of war and Agamemnon's concubine. And then to have my head chopped off?

First of all, it wouldn't be that easy. Take Vida's arm or leg, for instance, it's strong, and well-attached with those ligaments and joints and the stuff on Dr. Laird's skeleton charts. You would have to be very very strong, or insane, to actually sever anyone's limb. In Homer's time, people were always lopping off each other's parts but with axes or bayonets. The axe must be very sharp, and the axe-man strong. Those were only stories anyway and when you didn't write down a story, people added their own details; people exaggerated. War in general must be a grand exaggeration. It simply was not believable that people could do such terrible things to each other. But then, as Miss Morrow used to say, you are a gentle soul Cassie and you have been protected from the facts of life.

But these were not pleasant thoughts. Cassie tried to concentrate on the bits of Cassandra's life she would have enjoyed. Being a priestess, wearing the seer's net, making pronouncements. Being in a sacred trance of a sort, and departing from normal life, letting strange words escape her mouth.

She rolled lazily onto her side to look around the circle. They were passing a joint. People took such hard tokes that the tip turned an angrier, hotter red and then sank into the darkness once the smoker had inhaled and passed it on. Only Sara refused. Each one kept eyes and lips closed, afterward, to keep the smoke in. It looked like a highly secretive and even dangerous occupation; it looked like an indoctrination into a secret society.

"Come on, Cassie," said Vida. "Have some."

"She's stoned already," said Maureen/Delphine.

"Yes, she really doesn't need it. Think of what it might do to her."

Partly it was because she was tired of being spoken of in the third person. Partly it was because it had been a long and a terrible twenty-four hours, beginning the night before with the discovery that she might be a weird person who liked to kiss girls. Today had brought the bee escapade, and had gone on to the collapse and maybe death of her dearly beloved Headmaster. Add to that her certainty that she was a reissue from prehistory. Really, it had been a very long day. And so she said yes, she would take a drag.

She put the joint between her lips and sucked, the way she'd done when Vida showed her. A cloud of smoke came burning into her mouth and instantly her throat shut. Swallow, swallow they were shouting. She imagined her lips sewn together and suppressed the cough, held it in, using all her willpower and all her strength. She swallowed and then her mouth burst open and she spit out what air was left in her mouth.

"Again, again, I don't know how much she got."

Which was why Cassie held the joint for longer than anyone else did.

Eventually it was so short that she was burning her fingertips and the end of her nose too. Roxanne, who was a professional at this, took the tiny stub and sucked until she had an idiotic, pleased look on her face, and there was absolutely nothing left.

They all started to look small and far away to Cassie. She realized they were having fun and even that she was having fun with them. She observed herself playing tag and laughing uproariously; she observed herself crashing her shoulders against Roxanne's and then Maureen/Delphine's like a football player; she watched, too, as she put an arm around little Sara, who had not smoked or taken any drug and who was frightened. Then she wanted to sleep. The others got out their caps of crystal meth and began disappearing: they seemed to be going in twos into the woods; they would climb the stone seats and a small stone wall and then be lost behind tree trunks. All this was visible in the moonlight and with the special vision she had developed in the darkness. It became quieter and quieter and soon there were only a few left: Vida, Sara, Cassie, perhaps it was Dimitri whistling around the edges.

The wind came back and the sound far away of an occasional car on the road and even, who knew from where, balalaika music. Cassie sat with her back propped up against a stone coffin, the soles of her feet touching blocks of stone in what had to be significant positions, and watched Vida.

Vida had picked up two sticks from the forest floor and began to perform sinawali, the reticks, the eggbeaters, and heaven and earth. Her face was set and fierce as a cat's and her hair sprouted from her head like a blood fountain. Her tiny arms and legs seemed magically impelled. The compass on which she set herself and around the dial of which she moved, methodically, was at the same time full of meaning, and totally obscure. Like those languages the archaeologists had discovered and then set to work to decode, Cassie thought. She was Linear B. Cassie could watch her forever. Perhaps at the end of forever she would understand her, not simply what she said, but what she meant.

Vida is fierce and yet like the stroke of a gentle hand on me, she thought; when I think of her, even her furies, I smile and smile until people ask me what joke I'm remembering. But it is no joke; it's love, simple and powerful. Cassie adored Vida. She understood now that she was not even that weird because Vida was extraordinary and worthy of adoration.

She put her arm over Sara's little shoulder and in a minute Sara's head was leaning heavily against her. It was peaceful sitting there. Cassie tried to forget all the worrisome aspects of this venture. But they kept creeping into her mind. There were the facts: they had crept out of the hotel without permission and half the school was up in the bushes engaged in Dionysian rites, Dr. Laird was at death's door or beyond, and Amelia had gone AWOL. Cassie had inhaled some kind of smoke and what she feared now was that with all of this going on she would simply freak out. With all of this it was nearly impossible to hold on to what was secret and not to be spilled, the secrets of the Dead Ladies. The nervousness took hold and Cassie could no longer stay still. She shook herself free of Sara.

"Vida," said Cassie. "The thing is, we left Jacob back at the hotel and there's no telling what he might do when it's getting toward morning and nobody's back."

"You're right," said Vida. She froze in a kata and fixed her with a brilliant smile.

"So we should go back?"

"We should. And we will. Oh yes we will."

"Okay. But like, when?"

Vida began to laugh. "Oh, Cassie, get a life," she said. She threw a couple of kicks, flipped her sticks around wildly and kiai-ed. "Die!" Still laughing, she threw herself in the dust and rolled, holding her sides.

Cassie shrank back against her stone coffin. So Vida was finally sick of her. She hated her! Terrified, Cassie tried to make excuses for her idol. Okay, sure, Vida had bumped her head, and there was blood matted in what hair she had at the back of her shaven porcupine-prickly skull. It was also true that she had smoked up. It was probably two o'clock in the morning by now; they'd been up all day, maybe she wasn't thinking straight. Cassie reminded herself of all that. Still her heart fell and kept falling. Because it did not change the facts. Vida was tired of Cassie worrying, tired of Cassie being an old woman, tired of protecting her.

Roxanne emerged from the trees, with Chino; Maureen/Delphine, after having outrun Dimitri in foot races, left him panting on the ground. Ashley followed. The Dead Ladies gathered around Vida. Their eyes glinted in the moonlight; they were out of breath, their shoulders heaving. They looked dangerous. They looked the way they'd looked the night they mugged Ferdinand and wrecked his truck. They stared at Cassie.

"Why don't you just go back?" Vida said to Cassie. Maybe Cassie's worst fears made her say it.

Cassie stood up. She looked down at the tan-coloured earth. It seemed a long way down. Homo erectus, my fat white ass, she thought. If one of your tribe is hungry, let him eat from your food. If he is cold, let him sit by your fire. We walked through the bees together this morning. Or was that yesterday? Now they'd just as soon tear me limb from limb.

The Ladies shifted their feet. They steamed and belched like a pot of water about to boil. Ashley stumbled forward.

"Do you believe her?" she said, pointing to Cassie. "I am so fucked," she added as an afterthought, letting out a weird hoot of laughter.

Cassie felt a flash of anger. I am not one of you, she thought. I am of a different order of being altogether. It was always true. And it had never been more true. Even if I try to be like you guys I cannot be like you guys. I have a different destiny and it is calling out to me.

"I think you should go," said Vida.

Right. She was right. Go back to the hotel, find Amelia. Find out what has happened to Miss Morrow and Dr. Laird. Be inside, where it is safe, and wait for news. There is news coming. Something is about to happen.

"I have a sense of impending doom," Cassie said. She had said it before. She repeated it, almost with irony, knowing they'd laugh.

"Oh, that's so cute, she uses big words," cooed Ashley.

Vida laughed.

The doom began to hum all around Cassie in the air. She turned around to go. Sara was there: she hesitated. She could take Sara down with her. But it might not be safe. She tried to speak to Sara but she couldn't. The humming blocked out her voice. She walked away. She could feel them at her back but she did not run. She never ran.

Going down was more difficult than going up. "It will be different when you come down," she had said to Dr. Laird. Yes.

The moon had got itself to a place where the glow was hidden, or half-hidden. And the stones had gone dull so that they reflected back nothing. She was on the staircase but she could not see the next step when her foot went off the one she was standing on. Darkest before the dawn was the phrase that came to mind. She wandered along the horizontal path for a long way across the hill and then she saw the steep slope of the theatre below. When she came to the steps down, she took them. She was clumsy anyway and now she was cold, frightened, and possibly stoned. She tripped once, then again, falling. She was on her hands and knees. She stood to discover she had skinned her knees; little pebbles got stuck in the palms of her hands. She began to cry, in shuddering gulps. She forgot the route; now she was well past the theatre and into some other formation. The Temple of Apollo? Great bus-sized stones began to loom up in front of her and at the sides.

She bumped into a soft, porous rock that rose over her head and was wider than the reach of her arms.

Excuse me, she said.

She hoped it didn't fall down, ruining the ruins. Or fall on top of her. At home (how long ago and far away that was) she and Vida had read a story in the newspaper about a boy who overturned a pop machine while trying to get a free can; it fell on him and killed him. Like, forget the fuckin' loonie, Vida had said. Cassie felt sorry for the kids who discovered his pancaked body the next morning.

Vida would not be sitting here crying if she were lost at Delphi in the middle of the night. She would not howl at the moon. Cassie hated herself for not being brave; it was probably fitting that she should die. If she died she might go back to Ancient Greece. She might be stored for another several thousand years and re-emerge, a misfit all over again, in some ghastly science-fiction future. Oh god help us and save us, she said. It was her mum's expression. She felt along the wall that had materialized behind her and found a ledge to sit on. She let her crying rise like the howl of a wild animal. She heard the echo. Echo who speaks when there's a sound on a pond or a river. It was so frightening that she fell silent.

In the silence she heard a noise. Wind chimes? No. Wild animals? Only wild boars, in the myths, inhabited the slopes of Parnassus. They were silent and rushed through the undergrowth, their snouts leading, and had savage little hooves to kick you with. Thinking of wild boars made Cassie remember that ghastly novel she'd studied before she went to the Manor. *Lord of the Flies*. The wild boars were always chasing after the kids in it. Miss Morrow hated that book as much as Cassie did.

Hideous vision, she had remarked passingly, looking over Cassie's failing essay on it in her portfolio when she applied to enter the Manor. I have no idea why people insist on teaching it to innocent children. Right away Cassie had known she would love this woman. And where was she now? In some hospital weeping over the body of her fallen husband. She started to cry again. There was no one around to hear. Her sobs became theatrical. She sobbed to drown out the echo, which was too lonely a sound. She had never been anywhere before where she could howl with the certainty that she would be neither heard nor seen. She was impressed with her voice. She wished for a mirror so she could see the distortions in her face. She continued until her throat grew raw. Then she stopped and the silence bloomed around her like a wondrous plant.

"Blubbering, that's all you're doing," she said.

No answer. No sound.

"Just sitting here blubbering. You were going to go back for a reason."

Again it was a novelty to speak aloud to herself and to know that there wasn't anyone nearby to call her a freak.

"What was the reason you were going back, Cassie?"

Silence. The reason seemed far away. It seemed unimportant. Yet it nagged at the back of her mind.

"Reason, reason, you did have a reason."

Nothing.

"You said it to Vida and she said you're right." Vida was the powerful conjuror. The thing is, Cassie had said, Jacob is back at the hotel and there's no telling what he might do when it's getting toward morning and nobody's back. And then she had set out. At stake had been the security of their escape mission. If morning came and the kids were not back then Jacob would surely tell. And Amelia would get in trouble. But that wasn't all. It seemed imperative for Cassie to get back to the Dolphin Hotel. Remember that sense of impending doom? Yes, that was it. But first she would visit the oracle. She got up with determination. She sucked the palms of her hands and felt the tiny sharp pieces of rock embedded there loosen and come out in her mouth. She tasted her blood.

She began to work her way downhill. She thought she could remember where the actual room was where people came to consult. Where they waited and beyond the door the sibyl sat over her fragrant tripod and the fumes drifted up making her intoxicated, making her speak in riddles. It was in the Temple of Apollo. And the Temple of Apollo had a big stone wall and some columns, up on a platform. Beside it was the Cassiotis spring; she remembered because it was like her name. There was a ramp and some round bases from bigger columns and huge blocks of stone, which were set down close together.

She heard the tinkling again. It was getting near. There were lots of little tinklings, not all coming from one place. She went cold with fear. She could feel a living presence; it made the hair stand up on her head and her arms. Creatures! She couldn't stop herself from whimpering. One of them was so close she could smell it. Goats! Fucking local goats, that's what they were! She remembered the little flocks of them together with their herder, spilling across the highway.

"Go! Go! Go!" She whispered urgently to the goats.

They breathed stertorously in her direction. They were vague white ghostly shapes under the clouded moon.

It's just a stupid old billy goat, Cassie, went a voice inside her. You can scare it off easily. Don't be such a wimp. Just fight back. Fight back? Okay. She stamped her foot, she swung her arms: "Get the hell out! This is a sacred place!" she shouted. "Out, by order of the gods!"

The tinkling became louder. They responded to abuse, she saw. She stamped after the closest one and it broke into a run. As its little bell retreated she felt desperately lonely. She began to run after it.

Perhaps it was a sacred goat, because it took her to the Temple. Yes, there rising into the sky were the six round columns that used to support the roof. You could only tell where the rooms were by the level of the floor, which was uneven. One of the rooms was the adytum. Inside there were chasms and pediments and altars, even pipes carrying water. On the walls the mottos were written, Dr. Laird said: Know Thyself and Nothing in Excess. Dr. Laird said the Pythia was an older woman, the ancient equivalent of the guidance counsellor. Cassie had been to plenty of those. She should find the adytum and go in and ask for her help.

She climbed up to where she was not supposed to climb, the flat space between the columns. She walked in their tall presence. She could feel it, the ancient power. Knowing, secretive, solemn.

Remember, the oracle does not foretell the future, Dr. Laird had said, it only gives advice.

Thank god for that, thought Cassie. She did not wish to have the future foretold. She could see it herself, sometimes, a short distance away, and it was never pleasant. But somehow, she felt, it did not affect her. In her case, future tense did not apply. For herself there was only a blank, a respite from worry, a sinking away. Did this mean she was going to die?

There was more light now, as the moon reflected on the marble columns. Cassie walked to what she imagined was the secret room. She imagined the priests opening the door and giving her entry. She stepped down a big stair. Here it was darker, in moon shadow. She was cold, suddenly, her legs covered in goosebumps under her thin cotton pants. The rocks with their store of retained heat were far away. The earth had broken through the stone floor. Perhaps that was the hole the tripod sat over.

Suddenly Cassie had the idea that she needed smoke. For the

oracle to work there must be steam coming from under the earth. She scooped up the bits of dried wood that lay around, tucking dead leaves under it. Vida had given her matches to relight the joint; she found them in her pocket and struck one. The fire flared up reassuringly. She fanned the crackling with her hand. She walked to where the trees overhung, at the side, and picked up some dried dead branches and threw them onto the fire. When she returned, the oracle spoke.

"And what do you want to know?"

"I don't exactly know."

Not what shall I be when I grow up? Or, how shall I grow up? Or even, shall I grow up? Not why is life so hard? Or, should I continue bothering to live? Those would be the kind of questions the Dead Ladies would ask when they got here. And Vida? What would Vida ask?

But Vida was not here and she was tired of Cassie; she found her irritating, like everyone else did. The knowledge was a great sadness, which Cassie had carried like a boulder down the slope and which now threatened to roll over her, crushing and splintering everything in its path, down to the gulf. It was this problem of future. Even one question implied a belief in life beyond today.

Silence all around. The sibyl whistled in the dark.

"Your question, miss?"

To speak was like jumping off a cliff. You didn't fear jumping off a cliff if you knew you were dying, anyway. People did it all the time. She opened her mouth. She closed it again.

"What is it that you want?"

"I want—"

"You want. This is good." The returned voice mocked her self-importance.

"I want—"

The goats tinkled all around. Her fire was doing well. The branches had caught. She allowed the smoke to float up under her clothes and into her hair. It was pine smoke, not cedar, not as fragrant as she would have wished. The flames rose a little and she put on one more piece. It must have been dry indeed because it burned so well. There was a hot red glow in the core of the little pile. One, two, three, go, Cassie. She thought of the Dead Ladies. She felt the backed-up words of her protest coming up her throat.

"Is what happened to Dr. Laird—is it a curse because of what we did to Ferdinand?"

"Is it a curse you say if you say it is a curse"

The oracle true to its reputation gave her a puzzle, a puzzle without punctuation.

Cassie gathered her courage and her jumbled, too-big words. The words rose up like gorge, from a storehouse of riches only half-understood, but retained there in the recesses until one day she would know what they meant.

"But I want to know," said Cassie. "To know what gives with this cellular global porno java world. I don't want your palm-sized proverbs. I need to know what, under this toxic nimbus nauseous ozone doughnut burnt-out sun, is going to be left when the greedy all-terrain carnivores are done? Like, where are the streams without sewage, buried-underground polluted crap-loaded molecules mutating into cancer-causing radical cells?"

"Excuse me, Cassandra, but you must sit up straight and deliver your words clearly, with *breath*," said the Pythia. "Otherwise I cannot understand you and I know you have a great deal to say that is important."

"And the Dead Ladies, how where when can they score the cash they need to keep them in eye glitter hair gel velcro ornaments tattoos designer shoes compact disc pedicures hits of acid? Not to mention hot dogs."

"Say what?"

"And if you don't like it, where to go, to what left alone zone free of zebra mussels, child sex-trade, and school bombs, with no weirdo smut-peddling, wife-beating, till-pilfering freaks to ruin it? Without 'all things uncomely and broken, all things worn out and old'?

"So why not devote ourselves to a life of crime when nobody's home? And they don't get it even if you carve Help Me in your arm. At least you get attention if you do a B and E. Well that's what we thought. We didn't even get that when we beat up Ferdinand and wrecked his truck. He just went away. And nobody ever talked about him again. Doesn't anyone care that he disappeared? What does that mean?

"I know Hope stayed in the box when all the bad things flew out, but I haven't got it—"

The rocks beside her started to rumble.

"Please," Cassie said, "don't be mad."

But the noise began again, and there were voices with it, maybe Vida's voice.

"Help!" said Cassie. "There's so much coming." Did no one else feel the pressure of life out there, waiting to get at them? "I feel a sense of impending doom."

"You must be more specific," said the Pythia. "I cannot deal with a question that is not a question, but a speech. You sound like my husband. Is this about Ferdinand?"

"I cannot tell a lie: we beat him up, we pushed his truck into the lake."

"And for what reason, may I ask?"

"There was no reason. He was our friend."

"That's why?"

"No. To score the cash. To pay for my hot dogs."

"Pardon me?" Incredulous now.

"It's easy for you, you've had your life."

"That's rude, child."

"You've had the best, you're greedy, like the old tree that takes up the sun and the water too so the flowers die."

"Your time is up. What is your question?"

"Do you see what's coming?"

The rocks beside her rumbled.

"Because I do," said Cassie. "You know I do."

The noise began again, and there really were voices.

"Cassie! Cassie! Cassie!"

She could pick out Vida, and the others too, Maureen/Delphine and Ashley. She could just see them, coming down the slope, before the light of the fire blotted out their shapes.

"No, I'm here! I'm here!" she cried. But her voice did not come out loudly. They went on looking; they were moving past.

"Hey look, a fire!"

"Vida, it's me!" shouted Cassie. "I lit it."

Just as she said that she stepped over the flame. It was her intention to stand over the smoke the way the sibyl did, to become inspired to answer questions, to speak in riddles. But she was clumsy as always. She let the legs of her trousers catch the flame, her loose, fifteen-dollar Athens street-market army-surplus drawstring trousers in black cotton. She looked down. The fire seemed to deliberate on whether or not to consume this food, this weave of soft, girl-scented fibres. Then it bit. The flames jumped up her leg and ran across her back and her belly at the same time, flashing from the wrist elastics straight up the arm, as if to give Cassie wings of fire. They jumped into the escaped curls that had sprung up around her neck and ate, crackling like gryphons.

Her mouth opened in astonishment and closed on smoke. She looked down on her body as it acquired its raiments of fire. When she did cry out it was more of a gurgle, as she vomited from fear and pain, the already-shrieking pain of her skin's scorching as her pants fell away from her knees and shins. She screamed and screamed but stood frozen on the spot. And Vida was there.

"Run, Cassie! Spin, Cassie, Spin!"

She stepped blindly away from the fire; she did that much, at least. She could see for a moment through the smoke that rose from her own garments. And what she saw was Vida between the columns.

"Spin, Cassie!" Vida put her arms straight out to the sides and one foot behind the other and began turning. And even though Cassie was frozen she tried to do the step-toe-step-toe turn, her trademark, with arms lifted.

But Jacob was suddenly there, too, waving his arms like a film director and shouting, "No don't spin! It fans the flames. Get water! The spring, you guys, the spring, it's over there!"

Vida was running full speed toward her and tearing off her sweatshirt.

Perhaps Cassie believed that her spinning might quench the fire, but more than that she realized the spiral was her song, it was her shape and her self to express, and so she began, slowly but then faster and faster, to spin, her arms out like boards, her hair, or at least the bits that were left, flying behind.

At first, spinning opened up some space around her mouth in which she could breathe: the smoke was still there but it moved off a little and her open lips gulped in cool fresh air. But the more she spun the more the flames took heart. She was mad with fear and pain and choking on smoke now, coughing. Her eyes filled with tears so that she could not see.

"Stop Cassie down Cassie down *down*." Jacob put his arms around her, his little pudgy undertaker's arms that all the girls mocked. He threw something over her; there was a rough cloth full of cold water that smelled like earth and waste. Pieces of her clothing flew away, charred, frizzled. Her skin was coming off too she felt certain. Air touched her raw second layer of flesh and she screamed and screamed.

Then she was hit, collided with, simultaneously by two flying bodies. Maureen/Delphine and Vida knocked her down and smothered the fire in her remaining clothing with their sweatshirts, their own legs and chests and even their bare hands. Jacob was standing by, wringing his hands like the funeral director he'd always resembled. And Cassie was gone, screaming and screaming. Her voice echoed from the towering red rocks. And, dimly, she saw herself, Cassie, ascending the Phaedriades, the Shining Rocks. And from there, twirling off into the skies. She watched that girl called Cassie; she would twirl forever, like a tiny dervish, a volcano, a smear of black and blood and white skin and smoke and streaky flames.

Roll, Cassie, roll!! commanded Vida.

The body she'd been in was left in a heap, sinking into that place like sleep but a greater luxury. But she did hear Vida and the habit of obedience was strong, and so she gave her last efforts to rolling, painfully, oh excruciatingly, in the dry yellow dust of the ages, smearing it with blood and ashes.

BOOK THREE

19

THE TOPPLING TOWERS

THE BLUE BAY sighed and hissed with the cresting and tumbling waves. And it was full of goodbye: goodbye sunshine, goodbye knife-blade brilliance of light in the eye. Goodbye perfect crescent of beige sand. Goodbye as well all those perky blondes in short shorts although they were not to be regretted, thought Francesca. They, at least, with their brown legs stumpended in platform sneakers, which made them walk as if their pelvises were fused to their spines, Francesca would not miss.

But oh, how she would miss the patches of rough green that fringed the sand and the air-filled ribbons of white sails on the horizon. The curve of the beach and the sound of tennis balls—bok, bok, bok—and even the ongoing stream of infants in rolling stock, more and more babies to be raised, the astonishing and frightful task of educating their minds left to others. The Beach was the place to see the babies of Toronto, wee or pudgy, wrinkled or fresh-steamed, white, black, or khaki, incipient Torontonians who would grow up to take their *caffe latte* with skim milk. Little ones who would never come to the Manor and who would never be her rats. Born too late, they were. She pitied them.

One went by now, sound asleep on its gingham pouf, with gingham frills edging his stroller (blue-check, but it could be a girl, who knew?). She had half a mind to stop his mother to admonish her to take as good care of the child's brain as she did of its bottom. There was a familiar look to the mother's face, the set of her lips, a prominent chin that bespoke trouble—the "trouble face" Dugald would have called it. As he had designated Amelia when first he saw her. And certainly he had been right there. Of course the original trouble face still hung in the front hall of the Manor and belonged to Lily, Francesca's own mother. Dugald would have laughed to hear her finally admit it.

Would have? So was he gone? Is that what she believed in her heart?

Trouble faces were few and far between, but they were out there, and one had to beware. This one right in front of her was fetching and canny, selfish, smug and full of appeal. This was a look Francesca recognized; she could have been a Manor girl grown up and fulfilling her biological destiny. Motherhood was something of which Francesca approved and which she had always recommended, by word if not by deed. It made Francesca want to speak to the young woman. Hello and goodbye. I was Miss Morrow. Your babe was born too late. Perhaps even you were, Miss Pert. Too late to be—

To be what?

To be rescued?

Surely that was what she had intended to say.

Oh arrogance, Francesca, fatal arrogance. The city stood. The classics remained. Life remained, if anyone had the time or energy to live it. But it was too late. Of that Francesca was certain. Too late for the intangible, the nonquantifiable right way of existing. The sun was declining in the west. The ship was in the harbour. It would sail. And Toronto—what might have been—would be lost. Somehow this had happened while she was not looking. While she was in Greece, although it had only been a few weeks.

She and Dugald used to walk here, not so long ago. Perhaps a decade. No, three. Walk along the boardwalk and into Ashbridges

Bay and sometimes Cherry Beach, farther west, where the Taddle flowed into the lake, or once did, where the first settlers made their shelter, the creek Governor Simcoe once mistook for the Don and tried to canoe up. She remembered everything Dugald said although she often wished he would be quiet.

Yes, this year, or was it last, life here had changed unutterably. It was as if a silent, secret army had entered the city. The sellers in the marketplace were clones of one another, the honest women dressed as prostitutes. The drinking places where mugs had been lifted in song were infested with mercenaries. The great arena where the athletic contests were fought, won (more often lost, in fact), was to be sold for debt. The waves of spectators spelling out the team names turned their backs in disgust. Even here along the beachfront the bicycles with their winking silver spokes, the hunched brown biceps of those men who rode them, would be gone, gone, wheeled into oblivion, abandoned by the gods, eaten alive from within. And the brightest and the bravest of the youngsters would be sold into franchise-slavery or—their best hope—would run to hide in the wilderness.

The new world was upon them. Oh yes, Francesca could admit that now. You cannot live by the past. You may only be guided by it and, even then, it may guide you wrong. Because the new world would be surpassing strange. Of her students, her lovely ones, a precious few, perhaps four or five out of the thousands, would fit their own particular genius into the puzzle, become themselves the secret spring that fed the whole. Another few would distinguish themselves by infamy, god rest their souls. Most would lose themselves in the multitude but perhaps, occasionally, they would remember a line of poetry, the image from a great painting, a madrigal, a fine idea. For they had been well-educated. This she knew.

Francesca had taught some of these denizens of the new world. They turned up, didn't they, at the last Commencement Day. They had seen the future and determined to profit by it. But others were too innocent. Of this recent bunch, one had been a truth teller, a believer in pictures and dreams, a girl who rightly feared her gifts. She was unlucky.

Whereas she, Francesca Morrow, was a lucky woman.

Yes, lucky all her life. In loving and in having been loved. She had Dugald. They had met and fallen in love and joined their fates. She had adopted this city, into which she had walked on dusty roads barefoot (well, nearly). This podgy, stodgy pudding and pie town where for decades one could not even find a decent zabaglione. To Toronto she had given her passions; to her, Toronto had given its children.

Oh, Toronto.

Oh, the Manor.

Oh, Dugald.

Oh, my children. Wayward children of an affable philistine town destined by birth to comparative wealth, to based-in-ignorance ease, to unthinking almost happiness untouched by famine, torture and persecution.

Oh, Cassie, especially.

Coming now was the end of everything, perhaps. All the beautiful language, astonishing colours and textures that made your fingers curl, the ebb and flow of dreams, the marvels of statuary of muscled legs and slender waists under pleated fabrics. The secret springs that fed us from the deepest rivers of human art and endeavour, the bubbling source that dazzled the eye and heart.

Oh, Francesca, why so apocalyptic? No anniversary, no news flash, no petty complaint had brought this on. Is it because your husband has drifted away? Or is there a deeper waning, a loss of faith within yourself?

Over there, amongst the trees, she thought she could see the bronze Charioteer. He was a figure from the past and from her past, the one beautiful skirted man she had gazed on in childhood when her governess consented to take her to the excavation site. Now to her surprise she saw that he had come to Toronto, the mottled green and black of his oxidized surface camouflaging him perfectly, so he fit into the spaces between trees and became light and shadow. He stood tall, high-waisted, one-armed, the reins—attached to nothing—lying lightly across his palm. His Severe-style black stone eyes gazed across and down at her with gentle sadness.

"You've come," she said.

The perfect parted lips did not move but his head, only slightly wider than his muscled neck, seemed to nod slightly.

"Come for me? But I'm not ready. Not nearly ready!"

Of course not. He had not come across five hundred years before Christ and another two thousand after, he had not come across this gap, from the sacred spring at Delphi, for Francesca, who, despite the toppling towers around her, would carry on.

"Dugald, then?"

And a smile briefly lit the bronze features, either that or a cloud passed from before the sun, allowing a beam to do its work. Yet he stood so still she wasn't sure. Students asked, year after year, if this was a flaw, that the Charioteer—who clearly stood on the speeding chariot, driving the horses, showed no sign of speed. In fact he appeared to be the very definition of stillness. His snail-curled hair tied with a silver-plated band. His obsidian eyes. His chiton girdled below his chest. No breath of wind had left its trace in his frozen curls, or the folds of his garment. His eyes were fixed, his face too, with the perfect sadness of one who has been stopped in time. He seemed more likely to be driving a charnel wagon than a chariot. He was finality, which surely the Greeks understood.

"It is Dugald, then."

She turned her head from the bronze figure, wanting to escape the black depth of his eyes. She was nearly knocked over by a boy on rollerblades careening along, his ears cupped with black foam, his lips moving to some unknown lyric that thudded out of a tin box strapped to his belt.

"Dear God in heaven!" she exclaimed, giving the boy a furious glance to which he was oblivious. "Watch where you're going, young man." But her hauteur, her grand style was lost on the boardwalk; here she was not the reigning deity of the Manor, but a stalk-thin and infirm old woman. The boy's eyes, like the Charioteer's, were fixed on a place dead ahead of him.

Thus we observe the heartlessness of beauty, thought Francesca as she began to walk, a little unsteadily now, westward along the boardwalk. And now she noticed that the promenade was full of Greeks, Mediterranean sailors, men and women of the ancient world whose faces bore the dignity and the inflections of their language, their nations, whose eyes held reflections of sun and sea. They were dressed in the ugly Gap-inspired, tube-skirted, torn-off, studded black denim shrink-wrapped metallic neon mistakes that graced the corpi of young people today, but they were, she could tell, ancient folk. Their faces bore the serenity and cupidity one recognized immediately from the golden age.

They had simply never grown up, thinking perhaps that to never grow up was to never grow old. They imagined they might escape it all, that, put down here whole, the pockmarks and erosions, the ghastly mutilations and amputations that are the price of life might somehow pass them by. But that was futile. One simply became an aged child, and that was a sorry sight.

Francesca recognized them. There were the Korai, the maidens whose grace hid strength enough to hold the Erechtheion porch roof aloft, freed of their burden and in motion, pushing baby strollers and walking their dogs. There were the glorious women of Epidaurus, their tunics pressed back against perfect thighs, skating with shiny red helmets on their heads and black elastic padding around elbow and knee. There were the Corinthians, the Cretans and even the big-breasted smiling women of ancient Thera. There were short lusty Romans and blond chiselled-chinned Adonises. The crowd of Ancients did not assail her but slid silently by with vacant half-smiles. There went one of the dancing girls, acanthus leaves at her feet, only the cauldron on her head had become a turban of some kind. The leaves, now that Francesca looked more closely, were thick socks that rolled above her ankles. She wore gold hoops in her ears and her gaze, down at the pavement under her feet, turned inward to some beautiful but vacant mental landscape, was eerie.

But why have they all come here? wondered Francesca. What was the occasion? Was it by way of honouring Dugald in his last days? Their defender, the one who more than anyone had introduced their grandeur here to Troy-ronto?

She laughed. This was not Troy: the Hellespont was nowhere in the vicinity, only the toxic waters of Lake Ontario presiding over the eastward gates to the St. Lawrence Seaway and all the waters of the world, the waters plied by navigators from Odysseus' time. These were his sailors, then. Fetched up here through misadventure, escaping somewhere along on the journey to these more peaceful shores, dragging the shards and remnants of ancient cultures from antique hemispheres, visible today due to the mindless energy of human reincarnation.

Oh, Francesca, you are dramatizing. Shamelessly. But why not? She owed nothing to anyone now. She could do as she liked. It was a game, to populate the imagination with classical figures, with heroes and gods and the victims of fate. To pitch one's own voice in the same key as the great figures of history. It had always been her game, and a great game it was. As we are given this life to inhabit, why let it be little? Make it large, and copy the brilliant shapes already crafted.

And on they came, the figures. Here a Caryatid from the Siphnian Treasury, her long locks flat on her collarbone and a happy reflection on her sweet face, eyes like almonds, heavy-lidded, nearly closed, as she held her baby on her abdomen in one of those ugly front-pack devices. How do they stand it, the people who live out here on these beaches? Francesca thought in a moment of clarity. All this fecundity. All this empty-headed loveliness, this venality and avidity, the hunger to live, simply live, regardless of the consequences. That must have been what it was like in prehistory. But where was the turmoil and the despair of civilized times in Toronto's Beach? And the answer came to her: hidden. Hidden in her heart, and perhaps in the hearts of others. Not made evident. Not in this city. Not in these times, no matter how many poems she had the children memorize, how many great works they imbibed between Diet Cokes.

She would leave. She had recognized the colour of it as soon as she had come down to the water today, recognized the blue of goodbye. It was the agony garden of Van Gogh, the Gethsemane of Gauguin. That was what she was seeing. She was seeing this city for the last time.

She looked westward. There were the topless towers of Ilium. Never mind. New York had higher ones. Paris had more beautiful ones. There was nothing, nothing to keep her.

Go then, if you're going to be that way, the passersby seemed to be mouthing to her as they rolled mysteriously, handsomely, dispassionately by. If you don't like the way we are. We like it. We are happy. And Francesca saw her life as Headmistress roll away in their wake. Her past life, which was what it was now.

"Now that was a life, or was it a dream?"

Helen of Troy's words when she saw Menelaus, the husband she'd cuckolded for Paris, beautiful as he stepped onto the battlefield. Such a lovely phrase. "Now that was a life, or was it a dream?" It was the heart cry of regret, of loss. But it was not for the man, only for the life she had once lived. For herself, in other words.

There was Dugald, of course. She had to say goodbye to this man she loved. She had to, in fact, wrench him from her heart, wreck the illusions she'd cherished of the love he bore her. But more than that she had to say goodbye to her own life, to that part of it that had been lived in apparent security between marital sheets. To the way she had believed herself beloved. That lovely life she'd imagined herself to be living. Goodbye. It had all been in her mind anyway. Dugald had outlived his devotion. He had informed her that it was a hoax, of a sort. He had subsided after a rage, and the quarrel had never been mended. Now he would never speak again, though he was still alive in that hospital bed.

So it was left to Francesca to clean up, to do the difficult part. (As it always was, she noted.) He, Dugald, had been a bit naughty that way. He was a man only average in virtue. Because she had made him more than that she would have to kill him. Kill him with accurate assessment. Kill him with one of Cassie's truths. "How else to prepare a death for dangerous men who seem to love you?" Who said that? Clytemnestra, no doubt, as she was about to murder her husband.

This was not child's play, this business of a lifelong devotion, this matter of marriage. Not for the timid, that was for certain.

The swirl of passing classical beauties began, at last, to slow. One of them—Francesca thought perhaps it was one of the nymphs from the clay wheel at the Corycian Cave of Pan on Parnassus, a dancing nymph—slowed before her. Her very gestures calling up the music from the god's ivory flute, she slowed and actually looked Francesca in the face.

"Are you okay?"

Okay was not a word to which Miss Morrow was accustomed to responding.

"I beg your pardon?" Best Headmistress voice here.

"I mean, like, you're looking a bit lost—"

It was on Francesca's lips to exclaim that she was certainly not lost, or confused, that she was not the sort of woman to be discovered by a vacant beauty on the boardwalk, lost or confused. But instead she allowed her elbow to be taken, unsteadily, by the nymph-on-wheels, who had turned her toes inward in order to stop, looming from what seemed a great height, tottering sideways to a bit of grass.

Here was safety: out of the flow she, nymph, was no longer prone to losing her footing as the bearings shot out from under her and she, Francesca, was no longer in danger of being collided with by a skater.

"Okay?" The girl let go, and thrust her hands backward, forward, jerkily adjusting her balance. She was not as good on these skates as others.

"I'm fine, thank you," said Francesca in a tone that implied that she had always been fine. "Perfectly all right."

"Okay!" said the girl and with one step and a push from her grounded foot launched herself back into the traffic.

Francesca too straightened her dress and stepped back onto the wooden slats of the boardwalk. She was relieved to observe that the faces had reverted to those of ordinary Torontonians. But yet even watching the erratic flow of wheeled people—cyclists, strollers, small children on tricycles—she could see history. Here was a little Helen, a pouty, soft-fleshed girl of about ten. Her voice, directed at her mother walking alongside, cut the air with the whine of a saw.

"It's not working, Mum, it's broken it's too hard to push something's the matter with the chain."

And by she went in the onrush. How curious it was that they all seemed to be going in one direction. Perhaps there was an agreement. Only she, Francesca, appeared to be going against the flow, against the grain. To the west, into her own aging and into the renewal of history, she thought. While the world, or at least this local world, went east, trying to become younger, defying the passing of years and even of centuries.

Francesca began to walk again. She recalled a ferry dock in the vicinity. She would come to it before long if she continued to walk. She had a desire to stand on the deck of a gleaming white ship and watch the land sink into darkness behind her. To sail into the blue of goodbye. She walked along the boardwalk hearing the authoritative clomps of her heels as slightly hollow. She would walk until she found such a place, she would take note of it for later, and then she would go to see Dugald in the hospital. Sit beside him in the space created by his incapacitation. It was peaceful, there, and she could watch him sail out, as well. Her life's blood, the pulse in her veins. Say goodbye.

A little sob escaped her but she put her hand to her mouth and muffled it. Just then there was movement at her shoulder. A man sitting high up on a sleek horse. It was the Charioteer but he was wearing the uniform of a mounted policeman. As smooth and as cold as a mortuary attendant, a messenger of doom. But so sympathetic. He slowed his horse to exactly her pace with a subtle flick of the rein.

"Are you all right, ma'am?"

She gazed upward. It was on the tip of her tongue to snap that she was quite all right and why was he enquiring, but in fact she felt very unwell all of a sudden.

"I thought there were boats here," she said and was horrified to hear a quaver in her voice.

"That's quite a bit farther west, ma'am," he said. "They've boats at Cherry Beach." Cherry Beach: that was where the Taddle emptied into the lake. Suddenly, overwhelmingly, it was where she wanted to be.

"Cherry Beach," she said. "Can I get there by proceeding along this walkway?"

He looked down at her footwear, the three-inch, beige-suede platforms. "I would not attempt it, ma'am, if I were you," he said. "It's a good three miles."

"Oh my goodness." She stopped, aghast. Her calculations of size, her sense of proportion was far out of line.

"If you like, I can call you a taxi."

The helpful young man, even if he had on that too-smooth face, that boxy uniform that seemed to live in another time and space not the warm air of Toronto in late spring, consoled Francesca. The ease it conjured, hearing a male voice and offers to help, envisioning a taxi, even, was wonderful to her. Yes, in the old days, (now that was a life, or was it a dream?) she had had a man to help her, and a taxi at her beck and call. No reason she shouldn't have a taxi this minute.

"Why yes, that would help. That is an excellent idea."

"Very well, ma'am. I'll get one to come. You just walk ahead, to that bend in the road where it meets the boardwalk. If you can," he said.

It was the "if you can" that annoyed her.

Amelia arrived at the Ancient Agora shortly after eight in the morning; the birds were piping over an apricot sunrise. She had walked there, over the Acropolis, and down the back through the little village of Anafiotika. In all her trips to Greece, it had remained her favourite place. The doves filled her ears with their murmuring hoots. The old grey marble underfoot glistened and the walls of saffron were laced with potted plants with dark green foliage. The coffee tables tucked in against the rock face were silent at this hour. She passed a sign at the top of the Agora: Excavation in Progress, it said. Danger of Falling Down Wells. It was almost her favourite English sign in Athens, but had to take second place to Socrates Prison Tavern. Try Socrates light lunch. Open 11 'til 2.

She rejected the path across the open field with well holes as being too difficult, and walked down Panos, then Adrianou, to the gate, plodding along with an air of peaceful determination. She passed through a great crowd of men in black who were laying out their wares for the flea market. They had coffee in Styrofoam cups and shouted to their pals while spreading a blanket over a car hood and littering it with old pink Hawaiian sandals and plastic ashtrays, books and earrings and cheap baskets. Time was when their sort would have fascinated her: not now. The stolid Greek women who manned the Agora were just pushing aside the iron gates: she was the first one in.

But the near presence—across the railway tracks—and sudden

remove of the merchant class such as it was—made that entry into the Agora even more magical. The place was haunted, more so than any other shrine she had visited, haunted with the rustle and brawk of buying and selling, of voices raised for barter or debate, the chatter and friction of getting goods, or thinking in groups, of staying alive, in other words. Yet it was quiet. And simply beautiful. There was little else to say and happily, no one said it. Silent, empty of human folk, a maze of crumbled walls and steps to nowhere, it was stippled with tiny yellow wildflowers and, in spots, touched with the madness of those deep red poppies.

Some scent rose up, the early song of the birds—not only the doves' coo, but other, sharper trills—and it reminded her of a place so tender and sweet in memory that it stopped her breath. What was it? England in the spring? An otherwise forgotten childhood meadow? Her own childhood or the childhood of mankind? A train rumbled past and cut her last tie with the modern world. She walked on the rough cobbles in the first, cool haze of morning, past a brook, and through long sleeves of crimson poppies, the Thiseion, temple of Hephaestus, rising out of a rim of trees on a mound to her right.

Ahead was the Stoa, where statues on the open promenade stood exposed to weather and casual encounter. She stopped at the statue of Nike, headless of course, and compared her with a number of larger and equally headless Aphrodites in a desultory way. The Agora was flat and Mars Hill loomed huge above her: on it she could see a troop of black figures with backpacks picking itself up off the rock.

In the Stoa museum she cast her glance over Mycenaean-era burials unearthed here and all around the Acropolis. There was a casket of a girl in which her pelvis was still intact, as the rest of her dribbled away into a grainy brown substance, earth, maybe. She saw a chest with granaries set on top of it, all painted with those black, mazed lines. There it was, evidence of how those long ago peoples had cropped and hoarded and measured out their food (their days in coffee spoons). There were some red-figure vases from the sixth-century BC painted with little scenes like women washing, men boxing. One had a particularly tender profile of female breasts and thighs. A little boy statue was anatomically intact. She would have liked to have pointed him out to the Dead Ladies, who worried about such things.

A fabulous sphinx amphora from the seventh century diverted her, and then she studied a bronze rider that had somehow outlived the equestrian statue it had come with. We never know just what will last, do we? Posterity's selection is random, democratic, whimsical. Amelia was feeling somewhat jaded but at the same time full of tenderness.

This was the market, also the courts of law: somewhere near here, at the premises of Simon the Potter, Socrates had instructed his students. Fragments of the law codes had been found, written on stones. The laws were just graffiti. Just like those slogans on walls. What did they call them? Tags. That's how they wrote them down. They didn't have books. They didn't write on paper. The walls were their libraries.

There wouldn't be so much to read now if people had to carve it all on stone.

"This was the Euboulos. It was very orderly in classical times," Dugald had told the students, when they'd all been here together. "Every item for sale was kept in the same place as other examples of the same thing. For instance, the figs would be here, the honeycomb there. The lambs would be there, and the perfume over there. The fish, then the garlic. All together. All in its proper place. The Athenian named each little passageway or corner after what was being sold there. He might say, I'll meet you at the fig. Or, I am going to the fish."

"Or maybe, I was at the perfume and I ran into Diana," ventured Vida.

Oh, definitely they met people here; this was how the news was spread. Recall the word: *agiro*, to gather. The men came and stood around and talked politics, who was going to be ostracized, how much money should go to the fleet. They bought their roasted meat or tomatoes. Some of them stayed all night in case there was an emergency and the city had to be called to arms. Dugald's pale face had been enlivened as he called up the scene: the torch by the watcher's station; two men on their stools at the entryway to the market, the sleeping city under their eye.

Amelia mourned for Dugald.

In the metal workers' area on a low rocky hill was Hephaestus' temple. Hephaestus, lover, craftsman, troll; Ferdinand of the canteen truck, the one who brought earthy humour and warmth, who had the continual fire in his workshop. The destabilizer of Olympus, the one who created Pandora, and look at what she wrought.

Amelia missed Ferdinand, too. Here in the land of Aphrodite and Eros, the cradle of the stories of strange liaisons and sexual obsessions that destroyed humans and gods alike, she woke to an ache in her pelvis. That man! She could almost feel his body hovering near her.

She turned to the open field again. It was achingly beautiful. The orange trees were in bloom; the blue doves flew overhead with twigs in their beaks. The velvety red poppies with their black centres bubbled like a stream across the rough, pale rock.

Right in the centre of the Agora was a little church. A small church, Byzantine—recent, by comparison to the Thiseion—and restored by American students. Its only windows were round holes in the midst of arches, which seem to be made by cookie cutters; its walls were white and the tiles grey. Murals found under the plaster were now in view, patched with the stillness of new plaster.

And standing alone in its cross-shaped interior, its grey, cool peace, Amelia thought, perhaps it is possible to begin again. To return to innocence, as this church has been returned. She drank in the cool, cloistered air.

She stood in the centre of the floor, in the centre of the space, which was in the form of a cross, looking up. The frescoes with their colours now faded, now brighter, their bland spaces, their still-insistent story, held her entranced. It was a patched-up job, but it was beautiful for that reason. There was a peculiar salvaged peace in that building, and for the first time since the disasters at Delphi, Amelia let herself cry. She was a homeless exile; the Manor was washed up; Dugald vegetative or even compost; Cassie a crisp.

Perhaps Francesca had suffered enough. Or perhaps Amelia was defective in the area of carrying out revenge. She sometimes forgot for hours at a time that she hated the woman. She pondered this mystery whilst sipping on a frappé in the Plaka on the way to her class in Intermediate Modern Greek. She found herself wondering what, for instance, had happened to the rats. Here it was only a few days from the end of the term; would they all lose their year? Of course there was nothing she could have done, even if she'd gone back to Toronto. She, Amelia, had been fired. That had happened the night of *in flagrante* in the chapel, before the disastrous field trip to Greece, and there had never been any suggestion of her being un-fired, of Amelia apologizing, begging to be allowed to return, or indeed of the opposite, of Francesca begging the younger woman to stay on. Not especially after the night when she sat in the bar of the Dolphin Hotel and the kids ran amok at the site of the oracle and Cassie got burned.

As Francesca had her hands full with Dugald, Amelia had got the students back to Athens and onto a plane; then she set up shop outside the Burns Unit at the Athens International Hospital and waited, along with Cassie's mother, for news. Until, finally, Cassie was well enough to be flown home. Amelia kissed Cassie's thin adult face at the departure gate, mourning the strange child who had arrived only six weeks ago. Francesca did not need to fire Amelia again. No, that much was clear: it was over with the Manor and Amelia.

But she could not flout Francesca. Life was too brutal and in the end one's enemies became so sad and beaten down by its terrors that one absolutely could not take vengeance into one's own hands.

There was nothing Greek about that. She could not even hate Francesca now. She imagined her there in Toronto, Dugald as silent as he had once been voluble, as withholding of answers as he had once been bursting to give them. With his silence the school became silent. The grounds became silent. Even the waters of his beloved Taddle must be sinking farther underground.

Francesca stood at Dugald's bedside. He lay with his eyes mostly closed; only a slim crack showed between the upper and lower lashes, under which she thought she could see movement, as if he were watching a procession on the inside of his eyelids.

"I went to Cherry Beach. I saw the mouth of the Taddle," she told him. "I saw where the water goes into the lake. I gazed at the place, for long minutes. I was doing it for you. I saw it for you."

He said nothing.

He was gone from this place. He had been gone from this place since that day in Delphi. But Francesca would not believe it. She would not let go of him. Yes, she knew she was only dragging a stick through the pond. It only stirred up the sediment, the sinking decomposing bodies that made up pond life. Organic matter changing itself into other organic matter, as Dugald would have said. Life is energy. Energy is never destroyed. It simply becomes something else. Science 20. The frozen fish from the pond: her husband smacking it heroically against the countertop in the lab, the fish flying into smithereens.

Suddenly she laughed out loud. Dugald startled under his sheets.

"I'm sorry," she said. "I was just thinking... Do you remember the pond carp you froze with liquid nitrogen—"

"They weren't carp. They were goldfish. Our own, grown huge—"

It was one of the Myths of the Manor.

She remembered his triumphant waving of the frigid fish plank in the air and then the way he had slammed it on the counter and how it had fragmented, how it flew into thousands of small pieces unrecognizable as having ever been a fin or a scale or the sleek padded side fillets. "And the girls screaming and the boys laughing and falling out of their seats and the look of complete shock on your face, Dugald, and then the way you pulled it together, in one of those brilliant teaching moments, although it was the last thing you expected. What you expected was that you could show how the carp—"

"goldfish—"

"—how the fish overwintered in the pond, because you believed they froze solid in the ice and simply thawed out and swam away in spring. But you banged the fish on the lab counter, and it shattered, and you stood there gawping with the class in an uproar and then you acted as if it were just what you had planned."

"And where then had the energy gone that had been the salmon's life?" asked Dugald.

"What was it you said then about the energy? That it had become cold, and all those tiny fragments had entered the air, cooling it by nano-degrees? But, Dugald, I always wanted to ask, but never did, what use was that? Surely a salmon was of more value."

"Yet we are all subject to these changes of state. When I die I too will cool the air."

She sobbed.

Although Dugald had stood, and walked out of the Athens hospital, boarded the airplane on Francesca's arm and obediently sat in his executive-class seat all the way to Frankfurt and then to Toronto, Dugald had not spoken since Delphi. Once at home on Taddle Creek Drive he had remained silent but had indicated by furious gesture and utter refusal to cope with his own body that he wanted to go to the hospital. Once there he had allowed himself to be undressed, had lain down between the coarse sheets (not their calibre, not at all, not the silk sheets that had come to seem his due in life) and had looked once, gratefully, into Francesca's eyes, and then he had lapsed. He had lapsed into whatever waiting state this was, but he had not died.

Now, he spoke.

"It's not fair," he said.

"Dugald! No reprimands, please."

"It's not fair and I am sorry, my darling."

His speech was stiff and slurred at the same time; he spoke like a Hallowe'en Transylvanian with pointed eye teeth. Francesca could not connect these words to her husband. She did not answer right away and so he stopped.

"Don't go away, Dugald. Don't leave me." The words escaped her mouth, the expected words, despite the fact that she herself had already adjusted to his leaving.

A fin's flip of a smile twisted his lips and then was gone.

"I want to tell you the truth," he said.

"Yes, of course, my darling," she said, reaching for his hand. "I thought you already did." Truth was dangerous, and rarely welcome. She did recall in that second that she was furious with him, for all his final ramblings, for going back to Meryl, even if only in his imagination.

"That I realize how unfair it is."

"Oh, darling. Don't."

"Unfair that all of my rebellion—lately," he said lately with an immense sigh as if to contemplate the passage of time either forward or back was just too much of a reach at this point," has been taken out on you. It is coincidence. It could have been anyone. You were—" with an effort he changed the tense,—"you are... an exemplary wife."

So this was the goodbye speech. "Oh, Dugald, don't."

"That all my rebellion has been taken out on you. I want to tell you that it could have been anyone. You see? That it was only that you were there."

Francesca fled the room. She ran along the corridors of the Mount Sinai Hospital, her heels sounding the tattoo that had long created alarm in Manor students and now brought the nursing staff out of their huddles and cupboards and back rooms to see what was going on.

"Did the old man in Room 314 die?"

They went running in the opposite direction.

Francesca achieved the elevator, entered it, (antiseptic smell and claustrophobic, a bad combination) pressed the button for the main floor and held her breath until it began to move. It was all too humiliating, this venture, this leave-taking, and why did she deserve it? Being exemplary apparently did not bring one happiness or even respect in the final analysis.

She flew, her dress whipping against her shins in front and filling a little with the breeze she created in the rear, past the coffee cart, through the lobby and through the hideous revolving door that she found emblematic of Toronto.

Line beside line of stopped cars, eight abreast, spewing exhaust from their tailpipes. Curious stares of idle folk in their wheelchairs behind the plate-glass wall that fronted on the sidewalk. A small burst of people emerging from a hole in the ground, the subway exit. Pedestrians with averted eyes as if to tell her she was out of line in displaying emotion.

Francesca waved her hands around her head and shoulders as if the whole noxious environment were a cloud of smoke or insects and could be dispelled that way. The full impact of the last few expiring breaths of the twentieth century was contained in that still-petrified pageant: this is what he was leaving and he was tired of it and why should he not be? She was not to take it personally. That was what he meant. Not that she was immaterial, but that she "could have been anyone." That what happened to people happened regardless of who they tied themselves up with.

And so it was that at three o'clock on a Thursday afternoon in

June in the middle of the broad west sidewalk of University Avenue between College and Dundas streets, Francesca at last calmed herself after a two-month panic and let her husband go.

———————

Behind the hospital, in the west where Francesca could not see, thunderclouds massed. The rain would soon come. Under the street Taddle Creek ran silently through sewers, waiting for the great bursts that would make it rise into the basements of the great Toronto institutions, the hospitals, the museums, the concert halls. Dugald's sacred spring stirred, as if in sympathy with the man who had always believed in its power.

Upstairs the nurses stood by as the doctor read the chart and found instructions not to resuscitate.

"He's gone."

"How about that? Where's his wife? She was just here."

"Ran out a couple of minutes ago. What a shame."

"Can you catch her?"

A nurse ran to the elevator, watched the buttons and saw that it was on the way back up.

"I doubt it, I doubt it," she cried, running back along the hall. "Can someone go down?"

———————

Francesca held her position, at bay, in the middle of the sidewalk. There were no other pedestrians; a space opened around her.

There is no one for me, she thought wildly. I have seen him out. I stayed with him although he had forsaken me in his heart. I stayed by him and I saw him on his way. And who is there for me? Who will attend to me as I grow old and die?

A small girl with an orange plume bobbing on the top of her

head approached; she looked like a child but she was not a child. "Miss Morrow?" said Vida.

Francesca looked around, unprepared. "What is it? Who is it?" she said, clutching at Vida's arm.

"It's me, Vida."

"But what are you doing here? You should be in school, shouldn't you?"

"The substitute gave up on us."

"Oh, no," said Francesca. "That's not at all good. What about Amelia?"

"She didn't come back, remember? She stayed in Greece with Cassie. Only now Cassie's come home."

"Oh, our dead ones, our wounded ones. My poor husband. And poor Cassie."

"Cassie is going to be all right. She's right here, in this hospital. And Amelia is going to work in a museum. All she has to do is learn Greek."

"Are you certain, Vida? How do you know?"

"Because Cassie told me. And Cassie knows."

"Yes, Cassie knows. But Amelia—"

"It's good for Amelia. I know, too," said Vida. "There's a little bit of Cassie in me."

They stood in the street holding each other's hands and their eyes swam with tears.

"Mrs. Laird?"

It was the nurse from the ward. He, too, put his arm on Francesca's. "What is it?"

"Could you come back inside, please? It's your husband."

Amelia felt him go, in faraway Athens. A balm spread over her; she was touched by his spirit. "He's gone," she thought. And then, because like everyone she mostly felt for herself. "It's over. My life at the Manor is fully over."

It was over with Ferdinand, too. It was embarrassing now, how she'd slavered over Ferdinand. Good grief! The Portuguese troll. She remembered the panting and the way the blood had risen into her head and blotted out thought. But she could not for the life of her remember why. Or why it had been a problem.

Now the idea of unsuitable men seemed so silly. In Greece, in fact, all the men were unsuitable; they were Greek after all. And people understood. She would stay here. To do what, she did not know. Possibly to write captions for museum artifacts, as the girls had suggested. In this way a continuity could be achieved. It appeared that there was a thread, a connection still to the sacred spring. Her years at the Manor would become a prelude to whatever came next.

———————

Cassie had been crisp as an overcooked crepe, but Cassie was getting better. She would be improved by the skin grafts, the doctors joked. Her new skin would be thicker.

Vida sat with her.

"How I foretell the future," Cassie said, "is by remembering what they said would never happen. By listening and watching. Believing in the present. I do not, I cannot imagine it. Yet when the betrayal takes shape I recognize it. It rises up from the list of forsworn promises."

"Don't be bitter," said Vida.

"Like Miss Morrow's promise the first day I stepped into her office? 'You can absolutely count on me. I will never let you down.' And yet she has let me down; she has abandoned me. She promised that her calm would be stronger than my fear. But it wasn't. When the fit came over me that dreadful day at Delphi she was gone. And she is still gone."

"She's not really—" said Vida.

"She promised that the Manor would stand for as long as it took for me to finish. 'You must not worry, Cassie: there is life in me yet! Dr. Laird and I will see our little rats through their high-school graduation, without fail. We could never close our doors and leave you all in limbo.' She broke that promise too. She is not there at that school—"

"She hired a substitute. She tried to keep it going so we could finish our year—" Vida tried again.

"It was obvious, then, that these things would come to pass. The Manor School for Classical Studies must die; the principals must be gone; I would be thrust out into the world of the common everyday with no one to believe in me."

"Reduced to a number!" said Vida.

"Yes, you said that with glee whenever one of us threatened to move to Northern Secondary or North Toronto. And another thing. She promised that she and Dr. Laird's love would last forever. But I heard him talking; I saw them at the end. They'd quarrelled. He'd stopped loving her. She was mad at him."

"Zeus and Hera quarrelled too."

"And, finally, Miss Morrow promised she would always be my friend. I thought that even if the other promises were broken, if she got sick of me, if the school failed, even if she and Dr. Laird split up—unthinkable—because basically that meant the world would come to an end. And in a way it did. But I still believed, *still*, that she, Francesca Morrow, would be my friend for life."

"You don't know for sure—"

"I've lost everything. Do you see? A teacher who said she would not desert me, a school that would see me through, lovers who said they would never part, a friend who said she loved me. Every promise broken. Every haven lost. I have no teacher, no school, no gods, no friend."

"You have me."

Cassie was too agitated to hear. "Yes, but—"

Vida laughed. "What do you mean, but?"

"She who taught me to love gods took herself out of the pantheon of gods. She became mortal and not only mortal but dust. She's abandoned me."

"Why do you think she abandoned you?"

"Because she's gone. No one can find her anywhere."

"Maybe she had to go. Maybe she'll come back. You're being awfully dramatic, don't you think?"

"Yes, but I am dramatic. And I am bitter. I want to feel bitter. These betrayals came on me one by one and each one was a surprise. And strangely, with each one, I disbelieved what was happening, and believed her. I trusted her even as I saw that she lied. I am one of those people who love not wisely but too well, as her friend Shakespeare says. Unable to stop trusting even when they know their trust is misplaced. Even when the object of that love does his or her utmost to destroy it.

"Do you think Miss Morrow has betrayed herself along with me? That she has hypnotized herself into believing devotion to a cause and a child was a mistake? Could she have believed what she told me at the time? Was the act of naming me a way of convincing herself? I prefer this explanation."

"That's not what I think," said Vida.

"You know," said Cassie, "sometimes I feel there's a curse on us. The Dead Ladies, I mean. Because of what we did. That because of what we did we lost everything."

———

When they arrived back from Greece, the school opened with substitute teachers. The first day back the truck pulled up in front at eleven a.m. sharp. When the Dead Ladies saw the gleaming aluminum truck in front of the school, they panicked.

"Oh my god, he's come to get us."

"I'm leaving," said Ashley. "I'm outta here."

Vida caught her arm. "Wait. Maybe we'll get a chance—"

"You'll get a chance. I'm like on probation, remember. If I get caught I'm blown away, off to training school or some fuckin' thing." Ashley heaved her knapsack, solid with textbooks and binders, onto her shoulders in a great bounce to settle the weight in the middle of her back. "C'mon Spit," she said to the dog.

"Stay," commanded Vida.

"Stay," said Maureen/Delphine in her new voice like that of a medieval nun. She was wearing wispy clothing now, gauzy long skirts that flowed over the ankles of her boots, vests, and beads and ribbons in her long hair.

Spit had risen up to go, but now he stopped and looked from face to face.

"Maybe this is our chance to make amends."

They were big on making amends since everything terrible had happened.

"Aw, fuck," said Ashley. She dropped her bag.

Spit lay down again.

For a whole week they avoided the truck. They tried making do with Starbucks coffees but they were too expensive and they had vanilla and cream and other junk in them. The next day they ordered plain black but it was watery. Also, they had to wait in line, and listen to little smart-faced girls in uniform repeat their order down the line: one grande nonfat latte to go; one grande nonfat latte to go.

"This is just sick," said Vida, breaking out of line.

That whole week the truck came at eleven; the substitute and the boys bought snacks. Then it went away. It came back at one; the substitute and the boys bought lunch, and it went away.

"The truck's back. How come you don't use it?" said Jacob in his too smart to be real way.

"Oh, the food is like so gross."

"We're dieting."

"Those hot dogs really put on the weight," said Roxanne in an authoritative manner, looking askance at Jacob's pear shape.

"You didn't even bother him, look," whispered Maureen/Delphine. "He's not even embarrassed."

"He's so uncool he doesn't even know he's not cool."

"Yeah, but he knows we had something to do with the truck disappearing."

The Dead Ladies tried packing lunches but they either forgot them on the streetcar or got hungry and ate them at the end of second period. They desperately needed to eat at the one o'clock break and there was no café on Taddle Creek Drive. They had to run all the way up to St. Clair to the Real Jerk and eat firebrand-dried meat, not their favourite thing, or go to the convenience store and buy plastic-wrapped sandwiches that probably carried botulism. The teacher yelled at them for being late back to class. Avoiding the truck was attracting too much attention. By Friday it was clear: there was no way to get around Ferdinand.

"What the fuck does he come here for, anyway? Is he trying to creep us out?"

"I think he's just waiting to get us alone. He'll take his revenge."

"Maybe he's forgotten about it."

"Forgotten? Like, hello? Like, *brainer*."

Monday, Vida took a deep breath, sucked in her stomach and drew her hand alongside her cheek to pull the hair away from her face. The dark head was turned away from her, the short thick body addressed to the metal cabinets behind.

"I'll just have a coffee and a hot dog, please," she said.

He turned at the sound of her voice. And Vida found she was staring into the eyes of a near-Ferdinand, but not Ferdinand. A Ferdinand clone, a slightly taller, younger fellow with the same dog-like face.

"Oh my god," she said, "you freaked me right out. You're not Ferdinand."

The man did not even smile but looked down to where he was pulling a wiener out of plastic to put it on his shiny grill with the series of humps and hollows where it would slowly roll and turn a healthy brown.

"Ferdinand not here," he said. "I am the brother."

Vida flushed. The brother! He must know about them. He must hate them. She'd better check the hot dog for poison. Try it on Spit first. She wasn't hungry any more. And she missed Ferdinand dreadfully with a sudden pang, missed his kind rumpled face and those short, thick hands. What had they done? What was wrong with their brains?

"Oh no, is he sick?" she said in what she hoped was a neutral tone. She perused the chip packages: dill pickle, ketchup, sour cream and onion.

"Not sick. He gone to Portugal. His wife get baby."

"And the truck?" she ventured, not believing her nerve. "It's working okay?"

Ferdinand's brother shrugged.

"Some thugs they put it in the lake, last winter," he said, adopting the grimace of a tragic mask.

Vida whistled. She felt a cold thrill down her spine at her success in being the spy/traitor. "Ferdinand must have been so upset. He loves his truck."

"Oh yeah, but we Portuguese, we fix everything, so cheap. Ferdinand have a young guy who fixes everything electrical real good. Then another guy with a garage where they do body work. Now it looks good. Runs good. Forget about it!" He slapped his small plump hand on the metal serving counter. "Anything else?"

But why then, Vida wanted to ask, did he not come back? But of course she knew why he did not come back. He did not come back because he hated them and well he ought to, vile little criminals that they'd been.

"Did he, like, call the cops or anything?" said Vida.

The brother of Ferdinand looked in her face. His large wide

lips pulled themselves back up from the scowl and turned up at the edges. Something amused this man greatly. Vida felt her face go scarlet.

"No," said Ferdinand's brother.

Vida pushed on, face flaming.

"Why not?" Vida thought she knew the answer. The Ladies had discussed it amongst themselves. Immigrants were afraid of the police. Probably Ferdinand didn't call because he was scared of the authorities, fearful he might lose his licence, or that some nephew or second cousin who was working illegally in the country on a student visa would get sent home. So he kept quiet about it. But that was not what his brother said.

"He knows who did it. And he say he doesn't wanna get them in trouble. I think he's crazy but—"

Could his brother know he was speaking to one of the thugs at this minute? Could he not know? Vida felt like she was going to vomit. But it was time, was it not, to show that she could be a leader of women.

"Mr. Brother of Ferdinand," she said, directly, firmly. "Can you give him a message from all of us girls here at the Manor?"

"He's in Portugal."

"I know, but he'll come back. When he comes back say to him this. Say to him that the Ladies at the Manor School—remember that, Ladies—are sure that whoever did this terrible thing to him and his truck are very, *very* sorry and that these people, whoever they are, now realize they were total assholes."

The brother allowed himself a tiny smile. "You want me to remember all that? Maybe you better write it down."

"I dunno," said Vida. She paid (the brother's prices were higher but she did not dare ask to run a tab) and went inside. There, in the studio, hunger overcame caution; she decided that if the hot dog were poisonous she would just have to die, and she ate it.

"This is a dilemma and a mystery. The dilemma," she said to the Ladies after school (they were walking along St. Clair toward Yonge

Street where they would go for coffee at Futures), "is that if we write down we're sorry it's tantamount to a confession."

"No way," repeated Ashley. "I'm on probation."

They walked three abreast, Roxanne, Maureen/Delphine and Vida, followed by tall Ashley and short Sara, with Spit the dog between them. They all stared at the pavement in front of them. "The mystery is that by some intervention of the gods we now have a chance to make it up to Ferdinand."

"Like how?" asked Roxanne.

"We can't, you know," said Maureen/Delphine. "It was big, what we did. We just can't make something like that up to someone. You can't redeem yourself. We can't go over there and visit his baby or whatever and have him think we're like really nice kids, not now."

"That's right," said Sara in the second row.

"You know, tiny twat, you don't actually have a fucking clue what you're talking about," said Ashley to her.

"She doesn't. But she's right. We can't make it up to him. But then, what are we supposed to do?"

"We're going to write him a letter saying we're sorry."

"Oh sure, right. Like then he's got us. Just has to go to the cops and, bam, we're in juvenile court."

"Not necessarily."

The next day the Ladies stood around examining a giant card. On the front were a couple of Madonnas drawn by Ashley, a linocut transfer of a bee by Maureen/Delphine, the illuminated letter F contributed by Sara, and a pressed rose from the garden. In elegant cursive script, a specialty of Roxanne's, was written:

"Dear Ferdinand, The Ladies of the Manor have missed you and your truck. We are certain that the bad people who beat you and drove your truck into the lake have been punished for their wrongdoing, and that they are very sorry. They would probably never do anything like that again."

"This is an absolute piece of trash," Ashley said. "I'm like, having nothing to do with it. You wanna see me in reform school I guess."

"I guess," said Vida calmly.

"Don't worry," said Roxanne, "if they send you there you'll make great drug connections."

And so the card was sealed and duly delivered to the brother of Ferdinand. There was no response but, then, they had not expected one.

Sara left her French notes on the table after school. She came back the next morning, but they were gone. It was a surprise to her, because standards were not what they had been. Rules were not being upheld. The gardens were not what they should be. The students came in and out with their shirts untucked, and smoked openly on the grass. The substitute teacher said it was work enough for four, but that she would settle for one other to help her pull these kids up to standard for their final exams. Miss Morrow agreed to this, from somewhere, from wherever she was. Certain mothers arrived to assist. A teacher from decades ago was resurrected.

There was a pall on the place, most definitely. The pace of Dugald's decline had acted like a metronome over their hours and minutes, slowing them down and farther down, the shape of a tragedy forming as Miss Morrow lost her husband, and the students lost their Headmaster. And unspoken, but felt, everywhere was the suffering of poor Cassie. It was as if a crime had gone unpunished, observed Roxanne, swinging her legs against the stone wall where she sat.

"Fanciful, you are," said Vida, who had taken to speaking like Yoda.

"Even the plants look like shit."

"Works on them usually, she does, Miss Morrow."

"We could do that."

"We could, if we had the energy—"

A couple of the girls became gardeners but they had black thumbs.

Only James Janitor maintained his normal routine. He arrived at four o'clock each day to do the floors and get rid of the garbage, sweeping wallets and geography textbooks into his rolling garbage can without remorse, but returning early on Friday and Tuesday mornings to set out the cans for collection. At those times he revealed himself as reasonable and happy to negotiate, for an African violet or a pack of Player's Mild, no questions asked as to how the student had come by the latter. As James Janitor was now the only remaining adult of the original Manor regime, his shed at the side of the coach house became a gathering place for those students who hungered for their idols and sought comfort in familiarity.

Which was why Maureen/Delphine and Roxanne and Ashley and Vida were there on Friday morning early, rolling a Blunt before class to inaugurate Sara, who had been officially accepted as one of the Dead and Disbanded Ladies, now known as the DDL and having no further criminal aspirations.

"Fuck, it's early," said Maureen/Delphine, leaning back on the shed door and fishing in her breast pocket for the fixings for their joint. "I can't wait for this year to be over except at the end of it I've got to write exams. I don't see why we should do it, who needs grade twelve?"

"You need it," said James. "Otherwise you'll end up like me."

They looked into his dark shed sided with rotting cedar and saw the blades of the rusty lawn mower wink from a back corner. On a series of large-headed nails pounded into the wood was slung a series of implements, hoes, rakes, clippers and a snow shovel. Beneath was an old-fashioned double-buffered floor polisher with shearling pads.

"On second thought..." said Maureen/Delphine.

Cassie returned to school for the very last day. She came in a van that carried her wheelchair, with an attendant whose job it was to get her in and out and to make sure she did not injure herself. She came at eleven in the morning when the truck was waiting, and the kids all ran out the side door of the Manor and over the lawn t o gather around her ramp where it met the sidewalk. The Dead Ladies came up beside her chair. Roxanne and Maureen/Delphine were crying and Sara just stared. Jacob stood a little way away wringing his hands and looking like a very pleased undertaker. Vida stood at the arm of the chair, the manager (there it was, the mythic form of the press conference overtaking life), and handled the questions.

"Ohmigod, does she ever look great," squealed Roxanne, and Cassie wished a) that she could think of something more original than 'ohmigod' and b) that they wouldn't speak of her in the third person. She'd had quite enough of that.

"You're like, so thin."

"I almost died, twice," she said.

"We know, that's so weird. What did it feel it like?"

"Not so good," said Cassie and smiled. "It was like I realized, hey, I don't want to do this," she said. The truth was, when death came along she had begun to want, for the first time, to see herself in the future. She decided that she belonged there. And she would not die, not this time. In the hospital, she got to thinking about how absolutely marvellous life was. And how marvellous it was going to be. It would be full of sunlight and sex, for she no longer wanted to be a virgin forever, and the laughter of friends. What did it matter if people listened to her? The future would come and it would be as she saw it, whether others wanted to know or not.

"Tell them what you told me," said Vida.

"In my dreams, I can still feel the heat licking my shins and smell my own flesh burning—"

"Oooh gross—"

"I can hear my screams and your screams and I can feel Jacob wrap me up, and the weight of Vida and Maureen's bodies throwing me into the dust and even still taste the dust in my mouth."

In fact, wanting to live had begun right at the moment she'd been engulfed in flames. At the time she had seen the flaring begin to fade from her eyes. The piercing screams seemed to go on forever and then there was a silence that was even more frightening because it was so much like death.

No, Cassie had said over and over into the muffled darkness, this is not where I am going, it does not happen this way, this time. She refused to let the doubt take over and that was why she was alive. "And it wasn't just once I had to say it. I had to say it over and over."

"Ohmigod," said Maureen/Delphine. "I know just what you mean, it was just like that for me with the bees—"

"Aw, Delphine, forget it. It's not the same. Cassie was, like, critically injured. Most people would have died. You were just scared."

"No," said Cassie, "being afraid is the worst thing. Trust me."

The others smiled at her, so generous in her triumph. Cassie basked in their admiration. It was ecstasy she felt, not that of the Trojan trance, as Miss Morrow called it, but real joy. She looked around from her wheelchair seat and noticed the world that could so easily have gone on without her. The way Taddle Creek Drive led off into the flowering bushes of the Park, the way the girl's kilts and white blouses were super bright against the curtains of mature green, the way a simple thing like a silver truck pulling up against the curb leapt off the landscape and shouted at her to pay attention.

"We fixed it with Ferdinand," said Maureen/Delphine.

"I know," she said. "I felt it."

"Oh come on, Cassie, you're talking shit," Vida said.

But she wasn't talking shit.

She remembered what Miss Morrow had said about how artists work, that there is a moment when they see it all, the vision, just like that. When they are struck like a Chinese gong by the hammer of light; that this energy enters through the eyes and travels straight to the heart, to the solar plastic. Takes their breath, darkens their sight with tears, rends their heart. And then they have to hold on to themselves and hold on to the vision and they have their work—maybe for a year or two, maybe for a lifetime—to make it real for other people. It was like that; you had to wait for it and when it came to you had to stop yourself from foaming at the mouth and screaming and uttering weirdnesses.

This is what Cassie knew, now. Before, she did not understand; she was simply terrified. The truth was, this person, call her an artist, call her a priest, call her just anybody, a loser. When hit by the hammer, she rang like the gong. Now she knew that the vision exploded in you and you threw your net over it and captured it. You just snared it and held on for dear life. That was the lesson Miss Morrow had taught her and Cassie was grateful beyond words. And she knew how large the vision could be, at that moment, how large life could be. Fountains of desire had sprung up within her. She wanted to tell Miss Morrow thank you, thank you with my whole life for what you have done for me, but Miss Morrow was gone. She was so grateful that she was no longer bitter. It was very sad, but it felt like how life worked. Miss Morrow would not be paid back for the gifts she had given. In order to pay back Miss Morrow, Cassie would have to be her best self; she would have to give love and maybe never know if she would get it back.

All this Cassie thought while Vida stood beside her, fielding questions. Vida was growing up, even Cassie could tell, by the hollows forming in her cheeks and a new prominence to her chin. Be in my life, Vida, thought Cassie. Don't go from it. I want you to be in my life. I don't know how or in what way. It doesn't have to have a name, what we are. Just if you are there.

"Are you going to come back to school next year? If there is a next year at this school?"

"Don't tire her," snapped Vida. "I think that's too many questions."

Cassie watched Vida and saw that Vida would be taller but never very tall. She would be fierce and get her black belt and she would fight many battles. Other people's battles: she would be a leader of women. Oh yes, Vida will be the master, the sensei, Miss Morrow's true heir. Cassie could see Vida standing in the round open doorway of some huge airplane looking down into the dark ground with its tiny buried lights drawing lines on the surface of the earth. And all the people on the ground bid her farewell as she left. But she would return, Vida, she would clatter down the stairs like a little kid, her feet sounding the clear drumbeats of one who knows herself.

The future, its aura, grew a little wider and around the rim of Vida's life Cassie could see herself. Cassie would have her harbour, her little house in the sun, her point of departure, the place where the gap opened up between herself and the world. Cassie would do her slow work and watch the life of the city. She would need a city, a little cluster of people in houses around a harbour where the ships come in. There had to be a creek there, with fresh water coming from higher land. Over the ages the creek would fill up with shit, not to put too fine a word on it, and go underground. Then there would come a small tribe that believed the stream was sacred, and would strive once again to bring it to light.

"Cassie, can I go back with you in your van?"

"Not now," said Vida. "Can't you see she's tired?"

Yes, Cassie was tired. She was very tired of seeing what was coming. It was time to close her eyes. These moments drained her. And she had so much work to do to heal. When she had survived this, when she had new skin on her legs and her arms, when the pain was over, life would be wide open. But there would still be terrors. There would still be times when for Cassie the pain would be so great that she would have to spin.

The attendant was pulling her in her chair backward up the ramp. She looked down the slant and saw them all together on the sidewalk. Crying, Roxanne and Ashley and Maureen/Delphine.

Jacob waving, full of his own mystery, waving to her like a kindred soul from his own ship, which would set out soon. They were the last of the Manorites, the last to graduate, to have drunk from the sacred spring, the new Homo erectus, twenty-first-century variety.

Look out! Look out! She wanted to shout to her friends. Here comes the future.

Oh my god, she thought. How lucky it is that they don't know it. They don't know what will happen in their lives. If they knew, they'd be even crazier than they are now.

POSTSCRIPT

From the notebooks of Cassandra McVey:

A SPIRAL. A spiral is not proper, stiff, straight or tall. It changes size according to how it feels. A spiral is not fragile, but is stronger than a straight line. The spiral can go one of two ways, inward or outward.

CHAOS. The spiral tries to hold in the chaos. The inside is the Vortex. That's Miss Morrow's word, something to do with a bunch of English poets. You may begin spiralling at the outside or at the inside.

FEAR. If you fear you are losing control, begin at the outside. The winding in tightens everything. You can retreat. You become compacted to the point of disappearance.

TRUST. If you feel positive energy, begin at the inside, the vortex, and unwind. Then you are giving, and giving up control; you are putting your trust in life itself.

ACKNOWLEDGEMENTS

I had time and an office from which to consult numerous texts on Greece while acting as Fredelle Maynard Writer in Residence at the Toronto Reference Library. I thank the cheerful and helpful staff of the library, as well as Sydney Bacon, whose donation funded the program in memory of Dr. Maynard. I discovered the authoritative and highly readable *Delphi and the Sacred Way*, by Neville Lewis, in a second-hand bookshop across the street from the library. I should also express a debt of inspiration to the brilliant novel *Cassandra*, by Christa Wolf. Quotations from Euripides' *The Trojan Women* are from the John Davie translation, in the Penguin Classics edition.

My trips farther afield to the museums and sites of Athens and Delphi gave me joy. I was also helped by Ian Montagnes, who gave his Taddle Creek lecture and slide show at my house; Marnie Woodrow, who researched the story of Watts and Ellen Terry; and Kirsti Simonsuuri, who supplied Greek words. My son Robin Honderich and his friend Selina Schmocker shared their expertise on teenage dialogue over the kitchen table. My daughter Emily consulted on cover design, and helped type in editorial changes. Both Robin and Emily provided unquestioning love and support for me helping me to get through difficult days and sharing many good days as well.

And I thank, at Random House Canada, David Kent, who enthusiastically attended my readings even before he began to publish me, and Tanya Trafford, for her thorough and knowledgeable copy edit. Finally, there is my gratitude to Anne Collins, who has been a part of this book since it began. It seems fitting that Anne has re-entered my life now, many years after we first met at York University when neither of us was much older than the troubled young women of the Manor School. She assigned me a magazine piece on rebel girls; when they entered the novel she brought it with her to Random House. As my editor she has read draft after draft of *The Truth Teller*, finding a way through the story at moments when I myself was lost in it. I remain in awe of her gifts and her energy.